Op-Center

Tom Clancy's

Op-Center

Created by Tom Clancy and Steve Pieczenik

Thorndike Press • Chivers Press
Thorndike, Maine USA   Bath, Avon, England

This Large Print edition is published by Thorndike Press, USA and by Chivers Press, England.

Published in 1995 in the U.S. by arrangement with The Berkley Publishing Group.

Published in 1995 in the U.K. by arrangement with HarperCollins Publishers. 1̲92121

U.S. Hardcover 0-7862-0491-5 (Basic Series)
U.S. Softcover 0-7862-0492-3
U.K. Hardcover 0-7451-7899-5 (Windsor Large Print)
U.K. Softcover 0-7451-3723-7 (Paragon Large Print)

The text of this Large Print edition is unabridged. Other aspects of the book may vary from the original edition.

Set in 16 pt. News Plantin.

HOLLYHILL
BRANCH

Printed in the United States on permanent paper.

British Library Cataloguing in Publication Data available

Library of Congress Cataloging in Publication Data

Clancy, Tom, 1947–
    Tom Clancy's op-center / created by Tom Clancy and Steve Pieczenik.
        p.   cm.
    ISBN 0-7862-0491-5 (lg. print : hc)
    ISBN 0-7862-0492-3 (lg. print : sc)
    1. Large type books. I. Pieczenik, Steve R. II. Title.
[PS3553.L245T66 1995]
813'.54—dc20   95-17609

Acknowledgments

We would like to thank Jeff Rovin for his creative ideas and his invaluable contribution to the preparation of the manuscript. We would also like to acknowledge the assistance of Martin H. Greenberg, Larry Segriff, Robert Youdelman, Esq., and the wonderful people at The Putnam Berkley Group, including Phyllis Grann, David Shanks, and Elizabeth Beier. As always, we would like to thank Robert Gottlieb of The William Morris Agency, our agent and friend, without whom this book would never have been conceived. But most importantly, it is for you, our readers, to determine how successful our collective endeavor has been.
— Tom Clancy and Steve Pieczenik

ONE

Tuesday, 4:10 P.M., Seoul

Gregory Donald took a sip of scotch and looked across the crowded bar.

"Do you ever find yourself thinking back, Kim? I don't mean to this morning or last week, but — way back?"

Kim Hwan, Deputy Director of the Korean Central Intelligence Agency, used a red stirring straw to poke at the slice of lemon floating in his Diet Coke. "To me, Greg, this morning *is* way back. Especially on days like these. What I wouldn't give to be on a fishing boat with my uncle Pak in Yangyang."

Donald laughed. "Is he still as feisty as he used to be?"

"Feistier. Remember how he used to have two fishing boats? Well, he got rid of one. Said he couldn't stand having a partner. But sometimes I'd rather be fighting fish and storms than bureaucrats. You remember what it was like." From the corner of his eye, Hwan watched as two men sitting beside him paid their tab and left.

Donald nodded. "I remember. That's why I got out."

Hwan leaned closer, looked around. His eyes narrowed, and his clean-cut features took on a conspiratorial edge. "I didn't want to say anything while the *Seoul Press* editors were sitting here, but do you realize they've actually grounded my helicopters for today?"

Donald's brow arched with surprise. "Are they crazy?"

"Worse. Reckless. The press monkeys said choppers crisscrossing overhead would make too much noise and ruin the sound bites. So if anything happens, there's no aerial recon."

Donald finished his scotch, then reached into the side pocket of his tweed jacket. "It's upsetting, but it's like everywhere else, Kim. The marketers have taken over from the talent. It's that way in intelligence work, government, even at the Friendship Society. No one just jumps in the pool anymore. Everything's got to be studied and evaluated until your initiative is colder than Custer."

Hwan shook his head slowly. "I was disappointed when you quit to join the dip corps, but you were smart. Forget about improving the way the agency does business: I spend most of my time fighting just to maintain the status quo."

"But no one does it better."

Hwan smiled. "Because I love the agency, right?"

Donald nodded. He had withdrawn his Block meerschaum pipe and a packet of Balkan Sobranie tobacco. "Tell me — *are* you expecting any trouble today?"

"We've had warnings from the usual list of radicals, revolutionaries, and lunatics, but we know who and where they are and are watching them. They're like the kooks who call in to Howard Stern show after show. Same cant, different day. But they're mostly talk."

Donald's brow arched again as he tapped in a pinch of tobacco. "You get Howard Stern?"

Hwan finished his soda. "No. I heard bootleg tapes when we cracked a pirate ring last week. Come on, Greg, you know this country. The government thinks Oprah is too risqué most of the time."

Donald laughed, and as Hwan turned and said something to the bartender, his blue eyes once again moved slowly across the dark room.

There were a few South Koreans, but as it always was in the bars around the government building, it was mostly international press: Heather Jackson from CBS, Barry Berk from *The New York Times*, Gil Vanderwald from *The Pacific Spectator*, and others whom he didn't care to think about or talk to. Which was why he'd come here early and tucked himself in a far, dark corner of the bar, and why his wife Soonji hadn't joined them. Like Donald, she felt the press had never given him a fair shake — not when he was Ambassador to Korea twenty years ago, and not when he became the adviser on Korean affairs for Op-Center just three months before. Unlike her husband, though, Soonji got angry about negative press. Gregory had long ago learned to lose himself in his vintage meerschaum, a comforting reminder that, like a puff of pipe smoke, a headline is just for the moment.

The bartender came and went and Hwan turned from the bar, his dark eyes on Donald, his right forearm lying flat and stiff on the counter.

"So what did you mean by your question?" Hwan asked. "About thinking back?"

Donald put in the last of the tobacco. "Do you remember a fellow named Yunghil Oh?"

"Vaguely," Hwan said. "He used to teach at the agency."

"He was one of the founding fathers of the psychology division," Donald said. "A fascinating old gentleman from Taegu. When I first came here in 1952, Oh was just leaving. Being booted out, really. The KCIA was trying hard to establish itself as a U.S.-style, state-of-the-art intelligence group and, when he wasn't lecturing on psychological warfare, Oh was busy introducing aspects of Chondokyo."

"Religion in the KCIA? Faith and espionage?"

"Not exactly. It was a kind of spiritual, heavenly way approach to deduction and investigation he had developed. He taught that the shadows of the past and future are all around us. He believed that through meditation, by reflecting on people and events that were and will be, we could touch them."

"And?"

"And they would help us see today more clearly."

Hwan snickered. "No wonder they dismissed him."

"He wasn't for us," Donald agreed, "and frankly, I don't think Oh had all ten toes on the ground. But it's funny. More and more I find myself thinking he was on to

11

something — that he was in the neighborhood, if not knocking on the door."

Donald reached into his pocket for matches. Hwan watched his one-time mentor closely.

"Anything you can put your finger on?"

"No," Gregory admitted. "Just a feeling."

Hwan scratched his right forearm slowly. "You always did have an interest in unusual people."

"Why not? There's always a chance you can learn something from them."

"Like that old tae kwon do master. The one you brought in to teach us naginata."

Donald struck a wooden match and, cupping the bowl of the pipe in his left hand, he put the flame to the tobacco. "That was a good program, one they should have expanded. You never know when you'll be unarmed and have to defend yourself with a tightly rolled newspaper or a — "

The steak knife flew swiftly from under Hwan's right forearm as he slid from the bar stool.

In the same instant Donald arched back and, still holding the bowl of the pipe, his wrist twisted and swung the straight stem of the meerschaum toward Hwan. He parried the lightning thrust of the knife and, bringing the pipe around it counterclockwise, so the stem was pointing straight down, a counterparry of quarte, he knocked the blade to the left.

Hwan pulled the knife back and thrust forward; Donald flicked his wrist and batted it left again, and then a third time. His young opponent went low this time, slashing toward the right; Donald's elbow cocked to the side, brought the stem down to meet the knife, and parried the thrust again.

The delicate *clack-click-clack* of their sparring drew the attention of the people nearest them. Heads turned as the men dueled, forearms moving in and out like pistons, wrists pivoting with precision and finesse.

"Is this for real?" asked a techie with a CNN T-shirt.

Neither man said anything. They seemed oblivious to everyone as they fought, their eyes locked together, expressions flat, bodies motionless save for their left arms. They were breathing fast through their noses, their lips pressed tightly together.

The weapons continued to flash as the crowd closed around the combatants in a thick semicircle. Finally, there was a blinding series as Hwan lunged, Donald caught the knife in octave, bound it up to sixte, and then used a prise-de-fer move to roll Hwan's hand slightly. Donald followed up by releasing the blade briefly, then giving it a hard spank in septime, sending the blade to the floor.

His eyes remained fixed on those of Hwan; with a slight move of his right hand, Donald extinguished the match that was still burning there.

The crowd burst into applause and whoops, and several people moved in to pat Donald on the back. Hwan grinned and extended his hand and, smiling, Donald clasped it between both of his.

"You're still amazing," Hwan said.

"You were holding back — "

"Only on the first move, in case you were slow. But you weren't. You move like a ghost yourself."

"Like a ghost?" said a sweet voice from behind Donald.

Donald turned as his wife made her way through the dispersing spectators. Her youthful beauty drew stares from the men of the press.

"That was a shameless display," she said to her husband. "It was like watching Inspector Clouseau and his manservant."

Hwan bowed at the waist as Donald hooked his arm around his wife's waist. He pulled her close and kissed her.

"That wasn't meant for your eyes," Donald said, striking a new match and finally lighting his pipe. He glanced at the neon clock above the bar. "I thought I was supposed to meet you at the grandstand in fifteen minutes."

"That was ago."

He looked at her curiously.

"Fifteen minutes *ago*."

Donald's eyes fell. He ran a hand through his silver hair. "Sorry. Kim and I got to comparing horror stories and deeply held personal philosophies."

"Many of which turned out to be the same thing," Hwan noted.

Soonji smiled. "I had a feeling that after two years you would have a lot to talk about." She looked at her husband. "Honey, if you want to continue talking or fence with other utensils after the ceremony, I can cancel that dinner with my parents — "

"No," Hwan said quickly. "Don't do that. I'll have the post-event analysis to do, and that will run till late in the evening. Besides, I met your father at the wedding. He's a very large man. I'll try and come to Washington soon and spend some time with you both. Maybe I'll even find myself an American wife, since Greg took the best woman in Korea for himself."

Soonji gave him a small smile. "Someone had to show him how to lighten up."

Hwan told the bartender to put the drinks

on the KCIA tab, then retrieved the knife, laid it on the bar, and regarded his old friend. "Before I go, though, I do want to tell you this: I've missed you, Greg."

Donald gestured toward the knife. "I'm glad."

Soonji smacked him on the shoulder. He reached around and brushed her cheek with the back of his hand.

"I mean it," Hwan said. "I've been thinking a lot about the years after the war, when you looked after me. Had my own parents lived, I could not have had a more loving family."

Hwan bowed his head quickly and left; Donald looked down.

Soonji watched him go, then placed a slender hand on her husband's shoulder. "There were tears in his eyes."

"I know."

"He left quickly because he didn't want to upset you."

Donald nodded, then looked up at his wife, at the woman who had showed him that wisdom and youth are not mutually exclusive . . . and that apart from it taking a helluva long time to stand up straight in the morning, age really was a state of mind.

"That's what makes him so special," Donald said as Hwan stepped into the bright sunlight. "Kim's soft inside, hard outside. Yunghil Oh used to say that was armor for every eventuality."

"Yunghil Oh?"

Donald took her hand and led her from the bar. "A man who used to work at the KCIA, someone I'm beginning to wish I'd gotten to know a little bit better."

Trailing a thin line of smoke behind him, Donald escorted his wife onto broad, crowded Chonggyechonno. Turning north, they strolled hand-in-hand toward the imposing Kyongbok Palace, at the back of the old Capitol Building, first built in 1392 and rebuilt in 1867. As they neared, they could see the long blue VIP grandstand, and what promised to be a curious blend of boredom and spectacle as South Korea celebrated the anniversary of the election of its first President.

TWO

The basement of the condemned hotel smelled of the people who slept there at night; the musky, liquor-tinged scent of the poor and forgotten, those for whom this day, this anniversary, meant only a chance to get a few extra coins from the people who were coming to watch. But though the permanent boarders were gone, begging for their daily bread, the small brick room wasn't empty.

A man lifted the street-level window and slid in, followed by two others. Ten minutes before, the three had been in their own hotel suite at the Savoy, their base of operations, where each man had dressed in nondescript street clothing. Each man carried a black duffel bag without markings; two handled their bags with respect while the third man, who wore an eyepatch, took no care. He

18

walked to where the homeless had collected broken chairs and torn clothing, placed his bag on an old, wooden school desk, and drew open the zipper.

Pulling a pair of boots from within, Eyepatch handed them to one of the men; a second pair went to the next man, and Eyepatch kept the third.

Working quickly, the men removed their own boots, hid them among a pile of old shoes, and slipped on the new pair. Reaching back into the bag, Eyepatch removed a bottle of spring water before stowing the duffel bag in a dark corner of the room. The bag wasn't empty, but right now they didn't need what was inside.

Soon enough, Eyepatch thought. *If all went well, very soon.*

Holding the water in his gloved hand, Eyepatch returned to the window, raised it, and looked out.

The alley was clear. He nodded to his companions.

Squeezing through the window, Eyepatch turned and helped the others out with their bags. When they were back in the alley, he opened the plastic bottle and the men drank most of the water; with nearly a quarter of a bottle still remaining, he dropped the container and stepped on it, splashing water everywhere.

Then, with the two bags in hand, the men crossed the dirty alley, making sure they walked through the water as they headed toward Chonggyechonno.

Fifteen minutes before the speeches were to begin, Kwang Ho and Kwang Lee — K-One and K-Two, as they were known to friends at the government press office — were making a final test of the sound system.

Tall and slender, K-One stood at the podium, his red blazer a stark contrast against the stately edifice behind him.

Three hundred yards away, behind the grandstand, the tall and large K-Two sat in the sound truck, hunched over a console and snuggled beneath earphones that picked up everything his partner was saying.

K-One stepped before the leftmost of the three microphones.

"There's an extremely fat lady sitting on the top of the grandstand," he said. "I think the seats may collapse."

K-Two smiled and resisted the urge to put his colleague on loudspeaker. Instead, he pressed a button on the console before him: a red light went on under the microphone, indicating that the microphone was on.

K-One covered it with his left hand and moved to the center microphone.

"Can you imagine what it would be like making love to her?" K-One said. "Her perspiration alone would drown you."

The temptation grew stronger. Instead, K-Two pressed the next button on the console. The red light went on.

K-One covered the middle microphone with his right hand and spoke into the third.

"Oh," said K-One, "I'm terribly sorry. That's your cousin Ch'un. I didn't know, Kwang. Truly."

K-Two punched the last button and watched as K-One walked toward the CNN truck to make sure their feed from the press truck was secure.

He shook his head. One day he'd do it. He really would. He'd wait until the esteemed sound engineer said something really embarrassing and —

The world went black and K-Two slumped over his console.

Eyepatch shoved the big man to the floor of the sound truck and stuffed the blackjack in his pocket. While he began unscrewing the top of the console, one man gingerly opened the duffel bags while the third stood inside the door, a blackjack in hand in case the other man returned.

Working quickly, Eyepatch lifted the metal faceplate, leaned it against the wall, and examined the wires. When he found the one he was looking for, he looked at his watch. They had seven minutes.

"Hurry," he snarled.

The other man nodded as he carefully removed the brick of plastic explosive from each duffel bag. He pressed them to the underside of the console, well out of sight; when he was finished, Eyepatch removed two wires from the duffel bags and handed them over. The man inserted the end of a wire into each brick, then handed the other ends to Eyepatch.

Eyepatch looked out the small one-way window at the podium. The politicians had started to move in. The traitors and patriots both were chatting amiably among themselves; no one would notice that anything was amiss.

Punching off the three switches that controlled the microphones, Eyepatch quickly knotted the end of the plastique wires to the wires of the sound system. When he was finished, Eyepatch replaced the metal plate.

His two men each grabbed an empty duffel bag and, as quietly as they had entered, the three men departed.

THREE

Tuesday, 3:50 A.M., Chevy Chase, MD

Paul Hood rolled over and looked at the clock. Then he lay back and pushed a hand through his black hair.

Not even four. Damn.

It didn't make sense; it never did. There was no catastrophe in the offing, no ongoing situation, no crisis looming. Yet most nights since they moved here, his active little mind had gently nudged him from sleep and said, *"Four hours of sleep is enough, Mr. Director! Time to get up and worry about* something.*"*

Nuts to that. Op-Center occupied him an average of twelve hours most days, and sometimes — during a hostage situation or stakeout — exactly double that. It wasn't fair that it should also hold him prisoner in the small hours of the night.

As though you've got a choice. From his

23

earliest days as an investment banker through his stint as Deputy Assistant Secretary of the Treasury to running one of the world's most bizarre and intoxicating cities, he had always been a prisoner of his mind. Of wondering if there was a better way to do something, or a detail he might have overlooked, or someone he forgot to thank or rebuke . . . or even kiss.

Paul absently rubbed his jaw, with its strong lines and deep creases. Then he looked over at his wife, lying on her side.

God bless Sharon. She always managed to sleep the sleep of the just. But then, she was married to him and that would exhaust anyone. Or drive them to see an attorney. Or both.

He resisted the urge to touch her strawberry-blonde hair. At the very *least* her hair. The full June moon cast her slender body in a sharp white light, making her look like a Greek statue. She was forty-one, Nordic-Track slim, and looked ten years younger — and she still had the energy of a girl ten years younger than that.

Sharon was amazing, really. When he was the Mayor of Los Angeles, he would come home and have a late dinner, usually talking on the phone between salad and Sanka, while she got the kids ready for bed. Then she would sit down with him or snuggle on the couch and lie convincingly — tell him nothing important had happened, that her volunteer work at the pediatrics ward of Cedars went smoothly. She held back so that he could open up and dump his day's troubles on her.

No, he remembered. *Nothing important happened.* Only Alexander's terrible bouts with asthma or Harleigh's problems with the kids at school or hate calls and mail and packages from the radical right, the extreme left, and, even once, Express Mail from a bipartisan union of the two.

Nothing happened.

One of the reasons he opted not to run for reelection was because he felt his kids were growing up without him. Or he was growing old without them . . . he wasn't sure which disturbed him more. And even Sharon, his rock, was starting to push him, for the sake of all of them, to find something a little less absorbing.

Six months before, when the President offered him the directorship of Op-Center, a largely autonomous new agency that the press hadn't quite discovered, Hood had been preparing to go back into banking. But when he mentioned the offer to his family, his ten-year-old son and twelve-year-old daughter seemed thrilled by the idea of moving to Washington. Sharon had family in Virginia — and as Sharon and he both knew, cloak and dagger work had to be more interesting than check and dollar work.

Paul turned onto his side, stretched a hand to just an inch above Sharon's bare, alabaster shoulder. None of the editorial writers in Los Angeles ever got it. They saw Sharon's charm and wit, and watched her charm people away from bacon and doughnuts on the half-hour weekly *McDonnell Healthy Food Report* on cable, but they never realized how much her strength and stability enabled him to succeed.

He moved his hand through the air, along her white arm. They needed to do this on a beach somewhere. Someplace where she wouldn't worry about the kids hearing or the phone ringing or the UPS truck pulling up. It had been a while since they'd gone anywhere. Not since coming to D.C., in fact.

If only he could relax, not worry about how things were going at Op-Center. Mike Rodgers was capable as hell, but with his luck the agency would score its first big crisis while he was on Pitcairn Island, and it would take him weeks to get back. It would kill him if Rodgers ever handed him a win like that, neatly wrapped.

There you go again.

Paul shook his head. Here he was, lying next to one of the sexiest, most loving ladies in D.C., and his mind had wandered to work. It wasn't time for a trip, he told himself. It was time for a lobotomy.

He was filled with a mixture of love and need as he watched Sharon's slow breathing, her breasts rising — beckoning, he fancied. Extending his hand past her arm, he allowed his fingers to hover over the sheer fabric of her teddy. Let the children wake. What would they hear? That he loved their mother, and she loved him?

His fingers had just brushed her silken teddy when he heard the cry from the other room.

FOUR

Tuesday, 5:55 P.M., Seoul

"You really ought to spend more time with him, Gregory. You're glowing, do you know that?"

Donald tapped out his pipe against the seat of the grandstand. He watched the ashes fall from the top row to the street below, then put the pipe back in its case.

"Why don't you visit for a week or two at a time? I can run the Society alone."

Donald looked into her eyes. "Because I need you now."

"You can have both. What was that Tom Jones song my mother was always playing? 'My heart has love enough for two . . .'"

Donald laughed. "Soonji, Kim did more for me than he'll ever know. Taking him home from the orphanage each day helped keep me sane. There was a kind of karmic

28

balance to his innocence and the mayhem we were planning at KCIA and when I worked at the Embassy."

Soonji's brow knit. "What does that have to do with seeing more of him?"

"When we're together — I guess it's part cultural, and part Kim, but I was never able to instill in him that trait American kids embrace so easily: forget your folks and have a good time."

"How can you expect him to forget you?"

"I don't, but he feels as though he can't do enough for me, and he takes that very, very personally. The KCIA doesn't have a tab at that bar. He does. He knew he wouldn't win our fight, but he was willing to accept a public drubbing for me. When we're together, he carries his sense of obligation with him like a millstone. I don't want that eating at him."

Soonji hooked an arm through his and pushed back her hair with her free hand. "You're wrong. You should let him love you as he needs — " She froze for a moment and then shot erect.

"Soon? What is it?"

Soonji fired a look toward the bar. "The earrings you gave me for our anniversary. One of them is missing."

"Maybe you left it home."

29

"No. I had it in the bar."

"Right. I felt it when I brushed your cheek — "

Soonji shot him a look. "That had to be when I lost it." She stood and hurried to the end of the grandstand. "I'll be right back!"

"Why don't I call them?" Donald shouted. "Someone here must have a cellular — "

But she was already gone, making her way down the steps and, a moment later, hurrying down the street toward the bar.

Donald slumped forward and rested his elbows on his knees.

The poor girl would be devastated if it was lost. He'd just had the earrings custom-made for their second anniversary, with two small emeralds, her favorite stones. He could have it made over, but it wouldn't be the same. And Soonji would carry *her* guilt around.

He shook his head slowly. How was it with him that every time he showed someone love, it came back as pain? Kim, Soonji —

Maybe it was him. Bad karma or sins in a previous life or maybe he was a black cat with a résumé.

Leaning back, Gregory turned his eyes toward the podium as the President of the National Assembly stepped to the microphone.

FIVE

Park Duk had the face of a cat, round and unworried, with eyes that were wise and alert.

As he rose from his seat and moved to the podium, the people in the grandstand and the crowd standing below erupted into applause. He raised his hands in acknowledgment, framed majestically by the stately palace, with its walled grounds and collection of old pagodas from other parts of the country.

Gregory Donald clenched his teeth, caught himself, then returned his expression to neutral. As President of the U.S./Korean Friendship Society in Washington, he had to be nonpolitical as pertained to matters in South Korea. If the people wanted reunification with the North, he had to go along with

31

that in public. If they didn't, he had to go along with that in public.

Privately, he yearned for it. North and South both had a great deal to offer each other and the world, culturally, religiously, and economically, and the whole would be greater than the sum of its parts.

Duk, a veteran of the war and a fierce anti-Communist, was opposed to even talking about it. Donald could respect his politics, if he tried — but he could never respect anyone who found a subject so distasteful it couldn't even be debated. People like that were tyrants in the making.

After too-long applause, Duk put his hands down, leaned toward the podium, and spoke. Though his lips moved, nothing came out.

Duk drew back and, with a Cheshire grin, tapped the microphone.

"Unificationists!" he said to the politicians seated in a row behind him, and several applauded lightly. There were cheers from nearby members of the crowd who had heard him.

Donald allowed himself a little frown. Duk *really* bugged him, as much for his smooth manner as the growing size of his following.

A red flash caught Donald's eye as, from somewhere behind the august gathering, a figure in a red blazer went racing to the sound truck.

They'd have this fixed in no time. From the 1988 Olympics, Donald remembered just how good the focused, savvy South Koreans were at troubleshooting.

He lost the frown as he turned to look back toward the bar and saw Soonji running toward him. Her arm was raised in triumph, and he thanked God that at least something went right today.

Kim Hwan sat in an unmarked car on Sajingo, south of the Palace, two hundred yards behind where the podium had been erected. From here, he had a complete view of the square and of his agents on rooftops and in windows. He watched as Duk approached and then stepped back from the podium.

No sound from a bureaucrat: now *there* was his definition of a perfect world.

He raised the field glasses sitting beside him. Duk was standing there, nodding to acolytes in the crowd. Well, like it or not, this was what democracy was all about. It was better than the eight years that they had General Chun Doo Hwan running things as head of the martial law command. Kim didn't like his successor, Roh Tae Woo, any better when he was elected President in 1987,

33

but at least he *was* elected.

He turned the glasses toward Gregory and wondered where Soonji had gone.

If any other man had won his former assistant, Hwan would have hated him to his last breath. He had always loved her, but KCIA policy forbade relationships among employees; it would be too easy for infiltrators to get information by placing a secretary or researcher on staff and having her court an official.

She was almost worth quitting for, but that would have broken Gregory's heart. His mentor had always felt that Hwan had the mind and soul and sensitive political instincts of a KCIA man, and had spent a small fortune educating him and preparing him for that life. Even as thick as the red tape got at times, Hwan knew that Gregory was right: this *was* the life for him.

There was a beep to his left, and Kim lowered the glasses. A wideband radio was set in the dashboard of the car; when anyone needed to talk to him, a tone sounded and a red light flashed above the button that accessed their station.

A light came on from the operative stationed atop Yi's Department Store.

Hwan punched the button. "Hwan here. Over."

"Sir, we have a lone figure in a red blazer running toward the sound truck. Over."

"Will check. Over."

Hwan picked up the portable phone and called the office of the event coordinator at the Palace.

A harried voice said, "Yes — what *is* it?"

"This is Kim Hwan. Is that your man going to the sound truck?"

"It *is*. In case you didn't notice, our audio is down. Maybe one of your men did it when they were checking the stage for explosives."

"If they did, we'll take away their bones."

There was a long silence.

"Their dog bones. We had the sniff squad out."

"That's great," said the coordinator. "One of them might have urinated on a wire."

"Political commentary," Hwan said. "I want you to stay on the line till you hear something."

Another long silence. Suddenly a faraway voice crackled through the phone.

"My God! K-Two — "

Hwan was alert. "Turn up your radio. I want to hear what he says."

The volume rose.

"K-One, what's wrong?" the coordinator asked.

"Sir — K-Two is on the floor. His head's bleeding. He must have fallen."

"Check the console."

There was a tense silence. *"The microphones are off. But we checked them. Why would he have done that?"*

"Turn them back on — "

"All right."

Hwan's eyes narrowed. He squeezed the receiver tightly and was already starting out the door. "Tell him not to touch anything!" he shouted. "Someone may have gotten in there and — "

There was a flash, and the rest of his sentence was drowned out by a massive blast.

SIX

The STU-3 secured phone on the nightstand rang. The console had a rectangular, lighted screen on top with an LED display giving the name and number of the person calling, and whether or not the line was secure.

Not quite awake, President Michael Lawrence didn't look at the screen as he reached for the receiver.

"Yes?"

"Mr. President, we have a situation."

The President climbed to an elbow. Now he looked at the screen: it was Steven Burkow, the National Security chief. Below his phone number, it said Confidential — not Secret or Top Secret.

The President dug the palm of his free hand into his left eye. "What is it?" he asked as he rubbed his palm into the other eye and looked at the clock beside the phone.

"Sir, seven minutes ago there was an explosion in Seoul, outside the Palace."

"The celebration," he said knowingly. "How bad?"

"I just took a quick look at the video. There appears to have been hundreds of casualties, possibly several dozen deaths."

"Any of our people?"

"I don't know."

"Terrorism?"

"It appears to be. A sound truck was obliterated."

"Has anyone called to claim responsibility?"

"Kalt is on the phone with the KCIA right now. So far, no one."

The President was already on his feet. "Call Av, Mel, Greg, Ernie, and Paul and have them meet us in the Situation Room at five-fifteen. Was Libby there?"

"Not yet. She was en route from the Embassy — wanted to be late for Duk's speech."

"Good girl. Get her on the phone; I'll take it downstairs. And call the Vice President in Pakistan and ask him to come back this afternoon."

Hanging up, the President tapped the intercom beside the phone and asked his valet to take out a black suit, red tie. Power clothes, in case he had to talk to the media and didn't have time to change.

As he hurried across the soft carpet to the bathroom, Megan Lawrence stirred; he heard her call his name softly, but he ignored her as he shut the bathroom door.

SEVEN

Tuesday, 6:05 P.M., Seoul

The three men walked calmly down the alley. When they reached the window of the old hotel, the two men slid in while Eyepatch watched the street. When they were inside, he followed quickly.

Eyepatch hurried to the duffel bag he had left behind and pulled three bundles from inside. He kept the South Korean captain's uniform for himself, and tossed the noncom uniforms to the others. They removed their boots, stuffed them in the bag with their clothes, and quickly donned the uniforms.

When they were finished, Eyepatch went back to the window, climbed through, and motioned for the others to join him. Bags in hand, they quickly crossed the alley and walked away from the Palace, toward the side street where a fourth man waited in an

40

idling jeep. As soon as they were seated, the jeep pulled onto Chonggyechonno and headed away from the explosion, toward the north.

EIGHT

Quietly shutting the bedroom door, Paul Hood walked over to his son's bed, lay a hand over his eyes, and switched on the lamp beside his bed.

"Dad — " the boy wheezed.

"I know," Hood said softly. He cracked his fingers to admit the light slowly, then reached under the nightstand and took out the Pulmo Aide. Flipping the lid of the lunchbox-sized unit, Hood uncoiled the tube and handed it to Alexander. The boy put one end in his mouth while his father eyedropped the Ventolin solution into the slot on top.

"I suppose you'll want to kick my butt while you do this?"

The boy nodded gravely.

"I'm going to teach you chess, you know."

Alexander shrugged.

42

"It's a game where you can kick mental butt. That's a lot more satisfying."

Alexander made a face.

After switching on the unit, Hood walked over to the small Trinitron in the corner of the room, turned on the Genesis unit, then returned with a pair of joysticks as the *Mortal Kombat* logo blazed onto the screen.

"And don't put in the password for the bloody version," Hood said before handing one to the boy. "I don't want my heart being torn out tonight."

His son's eyes went wide.

"That's right. I know all about the A, B, A, C, A, B, B sequence on the Code of Honor screen. I watched you do it last time, and I had Matt Stoll tell me what it was all about."

The boy's eyes were still saucers as his father sat on the edge of the bed.

"Yeah . . . you don't mess with Op-Center technoweenies, kid. Or their boss."

With the nebulizer mouthpiece held firmly between his lips, Alexander made a point of pressing just the Start button. Soon, the room was filled with grunts and sharp slaps as Liu Kang and Johnny Cage battled for supremacy on the video screen.

For the first time, the elder Hood was beginning to hold his own when the phone rang. At this hour, it could only be a wrong number or a crisis.

He heard the floorboards creak, and a moment later Sharon poked her head in.

"It's Steve Burkow."

Hood was instantly energized. At this hour, it had to be something big.

Alexander had used the distraction to hit his father's proxy with two quick flying kicks, and as Hood rose Johnny Cage fell backward, dead.

"At least you don't get to rip out my heart," Hood said as he set the joystick down and headed toward the door.

Now his wife's eyes were wide.

"Guy talk," Hood said as he hurried past her, giving her a loving pat on the behind when he was behind the door.

The bedroom phone was a secure line, not a portable. Hood was on it for only as long as it took for the National Security Adviser to tell him about the explosion and to come to the meeting in the Situation Room.

Sharon sauntered in. From the bedroom, Hood heard the sounds of combat as Alexander battled the computer.

"Sorry I didn't hear him," she said.

Hood stepped from his pajama bottoms and pulled on his pants. "It's okay. I was up anyway."

She cocked her head toward the phone. "Is it big?"

"Terrorism in Seoul, a bomb blast. That's all I know."

She rubbed her bare arms. "By any chance, were you touching me in bed?"

Hood snatched a white shirt from the closet doorknob and half smiled. "I was thinking about it."

"Mmmm . . . must've come through in my dream. I could swear you did."

Sitting on the bed, Hood slid into his Thom McCanns.

Sharon sat down beside him and stroked his back as he tied his shoes. "Paul, do you know what we need?"

"A vacation," he said.

"Not just a vacation. Time away — *alone*."

He stood and grabbed his watch, wallet, keys, and security pass from the nightstand. "I was just lying here, thinking that."

Sharon didn't say anything; her twisted mouth said it all.

"I promise, we'll have it," he said, gently kissing her on the head. "I love you, and as soon as I save the world, we'll go and explore some part of it."

"Call me?" Sharon said, following him out the door.

"I will," he said as he jogged down the

hall, took the stairs two at a time, and flew out the front door.

As he backed the Volvo from the driveway, Hood punched in Mike Rodgers's number and put him on speaker.

The phone barely rang once. There was silence on the other end.

"Mike?"

"Yeah, Paul," Rodgers said. "I heard."

He heard? Hood scowled. He liked Rodgers, he admired him a great deal, and he depended on him even more. But Hood promised himself that if the day ever came that he caught the two-star General off-guard, he would retire. Because his professional life just wouldn't get any better than that.

"Who told you?" Hood asked. "Someone at the base in Seoul?"

"No," said Rodgers. "I saw it on CNN."

The scowl deepened. Hood himself *couldn't* sleep, but he was beginning to think Rodgers didn't require sleep. Maybe bachelors had more energy, or maybe he'd made a deal with the devil. He'd have his answer if one of his twenty-year-old girlfriends ever landed him, or when another six and a half years passed, whichever came first.

Since the car phone wasn't secure, Hood had to couch his instructions with care.

"Mike, I'm on my way to see the boss. I don't know what he's going to say, but I want you to get a Striker team on the field."

"Good idea. Any reason to think he'll finally let us play abroad?"

"None," Hood said. "But if he decides he wants to play hardball with someone, at least we've got a head start."

"I like it," Rodgers said. "As Lord Nelson put it at the Battle of Copenhagen, 'Mark you! I would not be elsewhere for thousands.'"

Hood hung up, feeling strangely uneasy about Rodgers's remark. But he put it from his mind as he called night-shift Assistant Director Curt Hardaway and instructed him to have the prime team in the office by five-thirty. He also asked him to track down Gregory Donald, who had been invited to the celebration — and who he hoped was all right.

NINE

Gregory Donald had been knocked down three rows from where he'd been sitting, but he'd landed on someone who had cushioned his fall. His benefactor, a large woman, was struggling to get up and Donald rolled off, taking care not to land on the young man beside him.

"I'm sorry," he said, bending close to the woman. "Are you all right?"

The woman didn't look up, and only when he asked again did Donald become aware of the loud ringing in his ears. He touched a finger to his ears; there was no blood, but he knew it would be a while before he heard anything clearly.

He sat there for a moment, collecting his wits. His first thought was that the grandstand had collapsed, but that clearly wasn't the

48

case. Then he remembered the crashing roar followed an instant later by the hit in his chest, a rolling impact that knocked him down and out.

His head cleared quickly.

A bomb. There must have been a bomb.

His head snapped to the right, toward the boulevard.

Soonji!

Rising unsteadily, Donald waited a moment to make sure he wasn't going to pass out, then hurriedly picked his way down the grandstand to the street.

Dust from the explosion hung in the air like a thick fog, and it was impossible to see more than two feet in any direction. As he passed people in the grandstand and then in the street, some were sitting in a state of shock, while others were coughing, moaning, and waving their hands in front of their faces to clear the air, many trying to get up or down or out from under debris. Bloody bodies lay here and there, riddled with shrapnel from the blast.

Donald hurt for them, but he couldn't stop. Not until he knew that Soonji was safe.

The muffled sound of sirens tore through the ringing in his ears, and Donald paused as he searched for their flashing red lights:

that would be where the boulevard was. Spotting them, he half walked, half stumbled through the powdery mist, sometimes stepping suddenly and awkwardly around victims or large pieces of twisted metal. As he neared the street he could hear muffled shouts, see hazy figures in white medical coats or blue police uniforms moving this way and that.

Donald stopped cold as he nearly walked into the wheel rim of a truck. The massive metal disk was turning slowly, shards of rubber hanging from it like dark seaweed from a galleon. Looking down, Donald realized that he was already *on* the boulevard.

He stepped back and looked to the right —

No. The other way. She'd been coming from the direction of Yi's.

Donald tensed as someone grabbed his arm. He looked to his right and saw a young woman in white.

"Sir, are you all right?"

He squinted and pointed to his ear.

"I said, are you *all right?*"

He nodded. "Take care of the others," he yelled. "I'm trying to get to the department store."

The woman looked at him strangely. "Are you *sure* you're all right, sir?"

He nodded again as he gently removed her fingers from his arm. "I'm fine. My

50

wife was walking there and I've got to find her."

The medic's eyes were strange as she said, "This *is* Yi's, sir."

As she turned to help someone leaning against a mailbox, Donald stepped back several steps and looked up. The words had hit him like a second blast and he struggled to draw breath into his tight chest. He could see now that the truck had not only been knocked on its side, but blown into the facade of the department store. He squeezed his eyes shut and clutched the sides of his head as he shook it vigorously, trying not to picture what might be on the other side.

Nothing happened to her, he told himself. She was the lucky one, they'd always known that. The girl who won door prizes. Who picked winning horses. Who'd married him. She was all right. She had to be.

He felt another hand on his arm, and turned quickly. The long black hair was flecked with white, and the fawn-colored dress was smudged with dirt, but Soonji was standing beside him, smiling.

"Thank God!" he cried, and hugged her tightly. "I was so worried, Soon! Thank God you're all right. . . ."

His voice trailed off as she suddenly went limp. He moved his arm to catch her around the waist, and the sleeve of his jacket stuck to her back.

With a mounting sense of horror, he knelt with his wife in his arms. Carefully shifting her to her side, he looked at her back and choked when he saw where the clothing had been burned away, the flesh and fabric both soaked with dark red blood, white bone peeking through. Clutching his wife to him, Gregory Donald heard himself as he screamed, heard clearly the wail that rose from the bottom of his soul.

A flashcube blazed, and the familiar face of the medic bent close. She motioned to someone behind her, and soon there were other hands pulling at his, trying to wrest Soonji from him. Donald resisted, then let them have her as he realized that his love was not what this precious girl needed now.

TEN

Tuesday, 6:13 P.M., Nagato, Japan

The pachinko parlor was a smaller version of the ones made famous in the Ginza district of Tokyo. Long and narrow, the building was nearly the length of ten railroad boxcars laid end to end. The air was thick with cigarette smoke and the clattering of ball bearings as men played the games that lined the walls on both sides.

Each game was comprised of a circular, upright playing surface a yard high, nearly two feet wide, and a half-foot deep. Under a glass cover, bumpers and metal flippers jutted out from a colorful background; when the player inserted a coin, small metal balls dropped from the top, banging pinball-like against the arms and falling this way and that. The player spun a knob in the lower right in an effort to see that each ball reached

53

the bottom; the more balls that were collected in the slot, the more tickets the player won. When the player collected enough tickets, he took them to the front of the parlor where he was given his choice of stuffed animals.

Though gambling was illegal in Japan, it was not against the law for a player to sell the animal he'd won. This was done in a small room in the back, small bears earning twenty thousand yen, large rabbits fetching twice that, and stuffed tigers selling for sixty thousand yen.

The average player spent five thousand yen a night here, and there were typically two hundred players at the parlor's sixty machines. While they enjoyed winning, few men came here to turn a profit. There was something addictive about the way the balls poured through the irregular maze, about the suspense of luck going for you or against you. It was really the player against fate, determining where he stood in the eyes of the gods. There was a widespread belief that if one could change their luck here, it would change in the real world as well. No one could explain why this was, but more often than not it seemed to work.

The parlors were scattered throughout the Japanese islands. Some were run by legitimate families, whose ownership went back centuries. Others were the property of criminal organizations, principally the Yakuza and the Sanzoku — one a league of gangsters, the other an ancient clan of bandits.

The parlor in Nagato on the west coast of Honshu belonged to the independent Tsuburaya family, which had run it and its predecessors for over two centuries. The criminal groups made regular, respectful overtures to buy the parlor, but the Tsuburayas had no interest in selling. They used their earnings to set up businesses in North Korea, potentially lucrative toeholds that they hoped to expand whenever unification became a reality.

Twice a week, on Tuesdays and Fridays, Eiji Tsuburaya sent millions of yen to North Korea through two trusted couriers based in the South. Both men arrived on the late afternoon ferry, carrying two empty, nondescript suitcases, walked directly to the back room of the parlor, left with full ones, and were back on the ferry before it turned about and left for the 150-mile trip to Pusan. From there, the money was smuggled north by members of PUK — Patriots for a Unified Korea, a group comprised of people from both the North and the South, everyone from businessmen to customs agents to street cleaners. It was their belief that profit for entrepreneurs and greater prosperity for the North Korean public in general would force the Communist leaders to accept an open market and, ultimately, reunification.

As always, the men left the parlor, climbed into the waiting cab, and sat quietly for the ten-minute ride to the ferry. Unlike other days, however, this time they were followed.

ELEVEN

Tuesday, 6:15 P.M., Seoul

Kim Hwan saw Donald sitting on a curb, his forehead in his hands, his jacket and pants covered with blood.

"Gregory!" he shouted as he jogged over.

Donald looked up. There was tear-streaked blood on his cheeks and in his disheveled silver hair. He tried to rise but his legs shook and he fell back; Hwan caught him and hugged him tightly as he sat down. The agent pulled away just long enough to make sure none of the blood was Donald's, then embraced him again.

Donald's words were swallowed by his sobs. His breath was coming in gasps.

"Don't say anything," Hwan said softly. "My assistant told me."

Donald didn't seem to hear him. "She . . . she was a . . . blameless . . . soul."

"She was. God will care for her."

"Kim . . . *He* shouldn't have her . . . I should. She should be here. . . ."

Hwan fought back tears of his own as he pressed his cheek to Donald's head. "I know."

"Who did she . . . offend? There was . . . no evil in her. I don't understand." He pressed his face into Hwan's breast. "*I want her back*, Kim . . . I want . . . her. . . ."

Hwan saw a medic turn toward them and motioned him over. Still holding Donald, Hwan rose slowly.

"Donald, I want you to do me a favor. I want you to go with someone. Let them make sure you're all right."

The medic put a hand on Donald's arm but he wrested it away.

"I want to see Soonji. Where have they taken . . . my wife?"

Hwan looked at the medic, who pointed toward a movie theater. There were body bags on the floor, and more were being carried in.

"She's being cared for, Gregory, and you need care yourself. You may have injuries."

"I'm all right."

"Sir," the medic said to Hwan, "there are others — "

"Of course, I'm sorry. Thank you."

The medic hurried off and Hwan took a step back. Holding Donald by the shoulders, he looked into the dark eyes, always so full of love but now red and glazed with pain. He wouldn't force him to go to the hospital, but leaving him here, alone, was not an option.

"Gregory, would you do me a favor?"

Donald was staring through Hwan, weeping again.

"I need help with this case. Would you come with me?"

Donald looked at him. "I want to stay with Soonji."

"Gregory — "

"I love her. She . . . needs me."

"No," Hwan said softly. "You can do nothing for her." He turned Donald around and pointed to the theater a block away. "You don't belong there, you belong with those of us you *can* help. Come with me. Help me to find the people who did this."

Donald blinked several times, then absently patted his pockets. Hwan reached into Donald's pocket.

"Is this what you want?" he asked, handing him his pipe.

Donald took it, his movements awkward and halting, and Hwan helped him put it in his mouth. When he didn't reach for his tobacco, Hwan took him by the elbow and walked him away, through the settling dust and increasing activity in the square.

TWELVE

The White House Situation Room was located on the first sublevel, directly below the Oval Office. There was a long, rectangular mahogany table in the center of the brightly lit room; there was a STU-3 and a computer monitor at each station, with slide-out keyboards underneath. Like all government computers, the computer setup was self-contained; software from outside, even from the Department of Defense or State Department, was debugged before it was allowed into the system.

On the walls were detailed maps showing the location of U.S. and foreign troops, as well as flags denoting trouble spots: red for ongoing and green for latent. There was already a red flag in Seoul.

Paul Hood had arrived at the west gate

of the White House and, after passing through a metal detector, took the elevator down one floor. When the door opened, his ID was checked by a Marine sentry, who escorted him to a small table that sat beside a door with no handle. Hood pressed his thumb lightly on a small screen that sat on the table: a moment later there was a buzz and the door popped open. Hood entered, walking past a guard who had checked his thumbprint against the print on file in the computer; if the two hadn't matched, the door would not have been opened. Only the President, the Vice President, and the Secretary of State were not subject to this security check.

The door to the Situation Room was open, and Hood walked in. Four other officials were already there: Secretary of State Av Lincoln, Defense Secretary Ernesto Colon, Chairman of the Joint Chiefs of Staff Melvin Parker, and CIA Director Greg Kidd were talking in a corner, away from the door; a pair of secretaries sat at a small corner table. One was there to take notes, in code, in a Powerbook, the other to bring up any data on the computer that might be called for. A Marine was putting out coffee butlers, pitchers of water, and cups.

The men acknowledged Hood with nods and salutes; only Lincoln walked over as soon as Hood entered. He stood just under six feet, powerfully hewn, with a round face and thinning widow's peak. A former Major League pitcher and Hall of Famer, he moved from the baseball diamond to the Minnesota state legislature to Congress quicker than his blinding fastballs. He was the first politician to get behind the candidacy of Governor Michael Lawrence, and the State Department was his reward; most agreed he lacked the diplomatic skills the job required, loved to treat the obvious like a revelation. But Lawrence was nothing if not loyal.

"How've you been?" Lincoln asked, extending his hand.

"Passing fair, Av."

"That was a good job your people did at Independence Hall on the Fourth. Very impressive."

"Thanks, but it's never really a good job when hostages are hurt."

Lincoln waved a hand with disgust. "No one was killed. That's what matters. Hell, when you've got to coordinate efforts between local police, the FBI, and your own Striker personnel, with the media looking over your shoulder, that's a goddamn miracle." He poured himself a cup of coffee. "It's like this situation, Paul. Already on TV, experts flapping their lips in the media — there'll be opinion polls before breakfast telling us why seventy-seven percent of the American public doesn't think we should even be in Korea or anywhere else."

Hood looked at his watch.

"Burkow rang down, said they were running late," Lincoln said. "The President's on the phone with Ambassador Hall. He doesn't want Americans moving into or being turned away from the Embassy unless he okays it, or any statements or actions that show any kind of panic."

"Of course."

"You know it's easy for these things to become self-fulfilling prophesies."

Hood nodded. "Any word yet on who did it?"

"None. Everyone's condemned it, including the North Koreans. But the government doesn't talk for the extreme hard-liners, so who knows?"

The Defense Secretary said from across the room, "The North Koreans *always* condemn terrorism, even their own. When they shot down that stray KAL jet, they condemned it even as they were combing the wreckage for spy cameras."

"And they found them," Lincoln said behind his hand as he wandered back toward the others.

Hood reflected on the shoot-first policy

of the North Koreans as he poured himself coffee. The last time he was here was when the Russians shot down a Lithuanian spy plane and the President decided not to press them hard on it. He would never forget the way Lincoln literally stood up and said, "What do you think world leaders would say if *we* ever shot down a foreign aircraft? We'd be crucified!"

He was right. For some reason, the rules were different for the U.S.

Hood took a seat at the northwest side of the table, as far from the President as possible. He liked to watch as the others jockeyed for authority, and this was the best seat in the house. Op-Center's Staff Psychologist, Liz Gordon, had told him what to look for in body language: hands folded on the table was submissive, sitting erect showed confidence while sitting forward was insecurity — *"Look at me, look at me!"* — and the head angled was patronizing. "It's like a fighter showing you his chin," she said, "daring you to hit it because he thinks you can't."

No sooner had he sat down than Hood heard the outside door pop open, followed by the resonant voice of the President of the United States. During the campaign two years before, one columnist had said that that voice was what won over the crucial undecideds: it seemed to start from some-where around the knees, and by the time it reached his mouth it was full of Olympian grandeur and power. That, plus his six-foot-four-inch height, made him look and sound presidential, though he had spent a lot of that capital explaining two foreign policy fiascos. The first was sending food and arms to Bhutanese rebels opposing an oppressive regime, a revolt that ended with thousands of arrests and executions and left the regime stronger than ever. The second was kid-gloving a border dispute between Russia and Lithuania, which ended with Moscow not only taking land from the small republic but placing soldiers there as well. That forced a massive exodus to the city of Kaunas, which resulted in food riots and hundreds of deaths.

His credibility in Europe was damaged, his clout on the Hill was hobbled, and he couldn't afford another misstep — especially with a longtime ally.

National Security Adviser Burkow did everything but pull out the President's chair for him as they walked in. He poured coffee for them both as they sat down, the President speaking even before everyone else was seated.

"Gentlemen," he said, "as you know, an hour and fifteen minutes ago a sound truck exploded in front of Kyongbok Palace in Seoul. Several dozen spectators and politicians were killed, and so far the KCIA hasn't a clue as to who, what, and why. There was no advance warning, and no one's called to take credit. Ambassador Hall has made no request other than that we reiterate our support for the government and people of South Korea, and I have authorized Press Secretary Tracy to do just that. Ambassador Hall will immediately issue a statement condemning the act in general." He sat back. "Ernie, in the event that it is North Korea, our standard operating policy would be what?"

The Defense Secretary turned to one of the secretaries and said, "File NK-AS." By the time he turned back to the table, the NORTH KOREA — ALERT SITUATION file was on the screen. He folded his hands.

"To summarize, Mr. President, our policy is to go to Defcon 5. We put our bases in the South and in Japan on High Alert and begin flying over troops from Ft. Pendleton and Ft. Ord. If intelligence picks up any sign that Korean troops are mobilizing, we go immediately to Defcon 4 and start moving in our ships from the Indian Ocean, so the Rapid Deployment Forces will be in position. If the North Koreans match our movements with further deployments of their own, the dominos fall fast and we move quickly through the accelerated deployment of Defcon 3, 2, and 1." He glanced at the screen and touched his finger to the chapter heading WAR GAMES. "When we reach the point of no return, we have three possible scenarios."

Hood looked from face to face. Everyone was calm, save for Lincoln who was leaning forward and tapping his right foot quickly. This was his kind of situation, his kind of big stick response. At the opposite end of the spectrum was Chairman of the Joint Chiefs of Staff Melvin Parker. His face and posture were subdued, like Ernie Colon's. In situations like these, it was never the military men who advocated force. They understood the price of even a successful operation. It was always the politicians and appointees who were frustrated or impatient and wanted to get themselves a victory, however quick and dirty.

The Secretary of Defense pulled on reading glasses and studied the monitor. He ran his finger down the menu and and touched the screen where it said DEFENSE WHITE PAPER UPDATE.

"If there's a war and the U.S. assumes a support role only, South Korea falls to the North in a matter of two or three weeks.

You can see the matchup between the North and ROKA for yourself."

Hood studied the figures. They looked as bad for the Republic of Korea Army as Colon had said.

Military Balance of the North and South is as follows:

	South	North
Number of Troops		
Army	540,000	900,000
Navy	60,000	46,000
Air Force	55,000	84,000
Total	655,000	1,030,000
Force		
Tanks	1,800	3,800
Armored Vehicles	1,900	2,500
Artillery	4,500	10,300
Force		
Combatants	190	434
Support Vessels	60	310
Submarines	1	26
Tactical Aircraft	520	850
Support Aircraft	190	480
Helicopters	600	290

After a few seconds, Colon brought up the menu again and touched U.S. 8TH ARMY UPDATE.

"The second scenario has our forces in the South becoming involved. Even then, the odds are not in our favor."

Hood looked at the new screen.

United States Forces in South Korea,
Number of Personnel

Army:	25,000
Navy:	400
Air Force:	9,500
Tanks:	200
Armored Vehicles:	500
Tactical Aircraft:	100

"The only value of us joining the South Koreans on the battlefield is the deterrent factor: does North Korea really want a war with the United States?"

CIA Director Kidd asked, "Isn't that same deterrent present if we're in a strictly support mode?"

"Unfortunately, no. If Pyongyang thinks we haven't got the belly for a scrap, he'll push to Seoul the same way Baghdad went after Kuwait when they thought we'd sit on the sidelines."

"And wasn't he surprised," Lincoln muttered.

The President said impatiently, "And the

third scenario is a preemptive strike?"

"Right," Colon said. "We and the South Koreans together take out communications centers, supply lines, and nuclear reprocessing plants with conventional weapons. If the war games simulations are correct, the North Koreans go to the negotiating table."

"Why wouldn't they turn to China and retaliate?" asked CIA Director Kidd.

Joint Chiefs of Staff Chairman Parker said, "Because they know that since the aid cutbacks of 1968, and the inability since 1970 of the twelve ROK and two U.S. divisions to successfully stave off an attack, our defense plans have been keyed almost entirely to the early use of nuclear weapons."

"Did we leak that information?" the President asked.

"No, sir. They read it in military journals. Christ, in 1974, *Time* or *Rolling Stone* or someone who hated Nixon did an article on our nuclear plans for Korea."

Kidd leaned back. "That still doesn't give us any kind of assurance they won't turn to China, and that Beijing won't support them with nuclear weapons."

"We just don't see that as happening." Colon went to the menu and touched the heading CHINA OPTION. "Mel, the CONEX games are your area — "

"Right." Despite the comfortable air-conditioning in the room, the diminutive Chairman of the Joint Chiefs was perspiring. "We ran a Conflict Exercise of a scenario similar to this a while back, after Jimmy Carter went to North Korea for his little chat with Kim Il Sung. Given the military situation in China and psychological profiles of its leaders — which your people provided, Paul — we found that if we loosened restrictions on business investments in China, and concurrently authorized the shipment of arms to anti-Chinese factions in Nepal through India, the Chinese would be unlikely to become involved."

"How unlikely?" the President asked.

"Eighty-seven percent chance of sitting on the sidelines."

"We came up with a slightly different percentage in our own SAGA simulations," Colon said, "about seventy percent. But the Studies, Analysis, and Gaming Agency didn't have up-to-date psych profiles, so I'm inclined to go with Mel's findings."

Though Hood was listening intently, his expression impassive, he found himself somewhat anxious about Liz's findings. He had a great deal of respect for his Staff Psychologist, just as he held his Operations Support Officer Matt Stoll in high regard. But he put computer analyses and psychology in the place and show slots, respectively, after good old-fashioned intuition. His Press Officer Ann Farris joked that he never met a gut feeling he didn't like, and she was right.

The President glanced at the clock on the bottom of the monitor, then steepled his hands. Colon motioned to the secretary to clear the screen, and Hood watched as screen saver missiles flew left and right across the monitor.

"Gentlemen," the President said after a long silence, "I would like all of you to serve on the Korean Task Force for the duration, and Paul" — he looked squarely at Hood — "I want you to head it up."

He caught the Op-Center Director off-guard — as well as everyone else in the room.

"You'll bring me an Options Paper in four hours. Barring further acts of terrorism or aggression, you'll proceed under the assumption that there will be some level of graduated deployment but no military action for the first twenty-four hours. That should give your people and the rest of the Task Force time to evaluate intelligence and write me an addendum." The President rose. "Thank you all. Av — meet me in the Oval Office at six so we can discuss the situation with our allies. Ernie, Mel — we'll brief the cabinet and members of the Armed Services Committee at seven. And, Paul, I'll see you at nine-thirty."

The President left, trailed by the Secretary of Defense and the Chairman of the Joint Chiefs of Staff. Av Lincoln walked over to Hood.

"Congratulations, Paul. I sense an ass-kicking." He leaned close. "Just make sure it isn't your ass that gets kicked."

He was right. The President had never given Op-Center a foreign crisis, and doing so now meant that he intended to strike hard and decisively, if given the chance. Should anything go wrong, he could pin it on the new kids on the block, shut down the agency, and suffer only minimal political damage. Then Hood could take a low-paying position at the Carter Center or the United States Institute of Peace, a convert to pacifism, a reformed sinner trotted out for public scourgings at dinners and symposia.

Av gave him a thumbs-up as he left, and after collecting his thoughts, Hood followed him to the elevator. In addition to having to take the fall for any failure, Hood wasn't keen on having to spend the next four hours playing ringmaster to a bureaucratic turf war as he teleconferenced with everyone who had been in attendance, formulating a cohesive strategy from six people with six very different agendas. It was part of the job, and he did it well, but he hated the way people did what was best for party and agency first and second, and for the country a distant third.

Still, there was the bright side to look at, the chance that he might just pull all this off. And as he contemplated that, the adrenaline began to flow. If the President was willing to take risks with Op-Center, Hood had to be willing to take greater risks to make sure that Op-Center earned its international credentials once and for all. Like one of his heroes, Babe Ruth, when you got your turn at bat you swung for the home run, not the double, and you didn't think about striking out. Even if, like the Babe, you did that sixty percent of the time you stepped to the plate. . . .

THIRTEEN

Tuesday, 5:25 A.M., Quantico Marine Corps Air Station, VA

The battle was long and hard-fought, bodies falling everywhere, faces twisting in anguish, commands and cries shattering the early morning silence.

"They're such assholes," Melissa Squires said to the other wives around the picnic table. She tapped the back of her husband's pager. "You'd think they could just have fun with this."

"The kids are," said one woman, wincing as she watched her daughter fall from her father's shoulders in the middle of the in-ground pool. "Oooh . . . that'll leave David in a bad mood today. He and Veronica were out there at four forty-five practicing their moves."

The eight women watched and picked at the bacon, eggs, and muffins that were fast becoming cold. The daily pool war had run over, but they knew better than to call their husbands to the table before it was through. They'd only get pissed off, and they wouldn't come anyway: not with their honor at stake.

There were just two chicken fighters left: lean Lt. Col. Charlie Squires and his spindly son Billy and pumped Private David George and his son Clark. The kids pushed hair from their eyes as their fathers circled each other slowly, each watching for an opening, for a kid who lost his balance, made a clumsy offensive maneuver, shivered and broke his concentration.

Sgt. Grey's wife Lydia said, "Last week, when we were visiting my folks in Alaska, Chick and I got stuck in a snowbank and he refused to call for a tow. He told me to put the car in neutral, then he got behind and *lifted* it out. He walked bent over for two days after, but he wouldn't admit he was sore. Not Hercules."

There was a shout from the pool as Clark lunged at Billy. Instead of stepping back, as he usually did, Lt. Col. Squires moved in: while Clark was leaning forward, Billy grabbed his outstretched arm, pulled down, and the boy flopped back-first into the water. Private George stood there, aghast, as he looked from his son to Squires. There was a smattering applause from the side of the pool, where the other defeated chicken fighters had been watching the showdown.

"That's it, sir?" George said to Squires. "Lor-*dee*, that was shorter than the first Clay-Liston fight."

"Sorry, Sonny," Squires winked. He reached up and high-fived his son.

"And when did you work that one out, sir?"

"While we were suiting up. Made sense, don't you think? Guy expects a retreat, gets an advance — he's gotta be surprised."

"He was, sir," George mumbled, wading toward the shallow end of the pool, his son in his wake.

"Nice fight," Clark said to Billy as he dog-paddled after his father.

"Don't talk like that," George muttered as he lumbered up the steps with the bearing and disposition of Gorgo. "You'll lose your edge for tomorrow."

Squires followed him out, his eyes drawn to headlights shining through the living-room window of his home in the base family quarters. He snatched a towel from a chaise lounge as the lights snapped off, then watched as a lone figure walked around the one-story cottage, silhouetted by the light blue horizon. No one could have gotten to this quarter without passing through the gate that separated his crew from the FBI Academy, and no one could have gotten through the gate without a call to him directly.

Unless they were from Op-Center.

Draping the towel over his shoulders and slipping on his sandals, the Lieutenant Colonel walked quickly toward the house.

"Charlie, your eggs are getting cold!"

"Be right there, Missy. Set 'em next to George, they'll stay warm."

Squires's Striker team of twelve full-time men and their support crews was established six months before, the same time as Op-Center. They were the so-called "black" side of the agency, their existence a secret from outsiders except those who needed to know: the heads of the other military and spy agencies, and the President and Vice President themselves. Their charter was simple: they were sent onto the field when offense was needed. They were an elite squad that could be counted on to strike hard and fast. Though all the Striker members belonged to the military and drew pay from their respective branches, they worked in nondescript camouflage pants and shirts without markings of any kind. If they screwed up, there was no way for anyone to trace them . . . or place blame.

Squires smiled as Mike Rodgers came around the side of the building. The tall man's arched nose — broken four times in college basketball — high, intelligent forehead, and light brown eyes that seemed almost golden were a welcome sight.

"I hope I'm glad to see you," Squires said, saluting the two-star General. When Rodgers returned the salute, the men shook hands.

"That depends on whether or not you were getting bored."

"Does diet Coke fizz? Yes, sir, we're ready for action."

"Good. Because I radioed the chopper: get one through eleven ready and have Krebs bring an extra grip. We leave in five minutes."

Squires knew not to ask where to or why only eleven men instead of the full Dirty Dozen were going — not while they were out in the open where their wives or children might hear. Innocent remarks, made over unsecured lines to friends or relatives, could be disastrous. He also knew not to ask about the small black bag Rodgers carried, or why there was a sewn-on design of what looked like a weed growing out of concrete. When and if the General wanted to tell him about it, he would.

Instead, Squires said, "Yes, sir," saluted again, and jogged back to the picnic table. The dozen other men were already on their feet and ready to go, the hostilities and disappointments of the morning's sport quickly forgotten.

After a word with Squires, eleven of the twelve men jogged to their homes to get their gear, none of them stopping to say good-bye to their wives or children: a sad face or teary eye might come to them when they were called on to risk their lives, cause them to hesitate. It was better to leave cold and make up later. The one man who hadn't been picked sat and hunkered down over his paper plate: this was not Private George's morning.

Like each man, Squires kept his grip handy and within four minutes they were running across the field beyond the fence, toward the Bell Jetranger that was being fired up for the half-hour ride to Andrews Air Force Base.

FOURTEEN

Tuesday, 7:30 P.M., Seoul

The sound truck looked like a gutted avocado, blasted panels peeled back by the force of the explosion, with only scraps and slag in the center.

For over an hour, Kim Hwan's team had picked over those scraps, looking for any leads. There were traces of plastic explosives stuck to the bottom of what used to be the sound panel, and those had been sent to the laboratory for analysis. Other than that, there was nothing. Nothing but the increasing numbers of victims being moved from the ranks of the injured to the list of the dead. The men on the rooftops had seen nothing unusual, one of the two video surveillance cameras they had placed on a rooftop was destroyed by shrapnel, and the other had been trained on the podium, not the crowd.

TV cameras were being collected, their tapes studied, to see if they had recorded anything unusual. Hwan doubted they would help, since it seemed as though all of them had been facing in the same direction: away from the truck. And his computer expert doubted that any of them had caught a useful reflection of the truck in a window, one large and complete enough to be enhanced and studied.

While he worked, Gregory Donald stood close by with his back against a charred streetlight, his unlit pipe still clenched in his teeth. He hadn't said a word and hadn't looked up from the ground; he was no longer crying and he didn't seem to be in shock, though Hwan couldn't begin to imagine the thoughts that had to be going through his mind.

"Sir!"

Hwan looked up as his assistant Choi U Gil came trotting over.

"Ri thinks he's found something."

"Where?"

"In an alley beside the Sakong Hotel. Shall I radio the Director? He asked to be told everything."

Hwan stepped down from the chassis of the exploded truck. "Let's wait and see what we've got. I'm sure he has his hands full."

Explaining the corner-cutting to the President, no doubt.

Hwan followed Choi toward the National Museum on the southern side of the Palace, surprised to see Donald walking after them slowly. Hwan didn't wait for him: he was happy that something was getting through to his friend, and he didn't want to put any pressure on him. Staying busy was all that kept Hwan himself from dwelling on the shattering loss they had suffered.

The wide-W ripple pattern in the dry dirt belonged to a North Korean army boot. There was no doubt about it. "Professor" Ri had suspected as much, and Hwan had confirmed it.

"They lead away from the abandoned hotel," the slight, white-haired chemist said.

"I've sent a team inside," Choi told Hwan.

"The perpetrators appear to have drunk from this" — the Professor pointed to the crushed and empty water bottle on the floor — "and then walked toward the sound truck."

The dirt in the alley was dry, but the hot air was still and the residue hadn't moved. Hwan knelt and studied the four complete prints and two partial ones.

"Has everything been photographed?" Hwan asked.

Choi nodded. "The footprints and the bottle. We're photographing the hotel basement now, as there seems to have been some activity there."

"Good. Send the bottle over for prints, and also have them check the mouth for any kind of residue — saliva, food, anything."

The young assistant ran to the car, removed a large plastic bag and metal tongs from a case, and brought them over. Lifting the bottle carefully, he placed it in the bag and marked the time, date, and place on a white strip at the top. Then he took a work order form from the case, filled it in, put both items in the case, and climbed into the window where a military policeman stood guard.

Hwan continued to study the boot prints, noting that the impression wasn't heavier in front, which meant that the terrorists hadn't been running. He was also trying to determine how much wear there had been on the soles and whether the markings belonged to one boot or many. There seemed to be at least two different right feet, and it struck him as odd that neither showed any wear in the ripples. The North Koreans tended to issue new boots after the winter, when they took the most wear — not during the summer.

"If the bottle was used by the terrorists, you won't find any fingerprints."

Hwan looked up at Donald. The voice was a barely audible monotone; his pipe was unceremoniously stuffed into his vest pocket and his flesh was the color of chalk. But he was here and he was alert, and Hwan was happy to see him.

"No," Hwan said. "I don't expect we will."

"Is that why they didn't take the bottle with them? Because they knew it couldn't lead you to them?"

The Professor said, "One would so conclude."

Donald took a few steps into the shadowy depths of the alley. His arms hung limp at his sides and his shoulders were rounded beneath his awful burden. Watching him move with such pain, Hwan had never felt so helpless.

"This alley, so near to the hotel," Donald said. "I would imagine it's picked clean by the poor. A clean bottle like that was sure to be noticed in your sweep — and, seeing it, you would also see the boot prints."

"I was thinking that myself," Hwan said. "We'd recognize the pattern and would jump to a conclusion about who was behind it."

"This is possible." The Professor shrugged. "But it's also possible that an inconsiderate jogger threw it there and the perpetrators never even noticed it."

"In which case someone's fingerprints will be on it," Hwan said.

"That is correct," said the Professor. "So I had best get to the matter. I'll see if there's anything to look at in the hotel, and then I'll return to the laboratory."

When the diminutive Professor left, Hwan walked to Donald's side.

"Thank you for what you did back there," Donald said, his voice tremulous, his eyes on the ground. "I heard you, but — I couldn't get a grip."

"How could you?"

"I'm not sure I have, even now." Tears spilled from his eyes as he looked around the alley. He breathed heavily and wiped his eyes with his fingers. "This thing, Kim — it isn't their way. They've always used incidents at the DMZ or assassination to send us messages."

"I know. And there's something else."

Before Hwan could continue, a black Mercedes with diplomatic plates screeched to a stop in front of the alley. A clean-cut young man got out on the driver's side.

"Mr. Donald!"

Donald stepped from the darkness. "I'm Gregory Donald."

Hwan moved quickly to his side. He didn't know who else might be a target today, and was taking no chances.

"Sir," said the man, "there's a message for you at the Embassy."

"From?"

" 'An enemy of the Bismarck,' I was told to say."

"Hood," he said to Hwan. "I was expecting that. Maybe he has some information."

As the men approached the car, the young Embassy official reached down and popped the electric door lock.

"Sir, I was also told to see to Mrs. Donald. Is there anything she needs? Perhaps she'd like to come with us?"

Donald pressed his lips together and shook his head; then his knees gave out and he fell against the side of the car, his arms folded beneath his chest.

"Sir!"

"He'll be all right," Hwan said, and waved for the young man to sit. He put an arm around his friend's waist and helped him up. "You *will* be, Gregory."

Donald nodded as he stood.

"I'll notify you there when we come up with something."

A somber Hwan opened the door and Donald slid into the car.

"Do me a favor, Kim?"

"Anything."

"Soonji loved the Embassy and she admired the Ambassador. Don't — don't let her go there. Not the way she was. I'll phone General Savran. Would you see that" — he breathed deeply — "that she gets to the base?"

"I will."

Hwan shut the door and the car drove off. It was quickly swallowed by the confusion of honking cars, buses, and trucks, the thick evening rush hour made worse by vehicles detoured from around the Palace.

"God be with you, Gregory," he said, then glanced toward the red sun. "I can't be with him, Soonji, so please — look after him."

Turning, Hwan walked back into the alley and looked down at the footprints. The shadows were more pronounced now in the slanting rays of the setting sun.

But there *was* one thing more, and it bothered him more than the too-convenient presence of the bottle and boot prints.

After telling the guard at the basement window to inform Choi that he'd gone to his office, Hwan hurried back to his car, wondering just how far Director Yung-Hoon would be willing to go to break this case. . . .

FIFTEEN

Tuesday, 5:55 A.M., Washington, D.C.

As soon as he was in his car, Hood phoned Op-Center and told his Executive Assistant, Stephen "Bugs" Benet, to start the count-down clock at twenty-four hours. That was something Liz Gordon had suggested: studies showed that most people work better with deadlines, something to shoot for. The clock was a constant reminder that although you had to run a marathon, really pour it on, there was an end in sight.

It was one of the few things on which Hood and Liz agreed.

As Bugs was telling Hood that Gregory Donald had been located and was being brought to the Embassy on Sejongno, just two blocks from the Palace, the Director's personal cellular phone rang. Telling Bugs he'd be there in fifteen minutes, Hood hung

90

up and answered the phone.

"Paul, it's me."

Sharon. He heard a ping in the background and muffled voices. She wasn't at home.

"Honey, what is it?"

"It's Alexander — "

"Is he all right?"

"After you left, he started wheezing worse than I've ever heard him. The nebulizer wasn't helping, so I brought him to the hospital."

Hood felt his own chest tighten.

"The doctors have injected him with epinephrine, and are watching him," Sharon said. "I don't want you coming here. I'll call as soon as we know something."

"You shouldn't have to do this alone, Sharon."

"I'm not alone — I know that. And what would you do here?"

"Hold your hand."

"Hold the President's hand, I'll be fine. Look, I want to call Harleigh and make sure she's all right. I think I scared her out of a year's growth when I went running through the house carrying Alex."

"Promise you'll beep the minute anything happens."

"I promise."

"And tell them both I love them."

"I always do."

Hood felt like hell as he drove through the early-morning traffic to Andrews Air Force Base, home of Op-Center. Sharon had had to shoulder a lot in seventeen years of marriage, but this was the capper. He could hear the fear in her voice, the trace of bitterness in her remark about the President, and he wanted to go to her. But he knew that if he did, she would only feel guilty for having pulled him away. And when she felt like that she got angry at herself, which wasn't what she needed now.

Unhappy as he was, there was nothing to do but go to Op-Center. But it was ironic, he thought. Here he was, the head of one of the most sophisticated agencies in the world, able to eavesdrop on hostages a mile away or read a newspaper in Teheran from Earth orbit. Yet there was nothing in the world he could do to help his son . . . or his wife.

His palms were damp, his mouth dry, as he swung off the highway and raced toward the base. He couldn't help his family because of whoever was behind the explosion, and he fully intended to make them pay.

SIXTEEN

Tuesday, 8:00 P.M., the Sea of Japan

The boat was pre-World War II vintage, a ferry that had been turned into a troop transport and then back into a ferry again.

As night fell over the sea, the two North Koreans sat on the foredeck benches, playing checkers with metal pieces on a magnetic board. The cases of money were laid flat between them, serving as a makeshift table.

A strong wind had begun to blow across the deck, misting them with seawater and rattling the heavy board. It drove most of the passengers into the cabin, where it was warm, dry, and light; one of the two men looked around.

"We should go in, Im," he said. It wasn't good to be alone: crowds dissuaded thievery.

Without finishing the game, one of the men began packing it up while the other stood, his hands on the handles of the cases.

"Make sure you don't jostle the board, Yun, and cost me my — "

A spray of red fell across the suitcases. Yun looked up and saw a dark figure standing behind his partner; the gleaming tip of a stiletto was protruding from the front of Im's throat.

Yun opened his mouth to scream, but he was cut short as a blade tore through his windpipe from behind. He scratched at his throat as his blood poured over his fingers, mingling with that of his companion. Both pools were softened by falling drops of sea and stirred by the wind.

The two assassins withdrew their blades and one of them bent over the dying men while the other walked aft, to the railing. He began shining his flashlight on and off in ten-second cycles while his associate severed the pinkie finger of each man. Only Yun managed a gurgled scream as the blade cut through his flesh.

His dark gray greatcoat flapping in the wind, the killer threw the fingers over the side; the signature of the Yakuza was upon the victims, and the authorities would spend weeks looking for the killers. By the time they realized they were chasing shadows, it

94

would be too late.

Going back to retrieve the suitcases, the assassin made sure they were secure and then glanced toward the cabin. There were no faces in the circular windows, and the darkness and sea spray would have made identification impossible in any event; the bridge was set well back, atop the cabin, leaving the crew without a clear view of the deck. With luck, no one would come outside and no one else would have to die.

His companion was still flashing his light. By the time he rejoined him, the hum of the distant engine was already audible, and they could see the dim outline of the amphibious plane, all but the running lights turned off. The LA-4-200 Buccaneer came up beside the rear transom door, pacing the ferry, prop-wash turning the sea spray into thousands of tiny darts. The killer shined his flashlight on the cockpit, and the pilot threw open the gull-wing hatch and tossed out an inflatable raft, the bow ring attached to several yards of steel cable. It landed heavily in the water, bucking against the wind.

By now, there was activity on the bridge as the crew saw the plane.

"Hurry," the man with the flashlight told his companion.

Setting the cases down, the man jumped

toward the raft. Landing in the water beside the inflatable, he grabbed the safety line, pulled himself in, then turned to face the ferry. Picking up one of the suitcases, his associate swung it toward the raft and released it. The other man caught it, then held out his arms for the second. He caught that too, then pulled his companion aboard when he jumped from the ferry.

Even as crew members reached the deck and found the bodies, the pilot was reeling the raft into the seaplane. Within moments, the men were on board, the aircraft's lights had flared on, and the plane and money were airborne, headed north. Only when it was out of view from the ship would it turn west — not to Japan and the Yakuza but to North Korea.

SEVENTEEN

Tuesday, 6:02 A.M., Op-Center

The evening and day shifts at Op-Center met at six A.M., at which time Paul Hood and Mike Rodgers took charge from Curt Hardaway and Bill Abram. Policy prohibited Hardaway and Abram from remaining in command after their shift: important decisions were best made by fresh minds, and at rare times when neither Hood nor Rodgers was available, duties were preassigned to different members of the prime day team.

Political Officer Martha Mackall had arrived minutes before and, after passing through the keycard and keypad entry and greeting the somber armed guards behind the Lexan, she replaced her own evening team counterpart, Bob Sodaro. Sodaro briefed her on what had happened since 4:11 that morning, when Op-Center first became involved in the Korean crisis.

Her stride confident, posture ramrod-straight, the handsome, forty-nine-year-old daughter of legendary soul singer Mack Mackall walked through the hub of Op-Center — the bullpen, with its maze of cubicles and operatives hurrying here and there. Since Hood's code hadn't been posted on the computer duty roster where she checked in upstairs, on ground level, she knew she'd be sitting in for him until he arrived. Passing through the bullpen to the action level office that ringed the hub of Op-Center, she heard her name on the intercom: there was a call from Korea for Hood. She paused, snatched a phone from the wall, and told the operator she would take the call for the Director in his office.

Hood's office was just a few steps away, in the southwestern corner. Located beside the Tank, it was the largest office in the building: he hadn't taken it for that reason, however, or for the view, since there were no windows anywhere. The fact was, no one else wanted it. The Tank was surrounded by walls of electronic waves that generated static to anyone trying to listen in with bugs or external dishes. There was some concern among the younger members of the team that the waves might affect their reproductive systems; Hood said that for all the use he got from his equipment anymore, he might as well have the leg room.

Unknown to him, Liz Gordon had noted the comment in his psych profile. Sexual frustration could impair his effectiveness on the job.

Martha entered her access code on the keypad of his office door.

Poor Pope Paul, she thought, reflecting on the latest nickname Ann Farris had given him. Martha wondered if the Director realized that all he had to do was crook his finger at his sexy Press Officer, and she'd do more to him than shower him with epithets. And he would have a reason to change office.

The door clicked open and Martha walked into the wood-paneled office. She perched herself on the corner of the desk and snatched up one of the two phones on the desk, the secure line; the LED ID at the bottom of the unit read 07-029-77, telling her that the caller was in the U.S. Embassy in Seoul. The prefix "1" instead of "0" would have indicated that the call was from the Ambassador. A third line, for teleconferencing, also secure, was integrated in the computer system.

Before she spoke, she switched on the dig-

99

ital tape recorder that translated words to type with amazing speed and accuracy. An almost simultaneous transcript of their talk appeared on a monitor on the desk beside the phone.

"Director Hood is unavailable. This is Martha Mackall."

"Hello, Martha. Gregory Donald."

At first she didn't recognize the slow, soft voice on the other end. "Sir, yes — Director Hood isn't in yet, but he's been anxious to hear from you."

There was a short silence. "I was . . . there, of course. Then we were looking at the blast site, Kim and I."

"Kim — ?"

"Hwan. Deputy Director of the KCIA."

"Did you find anything?"

"A water bottle. Some boot prints, North Korean military issue." His voice cracked. "Excuse me."

There was a much longer silence. "Sir, are you all right? You weren't injured, were you?"

"I fell — nothing broken. It was my wife . . . she was the one that was hurt."

"Not seriously, I hope."

His voice broke again as he said, "They murdered her, Martha."

Martha's hand shot to her mouth. She had

100

only met Soonji once, at Op-Center's first Christmas party, but her charm and quick mind had made an impression.

"I'm so sorry, Mr. Donald. Why don't we talk later — "

"No. They're taking her to the army base, and I'm going over when I finish here. It's best we talk now."

"I understand."

He took a moment to collect himself and then continued, his voice stronger. "There . . . were footprints in an alley, made by a North Korean army boot or boots. But neither Kim nor I believe that North Koreans were wearing them. Or if they were, that they were operating with the sanction of their government."

"Why do you think that?"

"The clues were out in the open, no effort made to conceal them. A professional wouldn't have done that. And the North Koreans have never attacked blindly like this."

As he was speaking, Hood walked into his office; Martha touched a button on the screen, scrolled the transcription back several lines, and pointed for Hood to see. After he read the passage about Soonji, he nodded gravely, then sat quietly behind the desk and rubbed two fingers against his forehead.

"Then you feel that someone wants to make this *look* like a North Korean attack," Martha said. "They've denied having had a hand in it."

"I'm saying it's an option we must explore before rattling any sabers at Pyongyang. For once, they may be telling the truth."

"Thank you, sir. Is — is there anything we can do for you?"

"I know General Norbom at the base, and Ambassador Hall has promised to do . . . whatever she can here. I appear to be in good hands."

"All right. But if you need help — "

"I'll call." His voice became stronger as he said, "Give Paul my best, and tell him — tell him that however Op-Center becomes involved in this, I want a part of it. I want to find the animals who did this."

"I'll tell him," she said as Donald hung up.

As soon as it heard the dial tone, the computer filed the conversation, marked the time, and cleared itself for the next call.

Martha placed the receiver in the cradle and slid off the desk. "Shall I call Ambassador Hall and make sure they give Donald whatever he needs?"

Hood nodded.

"You've got eye bags. Rough night?"

"Alex had a bad asthma attack. He's in the hospital."

"Ooo — sorry to hear that." She took a step forward. "You want to go to him? I'll watch things here."

"No. The President wants us to prepare the Options Paper on this thing, and I need you to get me the latest data on North Korea's financial ties to Japan, China, and Russia — black market as well as legitimate. If we've got a real situation, my feeling is that the President may want a military solution, but let's see what we can do with sanctions."

"Will do. And don't worry about Alex. He'll be fine. Kids are tough."

"They've got to be to survive us," Hood said, reaching for the intercom. Buzzing his aide Bugs, he told him to have Liz Gordon report to the Tank.

As she left, Martha hoped that she hadn't been too forward by offering to sit in for Hood. She felt bad for the way she jumped on Alexander's misfortune to improve her résumé, and made a mental note to have her secretary send him some balloons; but while Ann Farris had her heart set on the Director, Martha had her heart set on the directorship. She liked and respected Hood, but she didn't want to be Op-Center's Political Officer forever. Her fluency in ten languages and understanding of world economies made her more valuable than that. Co-managing an international crisis like this would have been a major notch in her portfolio, setting her up for advancement here or, if she were lucky, a move to the State Department.

There's always tomorrow, she told herself as she traversed the narrow corridor between the bullpen and the executive offices, passing Liz Gordon who looked like she had a serious head of steam and was in desperate need of a place to vent it. . . .

EIGHTEEN

Tuesday, 6:03 A.M., Andrews Air Force Base

"You really don't care if the boss blows a gasket, do you, sir?"

Lt. Col. Squires and Mike Rodgers were jogging across the field. It was less than a minute since the Jetranger had touched down and already it was airborne again, headed back to Quantico. The two officers were leading the line of Striker men toward the C-141B, which was revving up on the airstrip ahead. In addition to his gear, Squires was carrying a Toshiba Satellite portable computer with a specially designed side-mounted laserjet printer, which contained flight plans for 237 different locations, along with detailed maps and possible mission profiles.

"Now what would Hood blow a gasket about?" Rodgers asked. "I'm a quiet sort of guy . . . listen a lot. I voice my opinions politely and deferentially."

"Begging your pardon, sir, but Krebs is your size, and you had him bring an extra set of togs. Our play-books are all designed for a twelve-man squad. You're taking George's place, aren't you?"

"That's right."

"And I'll bet a month's pay that Mr. Hood hasn't okayed it."

"Why trouble him with details? He's got a lot on his mind."

"Well, sir — right there are two very good reasons why gaskets blow. Pressure, and a piece o'something where it doesn't belong. In this case, you . . . here."

Rodgers shrugged a shoulder. "Sure, he'll be pissed. But Hood won't stay that way. He's got a perfectly capable team back at Op-Center and, hell, we don't agree on much anyway. He won't miss me."

"Which brings up another point, sir. Permission to speak freely?"

"Shoot."

"I've got a perfectly capable team here too. Are you going to be running the show, or are you taking Private George's place?"

"I won't be wearing my stars, Charlie. You're in command, and I'll do whatever job needs to be done. You and your little laptop will have twelve hours to bring me up to speed."

"So this jaunt is just your idea of a good way to start the week. A chance to get out from behind the desk."

"Something like that," Rodgers said as they reached the huge, black transport plane. "You know how it is, Charlie. If you don't use the equipment, it gets rusty."

Squires laughed. "You, sir? Rusty? I don't think so. This kind of action is in the Rodgers's genes way back to — was it the Spanish-American War?"

"That's the one," Rodgers said. "Great-great-granddad Captain Malachai T. Rodgers."

The officers stopped on either side of the hatch, and as Squires shouted, *Go! Go! Go!"* the men climbed through without breaking stride.

Rodgers's heart swelled as the men went aboard, beat as proudly as it always did when he saw American soldiers running to do their duty. Young, afraid, and varying shades of green they went anyway, it was a sight that never failed to stir him. He was one of them during his first tour in Viet Nam and, after getting his Ph.D. in history from Temple University while he was stationed at Ft. Dix, he went back and led battalions of them in the Persian Gulf War.

Tennyson once wrote that Lady Godiva was a sight to make an old man young, and women did do that to him. But so did this. Twenty-six years slipped away in less than a minute, and he felt nineteen again as he followed the last enlisted man into the plane, allowing Squires to bring up the rear.

Despite his own somewhat glib assessment, Rodgers knew that the Lieutenant Colonel was right. Hood definitely would not be happy that he was going. For all his smarts and his often astounding skills as a mediator, Hood hated letting anything out of his control. And by going into the field, half a world away, Rodgers would effectively be out of his control. But above all, Hood was a team player: if it was necessary for the Striker team to go in and perform any covert actions, the Director wouldn't let ego stop him from letting the team — and Rodgers — do the job and grab the glory . . . or play the goat.

As soon as they were aboard, the men took their seats along the sides of the bare cabin while the ground crew finished prepping the massive plane. First introduced in 1982, the Lockheed C-141B Starlifter, with its 159-foot 11-inch top-mounted wings, was heir to the laurels of the earlier C-141A, introduced in 1964. That plane distinguished itself with year after year of daily nonstops to Viet Nam — its performance record one of the many unheralded benefits to come from the war. No other army had a troop transport that reliable, and that gave the U.S. an edge.

At 168 feet 4 inches in length, the C-141B — longer than its predecessor by 23 feet 4 inches — could accommodate 154 troops, 123 paratroops, 80 stretchers, and 16 sitting casualties or cargo. Flight refueling equipment located in the back added 50 percent to its normal range of 4,080 miles — longer if, like now, it was carrying less than its 70,847-pound payload. The jet would make it to Hawaii without any trouble, where it would be met and refueled in flight by a KC-135 tanker. From there, it was an easy run to Japan, and then a rapid half-hour chopper ride to North Korea.

While the crew finished up their preflight checklist, the Striker men went through their own inventory. In addition to his own gear — camouflage uniform, otherwise unmarked, a nine-inch knife, and one Beretta 92-F 9-mm automatic pistol, also unmarked — each man was responsible for bringing items the team would require, from the cardboard-box meals of ham sandwiches and candy bars to the field phones to the all-important TAC SAT radio with a parabolic antenna that unfolds for a satellite uplink.

Leaving the men, Squires and Rodgers headed for the cockpit followed by Sgt. Chick Grey. The Striker team had no special needs for the flight, but it was up to the Sergeant to find out if the flight crew required anything of the men, from weight distribution — not a problem on this mission, where they'd be rattling around the cabin — to the use of electronic equipment.

"You want to brief him?" Squires asked Rodgers — with a bit of an edge, the General thought. Or maybe he was just yelling to be heard over the four loud 21,000-pound st Pratt & Whitney TF33-P7 turbofan engines.

"Charlie, I told you — you're the head chef. I'm just here for dinner."

Squires smirked as they made their way down the ribbed cabin to the open door of the flight deck and introduced themselves to the pilot, copilot, first officer, navigator, and communications officer.

"Captain Harryhausen?" Sgt. Grey repeated the name as the Lieutenant Colonel booted the computer, the navigator looking over his shoulder. "Sir, are you by any chance the same Captain Harryhausen who flew a

United DC10 to Alaska last week?"

"I'm that very same Captain Harryhausen, U.S. Air Force Reserves."

A grin tore across the Sergeant's beefy face. "Now if that ain't one for Robert Ripley. My family and me were on that plane, sir! Jeez — what were the chances?"

"Actually very good, Sergeant," said the Captain. "I've had the Seattle-to-Nome route for seven months now. I put in for this assignment so I could finally fly into someplace with warm sunshine and no ice, unless it was in iced tea."

As the Captain proceeded to tell Sgt. Grey what he already knew — that his men should refrain from using Discmans and Game Boys until he gave the word — Squires pulled a cable from the laptop, plugged it into the navigator's console, pushed a button on his keyboard, and dumped the data into the C-141B's navigation computer. The process took six seconds; even before he'd closed the Toshiba, the onboard computer had begun matching the flight path with weather reports that would come in every fifteen minutes from U.S. bases along the route.

Squires faced the Captain and patted the computer. "Sir, I'd appreciate your letting me know the minute we can fire this up again."

The Captain nodded and returned the Lieutenant Colonel's salute.

Five minutes later they were taxiing down the runway, and two minutes after that they were banking away from the rising sun, heading southwest.

As he sat beneath the swinging light bulbs inside the wide, nearly empty cabin, Rodgers found himself reluctantly contemplating the downside of what he was doing. Op-Center was just half a year old, its modest twenty-million-dollar annual budget skimmed from CIA and Department of Defense budgets. On the books they didn't exist, and it would be an easy matter for the President to erase them if they ever screwed up big-time. Lawrence had been satisfied, if not impressed, with the way they handled their first job, finding and defusing a bomb onboard the space shuttle *Atlantis*. Their technoweenie, Matt Stoll, had really come through on that one — much to the pride and frustration of Director Hood, who had a deep and abiding distrust of technology. Probably because his kid was always whipping him at Nintendo.

But the President had been furious that two hostages had been shot in Philadelphia — even if the gunfire did come from the local police, who mistook them for terrorists.

The President saw that as a failure of Op-Center to completely control the situation, and he was right.

Now they had a new mission, though how much of it would be theirs remained to be seen. He'd have to wait for Hood to brief him on that. But this much he knew was true: if the Striker team veered so much as one step past their orders, and the number two man at Op-Center was there, the agency's plug would be pulled so fast Hood wouldn't have time to get pissed off.

Cracking his knuckles, Rodgers was reminded of the immortal words of Mercury astronaut Alan B. Shepard as he waited to be launched into space: "Dear God, please don't let me fuck up."

NINETEEN

Tuesday, 8:19 P.M., Seoul

The U.S. Army base in Seoul was a source of annoyance to many of the locals.

Sitting on twenty acres of prime real estate in the heart of the city, it housed two thousand troops on four acres, with ordnance and equipment stored in another two. The remaining fourteen acres existed for the amusement of the troops: PX's, two first-run movie theaters, and more bowling alleys than most large U.S. cities. With most of its effective military strength at the DMZ, thirty-five miles to the north, where a total of one million soldiers stood toe-to-toe, the base was a modest support system at best. Its role was part political, part ceremonial: it signified enduring friendship with the Republic of Korea, and it provided the U.S. with a base from which to keep an eye on

Japan. A DOD long-term study indicated that remilitarization of Japan was inevitable by the year 2010; if the U.S. ever lost its bases there, the base in Seoul would become the most important in the Asia-Pacific region.

But the South Koreans were more concerned about trade with Japan, and many felt that a few hotels and upscale stores on that site would serve them better than a sprawling U.S. base.

Major Kim Lee of the ROK was not among those who wanted the land returned to South Korea. A patriot whose late father was a top general during the war, whose mother was executed as a spy, Kim would have been happy to see more U.S. troops in South Korea, more bases and airstrips between the capital and the DMZ. He was suspicious of North Korean overtures over the past four months, in particular their sudden willingness to allow inspections by the International Atomic Energy Agency and a willingness to abide by the Nuclear Nonproliferation Treaty. In 1992, they had allowed six inspections of nuclear facilities, then threatened to withdraw from their obligations under the NPT when IAEA asked to inspect their nuclear waste disposal sites. Investigators believed that the Democratic People's Republic of Korea had accumulated at least ninety grams of plutonium through the reprocessing of irradiated reactor fuel, with the goal of using them to produce weapons. The North Koreans were using a small, twenty-five-megawatt thermal graphite-moderated reactor for this purpose.

The DPRK denied that, pointing out the U.S. wouldn't need IAEA to tell them whether the North had tested nuclear weapons; the U.S. said it wasn't necessary to conduct such tests to determine if a payload was in a deliverable state. Denials and accusations flew back and forth as the DPRK suspended its withdrawal, but the standoff continued for years.

And now it was over. The North Koreans recently surprised the world by agreeing to open their nuclear reprocessing facility at Yongbyon to the long-requested "special inspections," but while Russia, China, and Europe hailed the concession as real progress, many people in Washington and Seoul took a different view: that the North had simply erected small, lead-lined "hot room" facilities elsewhere — virtually anywhere — and terminated all weapons research in Yongbyon. Like Saddam Hussein and his milk factory, which the U.S. bombed in the Gulf War, the North Koreans probably built them under schools or churches. IAEA officials would be blissfully unaware of their presence and unwilling to push the matter: how unfair would they seem pressing for additional "special inspections" now that North Korea had fully complied with their initial request.

Major Lee didn't care about hurt feelings in North Korea or effusive praise and vigorous handclapping that had come from Moscow, Beijing, and Paris within minutes after Pyongyang made what they called their "great concession for peace and stability." The North Koreans couldn't be trusted, and he took a perverse satisfaction from the explosion at the Palace: if the world didn't understand that before this afternoon, they did now.

The question that bothered Major Lee and the other officers in Seoul was how would the government choose to respond. They'd wag a finger and rebuke the terrorists, and the U.S. would be prepared to move more troops into the region, but that was likely to be the extent of the response.

Lee wanted more than that.

After printing out the requisition order in the South Korean command center in the northern sector of the base, the Major and two junior officers went to the U.S. supply depot, while a third officer went to collect a truck. After passing through two checkpoints, where their IDs were examined and the day's password requested, they reached the HMV — Hazardous Materials Vault. The rubber-lined room had walls eighteen inches thick, and a door that was opened by a dual key system. Inside the unmarked room, and unknown to most of those on the base, the U.S. stored the agents for chemical weapons: if the people of Seoul weren't happy about the bowling alleys and movie theaters, they'd go nuts over the chemical weapons. But the North was known to have them and, in the event of a shootout, U.S. and South Korean policy was not to be the loser who fought fair.

The Major's requisition order was marked "Eyes Only" and was shown only to the officer in charge of the HMV. Major Charlton Carter rubbed his chin as he sat behind his desk down the hall from the HMV, and read the request for four quarter-sized drums of tabun. Major Lee stood watching him, his hands clasped behind him, his aides standing a step back on either side.

"Major Lee, I confess to being surprised."

Lee tensed. "About — ?"

"Do you know that in my five years sitting here, this is the first requisition I've had."

"But it's all in order."

"Perfectly. And I suppose I shouldn't be

surprised. After what happened in town today, nobody wants to get caught with their jockeys around their ankles."

"Well spoken."

Major Carter read from the requisition. " 'There exists a state of high alert in the southwestern corner of the DMZ.' " He shook his head. "And I thought relationships were improving."

"That, apparently, is what the North wanted us to believe. But we have evidence that they're in the process of digging up the chemical drums they've kept buried there."

"Really? Damn. And these quarter-size drums are going to do the trick?"

"If used efficiently. You don't need to hammer the enemy with it."

"You're right about that." Major Carter rose. He rubbed the back of his neck. "I assume you've been trained to handle tabun. It's not particularly volatile in the drum — "

"But it's easy to disperse in vapor or spray form, has little smell, is highly toxic, and works quickly when absorbed through the skin and even faster when inhaled. Yes, Major Carter. I've got Grade One certification, Colonel Orlando's class, 1993."

"And you have one of these?" He patted his chest.

Lee undid a button under his tie. He

reached beneath his undershirt and withdrew the key.

Carter nodded. Together, the men removed the chains from around their necks and walked to the vault. The keyholes were on opposite sides where one man couldn't possibly reach them both: when the keys were inserted and turned, the door retreated into the floor until a foot of the top remained: this impediment was designed like a speed bump, to keep soldiers from rushing off with the chemicals and having an accident.

Replacing the key around his neck, Major Carter returned to his desk to get an order fulfillment form while Major Lee supervised the careful loading of the two-foot-high orange drum onto a dolly. These dollies, specially designed to cradle different sized containers, hung on a rack on the back wall: if an enemy ever got through security and made it this far, they might not know that the dollies contained chips that sounded an alarm when they were taken more than two hundred yards from the HMV.

The drums were strapped to the dollies and taken outside, in turn, to the waiting truck. As each was loaded, an armed guard from HMV stood watch; she remained behind with the Korean driver each time Lee and his men returned to get another.

When they were finished, Lee went back in and signed the fulfillment order.

Carter gave Lee his copy. "You know to take this to General Norbom's office for his stamp. Otherwise, they won't let you out the gate with this."

"Yes. Thank you."

"I wish you luck," he said, offering Lee his hand. "We need men like you."

"And you," he replied flatly.

TWENTY

Paul Hood and Liz Gordon arrived at the Tank at the same time. Hood ushered her in with a sweep of his hand and then entered behind her. The heavy door was operated by a button in the side of the large oval conference table, and he pushed it when he was inside.

The small room was lit by fluorescent lights hung in banks over the conference table; on the wall across from Hood's chair, the countdown clock flashed its ever-changing array of digital numbers.

The walls, floor, door, and ceiling of the Tank were all covered with sound-absorbing Acoustix; behind the mottled gray-and-black strips were several layers of cork, a foot of concrete, and more Acoustix. In the midst of the concrete, on all six sides of the room,

122

was a pair of wire grids that generated vacillating audio waves; electronically, nothing could enter or leave the room without being utterly distorted. If any listening device did somehow manage to pick up a conversation from inside, the randomness of the changing modulation made reassembling the conversations impossible.

Hood sat down at the head of the table and Liz sat to his left. He turned down the brightness on the monitor that sat beside a computer keyboard at his end of the table; a tiny fiber-optic camera was attached to the top of the monitor, and a similar setup was located at Mike Rodgers's position, across the table.

Liz slapped her yellow pad on the table. "Listen, Paul. I know what you're going to say, but I'm *not* wrong. This wasn't his doing."

Hood looked into the hazel eyes of his Staff Psychologist. Her medium-length brown hair was pulled back by a black headband; a white streak on a lapel of her smart red pantsuit was the residue of a carelessly brushed ash from one of the Marlboros she chain-smoked in her office.

"I wasn't going to say you were wrong," Hood replied evenly. "But what I have to know is precisely how sure you are. The

123

President put me in charge of the Korean Task Force, and I don't want to tell him his North Korean counterpart is talking peace in our time while he's trying to egg us into crossing the DMZ."

"Eighty-nine percent," she said in her raspy voice, "that's how sure I am. If Bob Herbert's intelligence is accurate and we factor that in, our confidence level is ninety-two percent." She pulled a stick of Wrigley's from her pocket and unwrapped it. "The President of North Korea does not want a war. The short of it is, he's thrilled with the way the lower class is growing and he knows that the way to remain in power is to *keep* that class happy. The best way to do that is end their self-imposed isolation. And you know what Herbert thinks."

He did indeed. His Intelligence Officer believed that if the DPRK generals were opposed to the President's policies, they'd have thrown him out. The sudden death of long-time leader Kim Il Sung in 1994 left enough of a power void that they could have moved in if they didn't like what was happening.

Liz folded the gum into her mouth. "I know you don't think the psych division is very scientific, and you'd be happy as an elf if we were shut down. Okay. We didn't figure on the police overreaction in Philly. But we've worked on the North Koreans for years, and I'm sure we've got this right!"

A computer monitor to his left beeped. Hood glanced at the E-mail message from Bugs Benet: the other Task Force members were ready for the teleconference. Hood pushed the ALT key to acknowledge, then regarded Liz.

"I believe in first impressions, not in psychology. But I've never met the North Korean leaders, so I *have* to rely on you. Here's what I need."

Liz uncapped her pen and began writing.

"I want you to go back to your data and give me a fresh profile of the top North Korean leaders factoring in the following: even if they *didn't* endorse that attack, how will they react to a Defcon 5 mobilization on our part, to a possible South Korean reprisal in Pyongyang, and whether any of the DPRK generals are crazy enough to have authorized something like this without a presidential okay.

"I also want you to recheck that study you gave the CONEX people about China. You said that the Chinese wouldn't want to get into a war on the peninsula, but that a few officials *might* push for it. Write up who and why and send a copy to Ambassador

Rachlin in Beijing so he can do whatever stroking he feels is necessary."

When they were finished — indicated, as always, by the Director's exasperated exhaling, of which he probably wasn't even aware — Liz stood and Hood buzzed her out. Before the door had shut again, Op-Center's Interpol/FBI liaison Darrell McCaskey stepped in. Hood acknowledged the short, wiry, prematurely gray ex-FBI man and, when McCaskey was seated, Hood tapped the Control key on his keyboard. As he did, the monitor divided into six equal sections, three across and two down. Five of them were live television images of the other attendees at that morning's meeting; the sixth was Bugs Benet who would monitor the transcription minutes of the meeting. There was a black bar at the bottom for messages: if it was necessary for Hood to be updated on developments in Korea, the Op-Center Situation Room would send a concise message crawling across the screen.

Hood didn't understand why it was necessary to see the people he was talking to, but wherever hi-tech was available it was used, whether it was pertinent or not. The whole setup reminded him of the opening of *The Brady Bunch*.

The audio for each image was controlled

by the F buttons on the keyboard, and before he turned on the others he hit F6 to talk to Bugs.

"Has Mike Rodgers come in yet?"

"Not yet. But the team has taken the field, so he should be here shortly."

"Send him over when he arrives. Does Herbert have anything for us?"

"Also negative. Our intelligence people in the DPRK were as surprised as we were by all this. He's in touch with the KCIA, and I'll let you know when they have something."

Hood thanked him, then regarded the faces of his colleagues as he tapped F1 through F5.

"Can everyone hear me?"

Five heads nodded.

"Good. Gentlemen, it was my impression — and correct me if I'm wrong — that the President wants to be decisive in his handling of this crisis."

"And victorious," Av Lincoln's little image added.

"And victorious. Which means that the carrots we suggest may be a lot shorter than our sticks. Steve, you have the policy files."

The National Security Adviser turned slightly to look at another monitor in his office. "Our policy on the peninsula is governed, of course, by treaty with the South.

Within that framework, we are committed to the following: to work toward the stabilization of both sides, politically. To denuclearize the North and promote the NPT; to maintain a North/South dialogue; to follow our historic consultation procedure with Japan and China; to become immediately and closely involved in any initiatives undertaken by either side; and to make sure that no third party takes a more active hand in the foregoing than the United States."

"In short," said the Secretary of State, "we keep all our fingers in the pie."

Hood took a moment to look from face to face. There was no need to invite further comment: if anyone had anything to say, they'd say it.

"Strategies, then," he said. "Mel, what do the Joint Chiefs of Staff feel we should do?"

"We only spoke briefly," he said, using two fingers to smooth down his thin mustache. "But Ernie, Mel, Greg, and I were talking before you arrived at the White House, and we're all of a mind about this. Regardless of whether the bombing was an officially sanctioned act or not, we will seek to contain it through diplomatic channels. The DPRK will be assured of continuing bilateral talks, of increased trade, and of our help in maintaining the current regime."

"The only caveat," said blond, youthful-looking CIA Director Greg Kidd, "is whether economic and political rewards will be enough to deter them from a land grab. South Korea is the Holy Grail to them, particularly to some of the generals, who may not settle for anything less. Taking the South would also save them a fortune: the nuclear weapons program is a serious drain on the economy, and they could ratchet that down if they didn't have to worry about *our* nuclear presence in the South."

"So we may have a situation where it makes better fiduciary sense to unleash a conventional war rather than pursue an all-out nuclear arms race."

"Correct, Paul. Especially when they have to play catch-up against the U.S."

"If money is such a large part of this," Hood continued, "what can we do to put the screws to them financially?"

Av said, "I've got the Deputy Secretary of State on the phone with Japan right now, but it's a touchy situation. Both Koreas still harbor a great deal of antagonism toward Japan for atrocities during the Second World War, but the North and South are also trading partners with Japan. If they can't stay on the sidelines, they're going to try very hard to maintain normal relations with both sides."

"Typical," Mel muttered.

"Understandable," Av countered. "The Japanese live in dread of war on the peninsula and the possibility that it will spread."

Greg Kidd said, "There's something else to consider. Failing neutrality, it's very likely that Japan will side with the North."

"Against us?" Hood asked.

"Against us."

"Typical," Mel reiterated.

"The financial ties between Japan and the DPRK go deeper than most people realize. The Japanese underworld has been investing drug and gambling profits heavily in the North . . . we *think* with the tacit blessings of Tokyo."

"Why would the government sanction that?" asked Hood.

"Because of their fear that the North Koreans have Nodong 'Scud' missiles capable of crossing the sea. If there were a war, and the North Koreans wanted to play that trump card, the Japanese could take quite a pounding. Despite the great PR, our Patriot missiles took out a very small number of Scuds during the Gulf War. The Japanese will back us so long as they don't get their hair mussed."

Hood was silent for a moment. It was his job to pull threads and see where they took him, regardless of how bizarre it seemed on the surface. He turned to Deputy Assistant Director McCaskey.

"Darrell, what's the name of the super-nationalists in Japan, the ones that blew up the Mexico City stock exchange when Bush started pushing NAFTA?"

"The Red Sky League."

"That's the one. As I recall, they oppose close Japanese ties with the U.S."

"True, though they've always taken immediate credit for anything they do. But you've got a point: this may be a third party operation, maybe arms dealers in the Middle East looking to make a killing selling to the North. I'll put some people on it."

The ex-FBI agent went to the computer on the other side of the room and began E-mailing his sources in Asia and Europe.

"That's an interesting notion," Greg Kidd said, "one I had as well. But arms sales may not be what's behind this. I've got people looking into whether someone is trying to draw us into a war while they go hog wild somewhere else, Iraq or the Haitians, for example. They know the American public would never stand for our soldiers fighting in two wars at the same time. If they can get us waist deep in Korea first, that'll leave them free to fight their own war."

Hood regarded Bugs Benet's small image. "Put those in the Options Paper as a footnote under PROBLEM. Whenever the hell Rodgers gets here, he and Martha can hammer out an addendum." He looked back at the monitor. "Av, where do the Chinese stand in all this?"

"I spoke with their Foreign Minister just before the meeting. They insist they don't want war on their Manchurian border, but we also know they don't want a unified Korea there either. In time, it would grow into a capitalistic powerhouse that would spur envy and unrest among the Chinese. In the first case, you have refugees streaming into China, and in the second, Chinese trying to sneak into Korea for their bite of the apple."

"But Beijing is still providing money and military support to the North."

"A relatively modest amount."

"And if there's a war, will that increase or stop?"

Av flipped an invisible coin. "Politically, it could go either way."

"Unfortunately, we need a consensus on this for the President. Anyone care to commit?"

"What do *you* say?" Burkow asked.

Hood thought back to Liz Gordon's psych profile and took a leap of faith. "We assume they'll continue to support the North at present levels — even if war erupts. That would allow them to support their old allies without unduly antagonizing the U.S."

"That sounds reasonable," said National Security Adviser Burkow, "but — if you'll forgive me — I think you're missing an important point. If the Chinese *do* increase their support, and the President has relied on our paper, we'll all have egg on our faces. If, however, we urge him to move substantial manpower into the Yellow Sea — poised to strike at North Korea, but obviously keeping an eye on China — then he'll be greatly relieved when Beijing does nothing."

"Unless they perceive our sea power as a threat," said Defense Secretary Colon. "Then they might be forced to become involved."

Hood thought for several seconds. "I suggest we downplay the China role."

"I agree," said Colon. "I can see almost no circumstance that would cause us to attack supply routes in China, so there's no reason to move guns into their neighborhood."

Hood was glad, but hardly surprised, that Colon agreed. Hood had never served in the military — he lucked out on the draft lottery in 1969 — and one of the first things he learned about officers was how they're typically the last advisers to advocate the use of force. If they did, they wanted to know very clearly and explicitly the exit strategies for their troops.

"I'm with you on that, Ernie," said Av. "The Chinese have lived with our military presence in Korea for nearly half a century: they'll look the other way if war erupts and we use it. They don't want to lose favored nation trade status, not with their economy starting to percolate. And anyway, it will suit them to play the role of Great White Father and try to settle this thing for us."

Hood pushed F6 on the keyboard, then Control/F1 to see the current document. As the transcription had scrolled by Bugs Benet, he had merged the pertinent data with a blank Options Paper file. When the meeting was over, Hood would be able to go over the rough draft of the form, add or detract as necessary, and get it right over to the President.

His quick scan of the document revealed that they had everything they needed — save for military options and the Task Force's opinion as to whether or not they'd be necessary.

"All right," he said. "Good work. Now let's hammer out the rest."

Relying mostly on Defense Secretary Colon

and Chairman of the Joint Chiefs of Staff Parker, and referring to on-file policy papers, the team recommended a measured approach to full battlefield integration: continued slow deployment of troops, tanks, artillery, and Patriots, with nuclear, chemical, and biological depots on alert and ready to move.

Without new information from the KCIA and McCaskey's incomplete check on international terrorists, the Task Force recommended in addition that the President work through diplomatic channels to contain and resolve the crisis.

Hood gave the team members thirty minutes to look over the rough Options Paper and insert additional thoughts before he got to work on the final draft. As he finished up, Bugs cleared his throat.

"Sir, Deputy Director Rodgers would like to speak with you."

Hood looked up at the countdown clock; Rodgers had been out of touch for nearly three hours. Hood hoped he had a good explanation.

"Send him right in, Bugs."

Bugs looked like he wanted to loosen his collar; his round face grew red.

"I can't do that, sir."

"Why? Where is he?"

"On the phone."

Hood was reminded of the funny feeling he'd had when Rodgers quoted Lord Nelson. His features darkened. "Where is he?"

"Sir — somewhere over the Virginia-Kentucky border."

TWENTY-ONE

Tuesday, 9:00 P.M., Seoul

Gregory Donald walked for a while after leaving the Embassy. He was anxious to get to the base, to look after his wife, and to call her parents with the awful news. But he needed time to compose himself for that. To reflect. Her poor father and younger brother would be devastated.

He also had an idea he needed to mull over.

He made his way slowly down old Chongjin Way, past the markets with their brightly colored lanterns, banners, and awnings, all of them alive under the streetlights. The area was more crowded than usual, packed with the curious who had come to look at the blast site, to take pictures and videos and collect mementoes of scrap metal or shards of brick.

He bought fresh tobacco at an open-air stand, a Korean blend; he wanted a taste and smell to associate with this moment, one that would always bring back the aching love he felt for Soonji.

His poor Soonji. She gave up a college professorship in political science here to marry him, to help expatriate Koreans in the U.S. He had never doubted his wife's affection for him, but he had always wondered how much she was moved to marry him by love and how much because it was easier for her to come to the U.S. in his company. He didn't feel guilty thinking that, even now. If anything, her willingness to sacrifice a career that was important to her, to take a husband she barely knew, just to help others made her seem more precious in his eyes. If he had come to realize anything about people in his sixty-two years, it was that relationships between them shouldn't be defined by society, but by the people involved. And he and Soonji had surely done that.

He lit the pipe as he walked, the glow of the flame playing off his tear-filled eyes. It seemed like he should be able to turn around, pick up the phone at the Embassy, and call her, ask her what she was reading or what she'd eaten as he did every night they weren't together. It was inconceivable to him that he couldn't do that — unnatural. He wept as he waited to cross the street.

Would anything matter again?

Right now, he didn't see how. Whatever the level of love they shared, they were also a genuine mutual admiration society. He and Soonji knew that even when no one else appreciated what they were doing or trying to do, they themselves did. They laughed and wept together, debated and fought and kissed and made up together, and hurt together for the hardworking Koreans who were being brutalized in American cities. He could carry on alone, though he no longer seemed to have the desire. It would be his mind and not his heart that drove him. His heart died at a little past six this evening.

Yet, there was still a part of him that burned, that flamed hotter as he thought about the act itself. The explosion. He had known tragedy and loss in his life, had lost so many friends and colleagues through car accidents, plane crashes, and even assassination. But that was random or it was targeted: it was fate or it was an act aimed at a specific figure for a particular deed or philosophy. He simply couldn't comprehend the shocking impunity that drove someone to commit a blind act like this, to snuff out

Soonji's life along with the lives of so many others. What cause was so urgent that the death of innocents was the best way to get attention? Whose ego or ambition or singular world view was so strong that it had to be satisfied in this way?

Donald didn't know, but he cared. He wanted the perpetrators captured and executed. In ancient days, the Koreans decapitated murderers and left their heads on poles for birds to feed on, their souls blind, deaf, and speechless as they wandered through eternity. That was what he wanted for these people. That, and for them not to run into Soonji in the afterlife: in her boundless charity, she was liable to take them by the hand and lead them to a place where it was safe and comfortable.

He stopped walking in front of a movie theater and stood for a minute, thinking again about the footprints and the water bottle. He found himself wishing that he could be a part of Hwan's team, not just to bring the bombers to justice but to give himself something to focus on other than his grief.

Yet maybe there was a job for him, one that could get to the bottom of this quicker than men at the KCIA. He would need General Norbom's help and confidence to succeed, and he would have to know, somehow, that she would have approved, his Soonji.

Thinking about Soonji again brought tears spilling onto his cheeks. Stepping to the curb, Donald hailed a taxi and headed for the U.S. base.

TWENTY-TWO

Tuesday, 7:08 A.M., Virginia-Kentucky Border

Rodgers pressed the radio headset to his ear and, though the volume was turned way up, he was still having a tough time hearing what Paul Hood had to say. Which was just as well: when he'd pulled out his yellow earplugs to take the call, he'd known it wouldn't be warm and fuzzy — and it wasn't.

It would be better if he were screaming, because then he could have heard. But Hood wasn't a screamer. When he got angry he talked slowly, measuring his words with care as though afraid a wrong one might slip in on his wrath. For some reason, Rodgers had this image of Hood wearing an apron and holding a large pallet, feeding his words gingerly as though he were slipping pizzas into an oven.

". . . has left me dangerously understaffed,"

he was saying. "I've got Martha as my right-hand man."

"She's *good*, Paul," he yelled into the microphone. "I felt my place was with the team, first time overseas."

"That was not your decision to make! You should have cleared your itinerary with me!"

"I knew you'd have your hands full. I didn't want to bother you."

"You didn't want me to say 'no,' Mike. At least admit that. Don't jerk me off."

"Okay. I admit it."

Rodgers looked at Lt. Col. Squires, who was pretending not to listen. The General drummed the radio, hoping that Hood knew when to stop: he was as much a professional as the Director was, more so in military matters, and he didn't intend to take more than a bare-bones, there-I've-had-my-say dressing down. Especially from a guy who was busy fundraising with the likes of Julia Roberts and Tom Cruise while he was leading a mechanized brigade in the Persian Gulf.

"All right, Mike," Hood said, "you're there. How do we maximize your effectiveness?"

Good. He did know when to stop.

"For now," Rodgers said, "just keep me apprised of any new developments, and if we have to go into action make sure my staff runs the simulations through the computer."

"I copy on the sims, and the only new development is that the President put us in charge of the Task Force. He wants to play hardball."

"Good."

"We'll debate that over pizza and beer when it's all over. Right now, your orders are to continue to your destination. We'll radio if there are any updates or changes."

"Roger."

"And, Mike?"

"Yes?"

"Let the kids do the heavy lifting, Middle-Aged Man."

The men signed out and Rodgers sat back, chuckling over their favorite *Saturday Night Live* character. Yet what really got him was the pizza reference. Maybe it was just a coincidence, but Hood had an uncanny instinct for picking up people's vibes about things. Rodgers often wondered if Hood had developed those talents in politics or whether he'd been drawn to politics because of it. Whenever Rodgers felt like kicking Hood in the ass, he reminded himself that the guy got the top spot for a reason . . . however much he wished he'd been offered it himself.

He also wished Hood would join him at the

track once in a while, instead of doing the Family Man of the Year drill. They could probably make a fortune together, and some of the girls he knew might loosen Hood up a bit — make everyone's life a little less uptight.

Slipping off the headset, Rodgers lay back against the cold, vibrating aluminum rib of the transport plane. He ran a hand over his graying black hair, freshly buzz-cut the day before.

He knew that Hood couldn't help being what he was any more than Rodgers could change *him*self, and that probably wasn't a bad thing. What was it that Laodamas had said to Odysseus? *"Enter our games, then; ease your heart of trouble."* Where would any of them be without competition and rivalry to spur them on? Had Odysseus not participated in and won the discus throw, he would not have been invited to the palace of Alcinous and been given the gifts that proved so important on his journey home.

"Sir," said Squires, "do you want to start going over our playbook? We'll need a couple of hours."

"Absolutely," said Rodgers. "It'll ease my heart of trouble."

Squires shot him a puzzled look as he scooted closer on the bench and looked down at the oversize looseleaf binder.

TWENTY-THREE

Tuesday, 7:10 A.M., Op-Center

Liz Gordon was sitting in her small office, decorated only with a signed photograph of the President, a *carte de visite* of Freud, and, on the closet door, a Carl Jung dartboard given to her by her second ex-husband.

Across the Spartan metal desk, Associate Staff Psychologist Sheryl Shade and Assistant Psychologist James Solomon both worked on laptops that were plugged into Liz's Peer-2030 computer.

Liz used her old Marlboro to light a fresh one as she stared at her computer monitor. She blew smoke. "It would appear that our data adds up to the President of North Korea being a pretty solid citizen. What do you say?"

Sheryl nodded. "Everything is right in the middle of the chart, or toward the better adjusted. Relationship with his mother is strong . . . long-term girlfriend . . . remembers birthdays and anniversaries . . . no sexual aberrations . . . diet normal . . . drinks very moderately. We even have that cite from Dr. Hwong about how he uses words that communicate ideas rather than trying to impress people with his vocabulary, which is extensive.

"And there's nothing in the files of any of his executive staff that suggests they'd go against him," Sheryl added. "If we're dealing with a terrorist, he or she is not a member of the President's inner circle."

"Right," Liz said. "Jimmy, what've you got?"

The young man shook his head. "We've got a flat line on aggression in *Zhonghua Renmin Gonghe Guo*. In private conversations monitored here and by the CIA since we did our last report — the most recent at 0700 yesterday — the President, Premier, General Secretary of the Communist Party, and other leading figures in the People's Republic of China have all expressed a desire to sit out any kind of confrontation on the peninsula."

"Which all boils down to, we were right in the first place," Liz said through a stream of smoke. "The methodology is right, the conclusions are right, you can take our findings to the goddamn bank." She took another long drag, then told Solomon to fax the names of the most militant Chinese leaders to Ambassador Rachlin in Beijing. "I don't think we have anything to worry about from them, but Hood wants to cover all his bases."

Solomon flung her a two-fingered salute, unplugged his laptop, and hurried to his office. He shut the door behind him.

"I think that just about covers what Paul wanted," Liz said. She drew hard on her cigarette while Sheryl closed her computer and unplugged the cable. Liz watched her carefully. "What've we got here, Sheryl — seventy-eight people?"

"You mean at Op-Center?"

"Yes. There are seventy-eight here, plus another forty-two support personnel we share with DOD and the CIA, and the twelve Striker team members and the people they borrow from Andrews. Figure a hundred forty in all. So why, with all those people — so many of whom are friendly and open-minded and very, very good at what they do — why do I give a fig what Paul Hood thinks about us? Why can't I just do my job, give him what he asks for, and go have a double espresso?"

"Because we seek the truth for its own sake, and he looks for ways to manage it, use it for control."

"You think so, huh?"

"That's part of it. You're also frustrated by that male mindset of his. You remember his psych profile. Atheist, hates opera, never did mind-expanding drugs in the sixties. If he can't touch it, assimilate it in his day-to-day productivity, it's not worth the effort. Though that *is* a saving grace in one respect."

"How's that?" Liz seemed tired as her computer beeped for attention.

"Mike Rodgers is the same way. If they didn't have that in common, they'd maul each other to death with looks and innuendo — worse than they do now."

"The Bligh and Christian of Op-Center." The rail-thin blonde pointed a finger. "I like it."

"But you know, Dr. Shade, I think it's something else — "

Shade looked interested. "Really? What?"

Liz smiled. "Sorry, Sheryl. Thanks to the magic of E-mail, I see that I'm wanted at once by Ann Farris and Lowell Coffey II. Maybe we'll finish this later."

With that, the Staff Psychologist turned the key in her computer, dropped it in her pocket, and walked out the door — leaving a confused assistant behind her.

As she walked briskly down the corridor to the press office, folding more gum, more pure chewing satisfaction, into her mouth, Liz had to suppress a smile. It wasn't fair to have done what she did to Sheryl, but it was a good exercise. Sheryl was new, fresh out of NYU and brimming with book learning — kilobytes more than Liz had had at her age, ten years before. Yet she didn't have very much life experience, and her thinking was much too linear. She needed to explore some mental territory without a roadmap, discover routes of her own. And a puzzle like Liz left her with — *why does my boss care so much what her boss thinks* — will help take her there, make her go through the process of *"Does she have a crush on him? Is she unhappy with her husband? Does she want a promotion, and if so how will that affect me?"* A trail like that could take her to any number of interesting places, all of which would be beneficial to her.

The truth was, Liz enjoyed her espressos a great deal and didn't think about Hood when she had them. His inability — or un-willingness — to grasp the clinical soundness of her work didn't bother her. They crucified Jesus and locked Galileo away, and none of that changed the truth of what they taught.

No, what frosted her was how he was the consummate politician before the shit hit the fan. He courteously and conscientiously heard her out and incorporated snippets of her findings into policy papers and strategies — albeit not because he wanted to. That was what Op-Center's charter demanded. But because he didn't trust her work, she was always the first one he called on the carpet whenever something went wrong. She hated that, and swore that one day she'd leak his godless little psych file to Pat Robertson.

No you wouldn't, she told herself as she knocked on Ann Farris's door, but fantasizing about it did keep her cool whenever he turned on the heat.

The Washington Times once deemed Ann Farris to be one of the twenty-five most eligible young divorcees in the nation's capital. Three years later, she still was.

Standing five-foot-seven, her brown hair bunched behind her and tied with the designer kerchief-of-the-day, her teeth hardball-white, and her eyes a dark rust, she was also one of the least understood women in Washington. With her B.A. in journalism and M.A. in public administration from Bryn Mawr, the Greenwich, Connecticut, blue-blood

Farrises expected her to work on Wall Street with her father, and then at some blue-chip firm as V.P., then Senior V.P., then the sky was the limit.

Instead, she went to work as a political reporter for *The Hour* in nearby Norwalk, stayed two years, landed the job of Press Secretary to the iconoclastic third-party Governor of the state, and married an ultra-liberal public radio commentator from New Haven. She retired to raise their son, then left two years after that when funding cuts cost her husband his job and desperation sent him into the arms of a wealthy Westport matron. Moving to Washington, Ann got a job as Press Secretary for the newly elected junior Senator from Connecticut — a bright, attentive married man. She began having an affair with him shortly after arriving, the first of many intense, satisfying affairs with bright, attentive married men, one of whom held an office higher than Vice President.

That last part wasn't in her confidential psych file, but Liz knew because Ann had told her. She also confessed — though it was obvious — that she had a crush on Paul Hood and entertained some exotic fantasies about him. The statuesque beauty was remarkably frank about her relationships, at least to Liz: Ann reminded her of a Catholic schoolgirl she once knew, Meg Hughes, who was as careful and polite as she could be around the nuns, then uncorked her darkest secrets when they were away.

Liz often wondered if Ann confided in her because she was a psychologist or because she didn't perceive her as a rival.

Ann's husky voice told Liz to come in.

The smell of her office was unique, a blend of her pinelike, not-tested-on-animals Faire perfume and the faint, musky odor of the framed, archivally preserved newspaper front pages hung around her office, from before the Revolution to the present. There were over forty in all, and Ann said it was an interesting exercise to read the articles and ponder how she would have handled the crises differently.

Liz gave a quick smile to Ann, and blinked slowly at Lowell Coffey II. The young attorney stood when she entered; as always, he was fondling something rich — one of his diamond cuff links.

Masturbating the money, Liz thought. Unlike Ann, Coffey Percy Richkid had bought into his attorney-parents' Beverly Hills life-style and Alpha Gamma Crappa grandiloquence. He was always touching something that cost his family more than his yearly salary — Armani tie, gold Flagge fountain pen, Rolex wristwatch. She wasn't sure whether it was giving him pleasure, calling attention to how big his wallet was, or some of both, but it was transparent and annoying. So was the perfect, razor-cut dirty-blond hair, the manicured and polished fingernails, and the perfect, gray, three-piece Yves St. Laurent suit. She once begged Hood to put a spy eye in his office so they could settle once and for all not *if* he hit the lint remover every time he shut the door, but for how long.

"A cheerful good morning to you," Coffey said.

"Hi, Two. Morning, Ann."

Ann smiled and waved her fingers. She was sitting behind her big antique desk instead of on the front edge, as usual — a body-language barrier against Coffey, Liz imagined. The Yale grad was too smart or too chicken to indulge in overt sexual harassment, but his come-hither approach to Ann made him less popular than wage freezes among PR and psych personnel.

"Thanks for coming, Liz," Ann said. "Sorry to have to bring you in on this, but Lowell insisted." She swung her computer monitor around. "Paul wants a press release out there by eight, and I need you to sign off on an assessment of the North Korean leaders."

Liz leaned stiff-armed on the desk. "Isn't this Bob Herbert's area?"

"Technically, yes," Coffey answered, his voice like rolling skeins of velvet. "But some of the vocabulary Ann has chosen flirts with libel. If I can't make sure it's defensible, I want to ascertain whether the subject will seek relief."

"Like the President of North Korea is going to sue?"

"Ariel Sharon did."

"That was *Time*, not the U.S. government."

"Ah, but suing the government would be a marvelous way for beleaguered North Korea to fan the flames of sympathy." Coffey sat back down, released his cuff link, and fiddled with the knot of his black tie. "Would you want to undergo discovery, ladies, be forced to reveal sources, operating procedures, and the like? I wouldn't."

"You're right, Two, though it wouldn't be a lawsuit; you can't sue a sovereign government. Still, there is a risk."

He put on a just-do-it expression and held a hand toward the screen. Though she hated to comply, Liz studied the monitor.

"Thanks," Ann said, patting the back of her hand.

Liz chewed her gum hard as she read.

The highlighted passage was short and concise:

We do not believe that the Democratic People's Republic of Korea wants war, and we condemn rumors that its President personally ordered the terrorist attack. There is no evidence to suggest that he has been under pressure from hard-line officers opposed to reunification and compromise.

Liz turned to Coffey. "So?"

"I searched. Those rumors have not been published or broadcast elsewhere."

"That's because the explosion only happened three hours ago."

"Exactly. This would make us the first to consign said rumors to print — partly because Bob Herbert has been the only one voicing them."

Liz scratched her forehead. "But we're condemning the rumors."

"That doesn't matter. By introducing the issue, even in a censorious manner, we're at risk, legally. We must be able to show an absence of malice."

Ann folded her hands. "I need the paragraph, Liz, or something very much like it. What we're trying to do is let the North

Koreans know that if the President and his military advisers are behind this, we're onto them. And if they aren't, then our press release can simply be taken at face value: we're outraged by the rumors."

"And you want me to tell you how he's going to respond when he reads this."

Ann nodded.

Liz's chewing slowed. She hated to give Coffey an inch, but she couldn't let that influence her. She reread the passage.

"The President is not so naive that he wouldn't expect us to think these things. But he's also proud enough to take offense at the way you've singled him out."

Ann seemed disappointed. Coffey puffed slightly.

"Suggestions?" Ann asked.

"Two. In the line, '. . . *and we condemn rumors that its President personally ordered,*' I would change *President* to *government*. That depersonalizes it."

Ann regarded her for a long moment. "Okay. I can live with that. Next?"

"This one's a little dicier. Where you wrote, '*There is no evidence to suggest that he has been under pressure from hard-line officers opposed to reunification and compromise,*' I would say something like, '*We believe that the President continues to resist pressure from hard-line*

officers opposed to reunification and compromise.'
That still tells the DPRK that we're aware
of the hard-liners while making the President
look good."

"But what if he's not good?" Ann asked.
"Don't we look green if it turns out he's
behind the whole thing?"

"I don't think so," Liz said. "It makes
him look like an even bigger rat because
we trusted him."

Ann looked from Liz to Coffey.

"I approve." Coffey said. "We send the
same message with no downside."

Ann thought a moment longer, then typed
in the changes. She saved the document,
then handed the mouse to Liz. "You're good.
Want to swap jobs for a while?"

"No thanks," Liz said. "I prefer my psychos to yours." She shifted her eyes clan-
destinely to and from Coffey.

Ann nodded as Liz used the mouse to
access her password and switch it to the
margin of the document. Her code would
become part of the permanent file, right beside the changes, though it wouldn't appear
on the printed press release.

As Liz was about to save the annotated
file, the blue screen went black and the fan
behind the computer fell silent.

Ann ducked her head under the desk to

see if she'd somehow kicked the plug from the surge protector: the cord was right where it should be, and the green light on the surge protector was on.

There were muffled shouts from outside the office; Coffey strode to the door and opened it.

"It seems," he said, "that we're not alone."

"What do you mean?" Ann asked.

Coffey faced her, his expression grave. "It appears that all of the computers in Op-Center have gone down."

TWENTY-FOUR

Tuesday, 9:15 P.M., Seoul

After the taxi deposited him at the front gate of the U.S. base, Gregory Donald presented his Op-Center photo-badge to the guard. A call to the office of General Norbom and he was admitted.

Howard Norbom had been a Major in Korea while Donald was Ambassador. They met at a party celebrating the twentieth anniversary of the end of the war and had hit it off right away. Their liberal-leaning politics were the same, they were both looking for a wholesome little thing to marry, and both were devotees of classical piano, Frederic Chopin in particular, as Donald discovered when the honky-tonk pianist took five and the Major sat down and did a commendable job on the *Revolutionary Étude*.

Major Norbom found his wholesome little

thing two weeks later when he met Diane Albright of UPI. They were married three months after that and recently celebrated their twenty-fourth wedding anniversary. The General and Diane had two great kids: Mary Ann, a Pulitzer Prize nominated biographer, and Lou, who worked for Greenpeace

After an orderly showed him into the General's office, the men embraced and Donald's tears began again.

"I'm so sorry," the General said, embracing his friend, "so very sorry. Diane's on assignment in Soweto or she would have been here. She's going to meet us here."

"Thanks," Donald choked, "but I've decided to send Soonji to the U.S."

"Really? Her father agreed — "

"I haven't spoken to him yet." Donald laughed mirthlessly. "You know how he felt about the marriage. But I know how Soonji felt about the United States, and that's where I want her to be. I think it's where she'd have wanted to be."

Norbom nodded, then walked around his desk. "The Embassy will have to take care of the paperwork, but I'll see that that gets right through. Is there anything else I can do for you?"

"Yes, but tell me — is she here already?"

Norbom pursed his lips and nodded.

161

"I want to see her."

"Not — now," Norbom said, and looked at his watch. "I'm having our dinner brought over. We can talk for a while."

Donald looked into his friend's steel-gray eyes. Set in the craggy face of the fifty-two-year-old Base Commander, those eyes inspired trust, and Donald had always been quick to give it to him. If Norbom didn't want him to see his wife's body yet, Donald would defer. Only he had to see her soon, let her soul guide him, tell him that what he was planning was the right thing to do.

"All right," Donald said softly. "We'll talk. How well do you know General Hong-koo?"

Norbom's brow knit. "That's an odd question. I met him once at the DMZ meeting in 1988."

"Any firsthand impressions?"

"Sure. He's arrogant, blunt, emotional, and trustworthy in his own misguided way. If he says he's going to shoot at you, he will. Now I don't know him as well as General Schneider does, but I don't stare at him and his men across the DMZ every day, or listen to the loud North Korean folk songs they boom across the border in the middle of the night, or watch to see how many inches or feet he adds to his flagpole so it'll always be taller than ours."

162

Donald began filling his pipe. "Don't we send headbanger music back at him and raise our own flagpole?"

"Only when he does it first" — Norbom allowed himself a little smile — "you pinko sympathizer. Why do you ask?"

Donald noticed the framed photograph of Diane on the General's desk and glanced away. It took him a moment to collect himself.

"I want to meet with him, Howard."

"Out of the question. It's difficult enough for General Schneider to see him — "

"He's a soldier, I'm a diplomat. That may make a difference. In any case, I'll worry about contacting him. I need your help to get to the DMZ."

Norbom sat back. "Christ, Greg. What did Mike Rodgers do, give you a transfusion from his own right arm? What are you going to do, just walk across Checkpoint Charlie? Tie a note to a brick?"

"I'll use a radio, I think."

"Radio! Schneider wouldn't let you near one — that'd be *his* ass. Besides, even if you could see him, Hong-koo's the most militant nutcase they've got. Pyongyang sent him there as a signal to Seoul: go to the reunification talks with deep pockets and a giving heart, or you'll be staring across a rifle at him. If anyone would have come up

163

with a rogue operation like this, it's Hong-koo."

"What if he didn't, Howard? What if North Korea didn't do this?" Donald held the unlighted pipe in his right hand and bent closer. "As crazy as he is, he's proud and honorable. He wouldn't want to take credit *or* blame for any operation that wasn't his."

"You think he's going to tell you?"

"Maybe not with words, but I've spent my lifetime watching people and listening to exactly what they have to say. If I can talk to him, I'll know if he's involved."

"And if you learn that he is, what then? What are you going to do?" He pointed to the pipe. "Kill him with that? Or has Op-Center given you new ideas?"

Donald put the pipe in his mouth. "If he did it, Howard, I'm going to tell him that he killed my wife, that he robbed me of my future, and that this must not happen to anyone else. I'll go with very deep pockets, and with the help of Paul Hood I'll find some way to stop this madness."

Norbom stared at his friend. "You mean it. You really think you can square-dance right in and make him see reason."

"From the bottom of my soul I believe it. As much of it as is still alive."

The orderly knocked, entered with their

dinner, and set the tray between the men: Norbom was still staring at Donald after the orderly had removed the metal covers and left.

"Libby Hall and most of the government of Seoul will oppose your going there."

"The Ambassador mustn't know."

"But they'll find out. The North will make propaganda hay out of your visit, just as they did when Jimmy Carter went there."

"By then I'll be finished."

"You're not kidding!" Norbom dragged a hand through his hair. "Jesus, Greg, you've got to think long and hard about your plan. Hell, it's not even a plan, it's a hope. Doing an end run like this can upset whatever stage the negotiations are at now. It can destroy you *and* Op-Center."

"I've already lost what counts. They can have the rest."

"They'll take that and more, believe me. Making unauthorized contact with the enemy — Washington and Seoul will chow down on you, me, Paul Hood, Mike Rodgers. It'll be a turkey shoot."

"I know this will hurt you, Howard, and I don't take that lightly. But I wouldn't ask if I didn't think I had a chance to make a difference. Think of the lives that can be saved."

The color seemed gone from the Base Commander's weathered face. "Dammit, I'd do anything for you — but I've put my professional life into this base. If I'm going to chuck that, and write my memoirs in a nine-by-twelve cell, I want you to at least sleep on this. You're hurt, and you may not be thinking as clearly as you ought to be."

Donald lit his pipe. "I'm going to do better than sleep on it, Howard. We'll have our dinner and then I'm going to pay Soonji a visit. I'm going to stay with her awhile, and if I feel differently after that I'll tell you."

The General slowly picked up his knife and fork and began cutting his steak slowly and in silence. Donald set his pipe aside and joined him, the quiet meal broken by a knock at the door and the arrival of a man with a fixed scowl set beneath a shiny black eye-patch.

TWENTY-FIVE

Tuesday, 7:35 A.M., Op-Center

"This can't happen, this can't happen, this can't *happen!*"

The normally passive, cherubic face of Operations Support Officer Matt Stoll was pale as an unripe peach, with Kewpie doll smears of red on the cheeks. He was whining under his breath as he worked feverishly to plug his computer into a backup battery pack he kept in his desk. He couldn't find out why the entire system had gone down until he got it back on-line and crawled into the wreckage — what hackers humorlessly referred to as the black box system of making *your* flight safe.

Perspiration dripped to his eyebrows and spilled into his eyes. He blinked it away, spotting his glasses with sweat. Though it had only been a few seconds since the crash,

Stoll felt like he'd aged a year — a year more when he heard Hood's voice.

"Matty — !"

"I'm working on it!" he snapped, fighting down the urge to add, *But this just can't happen.* And it shouldn't have. It made absolutely no sense. The main power from Andrews hadn't gone down, just the computers. That was impossible to do from the outside: it had to be a software command. The computer setup in Op-Center was self-contained, so the shutdown had to come from a software command issued here. All incoming software was searched for viruses, but most of the ones they found were nonmalicious — like the one that flashed "Sunday" on the screen to tell workaholics to get away from the keyboard, or "Tappy" that created a clicking sound with every keystroke, or "Talos" that froze computers on June 29 until the phrase "Happy Birthday Talos" was typed in. A few, like "Michelangelo," which erased all data on March 6, the artist's birthday, were more malevolent. But this one was something incredibly new, sophisticated . . . and dangerous.

Stoll was as intrigued and amazed as he was distressed by all of this — the more so as the screen blinked back on a moment before he plugged in his battery pack.

The computer hummed to life, the hard drive whirred, and the DOS screen flashed by as his customized Control Central program booted. It locked on the title screen as the synthesized voice of Mighty Mouse sang operatically from a speaker in the side of the machine.

"Are any other programs currently running, Matty?"

"No," Stoll said glumly as Hood swung into his office. "How long were you off fighting Mr. Trouble?"

"Nineteen point eight-eight seconds."

The computer finished accessing the program and the familiar blue screen appeared, ready to go. Stoll hit F5/Enter to check the directory.

Hood leaned on the back of Stoll's chair and looked down at the screen. "It's back — "

"Seems to be. Did you lose anything?"

"I don't think so. Bugs was saving everything. Nice work getting it running again — "

"I didn't do anything, boss. Not unless you count sitting here, *shvitzing*."

"You mean the system came back by itself?"

"No. It was instructed to do that — "

"But not by you."

"No." Stoll shook his head. "This can't happen."

169

Lowell Coffey said from the doorway, "And Amelia Mary Earhart had a map."

Stoll ignored the attorney as he finished checking his directory: all the files were there. He entered one; when he didn't get an Error prompt, he felt confident the files themselves hadn't been burned.

"Everything looks okay. At least the data seems to be intact." His thick, piston-fast index fingers flew across the keys. Stoll had written a WCS program as a lark, never expecting to have to use it. Now he hurriedly dumped the worst-case-scenario diagnostics file into the system to give it a top-to-bottom physical. A more detailed diagnostics examination would have to be made later, using classified software he kept under lock and key, but this should spot any big problems.

Hood chewed on his lower lip. "What time did you get here, Matty?"

"Logged in at five forty-one. I was down here two minutes later."

"Ken Ogan report anything unusual?"

"Nada. The night shift was smooth as glass."

"As the sea when the *Titanic* sunk," Coffey noted.

Hood seemed not to have heard. "But that doesn't mean something didn't happen in the building. A person at any station could have gotten into the system."

"Yes. And not just today. This could have been a time bomb, entered at any time and set to go off now."

"A bomb," Hood reflected. "Just like the one in Seoul."

"Could it have been an accident?" Coffey asked. "Mightn't someone simply have pressed a wrong key somewhere?"

"Nearly impossible," Stoll said as he watched the diagnostics checklist begin working its magic. Numbers and characters scrolled up at lightning speed as it looked for aberrations in any of the files, commands that didn't gel with existing programs or weren't entered "on the clock."

Hood drummed the back of the chair. "What you're saying then is that we may have a mole."

"Conceivably."

"How long would it have taken for someone to write a program to bring down the whole system?"

"Anywhere from hours to days, depending on how good they were. But that doesn't mean the program was written on-premises. It could have been created anywhere and piggybacked in on the software."

"But we check for that — "

"We check for sore thumbs. That's basically what I'm doing now."

"Sore thumbs? You mean something that sticks out?"

Stoll nodded. "We tag our data with a code, stored at specific intervals — like a taxicab, either every twenty seconds or every thirty words. If the code doesn't show up, we take a closer look at the data to make sure it's ours."

Hood clapped a hand on his shoulder. "Keep at it, Matty."

Sweat trickled into his left ear. "Oh, I will. I don't like being coldcocked."

"Meantime, Lowell, have the Duty Officer start running through the videos they took last night, all stations inside and out. I want to know who might have come and gone. Have them blow up the badges and check them against file photos — make sure they're authentic. Put Alikas on that. He's got a good eye. If they don't find anything unusual, have them go to the day before and then the day before that."

Coffey toyed with his class ring. "That'll take time."

"I know. But we've been blindsided, and we better find out by whom."

The two men left just as Bob Herbert wheeled in. The thirty-eight-year-old Intel-

172

ligence Officer was in a high dudgeon, as always. Part of him was angry at whatever had gone wrong, the other ninety percent was mad at the die toss that had dropped him in a wheelchair.

"What gives, techboy? Are we pregnant?" There were traces of a Mississippi youth still in his voice, edged with urgency born of ten years in the CIA and lingering bitterness over the bombing of the U.S. Embassy in Beirut in 1983 that had left him crippled.

"I'm checking on the degree and type of penetration," Stoll said, pressing his lips shut before he added, *"Major Pain in the Ass."* The dogged Herbert took that from Hood and Rodgers but not from anyone else. Especially someone who had never worn a uniform, pulled the Libertarian Party lever most Novembers, and still carried as much weight around Op-Center as he did.

"Well maybe, techboy, it'll help if you know that we weren't the only ones who got slam-dunked."

"Who else?"

"Portions of Defense went down — "

"For twenty seconds?"

Herbert nodded. "So did parts of the CIA."

"Which parts?"

"The crisis management sectors. Every

place we supply with data."

"Shit — "

"Horse apples is right, boy. We knocked up a whole lot of people, and they're gonna want someone's ass."

"*Shit,*" Matt said again, turning back to the screen as the first wave of figures stopped.

"The first directory is clean," sang Mighty Mouse. "Proceeding to second."

"I'm not saying it's your fault," Herbert said. "I'd be walking if good men didn't get blindsided now and again. But I need you to get me some intelligence from the NRO."

"I can't do that while the system is in the diagnostics mode, and I can't exit while it's in a file."

"I know that," he said, "junior technoboy Kent told me. That's why I rolled on in here, to keep you company till you get the damn system on-line again and can provide me with the information I need."

"What information is that?"

"I need to know what's happening in North Korea. We've got a pile of dead people wearing what seems to me *Made in the DPRK* death masks, there's a planeload of Striker boys en route, and the President wants to know what the troops up there are doing, the current status of missiles, if anything is

happening at the nuclear power plants —
that sort of thing. We can't do that without
satellite surveillance, and — "

"I know. You can't do *that* without the
computers."

"The second directory is clean," Mighty
Mouse reported. "Proceeding to — "

"Cancel," said Matt and the program shut
down. Using the keyboard, he exited to DOS,
entered the password to go on-line with the
National Reconnaissance Office, then folded
his arms, waited, and hoped to God that
whatever had invaded the computers hadn't
gotten through the phone link.

TWENTY-SIX

Tuesday, 7:45 A.M., the National Reconnaissance Office

It was one of the most secret and heavily guarded sections in one of the world's most secretive buildings.

The National Reconnaissance Office in the Pentagon was a small room with no overhead lighting. All of the room's illumination was provided by the computer stations, ten neat rows of them with ten stations in each row, laid out like a NASA control room; one hundred lenses in space watching the Earth in real-time, providing sixty-seven live, black-and-white images a minute at various levels of magnification, wherever the satellite eyes were pointed. Each picture was time-encoded to the hundredth of a second so that the speed of a missile or the power of a nuclear explosion could be determined by comparing successive shots or by factoring in other data, such as seismic readings.

Each station had a television monitor, with a keyboard and a telephone below each monitor, and two operators were responsible for each row, punching in different coordinates for the satellites to watch new areas or provide hard copy of images for the Pentagon, Op-Center, the CIA, or any of America's allies. The men and women who worked here went through training and psychological screening nearly as thorough as that of the people who worked in the control centers of the nation's nuclear missile bases: they couldn't become anesthetized by the steady flow of black-and-white images, they had to be able to tell in seconds whether a plane or tank or soldier's uniform belonged to Cyprus, Swaziland, or the Ukraine, and they had to resist the temptation to check in on their folks' farm in Colorado or brownstone in Baltimore. The space eyes could look at any square foot on the planet, were powerful enough to read a newspaper over someone's shoulder in a park, and the operators had to resist the temptation to play. After looking at the same mountain range, plain, or ocean day after day, the urge to do so was intense.

Two supervisors watched the silent room from a glass control booth that occupied one full wall. They notified the operators of all requests from other departments, and double-checked any changes in satellite orientation.

Supervisor Stephen Viens was an old college buddy of Matt Stoll. They'd graduated one and two in their MIT class, jointly held three patents on artificial neurons for silicon brains, and in a national mall-tour shootout were, respectively, the number two and number one highest scorers on Jaguar's *Trevor McFur* game. Atari executives had to agree to pay for overtime as Stoll's game continued four hours past mall closing time. The only thing they didn't share was Viens's passion for weight lifting, which gave their wives the idea for their nicknames: Hardware and Software.

Stoll's E-mail arrived just as Viens was settling in with his coffee and chocolate-chip muffin before starting his eight o'clock shift.

"I'll take it," he told night Supervisor Sam Calvin.

Viens rolled his chair in front of the monitor; he stopped chewing as he read the message:

Facehugger successful. Operating now. Send 39/126/400/Soft. Check own Alien?

"Whoa Nellie," Viens muttered.

"*Que pasa,* Quickdraw?" asked Calvin. The

night and day Deputy Supervisors also came over.

"Facehugger?" said day Deputy Supervisor Fred Landwehr. "What's that?"

"From the movie *Alien*. The thing that put baby aliens into people to incubate. Matt Stoll says they've got a virus, which means we could have it too. He also wants to see Pyongyang." Viens snapped up the phone. "Monica, take a look at longitude 39, latitude 126, magnification 400 and send it over to Matt Stoll at Op-Center. No hard copy." He hung up. "Fred, run a diagnostics on our software. Make sure everything's okay."

"Am I looking for anything in particular?"

"Don't know. Just scan everything and see what beeps."

Viens turned back to the computer and typed:

Looking for Chestburster. Kick butt Ripley. 39/126/400 Soft copy.

Sending it, he looked out across the rows of monitors, still not quite believing what he'd read. Stoll had come up with what they'd both agreed was as virus-proof a system as someone could design. If it had been compromised, that would be something. He hurt for his pal but he also knew that, like him,

179

Stoll had to be fascinated by the prospect that it had been done at all . . . and determined to get to the bottom of it.

TWENTY-SEVEN

Tuesday, 9:55 P.M., Seoul

Major Lee saluted as he walked into the General's office, and Norbom returned the salute.

"Greg Donald," he said, "I believe you know Major Kim Lee."

"Yes, we've met," Donald said, touching a napkin to his lips. He stood and offered the Major his hand. "Several years ago, at the parade in Taegu as I recall."

"I'm impressed and flattered that you remember," said Lee. "You are here on official business?"

"No. Private. My wife — was killed this afternoon in the explosion."

"My condolences, sir."

"What are your thoughts on that, Major?" Norbom asked.

"It was ordered in Pyongyang, perhaps

181

by the President himself."

"You seem pretty certain," Donald said.

"You are not?"

"Not entirely, no. Neither is Kim Hwan of the KCIA. The evidence is very thin."

"But not the motive," said Lee. "You are in mourning, Mr. Ambassador, and I mean no disrespect. Yet the enemy is like a snake: it has changed its skin, but not its heart. Whether through war or by sinking its fangs into our economic well-being, they will try to sap us. To destroy us."

There was sadness in Donald's eyes and he looked away. Now as in the 1950s, the biggest impediment to lasting peace was not greed or territorial disagreements or indecision over how to unify two separate governments. They were formidable problems, but not insurmountable. The biggest impediment was the suspicion and deep-seated hatred that so many of the people of one nation had for the other. It distressed him to think that real unification could not occur until the generation touched directly by the war had died out.

"This is Kim Hwan's bailiwick," said General Norbom, "so why don't we leave it to him, Major?"

"Yes, sir."

"Now, what is it you wanted to see me about?"

"This transfer order, sir. It requires your stamp."

"What's it for?"

Lee handed him the paper. "Four quarter-sized drums of tabun, sir. I'm to take it to the DMZ."

The General put on his glasses. "What on earth does General Schneider want with gas?"

"It's not for the General, sir. Military intelligence reports that chemical drums are being dug up at the border, and that more are on the way from Pyongyang. We are to bring these to Panmunjom in the event that they're needed."

"Christ," sighed Donald. "I told you, Howard, this is going to get out of hand."

Lee's face was impassive as he stood stiffly beside Donald, watching Norbom read.

"You requisitioned the gas," the General said to Lee. "To whom is it being delivered?"

"I will be staying with the shipment, sir. I have orders from General Sam." He removed the papers from his shirt pocket and held them out.

Norbom gave them a cursory glance, then tapped his intercom. "Shooter."

"Yes, sir?"

"Authorize Major Lee's transfer and get me General Sam on the phone."

"Yes, sir."

Norbom handed the papers to the officer. "I have only two things to say, Major. One is drive carefully. The other is when you get to Panmunjom, err on the side of caution."

"Of course, sir," said Lee, saluting, bowing curtly to Donald, his eye lingering on the diplomat's and chilling him inexplicably before he turned smartly and left.

Lee's face remained expressionless, but he was smiling inside. The months and money he had spent persuading Sgt. Kil to join them was paying off. General Sam's aide had signed his superior's name so many times it was indistinguishable from the real thing. And he'd be the first to get Norbom's call, finding ways to make the General unavailable until it slipped Norbom's aging mind or it was too late. In either case, Lee and his team would get what they wanted: the chance to put the second and deadliest phase of their operation into effect.

He met his three men at the canvas-backed truck, an old Dodge T214. U.S. soldiers had nicknamed this vehicle the Beep — the Big Jeep. It was three quarters of a ton, with sturdy shocks and a low center of gravity that was perfect for some of the off-road traveling they'd be doing.

The men saluted as Lee approached and he climbed into the passenger's seat. The other two men sat in the back, under the canvas.

"When we leave the base," he said to the driver, "you will return to the city, to Chonggyechonno." He half turned toward the back "Private, the Deputy Director of the KCIA does not believe that the enemy is behind this afternoon's attack. Please see to it that Mr. Kim Hwan does not perpetuate falsehoods. Make certain he does not report for work in the morning."

"Yes, sir. An act of God?"

"No, no accidents. Go to the hotel, put on civilian clothes, take one of the IDs, and steal a car from the garage. Find out what he looks like, follow him, and hack him, Jang. Brutally, the way the North Koreans hacked the American servicemen who were trimming trees. The way they mercilessly killed seventeen people in the bombing in Rangoon. The way they murdered my mother. Show them, Jang, what animals the North Koreans are and how they have no part in joining the civilized world."

Jang nodded and Lee settled back in his seat to place a call to Captain Bock at the DMZ. At the gate, he presented the stamped document to the U.S. guard, who went to

185

the back of the truck, checked the drums, returned the paper, and waved the truck on. When they reached the boulevard, Jang slipped from the back and hurried to the Savoy, the hotel where their long and eventful day had begun.

TWENTY-EIGHT

Tuesday, 7:57 A.M., Op-Center

Paul Hood's telephone rang. That didn't happen very often. Most of his communications came through E-mail, or through the special phone lines in his terminal.

It was especially odd because his intercom hadn't alerted him to the incoming call. Which meant it was someone with the clout to bypass Op-Center's main switchboard.

He picked up. "Hello?"

"Paul, it's Michael Lawrence."

"Yes, sir. How are you, sir?"

"Paul, I understand your boy went into the hospital this morning."

"Yes, sir."

"How's he doing?"

Paul frowned. There were times to give the President good news, and times to give him the truth. This was one of the latter.

"Not well, sir. They're not sure what's wrong, and he's not responding to treatments."

"I'm sorry to hear that," the President said. "But, Paul, I need to know, how much of a distraction will this be?"

"Sir?"

"I need you, Paul. I need you on top of this Korean situation. I need you focused and in control of things. Or I need someone else in charge. It's your call, Paul. Do you want me to hand this off to someone else?"

It was funny. Paul had been thinking that very thing not five minutes before, but now, hearing the President ask him flat out, there was no longer any doubt in his mind. "No, sir," he said. "I'm on top of it."

"Good man. And, Paul?"

"Yes, sir?"

"Let me know how your boy does."

"I will, sir. Thank you."

Hanging up the phone, Paul thought for a moment, then pressed the F6 key to talk to Bugs Benet. "Bugs," he said, "when you get a chance, call up one of our resident technoweenies. I need a new code sequence for *Mortal Kombat*, something that'll really knock Alexander's socks off when he gets home from the hospital."

188

"You got it," Bugs said.

Paul smiled, nodded, and then pulled up the next document in the queue and got back to work.

TWENTY-NINE

Tuesday, 10:00 P.M., Seoul

The brand-new, modern, four-story, steel and white brick building was set back from Kwangju, gleaming brightly behind a long, rectangular courtyard. Except for the high iron fence surrounding the courtyard, and the drawn shades behind the windows, a passerby might think the building was the office of a corporation or university. It was unlikely anyone would suspect that it was the headquarters of the KCIA and housed some of the most delicate secrets in the East.

The KCIA building was protected by video cameras on the outside, sophisticated motion detectors at every door and window, and electronic waves to prevent eavesdropping. Only upon entering the brightly lighted reception area and encountering the two armed guards behind bulletproof glass would one get a hint of the delicacy of the operations that went on inside.

The office of Deputy Director Kim Hwan was on the second floor, down the hall from the office of Director Yung-Hoon. Right now, the former police chief was having dinner in the fourth-floor café with friendly contacts in the press to try to find out what they knew. Hwan and Yung-Hoon had very different but complementary methods of working: Yung-Hoon's philosophy was that people had every answer investigators needed, as long as the proper people were asked the proper questions. Hwan believed that, intentionally or not, people lied — that facts were best learned through scientific means. Each admitted that the other's approach was perfectly valid, though Hwan didn't have the stomach for the smiles and chatter Yung-Hoon's work required. Back when he'd been a smoker, his attention span for bullshit was roughly an unfiltered Camel; now it was less.

His small desk stacked with papers and files, Hwan was studying the report that had just come in from the lab. He skipped the Professor's analyses of "hybridized sp-orbitals" and "direction of electronegativity" — details not required by the KCIA but by the courts, if the evidence were ever used in trial —

and went right to the summary:

Analysis of the explosives reveals them to be standard North Korean plastique: composition typical of production facility in Sonchon.

There are no fingerprints on the water bottle. There should at least have been partial fingerprints of a store clerk. We conclude that the bottle was wiped clean. The traces of saliva found in the drops of water that remained are unremarkable.

The soil particles themselves tell us nothing. The principal components, sandstone and bauxite, are common throughout the peninsula and cannot be used to locate the point of origin.

However, a toxicology study reveals concentrated traces of sublimation of the salt $NaCl$ ($Na+$ from the base $NaOH$, $Cl-$ from the acid HCL). This is commonly found in petroleum products from the Great Khingan Range of Inner Mongolia, including diesel fuel used by mechanized forces of the DPRK. The concentration of 1:100 $NaCl$ in the soil seems strongly to preclude the possibility that particles blew from the North. Computer simulation suggests that such a ratio would have been 1:5,000.

Hwan let his head flop back on the chair. He let the cooling waves from the ceiling fan wash over his face.

"So we have bombers who were in the North. How could they not be North Korean?" He was beginning to think that there was only one way to find out for certain, though he was reluctant to play a card as important as that.

As he reread the summary, the intercom beeped.

"Sir, this is Sgt. Jin at the desk. There's a gentleman who wishes to see the officer in charge of the Palace bombing."

"Does he say why?"

"He says he saw them, sir. Saw the men who ran from the sound truck."

"Keep him there," Hwan said as he leapt to his feet and tightened his tie. "I'll be right there."

THIRTY

Bob Herbert and Matt Stoll both watched in shocked silence as the photos from the NRO came up on Stoll's monitor.

"I'll be diddled," Herbert said. "They are out of their freaking *minds.*"

The photographs of Pyongyang showed tanks and armored vehicles rolling from the city, with antiaircraft artillery being moved into the surrounding countryside.

"These bastards are preparing for war!" Herbert said. "Have NRO look at the DMZ. Let's see what's happening there."

He snapped up the phone on the armrest of his wheelchair. "Bugs — put me through to the chief."

Hood came on at once. "What've you got, Bob?"

"A job for you — rewriting the Options

194

Paper. We've got at least three mechanized brigades moving south from the North Korean capital, and at least . . . I count one, two, three . . . four AA guns ringing the southern perimeter."

There was a long silence. "Get me the hard copy and keep monitoring the situation Has Matty found anything yet?"

"No."

There was another long silence. "Call Andrews and ask them to get us firsthand recon from the East Korea Bay west to Chungsan Bay every two hours."

"You want flyovers?"

"Mike and a Striker team are headed over. If the computers go down again and we lose our uplink, I don't want them going in blind."

"Gotcha," Herbert said. "Tell me, chief. You still think those bastards don't want war?"

"The White House or DPRK?"

Herbert swore. "Dee-Perk. We didn't start this — "

"No, we didn't. But I still think that North Korea doesn't want war. They're deploying because they assume we will. The problem is, the President can't appear soft and he won't blink. Will they?"

Saying he'd report back as soon as he had any information, Herbert muttered under his breath about Hood's suspicious nature. Just because he was a politician's politician when he was Mayor, consulting every adviser and poll, didn't mean that everyone was. He did not believe that this President would put American youths at risk to enhance his image as a tough guy. If he didn't blink, it was for the same reason that Ronald Reagan sent Tripoli a high-explosive wake-up call when Libyans bombed a bar in Berlin. You hurt us, we're going to draw blood. He wished that policy were standard operating procedure, instead of hollow chest pounding at the United Nations. He still wished that someone would pay back the Moslem terrorists who cost him the use of his legs in 1983.

Ringing his assistant, Herbert asked to be put through to General McIntosh at Andrews.

The plane was a Dassault Mirage 2000, built under contract by the French government and designed as an interceptor. But it had quickly proven itself to be one of the most versatile planes in the air, formidable in both close-support and low-altitude attack missions as well as aerial reconnaissance. In its latter capacity, the fifty-foot-long two-seater was able to fly at speeds of up to Mach 2.2 at fifty-nine thousand feet; it could achieve both just under five minutes from brake-release. The U.S. Air Force had purchased six of the planes for use in Europe and the Far East, partly to cement military ties with France and partly because the jet was state-of-the-art.

The jet roared into the night sky from the U.S. air base in Osaka. Planes coming toward the North from the South had to fly higher and were easier to pick up on radar; planes coming from Japan could fly in low over the sea and be in and over North Korea before the military could respond.

The Mirage reached the eastern coast of North Korea fifteen minutes after takeoff; as its M53-2 turbofan engine kicked it into a nearly vertical climb, Recon Officer Margolin seated behind the pilot began snapping photographs. She was using a Leika with a 500x telephoto lens, modified for night vision.

The officer had been briefed on what to watch for: troop movements and activity around the nuclear power plants and chemical storage sites. Anything similar to what the NRO spy satellite had seen around the capital.

What she saw as the Mirage passed Pyongyang and swept southwest over the bay and toward the Yellow Sea astounded her. She told the pilot to forget the sweep back for a second look: they raced toward the thirty-eighth parallel, and as soon as they were across, Margolin broke radio silence to talk to the mission commander.

THIRTY-ONE

Tuesday, 10:10 P.M., Seoul

For several minutes, Gregory Donald stood in the doorway of the small base chapel, unable to move. He looked at the plain pine coffin, unable to see inside, unwilling to do so until he was ready.

He had just gotten off the phone with her father, who admitted that he had become concerned when Soonji hadn't called him. He knew she'd been going to the celebration, and whenever there had been a problem, anyplace she went, she'd always phoned to say she was all right. She hadn't done that today. And when there was no answer at home and no record of her at any hospital, he'd feared the worst.

Kim Yong Nam took it the way he took everything that upset him: by withdrawing. Immediately after hearing about Soonji's death and Donald's plans for a funeral in America, he had hung up without uttering a word of thanks, sorrow, or condolence. Donald had never held Kim's manner against him, and he hadn't expected a word or two — welcome though they would have been. Everyone had their own way of dealing with grief, and Kim's was to shut it in, others out.

Breathing deeply, he forced himself to think back to the way he had last seen her — not as his wife, not as Soonji, but as a torn figure cradled lifelessly in his arms. He prepared himself, told himself that the mortician's art was one of suggestion, transforming the dead into the vision of peace and red-cheeked health — but not ever recreating life as we remembered it. Yet it would be more, he knew, than death as he remembered it. More than that broken and bloodied flesh he held —

His breathing was tremulous, his step unsteady as he entered the room. There were large candles burning on either side of the coffin, toward the head, and he walked around to the foot without looking in. From the corner of his eye he could see the dress they had sent a soldier to collect, the plain, white silk gown she wore when they were married. He could see the red and white of

200

the bouquet they had placed in her hands, on her waist. Donald had asked for that: though Soonji didn't believe that red and white roses brought you to the side of God, her mother, who believed in Chondokyo, had been buried that way. She might not find God, in whose existence she had more faith than he, but perhaps Soonji would find her mother.

Facing the coffin, he raised his eyes slowly.

And smiled. They had taken care of his girl. In life she had worn only the slightest touch of rouge, and she had on only a hint of it now. Her lashes were lightly brushed with mascara, and her skin wasn't caked with powder or paint but fair-looking, as it had been in life. Someone must have brought her perfume from their apartment, for he became aware of it now that he stood so close. Donald resisted the urge to touch her, for to the senses of sight and smell she was asleep . . . and at peace.

He wept openly as he moved to the left side of the coffin, not to gaze more closely at her but to kiss his finger and touch it to her gold wedding band, a ring inscribed with their names and the date they were married.

After allowing himself to touch the ruff of her sleeve, and remembering how soft and young and vital she had been the day they were wed, Donald walked from the chapel stronger than when he had entered, with reason in control of the anger he had shown General Norbom.

But he still intended to go north, with or without his friend's help.

THIRTY-TWO

Tuesday, 10:15 P.M., Seoul

When Kim Hwan entered the guardroom, the Desk Sergeant gave him a photo ID. Hwan read the information: *Name: Lee Ki-Soo. Age: Twenty. Address: 116 Hai Way, Seoul.*

"Did you check it?" he asked.

"Yes, sir. The apartment is leased to a Shin Jong U, whom we haven't been able to contact — this man says he lives in a room and that Mr. U is away on business. He works at the General Motors factory outside of town, but the personnel department is closed until tomorrow."

Hwan nodded, and as the Desk Sergeant prepared to take notes, the Deputy Director studied the man who had come to see him. He was short but well muscled; Hwan could see that in his neck and forearms. He was dressed in a factory worker's drab grays; he played with his black beret, shifted uneasily from foot to foot, and bowed several times when Hwan first entered. But his eyes never left Hwan, and they were strangely unsettling: they had a hard but lifeless glaze, like the eyes of a shark.

Strange combination — odd man, he thought. But today affected many people, and perhaps he was one of them.

Hwan moved up to a circular metal grid in the glass. "I'm Deputy Director Kim Hwan. You asked to see me?"

"You are in charge of this — this terrible thing?"

"I am."

"I saw them. As I told this fellow, I saw three men. They were walking away from the truck toward the old section — carrying bags."

"Did you see their faces?"

The man shook his head quickly. "I was not close enough. I was standing right out there — " He sidled to the door and jabbed with his finger. "By the benches. I was looking for — you know, sometimes they put lavatories out for the public. But not today. And while I was looking, I saw them."

"Are you certain you couldn't identify them? Color of their hair — "

"Black. All three."

"Facial hair? The size of their noses? Thin lips, large lips, prominent ears?"

"I'm sorry, I didn't see. As I said, I had other things on my mind."

"Do you recall what they were wearing?"

"Clothes. I mean, ordinary street clothes. And boots. I think they had boots on."

Hwan regarded the man for a moment. "Is there anything else?"

The man shook his head.

"Would you be agreeable to signing a statement regarding what you saw? It will only take a few minutes to prepare."

The man shook his head vigorously and quickly closed the small distance between himself and the door. "No, sir. I couldn't do that. I was not on my break when I went to the ceremony, so I slipped out. I wanted to *be* there, you understand. If my bosses knew, I would be disciplined — "

"They needn't know," said Hwan.

"I'm sorry." He put his hand to the door. "I wanted you to have this information, but I don't wish to become involved. Please — I hope this was helpful to you, but I must go."

With that, the man pushed open the door and ran into the darkness. Hwan and the Desk Sergeant looked at each other.

"Seems to have had a few beers too many before stopping by, sir."

"Or not enough," Hwan said. "Would you type that up and give it to me unsigned? There was some useful information there."

At least, it corroborated some of the facts he had come up with in the alley. He toyed briefly with the idea of having the curious little man followed, but decided the manpower was best utilized where it was, interviewing other attendees, checking video footage and photographs, and searching the area and abandoned hotel for other clues.

Climbing the stairs — he refused to take elevators when he had the time and energy to walk — Hwan returned to his office to consider his next move.

When the Director returned, he would be unhappy with the state of the investigation: their skimpy evidence pointing to North Korea, but no leads to who perpetrated the deeds.

After using his radio to check with the field forces, and learning that they were coming up empty, Hwan decided that to get that evidence quickly he would have to move in a way he'd been loath to, a way that might cost them as much as they would gain.

Reluctantly he picked up the phone. . . .

THIRTY-THREE

Tuesday, 10:20 P.M., Kosong, North Korea

Traveling at an average speed of 120 miles an hour, the sleek, modern Lake LA-4-200 Buccaneer four-seater flew low over the sea as it headed toward the coast of North Korea, its top-mounted Lycoming 0-360-A1A engine humming as the pilot kept the plane steady. The air was turbulent this close to the surface — just under one thousand feet and descending quickly — and the pilot didn't want to have to ditch her. Not with these two onboard. He dragged a handkerchief across his sweaty forehead, not daring to contemplate what they might do if he had to land fifty miles from shore.

The twenty-five-foot-long plane bucked as he dropped below five hundred feet — faster than he should have, given the down draft, but not as fast as he would have liked. The dark outline of the shore was visible now, and the pilot knew he wasn't going to have time to make a second pass: his passengers needed to be ashore by eight-thirty, and he wasn't going to disappoint them. Not by so much as a second.

He also wasn't going to let his dear friend Han Song get him any more off-the-book flights. Sons wanting to sneak in and visit fathers or even spies from the South were one thing. The gambler had said that these two were businessmen, but he didn't say their business was murder.

He set the boat-shaped belly of the aircraft down with a gentle thud, water kicking up on both sides as he braked quickly; he wanted to get the men off and the plane turned around before any curious fishermen or constables decided to check him out.

He unlatched the hatch and flipped it open. The entire cockpit was exposed. Snatching the raft from the copilot's seat, he lowered it over the side while the men in the back seats stood. The pilot extended his hand to help the first man into the raft. The killer grabbed the pilot's wrist and looked at his phosphorescent aviator's watch.

"We — we made it!" the pilot said.

"You've done well," the killer replied as his companion edged around him and climbed into the raft. He reached into the pocket of his greatcoat and handed the pilot a bundle of money. "As your agent and I agreed."

"Yes, thank you."

Then he reached into his pocket and withdrew the bloody stiletto, held it in front of him. The pilot's heart drummed so hard he was sure it and not the engine was causing the plane to shake. The killer laughed, cocked his arm suddenly to the side, and threw the blade out to sea; the pilot deflated so quickly he lost his balance and fell against the seat.

"Good night to you," said the killer as he turned and joined his friend in the raft.

It was several minutes before the pilot felt calm enough to taxi back to sea. By that time his passengers had been swallowed by the darkness.

The men were guided to shore by the flashing light of a soldier on the beach. The tide was low and they arrived in minutes, one of them deflating the raft while the other took the suitcases and walked toward two jeeps parked in the shadows beneath a sea cliff.

"Colonel Oko?" said the new arrival.

"Colonel Sun," the other bowed. "You're early."

"Our pilot was anxious to be rid of us." Sun glanced at the armed soldier standing beside the jeeps. "You have the uniforms, documents, and — package?"

"They're in the jeep. Would you care to check?"

Sun smiled and set the cases in the sand. "Major Lee trusts you." The smile broadened. "And we have a common goal, after all. To remain enemies."

"I need no war for that."

"You are not a politician, Colonel. We do not need to be reminded of what is in our blood. Would you care to check the money?"

Oko shook his head and motioned for his aide to take the case. "To be frank, Colonel, even if we were not recompensed for the bribes we've paid, the cost would have been worth it."

Bowing again to Colonel Sun, Oko climbed into the jeep, and did not look back as they drove up the steep dirt road into the hills.

Colonel Sun's aide, Corporal Kong Sang Chul, approached as he watched them go. "And they say the North and South can never agree on anything."

Ten minutes later, dressed in the uniforms of a North Korean Colonel and his orderly, and having checked the package to make

210

sure everything was there, the South Koreans followed the same road, headed toward a spot marked in red on the map among the folder of documents.

THIRTY-FOUR

Tuesday, 8:40 A.M., Op-Center

"This can't happen, this can't happen, *this* can't happen!"

"But it did, techboy. It did."

Stoll and Herbert were sitting at the conference table in the Tank with Hood and the rest of Op-Center's prime team, save for Rodgers who would be briefed. Ann Farris sat to Hood's right, Stoll and Herbert beside her, and Lowell Coffey II to his left; on the opposite side of the table were Martha Mackall, Liz Gordon, and Environmental Officer Phil Katzen. Darrell McCaskey sat down between Gordon and Katzen, having just presented Hood with a one-page summary of the activities of the Red Sky League and other terrorist organizations. It appeared that none of them was involved with the blast in Seoul.

212

Resting on the table in front of Hood were McCaskey's paper and the photo the NRO had sent over showing extensive troop movements around Pyongyang; beside it was the just-wire-photoed snapshot taken by Judy Margolin from the Mirage. They showed no tanks moving out, no artillery ringing the city, and no other preparations indicating that the DPRK was preparing to go to war. "What do you make of the discrepancy, Matty? Other than that it can't happen."

The portly Operations Support Officer sighed bitterly. "The key landmarks in both photographs are the same, so the satellite wasn't just misdirected, taking pictures of someplace else. They're both Pyongyang."

"We had NRO send us an update," Herbert said, "and I confirmed it with a secure call. The photo on the monitor showed a natural progression of the deployment seen in the first photograph."

"A deployment which probably isn't taking place," McCaskey pointed out.

"Correct."

"So, Matty?" Hood said. "I'm due at the White House in just about a half hour. What do I tell the President?"

"That there's a software glitch of some kind. A glitch like we've never seen before."

"A *glitch!*" Herbert roared. "In twenty

million dollars worth of computer widgetry that *you* designed?"

"That's *right!* Sometimes bright guys miss something, and sometimes trucks full of bombs get through cement barricades — !" Stoll regretted he'd said it even as the words were coming out. He pressed his lips together and slumped in his chair.

"Nice one, Matt," Coffey said to break the tense silence.

"I'm sorry, Bob," said Stoll. "That was out of line."

Herbert glared at him. "You got that right, techboy." His gaze fell to the leather seat of his wheelchair.

"Look," Liz said, "we're all going to make mistakes. But we can work them out better if we cooperate rather than point fingers. Besides, guys — if this is how we're going to react in the early stages of a crisis, we'd all better think about new lines of work."

"Point well taken," Hood said. "Let's move on. Matty, give me your best guess as to what it is we're dealing with."

Stoll sighed even deeper. He didn't look at Herbert. "My first thought was that when we went down, it was just a display of some kind. Someone showing us that they'd gotten into the system *somehow* and could do it again. I half expected we'd get an E-mail ransom note when we came back on-line."

"But we didn't," Coffey said.

"No, we didn't. Still, I figured there was a bug in the original program or one that slipped in with some software, and that it went from us to DOD to the CIA or vice versa. Then the photo came in from Osaka, and now I'm thinking that *that* was when we were really invaded."

"Explain," said Hood.

"The shutdown was either a smokescreen or a distraction to cover the real goal, which appears to have been the compromising of our satellite surveillance system."

"From space?" Coffey asked.

"No. From Earth. Someone else is controlling at least the Geostationary 12-A eye . . . perhaps more."

"The President's going to love that," Coffey noted.

Hood glanced at the countdown clock, then down at Bugs's image on the computer screen.

"Have you got that?"

"Yes, sir."

"Tack it to the end of the Options Report — with this." He looked at Stoll. "Our Operations Support Officer is working on the problem now, and assures me that the problem will be identified and solved. Time frame to follow. In the interim, Op-Center will function without its computers, since we can't trust any of the data. We'll rely on aerial surveillance, on agents in key areas, and on crisis simulation papers. Signed, etc. Print it all out, Bugs. I'll be there in a minute." Hood rose. "What's that phrase you're fond of, Matty? 'Make it so'? Well, make it so. This setup was supposed to be invasion-proof. That's how the President helped sell Op-Center to Congress nearly one year and a quarter billion dollars ago. I want the invader found and killed, and the hole patched." He turned to the sandy-haired Environmental Officer. "Phil — I don't think we'll be needing your division at this stage. You've got an M.A. in computer science — would you work with Matty on this?"

Phil's blue eyes went from Hood to the countdown clock. "My pleasure."

Stoll stiffened but said nothing.

"Bob, call Gregory Donald at the base in Seoul. He lost his wife in the explosion, but see if he feels up to a visit to the DMZ for some firsthand reconnoitering. We can't trust the satellites, I want one of our people there — and this may be good for him."

"He sounded out of it before," Martha noted, "so tread lightly."

Herbert nodded.

"Then I'd like you to brief Rodgers," Hood said. "Tell him to continue in at his discretion, unmarked. If Rodgers is up to it — and I suspect he will be — have his team report back to us on the Nodong missiles in the Diamond Mountain region."

Herbert nodded again, then wheeled himself from the table, still clearly smarting from what Stoll had said.

Hood hit the buzzer and left, followed by Herbert and the other team members.

Stoll thundered down the corridor to his office, Phil Katzen racing to keep up with him.

"Sorry he did that to you, Matty. I know there isn't much I can do to help."

Stoll grumbled something that Phil couldn't quite make out. He wasn't sure he wanted to.

"People don't understand that so much of progress comes from learning by our mistakes."

"This wasn't a mistake," Stoll snapped. "This is something we've never seen before."

"I see. Reminds me of when my older brother hit forty-five, chucked his wife and his job at Nynex, and decided to walk around the world. He told me that was a life-style change and not a midlife crisis."

Stoll stopped short. "Phil, I came to work today and got hit with the equivalent of the Cretaceous asteroid. I'm an apatosaurus fighting for his life, and this just isn't helping me." He started walking again.

Phil continued after him. "Well, maybe this will. When I was writing my dissertation on Soviet whale hunting, I went on a Greenpeace rescue mission to the Sea of Okhotsk. We weren't supposed to be there, but never mind. We found out that the Soviets had a way of creating false sonar images using sound transmitters at sea; we'd pick up an echo and rush off to protect a pod that wasn't even there, while the hunters were killing whales somewhere off our screen."

The two men entered Stoll's office.

"This isn't a sonar blip, Phil."

"No. And that's not the relevant part of the story. We started keeping video records of the images for future reference and found that whenever the transmitters were turned on there was an almost imperceptible burst of energy — "

"A start-up surge. That's common."

"Right. The point is, the signal had a fingerprint, a signature we could check before running off on a wild whale chase. The computers went down here for almost twenty seconds — you called it a smokescreen, and you may be right. But as I was watching the countdown clock in the Tank, I realized that there's one eye that wouldn't have blinked."

Stoll stood beside his desk. "The computer clock."

"Right."

"How does that help us? We know from when to when the shutdown occurred."

"Think. The satellite continued to store images, even when it couldn't transmit them to Earth. If we could compare an image from the instant before with one taken an instant after, we might be able to figure out what was done to the system."

"Theoretically. You'd have to superimpose two at a time and compare them for subtle changes — "

"The same way astronomers search for asteroids moving against a star field."

"Right," said Stoll, "and it'd take a long time to compare the dozens of images pixel-by-pixel. We can't even trust the computer to compare them for us, since it may have been programmed to overlook certain artifacts."

"That's just it. We don't need the computer. All we have to do is study the one set of before-and-after shots. That's what I meant about the computer clock. It wouldn't have shut down, even if a virus crawled in. But it *would* have taken a fraction of a second for a false image to supplant a real one — "

"Yes, *yes*." Stoll said. "Shit, yes. And that would show up in the time-encoding on the photographs. Instead of coming in at — what is it, every .89-odd seconds, there'd be an infinitesimal delay on the first bad egg."

"And that delay would show up right on the bottom of the photograph."

"Phil, you're brilliant." Stoll reached around and snatched his calculator from the desk. "Okay — the photographs should advance in increments of .8955 seconds. When we find one that's .001 second late, we have the first of our fakes."

"You've got it. All we have to do is ask NRO to run a check backward until they hit the time discrepancy."

Stoll dove for his chair, got Steve Viens on the line, and explained the situation. While he waited for Viens to run his time check, Stoll unlocked his desk drawer, pulled out a tray full of diagnostics diskettes, and began his check of the inner workings of the system.

THIRTY-FIVE

Tuesday, 8:55 A.M., Op-Center

Bob Herbert stewed as he rolled his wheelchair into his office. His mouth was locked in a frown, his teeth clenched, his thin eyebrows pinched in the center. He was angry in part because Stoll had been tactless enough to say what he did, but also because, in his heart, Herbert knew that he was right. They were no different, the glitch in software Matt wrote and the breakdown in security he'd helped to organize — they were all part of the same SNAFU scheme of things. You couldn't avoid it, however hard you tried.

Liz Gordon was right too. Rodgers had once quoted Benjamin Franklin, the gist of which was that we must all hang together or we'll all hang separately. Op-Center had to run that way, and it was difficult. Unlike the military or NASA or any organization

221

where the people were of a vaguely similar background or orientation, Op-Center was a potpourri of talent, education, experience — and idiosyncrasies. It was wrong and, worse, counterproductive to expect Stoll to act like anyone but Matthew Stoll.

You're going to give yourself a stroke —

Herbert slid behind his desk and locked the wheels. Without lifting up the receiver, he punched in the name of the U.S. military base in Seoul. The main number and direct lines came up on a rectangular screen below the keypad. Herbert scrolled through them with the ✳ button, stopped at General Norbom's office, lifted the receiver, and punched # to enter it. He tried to think of what he could say to Gregory Donald, since he had lost his own wife Yvonne, a fellow CIA agent, in the Beirut blast. But words were not his forte. Only intelligence . . . and bitterness.

Herbert wished he could relax, just a little, but it wasn't possible. It had been nearly a decade and a half since the blast. The sense of all he'd lost haunted him, every day, though he had gotten used to the wheelchair and to being a single father to a sixteen-year-old girl. What didn't diminish with time, what was as wrenchingly vivid today as it was in 1983, was the sheer chance of it all.

If Yvonne hadn't popped in to tell him a joke she'd heard on a *Tonight Show* tape, she would be alive today. If he hadn't gotten her that Neil Diamond tape, and Diamond hadn't been on that night, and she had never asked her sister to record it —

It was enough to make his heart sink and his head spin each time he thought about it. Liz Gordon had told him it was best not to, of course, but that didn't help. He kept going back to that moment when he stood in the music store, asking for anything by the singer who did the song about the heart-light. . . .

General Norbom's orderly answered the phone and informed Herbert that Donald had accompanied his wife's body to the Embassy to see to her return to the U.S. Herbert brought up Libby Hall's number and entered it.

God, how she loved that dopey song. As many times as he'd tried to interest his wife in Hank Williams and Roger Miller and Johnny Horton, she kept going back to Neil Diamond and Barry Manilow and Engelbert.

Hall's secretary answered and put Herbert through to Donald.

"Bob," he said, "it's good to hear from you."

Donald's voice sounded stronger than he'd expected. "How are you, Greg?"

"Like Job."

"I've been there, friend. I know what you're going through."

"Thanks. Do you know anything more about what happened? They're working hard at KCIA but coming up short."

"We've, uh, got a bit of a situation here ourselves, Greg. Seems our computers have been violated. We can't be sure of the data we're getting, including the pictures from our satellites."

"It sounds like someone did their homework for today."

"They did indeed. Now we know what your situation is, and with God himself holdin' the Bible I swear I'll understand if you say no. But the chief wants to know if you'd consider going to the DMZ and eyeballing the situation up there firsthand. The President's put him in charge of the Korea Task Force, and he needs reliable people on the scene."

There was a brief silence, after which Donald replied, "Bob, if you'll arrange the necessary clearances through General Schneider, I'll be available to go north in about two hours. Will that be acceptable?"

"I'm sure it will," said Herbert, "and I'll see to the clearances and a chopper. Good luck, Greg, and God bless."

"And God bless you," said Donald.

THIRTY-SIX

Tuesday, 11:07 P.M., the DMZ

The Demilitarized Zone between North and South Korea was thirty-five miles north of Seoul and one hundred miles south of Pyongyang. It was established concurrent with the truce of July 27, 1953, and since that time, soldiers from both sides have watched their counterparts with fear and suspicion. At the present time a total of one million soldiers were stationed on either side, most of them housed in modern, air-conditioned barracks. These were arranged in rows and covered nearly two hundred acres, beginning less than three hundred yards from either side of the border.

The zone was demarcated from northeast to southwest by a ten-foot-high chain-link fence on both sides, with another three feet of barbed wire running along the top. Between them was an area nearly twenty feet across from coast to coast — the DMZ itself. Soldiers armed with high-powered rifles and German shepherds patrolled the outer perimeter of both sides. There was only one way through the DMZ, a narrow roadway that was wide enough for just one vehicle to pass; until Jimmy Carter went to Pyongyang in 1994, no individual had ever crossed from this region to the capital of North Korea. The only direct contact between both sides occurred in a one-story structure that resembled the barracks. There was a single door on each side, two guards beside that door, and a flagpole to the left of the guards; inside was a long conference table that, like the structure itself, neatly straddled the border between North and South. On those rare occasions when meetings were held, the representatives from the North remained on their side of the room, the representatives from the South on theirs.

Well east of the last of the barracks on the South Korean side of the DMZ was scrubland spotted with low-lying hills and occasional thickets. The military held maneuvers beyond the hills; though difficult to see from the north, the sounds of tanks and artillery fire, especially during nighttime activity, could be alarming.

One of the thickets, nearly twenty yards across, grew over a rocky depression nearly a half mile from the DMZ. It was a mined area that Captain Ohn Bock personally checked at least twice a day. There, just seven weeks before, ROK forces had quietly built a tunnel four feet in diameter: unknown to the North Koreans, it allowed the South to keep an eye on activity in the network of tunnels that the enemy had excavated under the DMZ. The South Korean tunnel didn't actually connect with the North Korean tunnel; audio devices and motion detectors had been poked through the tunnel walls to keep track of spies being smuggled into the South from an exit hidden beneath rock and shrubs a quarter mile farther south. These operatives were then followed, their identities reported to both Military Intelligence and the KCIA.

As planned, Captain Bock had arranged his evening trip to the tunnel to coincide with the arrival of his childhood friend Major Kim Lee. The Captain and an aide drove up shortly after Lee arrived. They were already unloading the chemical drums. Bock saluted his superior.

"I was happy to get your call," Bock said. "This has been a great day for you."

"It's not yet over."

"I've heard bodies were discovered on the ferry and that the seaplane pilot returned on time. Colonel Sun's operation, too, appears to be going as planned."

In the two years that he'd known him, and in the year that this operation had been in the planning stage, Bock had never once seen the stoic Major show any emotion. But that was especially true now. Whereas another man might be expected to show relief at what had been accomplished, or anticipation over what was still to come — Bock himself was more anxious as the hour grew closer — Lee seemed almost supernaturally calm. His sonorous voice was soft, his movements unhurried, his manner slightly more reserved than normal. And he was the man going into the hole, not Bock.

"You've taken care of the tunnel watch for tonight?"

"Yes, sir. My man Koh is on the monitors. He's my computer genius. He'll make sure the surveillance equipment registers nothing until you've returned."

"Excellent. We're still planning to move at 0800 hours."

"I'll be waiting here for you."

With a smart salute, the Captain turned, climbed into his jeep, and returned to his post and to his job reviewing reports from along the DMZ and shuffling them off to Seoul. If all went well, after tonight he would be reviewing troops and not papers as they prepared to fend off an attack from the North.

THIRTY-SEVEN

Tuesday, 9:10 A.M., Washington, D.C.

With both hard copy and a diskette of the Options Paper in his small black briefcase, Paul Hood hurried to his car in Op-Center's underground parking lot. Once inside, he handcuffed the briefcase to his belt and locked the doors — he also carried a .38 in a shoulder holster when he was carrying secret documents — then logged himself out using the keypad at the gate; the sentry visually ID'd his badge and marked the time of his departure on a separate computer. This process was virtually identical to the procedure each employee went through upstairs. The code here was different from the one upstairs, and the feeling was that security might be compromised at one point, but rarely two.

Which doesn't matter much, Hood mused, *if we've got someone slipping into our computers without getting near the place.*

Distrustful of technology, Hood had little understanding of the way it worked. But he was keenly interested to hear what had happened this morning: Stoll was the best at what he did, and if something got past him it had to be one for the books.

As he cleared the concrete structure and drove toward the gate at Andrews — a third and final checkpoint, card ID only — he snapped up the phone. He called information, got the number of the hospital, and punched it in. He was connected to their son's room.

"Hello."

"Sharon — hi. How is he?"

She hesitated. "I've been waiting for you to call."

"Sorry. We've got a . . . situation." The phone was not secure; he couldn't say more. "How's Alex?"

"They have him in a tent."

"What about the injections?"

"They didn't work. His lungs are too full of fluid. They have to control his breathing until — until he clears up."

"Are they concerned?"

"*I* am," she said.

"So am I. But what do they say, honey?"

"This is standard. But so are the injections, and those didn't work."

Shit. He looked at his watch and cursed Rodgers for not being here. What the hell kind of goddamn business was he in where he had to choose between being at his ailing son's side and being with the President — and picked the latter. He thought of how unimportant this would all seem if anything happened to Alexander. But what he did today would affect thousands of lives, maybe tens of thousands. He had no choice but to finish what he'd begun.

"I'm going to call Dr. Trias at Walter Reed and ask him to come over. He'll make sure that everything possible is being done."

"Will he hold my hand, Paul?" she asked, and hung up.

"No," he said to the dial tone. "No, he won't."

Hood lay the receiver back in the cradle. He squeezed the rim of the steering wheel until his forearms ached, angry because he couldn't be there, but also frustrated because Sharon was exacting her pound of flesh. In her heart, she knew that as much as he loved her and Alex and wanted to be at the hospital, there wasn't much he could do there. He would sit, hold her hand for a few minutes, then walk around and be otherwise useless . . . just as he was when his children were born. The first time he'd tried to help her breathe through a contraction, she'd screamed for him to get the hell away from her and find the nurse. It was an important lesson: Hood learned that when a woman wanted you, it wasn't the same as her needing you.

Now if only he didn't feel so guilty. Swearing, he hit the Speaker button, called Op-Center, and asked Bugs to patch him through to Dr. Orlito Trias at Walter Reed.

While he waited, picking his way through late rush-hour traffic, Hood cursed Rodgers again — though he knew he really didn't blame him for anything. After all, why had the President appointed him? It wasn't just because he was a second-string quarterback who could come in and win the game. It was because he was a seasoned soldier who would be a voice of experience and caution in situations like these, a combat veteran and historian with a profound respect for fighting men, strategy, and war. A man who stayed in shape by walking on his office treadmill for an hour each afternoon, reciting *The Poem of The Cid* in Old Spanish when he wasn't conducting business. And sometimes while he was. Of course a man like that would want to be in the field with a team he'd helped organize: once a general, always a general. And didn't Hood always encourage his people to think independently? Besides, if Rodgers had been less of a cowboy, he would be Assistant Secretary of Defense, the post he'd wanted, instead of getting the consolation prize, the number two spot at Op-Center.

"Good morning, Dr. Trias's office."

Hood turned up the volume. "Good morning, Cath, this is Paul Hood."

"Mr. Hood! The doctor missed you at the National Space Society meeting last night."

"Sharon rented *Four Weddings and a Funeral*. I kind of had no choice. Is he in?"

"I'm sorry, but he's giving a lecture in Georgetown this morning. Is there a message?"

"Yes. Tell him that my son Alexander had an asthma attack and is in pediatrics. I'd like him to check on him, if he has the time."

"I'm sure he will. Give your boy a hug for me when you see him — he's a button."

"Thanks," Hood said, punching off the phone.

That's great, he thought. *Just great.* He couldn't even deliver the doctor.

Hood considered and quickly dismissed the idea of asking Martha Mackall to go to the White House in his stead. While he respected her abilities, he couldn't be sure whether she would be there representing his positions and Op-Center, or promoting the career and best interests of Martha Mackall. She'd come up from Harlem the hard way, learning Spanish, Korean, Italian, and Yiddish as she hand-painted signs for shops all around Manhattan, then studied Japanese, German, and Russian in college while earning her master's degree in economics on a full scholarship. As she'd told Hood when he first interviewed her, at forty-nine she wanted to get out of the Secretary General's office at the U.N. and continue to deal directly with the Spanish, Koreans, Italians, and Jews — only this time shaping policy, not serving as just a mouthpiece. If he hired her to collect, maintain, and analyze a database on the economies and key political operatives of every country in the world, he was to stay out of her way and let her do her job. He'd hired her because she was the kind of independent thinker he wanted at his side going into battle, but he wouldn't trust her to lead the charge until he was sure that Martha Mackall's agenda wasn't more important to her than Op-Center.

As he swung down Pennsylvania Avenue, Hood was bothered by the fact that he was able to overlook Mike's flaws more readily than Martha Mackall's . . . or Sharon's, for that matter. Martha would have called it sexism, but Hood didn't think so: it was a question of selflessness. If he got on the horn and asked Mike to bail out over Little Rock, hitch back to D.C., and fill in for him, he'd do it, no questions asked. If he paged Orly, he would leave the lecture in midsentence. With women, it was always a dance.

Feeling as though he had two left feet, Hood pulled up to the White House gate, one of two that protected the narrow private road that separated the Oval Office and the West Wing from the Old Executive Office Building. Presenting his pass, he parked amid the cars and bicycles there and, briefcase in hand, hurried to meet the President.

THIRTY-EIGHT

Tuesday, 11:17 P.M., Sea of Japan, twelve miles from Hungnam, North Korea

The policy among most Communist nations regarding territorial waters was that the boundaries, as decided by international treaty, did not apply to them. That the limit was not three miles but twelve, and often fifteen where enemy troops have been known to patrol.

North Korea had long maintained that it owned waters that stretched well into the Sea of Japan, a claim disputed by Japan and the United States. Navy patrol boats routinely pushed the envelope, sailing within four and five miles of the North Korean coast, and were occasionally challenged; when they were, they came no closer but rarely retreated. In more than forty years, confrontations had been few. The most famous incident was the North's seizure of the USS

Pueblo in January of 1968, accusing the sea-men of being spies; it took a day shy of eleven months of negotiations before the eighty-two-man crew was released. The deadliest encounter occurred in July of 1977, when a U.S. helicopter strayed over the 38th parallel and was shot down with the loss of three crew members. President Carter apologized to the North, admitting that the men had been in error; the three bodies and one survivor were returned.

After a brief stopover in Seoul to deliver her film, Recon Officer Judy Margolin and pilot Harry Thomas were skyborne again for their second pass over the North. This time, however, they were obviously expected and picked up by early warning and tracking radar on the ground as they swept in over Wonsan. A pair of airborne MiG-15P interceptors quickly entered their attack zones, one coming in low from the north, one high from the south. Harry expected a chase toward the sea, and knew he could outrun the old planes easily if he was facing in the right direction.

Pulling his nose up, he started to roll while ascending and accelerating. Temporarily losing sight of the Russian-made jets, he found them again when one MiG's twin 23mm NS-23 cannons caught the fuselage on the starboard side. The loud *pock-pock-pock* sounded like balloons popping and took him totally by surprise.

Despite the screaming of the engine, he heard Judy moan into her mouthpiece; from the corner of his eye, he saw her slump against her harness. Finishing his roll, hc banked south and continued to accelerate.

"Sir, are you all right?"

There was no response. This was insane. He'd been fired on without so much as a warning. Not only did that run counter to the four-stage method of North Korean aerial engagement, with contact coming during stage one, but the first burst was supposed to be fired below the aircraft — away from the direction it would typically fly after being spotted. Either the North Korean gunner was a poor shot, or he had been given some dangerous orders.

Breaking radio silence, Thomas sent a Mayday to Seoul and said he was coming in with a wounded crew member; the MiGs followed him toward the south, neither firing as they shrunk in the wake of his Mach 2 retreat.

"Hang on, sir," he said into his mask, not knowing whether the Recon Officer was dead or alive as he soared into the starlit night sky.

THIRTY-NINE

Tuesday, 8:20 A.M., the C-141 over Texas

Rodgers had to hand it to Lt. Colonel Squires. When he'd seconded the twenty-five-year-old from the Air Force to head up the Striker team, he'd told him to set up their offense, take pages from every military book that worked. And so he had.

As he sat there with the binder in his lap, he saw maneuvers and battle tactics that instinctively duplicated plans from Caesar, Wellington, Rommel, the Apaches, and other warrior-strategists, as well as from current U.S. plans. He knew that Squires hadn't had formal training in these matters, but he did have an eye for troop movement. It probably came from playing soccer as a kid growing up in Jamaica.

Squires was napping beside him, or he would have poked him in the ribs and told him what he thought of his single echelon offensive deployment against a primary avenue of enemy approach. When he got back, he'd pass this one to the Pentagon: it should be SOP for a battalion or regiment that had suffered heavy losses. Instead of setting up an operational belt along defensible terrain, he set up a small second echelon and sent his first echelon group in a flanking maneuver to pin the enemy in a crossfire. What was unique — and ballsy — was the way he moved his second echelon group forward, then, through the defensible terrain, to push the foe toward the heavier line of fire.

Squires also had a humdinger of a plan for a raid on a command and control installation, with a four-pronged attack from the drop zone: one frontal, one from each side, and one from the rear.

Private Puckett stepped around the Lieutenant Colonel and saluted. Rodgers removed his earplugs.

"Sir! Radio for the General."

Rodgers saluted and Puckett handed him the receiver. He wasn't sure whether it had gotten quieter in here or if he'd gotten deafer, but at least the tremorlike droning of the four big turbofans didn't seem quite as bad as before.

He put one plug back in and pressed the

receiver to his other ear. "Rodgers here."

"Mike, it's Bob Herbert. I've got an update for you — it's not what you might have been hoping for."

Well, it was fun while it lasted, Rodgers thought. *We're going home.*

"You're going in," said Herbert.

Rodgers snapped alert. "Repeat?"

"You're going into Dee-Perk. NRO has a problem with satellite recon, and the chief needs someone to eyeball the Nodong site."

"The Diamond Mountains?" Rodgers asked, nudging Squires, who was instantly awake.

"Bingo."

"We need the North Korea maps," he said to the Lieutenant Colonel, then was back on the phone with Herbert. "What happened to the satellites?"

"We don't know. The whole computer system's gone bugshit. Techboy thinks it's a virus."

"Is there anything new on the diplomatic front?"

"Negative. The chief's at the White House right now, so I'll have more for you when he gets back."

"Don't let us slip through the cracks," Rodgers said. "We'll be in Osaka before dinner, D.C. time."

"We won't forget you," Herbert said, then signed out.

Rodgers returned the handset to Puckett, then faced Squires. He had brought up the map on the laptop; his clear eyes were expectant.

"This one's for real," Rodgers said. "We're to check up on the North Korean Scuds."

"Just check?"

"That's all the man said. Unless we're at war before we land in Osaka, we don't go in with explosives. If necessary, my guess is they'll use us to coordinate an air strike."

Squires angled the screen so Rodgers could see; he asked Puckett to unscrew the bare light jiggling overhead so he could see the screen without glare.

As he looked at the map, he contemplated the suddenness with which his expectations and mood had changed. He'd gone from complacency and academic appreciation of Squires's work to readiness and an awareness that the lives of the team would depend on those plans and on the rest of Squires's preparations. He was sure those same thoughts — and a few doubts — were going through the Lieutenant Colonel's mind as well.

The map, just six days old, showed three truck-mounted Nodongs in a crater nestled between four high hills in the foothills of the mountain range. There were mobile artillery emplacements ringing the perimeter, in the hills, making a low flyover too risky. He scrolled the map westward, to bring in more of the eastern side. The map showed radar facilities at Wonsan.

"It'll be a tight squeeze," said Squires.

"I was just thinking that." Rodgers used the cursor to indicate a course. "The chopper will have to fly up from Osaka, in the southeast, and veer out to sea just above the DMZ: south of Mt. Kumgang looks like the best spot. That will put us down about ten miles from our target."

"Ten downhill miles," Squires said. "That's ten uphill back to get picked up."

"Right. Not a good exit strategy, especially if any of the troops down there are looking for us."

Squires indicated the Nodongs. "They haven't got the bomb on these things, have they?"

"Despite all the hoopla in the press, they aren't quite there yet, technologically," said Rodgers, still studying the map. "Though a payload of a couple hundred pounds of TNT per Nodong will put a helluva dent in Seoul."

He pursed his lips. "I think I've got it, Charlie. We don't leave where we came in but about five miles farther south, which

244

the enemy will never expect."

One of the clear eyes squeezed shut. "Come again? We make it *tougher* on ourselves?"

"No, easier. The key to getting out isn't to run, but to fight and then walk. Early in the second century A.D., during the first Trajanic campaign, legionary infantry of Rome were engaged by a smaller number of Dacian warriors in the foothills of the Carpathian Mountains. It was the mail and heavy javelins of Rome against bare chests and spears, but the Dacians were victorious. They snuck in at night, took the Romans by surprise, then led the enemy into the hills where the legionnaries were forced to spread out. When they did, the soldiers were picked off by enemies working in pairs. With the Romans dead, the Dacians were literally able to stroll back to their camp."

"That was spears, sir."

"Doesn't matter. If we're spotted, we'll lead them off and use knives. The enemy wouldn't dare use firearms at night, in the hills, or they might start picking off their own people."

Squires looked at the map. "The Carpathian Mountains doesn't exactly sound like home turf for the Romans. The enemy probably knew that land as well as the North Koreans know *their* terrain."

"You're right," Rodgers said. "But then, we've got something the Dacians didn't have."

"A Congress wanting to cut back our asses?"

Rodgers grinned and pointed toward the small black bag he'd been carrying earlier. "EBC."

"Sir?"

"Something Matty Stoll and I cooked up: I'll tell you about it after we've finished making our plans."

FORTY

Kim Chong wondered if they'd figured the cipher out.

She'd been playing piano at Bae Gun's bar for seventeen months, sending messages to men and women who stopped by irregularly — watched most of the time, she knew, by agents of the KCIA. Some of them were dashing, some beautiful, some scruffy, all of them doing a good job playing the successful businesspeople or models or factory workers or soldiers they were supposed to be. But Kim knew what they really were. The same talent that enabled her to memorize musical pieces allowed her to memorize distinctive features or laughs or shoes. Why is it that undercover operatives who took such pains to change their attire or makeup or hairstyle came back wearing the same shoes or holding

247

their cigarettes the same way or fishing the almonds from the peanut bowl first? Even Mr. Gun had noticed that the scraggly artist type who came in now and then had the same chronic bad breath as the ROK Private who showed up once a week.

If you're going to play a part, you must play it completely.

Tonight, the woman she'd nicknamed Little Eva was back. The lithe woman watered her drinks with a lot of ice; obviously a health nut, obviously not accustomed to drinking, obviously not drowning her sorrows alone but nursing her scotch while she kept a close eye and ear on the piano player.

Kim decided to give her something to chew on.

She rolled from "The Worst That Could Happen" into "Nobody Does It Better"; Kim always used songs from movies to send her messages. She played the first note of the second measure, a "C," an octave lower than it was written. She trilled the "A" below middle "C" in the third measure, then played the entire twentieth measure without the pedal.

Anyone who knew the music well would recognize the discrepancies. The "C" and "A" were wrong, and a pedal measure corresponded to a letter of the alphabet: in this case twenty, or "T."

She'd spelled CAT for the KCIA, and wondered if they'd get it; there was no letter frequency ratio, nothing a cryptanalyst could hook onto in the way of a regular substitution or transposition cipher. Kim watched as her man Nam left, his departure noted by Little Eva. The counterintelligence agent didn't go after him; maybe someone else did. Nam said he never saw anyone following him home, but he was old and half blind and when he came here he drank most of what she paid him. She could just imagine the contortions the KCIA went through trying to figure out how Nam and her other letter boxes sent their messages.

It was almost a shame to take money for this — money from the North as well as a salary to play here. If she were back in her hometown of Anju, north of Pyongyang, she'd be living like an empress.

If I were back home —

Who knew when that would be? After what she had done, she was lucky to be alive. But she *would* go back one day, when she had enough money or had her fill of the self-righteous South or learned something of the whereabouts of Han.

She finished playing the James Bond song and segued into a honky-tonk version of

249

"Java." The Al Hirt song was her favorite, the first one she remembered hearing as a child, and she played it every night. She often wondered if the KCIA thought it had something to do with her code: the next song after it was the one with the message, or maybe information was hidden in the little improv she did with the right hand in the second section. She couldn't even begin to imagine what the intelligence minds on Chonggyechonno were coming up with. And at the moment, she couldn't care less.

Ba-da da-da da-da. . . .

She shut her eyes and hummed along. Wherever she was, whatever she was doing, "Java" always brought her back to when she was just a baby, being looked after by her much older brother Han and their mother. Her mother's husband, Han's father, had died in the war, and her mother had no idea which soldier passing through was Kim's father, whether he was even Korean or whether he was Russian or Chinese. Not that it mattered: she loved her daughter just the same, and food had to be put on the table somehow. And when they found that box of 45s stolen from the South, her mother used to put Java on an old hand-cranked record player and they'd dance around their small shack, causing the tin roof to rattle

250

and scaring the chickens and goat. Then there was the priest who had a piano and saw Kim sing and dance and thought she might like to play —

There was a commotion in the nightclub and her eyes snapped open. Little Eva rose as two clean-cut men wearing suits and hard expressions entered by the front door and another pair came in through the kitchen door, behind a beaded entranceway to her left. Remaining otherwise motionless, Kim reached down with the toe of her right foot and lifted the wheel lock that held the piano in place. When she saw Little Eva look at her and knew why the men had come, she jumped to her feet and pushed the piano lengthwise across the beaded passage, blocking it. Little Eva and the other men still had to make their way through the tables, which gave Kim a few seconds head start.

Grabbing her purse, Kim ran for the rest rooms that were in the other direction. She swung into the men's room, remarkably calm and focused. Her six months of training in North Korea had been brief but effective: she had learned how to plan and walk through her exit routes with care, to keep money and a variety of handguns hidden.

The window was always open in the men's room, and climbing on the sink, she slipped through. Once outside, she discarded her purse after fishing out the switchblade she kept there.

Kim was in the small backyard of the bar. It was cluttered with broken stools, discarded appliances, and surrounded by a high wooden fence. Clambering on top of the row of garbage pails, cats scurrying in all directions, she held the knife in her teeth and put her hands on the top of the slats; as she was about to vault over, a shot chewed the fence just inches from her left underarm. She froze.

"Think it over, Kim!"

Kim's stomach tightened as she recognized the voice. She turned slowly and saw Bae Gun standing there, holding the smoking Smith & Wesson .32 automatic he kept to protect the bar and its take. She raised her hands.

"The knife — " he said.

She spat it out. "You bastard!"

Two other agents ran up behind him, guns drawn. They ran over, and while one of the men helped Kim down from the garbage pails, the other pulled her arms behind her back and cuffed her.

"You didn't have to *help* them, Bae! What lies did they tell you about me?"

"No lies, Kim." The light from the bathroom window spilled onto his face and she saw him smile. "I've known about you from the start, just as I knew about the singer who was here before you and the bartender who worked here before him. My boss, Deputy Director Kim Hwan, keeps me well informed about DPRK spies."

Fire in her eyes, Kim didn't know whether to curse or congratulate him as she was ushered past, half walking, half stumbling toward the street and the waiting car.

FORTY-ONE

Tuesday, 9:30 A.M., the White House

Hood remembered the first time he'd come to the Oval Office. It was when President Lawrence's predecessor had asked to meet the mayors of New York, Los Angeles, Chicago, and Philadelphia to see what could be done to prevent riots. The gesture, intended to show his concern for the inner cities, backfired when the President was accused of being racist for anticipating that blacks might riot.

That President was a tall man, like Lawrence, and while both may have appeared a little too short for the job itself, they seemed too large for the desk and for the office.

It was a small room by any reckoning, made smaller by the large desk and chair and clusters of top-level aides who were always coming and going from the senior staff offices down the hall. The desk was built from oak planks that once belonged to the British frigate HMS *Resolute*, and it took up fully twenty-five percent of the Oval Office, beside the window. The leather swivel chair was also larger than life, designed not just for the President's comfort but his protection: the back was lined with four sheets of Kevlar, the bulletproof fabric that was designed to protect the Chief Executive from gunfire originating outside the picture window. It was designed to withstand a hit from a .348 Magnum, fired at point-blank range. The desk itself was free of clutter: there was a blotter, pen stand, photograph of the First Lady and their son, and the ivory-colored STU-3 telephone.

Across from the desk were two thick-cushioned armchairs dating back to the administration of Woodrow Wilson. Hood was in one, and National Security chief Steve Burkow was in the other, away from his empire, the spacious National Security Council suite located on the other side of the lobby and accessible through double doors under a portico. The Op-Center Director had presented them both with copies of the Options Paper, which they read through quickly. Since Hood had told them about the surveillance breakdown at NRO and Op-

Center, the President had been curt at best.

"Is there anything you haven't put in here," Burkow asked, "anything off the books?"

Hood hated questions like that. *Of course there were.* Clandestine operations were always going on. They went on long before Ollie North oversaw the arms-for-hostages deal, kept going on after his activities were exposed, and would continue going on in the future. The difference was, presidents no longer took credit, even in private, for covert operations that succeeded. And people like Hood were castigated, in public, if they failed.

The effete Burkow just liked to hear it. He liked officials to admit that they were doing something illegal so he or the President could point out that they were on their own. It reminded them who was President and who was his cousin and most trusted adviser.

"We've been flying one surveillance mission an hour to make up for the loss of satellite recon, and I sent a Striker team over minutes after the explosion. It's a twelve-hour flight, and I wanted them in place if they were needed."

"In place," said Burkow. "Meaning — "

"North Korea."

"Unmarked?"

"No uniforms, no identification of any kind on the weapons."

Burkow looked at the President.

"What's the mission profile?" the National Security head asked.

"I've ordered the team to go in near the Diamond Mountain range and report back on the status of the Nodong missiles."

"You sent all twelve men?"

Hood nodded. He didn't bother to tell them that Mike Rodgers was one of them; Burkow would have a shit. If the team were captured, war-hero Rodgers was well known enough that he might be identified.

"This conversation never took place," Lawrence said predictably, then closed the report. "So the Task Force recommends that we continue a slow, steady deployment until we've determined whether or not North Korea was responsible for the explosion. And even if the government or one of its representatives was responsible, that we exert diplomatic pressure only, though without standing down militarily. Assuming, of course, that there are no additional acts of terrorism."

"That's it, sir. Yes."

The President drummed the top of the report. "How long have we been piddling with the Palestinians about those Hezbollah terrorists who hit the Hollywood Bowl? Six months?"

"Seven."

"Seven months. Paul, we've been kicked in the ass way too often since I took office, and we keep turning the other cheek. It's got to stop here."

"Ambassador Gap called earlier," said Burkow, "and offered the most obligatory of regrets. He said nothing to assure us that they weren't responsible."

"Martha says that's the way they are," Hood said. "And while I don't disagree with the need to be decisive, we have to make sure we hit the right target. I repeat what's in the report: we see no unusual military activity in the North, no one has claimed responsibility for the explosion, and even if certain factions in North Korea *were* responsible, that doesn't implicate the government itself."

"It doesn't let them off the hook, either," said the President. "If General Schneider started lobbing shells over the DMZ, you can bet Pyongyang wouldn't check with me to see if it's okay to start firing back. Paul, if you'll excuse me now, I've got to meet — "

The STU-3 rang and the President picked it up. His face clouded over as he listened, saying nothing. After several seconds, he thanked the caller and said he'd get back to him. After hanging up, he rested his forehead in his steepled hands.

"That was General MacLean at the Pentagon. We have had now, Paul, unusual military activity in the North. A DPRK MIG fired on one of your spy planes, killing the Recon Officer."

Burkow swore.

"Was it a warning shot that went bad?" Hood asked.

The President glared at him. "Whose side are you *on*, for Christ's sake?"

"Mr. President, we were over their airspace — "

"And we will not apologize for that! I will instruct the Press Secretary to tell reporters that in light of what happened this afternoon, we had to step up security in the region. North Korea's overreaction simply confirms our concerns. I will further instruct General MacLean that as of ten A.M. this morning, all U.S. forces in the area are to go to Defcon 3. Put the screws to your friends in Seoul, Paul, and huddle with the DOD to get me a military update to this by noon. Fax it — you're too valuable to have running back and forth." He picked up the Options Paper and dropped it. "Steve, tell Greg I want the CIA out there turning over every rock until they find out who was responsible for the explosion. Not that it matters: whether or not the North was in it before, Paul, they're in it now — up to their necks!"

FORTY-TWO

Tuesday, 11:40 P.M., Seoul

The hearse sped south toward the airstrip, traveling highways that were thick with military traffic heading north, away from Seoul.

As he sat in the backseat of the Ambassador's Mercedes, following the hearse, Gregory Donald noticed the increased troop movements away from the city. In light of Bob Herbert's phone call, he could only imagine that things were heating up between the two governments. He wasn't surprised; this close to the DMZ, high alerts were as common in Seoul as pirated videotapes. Still, this level of activity was unusual. The numbers of soldiers being moved suggested that generals didn't want to have too many people in one spot, lest the North attack with rockets.

For the moment Donald felt detached from it all. He was trapped in a cocoon two car-lengths long and too few years wide, locked in with the reality that that was his wife in front of him and that he would never see her again. Not on this earth. The hearse was illuminated by the headlights of the Mercedes, and as he gazed at the black drapes drawn in the back he wondered if Soonji would have been pleased or bothered to be riding in a state vehicle . . . in that car in particular. He remembered how Soonji had shut her eyes after he told her the story, as though that would somehow close out the truth —

The black Cadillac was shared by the American, British, Canadian, and French embassies in Seoul, and was parked at the latter when not in use. Sharing official hearses was not uncommon, though there was almost an international incident in 1982, when both the British and French ambassadors unexpectedly lost relatives on the same afternoon and both requested the official hearse at the same time. Since the French kept it garaged, they felt they deserved first use; the British maintained that since the French Ambassador had lost a grandmother and the British Ambassador a father, the closer relation took priority. The French countered that, arguably, the

262

Ambassador was closer to his grandmother than the British Ambassador was to his father. To defuse the conflict, both ambassadors hired outside funeral homes and the official hearse remained unused that day.

Gregory Donald smiled as he remembered what Soonji said, with her eyes still tightly squeezed: "Only in the diplomatic corps could a war and a car reservation carry equal weight." And it was true. There was nothing too small, too personal, or too macabre to become an international issue. For that reason, he was touched — and felt Soonji would have been too — when British Ambassador Clayton phoned him at the embassy to offer his condolences and to tell him that the embassies would not use the hearse for their own victims of today's blast until after he was finished with it.

He refused to take his eyes off the hearse, though his tired mind roved in a stream-of-consciousness state, thinking of the last meal he had with Soonji, the last time they made love, the last time he had watched her dress. He could still taste her lipstick, smell her perfume, feel her long fingernails on the back of his neck. Then he thought back to how he had first been attracted to Soonji, not by her beauty or poise but by her words — her incisive, clever words. He remembered the conversation she had had with a girlfriend who worked for outgoing Ambassador Dan Tunick. As the Ambassador finished his farewell speech to the staff, the girlfriend said, "He looks so happy."

Soonji regarded the Ambassador for a moment, then said, "My father looked like that once, after passing a stone. The Ambassador looks relieved, Tish, not happy."

She'd hit it on the head in her open, irreverent way. As the crowd drank champagne, he'd walked over to her, introduced himself, told her the hearse story, and was smitten even before her eyes had opened. As he sat here now, out of tears but not memories, he took consolation from the fact that the last time he saw Soonji alive, as she ran back to his side after finding her earring, she was wearing a look of profound relief *and* happiness.

The Mercedes followed the hearse off the highway and toward the airfield. Donald would see his wife to the TWA flight that was taking her to the States, and as soon as it had taken off, he would board the waiting Bell Iroquois for the short hop to the DMZ.

Howard Norbom would assume Donald had gone around him to get what he wanted, and he felt some guilt over that. But at least the General wouldn't be implicated when he tried to contact the North. Thanks to the phone call, whatever fallout there was would land on him . . . and on Op-Center.

FORTY-THREE

Tuesday, 11:45 P.M., KCIA Headquarters

When he got the call from Bae Gun that the arrest had been successful, Hwan was of two minds: they'd done the right thing, though he was sorry to lose a most interesting figure in Ms. Chong. His cryptanalysts had not yet cracked her code, even though they knew the contents of some of the data she was sending, having fed it to her through Bae, who told her he had a son in the military and occasionally gave her real but unimportant troop strength, map coordinates, and changes in command. Now that she was in custody, Hwan doubted that she would help them along.

The KCIA had spent four years monitoring but not interfering with the current crop of North Korean agents in Seoul. By watching one they had found another, then another and another. The five operatives seemed to form a closed loop, with Kim Chong and a pretzel-maker at their hub, and Hwan felt he had them all. With the woman's capture, he would have the others watched round the clock to see whom they contacted or what new agent might be moved in to take her place.

It bothered him, though, that in what little of her code they had broken, there hadn't even been a hint of today's attack. Indeed, the pretzel-maker — who baked information into salt-free nuggets — had even been told to attend the festivities and gauge the mood of the crowd toward reunification. While it was true the North could have executed the attack on a need-to-know basis and not told their operatives, Hwan doubted they would have put one in danger like that. Why bother sending him at all if they intended to terrorize the celebration?

The Desk Sergeant phoned up when the agents arrived, and Hwan stood behind his desk to receive them — and Ms. Chong. He had never seen Kim Chong herself in the flesh, only in photographs, and went through a traditional exercise Gregory had taught him to do when meeting someone he knew only by picture or voice or reputation. He tried to fill in the blanks, to see how close his guesses came to reality. How tall they were, what they sounded like — in the case of suspected enemies whether they would be irate, abusive, or cooperative. The process served no purpose other than as a useful review of what Hwan knew about the people before meeting them.

He knew Ms. Chong was five-foot-six, twenty-eight, with fine, long, coal-dust hair and dark eyes. And that according to what Bae had told his contact here, she was a tough nut. Hwan suspected that she would also have a musician's sensitivity, the thorny temperament of a woman who had to endure the advances of men at Gun's bar, and the habit of all foreign agents to listen more than she spoke, to learn rather than divulge. She would be defiant; most North Koreans were when dealing with the South.

He heard the elevator door slide open followed by footsteps in the corridor. Two agents walked in with Kim Chong between them.

Physically, the woman was exactly as he'd pictured her: proud, intense, alert. She was dressed more or less as he'd expected, in a tight black skirt, black stockings, and a white blouse, the top two buttons open — the uniform for women who played in lounges and bars. He'd missed the skin, though, not having imagined it to be so sun-bronzed. But of course it would be, since her days were free and she spent them poking about the city. He was also surprised by her hands, which he saw when he told the men to uncuff her. Unlike other musicians he had known, the fingers were not thick and strong but slender, delicate.

He asked the men to shut the door and wait outside, then gestured toward an armchair. The woman sat down, both feet on the floor, knees together, those graceful hands folded upright in her lap. Her eyes were on the desk.

"Ms. Chong, I'm Kim Hwan, Deputy Director of the KCIA. Would you — care for a cigarette?"

He picked up a small case on his desk and raised the lid. She took a cigarette, caught herself as she went to tap it on the face of her watch — it had been taken from her, lest she use the glass to try to slit her wrists — then put the cigarette in her mouth.

Hwan walked around the desk and lit it for her. The woman drew deeply and sat back, one hand still on her lap, the other on the armrest. She still didn't allow her eyes to meet his, which was more or less standard with women during an interrogation. It prevented any kind of emotional connection from being made, which kept the meeting formal and tended to frustrate many interviewers.

Hwan offered her an ashtray and she set it on the armrest. Then he sat on the edge of the desk and regarded the woman for nearly a minute before speaking. For all her polish, there was something about this one he couldn't quite get a handle on. Something *wrong*.

"Is there anything I can get you? A drink?"

She shook her head once, still staring at the desk.

"Ms. Chong, we've known about you and your work for quite some time. Your mission here is over, and you'll be tried for espionage — within the month, I imagine. The mood running as it is after today, I suspect that justice will be quick and unpleasant. However, I can promise you some measure of leniency if you help us find out who was behind the explosion at the Palace this afternoon."

"I know nothing more than what I saw on television, Mr. Hwan."

"You were told nothing in advance?"

"No. Nor do I believe that my country was responsible."

"Why do you say that?"

She looked at him for the first time. "Because we are not a nation of lunatics. There are some madmen — but most of us don't want war."

That was it, he thought. That's what was wrong. She was following the rules for interrogation, and would probably stonewall wherever she could. But her heart wasn't in this. She'd just made a very clear distinction between "some madmen" and "us." Us *who?* Most operatives came from the military and would never say anything against their countrymen. Hwan wondered if Ms. Chong might be a civilian, one of those North Koreans who served against their will because they had a criminal record, were fighting to regain lost family honor, or because a sibling or parent needed money. If that was true, then they did have something in common: both of them desperately wanted peace.

Director Yung-Hoon would not approve of revealing privileged information to the enemy, but Hwan was willing to take that risk.

"Ms. Chong, suppose I were to tell you that I believed you — "

"I'd ask you to try another tack."

"But what if I meant it?" Hwan slid off the desk and squatted in front of her where she had to turn away or look at him. She looked at him. "I did poorly in the reverse psychology training, and I'm a terrible poker player. Suppose I also told you that while someone tried very hard to make this look like the work of your military, and the evidence points to that, I don't believe it is."

She frowned. "If you were to tell me *that,* then I'd implore you to persuade others."

"Suppose they didn't believe me. Would you help me prove my suspicions?"

Her expression was wary but interested. "I'm listening, Mr. Hwan."

"We found footprints near the bomb site — the prints of North Korean military boots. For someone to frame your military, they'd need the footwear, of course, as well as the proper explosives and possibly weapons from the North. We don't know in what quantities these might have been taken — not a large amount, I'd imagine, since a group like this would want to remain close and very small. I need you to try and find out if such a theft has occurred."

Kim stubbed out the cigarette. "I think not."

"You won't help?"

"Mr. Hwan, would your superiors believe me if I came back with such information? There's no trust between our nations."

"But I'll trust you. Can you contact your

people any way other than through the bar?"

"If I could," Kim said, "what would you do?"

"Go with you and hear what they have to say, find out if any other matériel was taken. If these terrorists are as desperate as I suspect, they may be planning other attacks to push us toward war."

"But you said yourself that your superiors don't agree with your suspicions — "

"If we can find evidence," Hwan said, "*anything* to support my suspicions, I'll by-pass my people and contact the head of the crisis Task Force in Washington. He's a reasonable man, and he will listen."

Kim continued to look at the Deputy Director. He sighed and rested his temples in his thumb and index finger.

"Time is very short, Ms. Chong. The result of today's explosion may not just be war, but the end of reunification talks for our lifetime. Will you help me?"

She hesitated, but only for a moment. "You're certain that you trust me?"

He smiled faintly. "I won't give you the keys to the car, Ms. Chong, but in this matter — yes, I trust you."

"All right" — she rose slowly — "we'll work together on this. But understand, Mr. Hwan, I have family in the North — and

I will only go so far for you . . . or even for peace."

"I understand."

Hwan walked briskly back to his desk and punched the intercom. He told the Desk Sergeant to arrange for his car and driver, then regarded his prisoner.

"Where are you taking me?"

"I'll direct your driver as we go, Mr. Hwan. Unless you *would* care to give me the keys, in which case — "

"I'll let you guide us, thanks. However, I'm required to file an itinerary in case there's a problem, and that's the first thing the Director will ask for when he returns. Give me a general direction."

Kim smiled for the first time and said, "North, Mr. Hwan. We're going north."

FORTY-FOUR

Tuesday, 10:00 A.M., Washington, D.C.

Hood felt as though he'd been cut off at the knees, but he didn't dislike the President. He couldn't.

Michael Lawrence wasn't the brightest man who ever held the office, but he had the touch, he had charisma, and that worked on TV and at rallies. The public liked his style. He certainly wasn't the best manager to hold the office. He didn't like getting his hands dirty with the nitty-gritty of running the government: he wasn't a detail man like Jimmy Carter. Trusted aides like Burkow and Lawrence's Press Secretary Adrian Crow had been allowed to create their own little fiefdoms, power bases that won over or alienated other government agencies by rewarding cooperation and success with access to the President and increased responsibilities, punishing failure with backwater assignments and busywork. Even when he was making his rookie failures in foreign policy, this President didn't suffer the kind of bad press that dogged his predecessors: by wining and dining the Press Corps, increasing perks and amenities for reporters, and carefully doling out leaks and exclusives, Crow had put all but a few crusty columnists in her hip pocket. And no one read the Op-Ed pages anyway, she maintained. Sound bites and advertising controlled the voters, not George Will and Carl Rowan.

Lawrence could be ruthless, blind, and stubborn. But if nothing else, he had a vision for the country that was bold and intelligent and was just starting to work. For a year prior to announcing his candidacy, Florida Governor Lawrence had met with industrial leaders and asked if, in exchange for considerable tax breaks and deferments, they would buy into the privatization of NASA with the government managing all launches and facilities, the companies assuming most costs for personnel and R&D. In effect, Lawrence was proposing to boost the space agency's budget nearly threefold without going through Congress. Moreover, government expenses on space would be cut by two billion dollars, money that Lawrence earmarked for crime fighting and education. He also suggested that one third of the new blue-collar work force for NASA be culled from welfare, making for an annual savings of half a billion dollars.

U.S. industry agreed to the plan, and Lawrence's campaign advertisements reminded Americans of the lost glory of the Mercury, Gemini, and Apollo days, of blue-collar and white-collar workers laboring side by side for a common goal, of high employment and low inflation. He tied them all together, and hammered voters with views of existing spinoffs — personal computers and calculators, communications satellites and cellular phones, Teflon and portable video cameras and video games — and with visions of anticipated spinoffs — medicines to cure cancer and AIDS, space-based generators to convert solar energy into electricity to reduce costs and reliance on foreign oil, and even weather control. During the campaign, every time his opponent argued that the money would be better spent on Earth, Lawrence countered that Earth had become a sinkhole, swallowing up jobs and tax dollars, and that his plan would put an end to that . . . and also end foreign inroads in technological advances that were stealing American jobs.

Lawrence won handily, and as soon as he

was elected he met with those same business leaders and the new heads of NASA to get some tangible results, fast, while they worked on getting the space station into orbit before the end of his first term. Leasing the abandoned Russian space station *Nevsky*, they put medical researchers and engineers in space, and within eighteen months Adrian Crow's press machine was touting the developments: most startling of all were images of a young medic, paralyzed below the waist in Desert Storm, playing zero-gravity basketball with an astronaut. The President had cured the lame, and it was an image people would never forget.

You could be frustrated with the man for his faults and for his frequent heavy-handedness, but you had to admire his vision. And even though his foreign policy faltered badly in the early going, he was smart enough to put together Op-Center to help run things. Burkow had argued that less bureaucracy and not more was what they needed to make things work abroad, but the President had disagreed with him on that — creating the ongoing tension between Hood and the National Security Council.

But that was okay: Paul could live with that. Compared to some of the special interest groups and political correctness monitors he'd had to deal with in Los Angeles, Burkow was a day at the beach.

Hood pulled up to the hospital, parked in the Emergency area, and hurried to the elevator. He had the room number, 834, from phoning earlier and went right up. The door of the private room was open; Sharon was slumped in the chair, eyes shut, and started when he entered. He kissed her on the forehead.

"Dad!"

Hood walked over to the bed. Alexander's voice was muffled by the clear tent, but his eyes and smile were luminous. He was wheezing slowly, his strong little chest fighting hard to skim air off the top of each breath. Hood knelt on one knee.

Hood asked, "Koopa Lord knock you for a loop, Super Mario?"

"It's the Koopa King, Dad."

"Sorry. You know me and video games. I'm surprised you haven't got your Game Boy in there."

The boy shrugged a shoulder. "They wouldn't let me have it. I can't even have a comic book in here. Mom had to read me *Supreme* and hold up the pictures."

"We'll have to talk about some of the comics he's been reading," Sharon said, walking over. "Ripping off arms and punching out teeth — "

"Mom, it's good for my imagination."

"Don't get agitated," Hood said. "We'll talk about it when you're better."

"Dad, I love my comics — "

"You'll have them," Hood said. He touched the tent with the back of his hand, rubbing his son's cheek through it. Just now, medical advances seemed very important. He leaned closer and winked. "You worry about getting on your feet, and we'll see about convincing your mom later."

Alexander nodded weakly, and his father rose.

"Thanks for coming," Sharon said. "Crisis over?"

"No." He wasn't sure if that was a dig, but gave her the benefit of the doubt. "Look, I'm sorry about before, but we're really swimming through it. What are you doing about Harleigh?"

"She's going to my sister's."

Hood nodded, then kissed Sharon. "I'll call you later."

"Paul — "

He looked back.

"I really *don't* think those comics are good for him. They're very violent."

"So were the comics when I was a kid, and look how well adjusted I am. Severed

heads, zombies, and Uncle Creepy notwith-
standing."

Sharon arched her brows and sighed heavily
as Hood kissed her again. Giving Alexander
a thumbs-up, he hurried to the elevator, not
daring to look at his watch until he was
safely inside.

FORTY-FIVE

Tuesday, 10:05 A.M., Op-Center

"What the hell's taking Viens so long?" Matt Stoll asked as he stared at his monitor. "You program in the time differential, hit Search, and it should go to the start of your bogus satellite imagery."

Phil Katzen was sitting on a bridge chair beside him, also watching the screen. While the NRO searched back through the morning's photo-file, Stoll and Katzen were running the detailed diagnostics programs on the system. The eleventh and final program was nearly completed.

"Maybe Viens didn't find anything, Matty."

"Hell, you know that's not possible."

"*I* know that. But maybe the computer doesn't."

Stoll's lips puckered. "Touché." He shook

his head as the last diagnostics self-exited with an AOK graphic. "And we know *that's* not true either!" He resisted the urge to slap the computer. The way his luck was running, the entire system would go down again.

"There's no way the diagnostics could have been corrupted, is there?" Katzen asked.

"None. But that's what I thought about the rest of the software too. I hate to say it, Phil, but I'd give my left nostril to meet the son of a bitch who did this to me."

"You're taking it personally, huh?"

"You bet. Hurt my software, hurt me. What gets me is not only that he outsmarted me, but he didn't leave any footprints. Not a one."

"Let's wait and see what the NRO — "

The phone rang and the caller's ID number flashed on the rectangular screen. "Speak of the devil," Stoll said as he hit the Speaker button. "Stoll here."

"Matty, it's Steve. Sorry it took so long, but the computer showed that there was no problem so I decided to check the photos themselves."

"My apologies."

"For what?"

"For bitching to my pal Phil, here, about you taking so long. What'd you find?"

"Just what you said we would. A photo that came in at 7:58.00.8965 this morning . . . exactly .001 seconds late. And guess what? It's full of rolling thunder that wasn't there .8955 seconds before."

"This is fucking amazing," Stoll said. "Put 'em on my screen, would you? And, Steve — thanks much."

"You're welcome. Meanwhile, is there anything we can do to purge the system?"

"Can't say until I've looked at the pictures. I'll get back to you ASAP."

Stoll punched off even as the pictures were scanning onto his monitor. The first photograph showed the terrain as it really was: no troops, no artillery, no tanks. The second photograph had them edging into the frame. Everything from the grain to the shadows looked authentic.

"If it's a fake, it's a damn good one," Katzen said.

"Maybe not. Look here."

Stoll hit F1/Shift, then went to the magnify option. The screen returned with a cursor, and he moved it over the windshield of a jeep at the top of the screen. He pressed Enter, and the windshield filled the monitor.

"Get a load of that."

Katzen looked, squinted, then exhaled loudly. "No way."

"Way," said Stoll, smiling for the first time in hours. He grabbed his mouse, hit the button on top, and rolled the cursor across the windshield, drawing a fine yellow line around the reflection of an oak tree. "No trees in the neighborhood, Phil. This image was lifted from another photo or it was shot somewhere else and inserted, digitally." Leaving the photo on document one, he switched screens to document two and asked the computer to search the NRO files for a matching shot. Two minutes and twelve seconds later, the photograph was on the screen.

"Unbelievable," Katzen said.

The technical data on the photograph appeared in a sidebar: it was taken 275 days before in the woods near the Supung Reservoir near the Manchuria/North Korea border.

"Someone went through our photo files," Stoll said, "selected all the images they wanted, and created a new program."

"And loaded it in .001 seconds," Katzen said.

"No. The loading was what the shutdown was all about. Or at least, what seemed like a shutdown to us."

"I don't follow."

"While we thought the computers were

off-line, someone, somehow, used the twenty seconds to dump this photo and every successive photo into the system. It took .001 seconds to kick in, and now, like a recording, those prefabricated images are being played back to us every .8955 seconds."

"This is too goddamn fantastic — "

"But the fact remains that we — the NRO, DOD, and the CIA — are all closed systems. No one could get to any of us over the phone lines. To download that much data, someone would have to have been sitting somewhere in Op-Center popping in diskettes."

"Who? The security videos turned up nothing."

Stoll snickered. "What makes you think you can trust them? We've got someone screwing with our satellites. A camcorder isn't going to be much of a challenge."

"Christ, I didn't think of that."

"But you're right. I don't think this was done on premises. It would mean that someone here's a bad penny, and whatever I think of Bob Herbert personally, he's one very careful cashier."

"I like that."

"Thanks." Stoll went back to document one and looked at the windshield. "So what've we got? Somewhere in this system is a rogue program, and on it are photographs that the NRO satellites haven't even taken yet — photographs that they will *appear* to take every .8955 seconds. That's the bad news. The good news is, if we can get to that program, we can drop-kick it, restore our space eyes, and prove that someone's out to stir up big trouble in Korea."

"How can you do that if you don't know where the file is or what it's called?"

Stoll saved the blowup and exited the file, then went to Directory. He selected Library and waited while the massive list loaded.

"The photos the infiltrator used were taken before there even was an Op-Center, so this obviously took a long time to write. It's a big one. Now, it had to have come in on the coattails of some other file or we would have spotted it when we sterilize incoming software. That means the host file has to be seriously bloated."

"So we look at the file of, say, traffic light patterns in Pyongyang, and if it's thirty megabytes fat we probably have our rogue program."

"That's the drill."

"But where do we start looking? Whoever wrote the program had access to surveillance photos of North Korea — which would make it someone at Op-Center, the NRO, the

Pentagon, or ROK."

"No one at Op-Center or the NRO stands to gain by mobilization up and down the peninsula," Stoll said. "Either way, it's business as usual. Which leaves us with DOD and ROK." Stoll began running a search through the Library listing, counting the number of diskettes from each source. In order to obtain diskettes he wanted, it would be necessary to star each file and E-mail his request to Op-Center's archives; the diskettes would then be copied, hand-delivered, signed for, and erased upon their return.

"Shit," Katzen said as the number grew. "We've got about two hundred diskettes from DOD and forty-odd from ROK. It'll take days to go through them all."

After thinking for a moment, Stoll highlighted the entire ROK file.

"Starting with the shorter one?"

"No," said Stoll, "the safer one." He tapped the Star button, then Send. "If Bob Herbert ever found out I suspected our guys first, he'd kick my ass."

Katzen clapped a hand on his shoulder and rose. "I'll go bring Paul up to speed, but, Matty, I need you to do me a favor."

"Name it."

"Tell Paul that I spotted the oak."

"Okay, but why?"

"Because if our Director ever finds out that his Environmental Officer couldn't see a tree two feet in front of him, he'll kick *my* ass."

"Done deal," Stoll said as he sat back, folded his arms, and waited for the disks to be delivered.

FORTY-SIX

Wednesday, 12:30 A.M., outside of Seoul

The highways leading from Seoul to the DMZ were still crowded with military traffic, and Hwan had told his driver Cho to stick to the back roads. They followed Kim Chong's directions, a fine drizzle falling as the car headed north from the city. Cho switched on the defroster and it breathed smoothly; Hwan wished his own insides were as well tuned.

As he sat in the backseat beside Kim, Hwan wondered if this was a good idea — ignoring the fact that for the time being, it was the only idea. Cooperating with Kim went against everything he'd been trained and raised to believe: he was going to trust a North Korean spy about matters pertaining to DPRK security. As he sat next to the young woman who gazed silently from her own window, he began having serious doubts about what he was doing. He wasn't afraid that she would try to lead him into an ambush or a nest of North Korean vipers. Hwan had made a point of sitting with his coat open, so she could see the .38 in his shoulder holster. If anything happened, she'd get a part of it. But Kim had surrendered to Bae rather than take a bullet. She wanted to live.

He was concerned that she might mislead him — it was possible, despite her apparent sincerity — and he would help set his nation's military up for a fall. He was even worried that she might not mislead him. If everything worked out, if her information were accurate and a conflict was averted, he could still be accused of collusion with the enemy. Whatever good might come of this would be outweighed by the shame of being charged with treason.

He resisted the urge to talk to her, to try to find out more about her. He didn't dare show weakness or doubt, or she might try to take advantage of it. Hwan's driver Cho apparently had no such concerns as he kept glancing into the rearview mirror. Beneath the sharp brown edge of his snap-brim hat, there was concern in Cho's eyes. Each time Kim gave them a new direction they headed farther into isolation, deeper into the hills of the northeast, and with every turn Cho would fire a glance toward the radio set in the bottom of the dashboard, pointing with his eyes, quietly urging Hwan to let him radio headquarters with their location.

Hwan would just shake his head once, slowly, or break eye contact.

Poor Cho, he thought. Three months before, he'd taken a bullet in his right hand and had been moved from fieldwork to driving. He so very much wanted to get back into it, to rack 'em up and break a few heads.

But no. No backup, no reinforcements, and no doing anything to cause Ms. Chong to doubt their sincerity. They were in for the whole ride — in it with a woman who knew that if she didn't escape, she was going to prison or perhaps the gallows. Hwan only hoped that her sense of duty was as strong as his.

"May I say something?" Kim asked, still staring out her window.

Hwan looked at her with barely concealed surprise. "Please."

She faced him now, her eyes softer than before, her mouth less rigid. "I've been thinking about what you're doing, and it's very courageous."

"An intelligent risk, I think."

"No. You could have stayed where you were — there's no shame in that. You don't know where I'm leading you."

Hwan felt Cho let up on the gas and fired him a look. The car got back up to speed.

"Where *are* you taking us?" Hwan asked.

"To my cottage."

"But you live in the city."

"Why do you say that? Because your agents followed me there? The woman who doesn't like to drink, and the man who changed his disguises but not his bad breath?"

"Those were trainees. You were supposed to see them."

"I understand that now. So I wouldn't suspect that Mr. Gun was the one who was watching me. But he never took me home. You had to be getting some of your information from the cadets."

Hwan said nothing.

"It isn't important. I had a motor scooter in the back, and I would come out here to send my real messages. Make a right onto the dirt road," she said to Cho.

Cho looked at Hwan in the mirror. This time Hwan ignored him.

"You see," Kim went on, "you weren't the only one engaging in a deception. We've known for years that you were watching the bar, and I was sent there to tie up your personnel. My code was real enough, but the people I was playing them to — the people who came in, who you would follow home — had no idea what I was doing. They were all South Koreans I hired for the night to sit for an hour or two at the bar and then leave."

"I see," said Hwan. "Assuming I were to believe you — which I'm not entirely prepared to do — why are you telling me this?"

"Because I need you to believe something I have to say, Mr. Hwan. I did not come to Seoul because I wanted to. My brother Han broke into a military hospital to get morphine for our mother. When the police came, I helped him to escape — and they arrested my mother and me. I was given a choice: we could remain in prison, or I could go to the South and gather intelligence."

"How did you get here?"

Kim's eyes flashed. "Don't misunderstand me, Mr. Hwan. I'm not a traitor. I'll tell you only what you need to know, and no more. Shall I continue?"

Hwan nodded.

"I agreed to come here, provided my mother was taken to a hospital and my brother was pardoned. They consented, though I was unable to find Han after that.

Since then, I've learned that he made his way to Japan."

"And your mother?"

"She had stomach cancer, Mr. Hwan. She died before I came here."

"Yet you still came."

"My mother was comfortable until the end. The government had kept its word, and I would keep mine."

Hwan nodded. He continued to ignore Cho's eyes, which were shifting like Ping-Pong balls.

"You said you wanted me to believe something, Ms. Chong. Your story — ?"

"Yes, but also this. You'll die at the cottage without my help."

Cho eased the brake to the floor; the car skid slightly on the muddy road before coming to a stop.

Hwan regarded his passenger, angrier at himself than at her. The doors were locked, and he was prepared to use his gun if he had to.

"And you'll die in Masan Prison without my help," he said. "Who's at the cottage?"

"No one. It's booby-trapped."

"How?"

"There's a radio inside the piano. If you don't play a specific melody before raising the lid, a bomb will explode."

"You'll play the melody for us. You don't want to die."

"You're wrong, Mr. Hwan. I'm willing to die. But I'm also willing to live."

"Under what conditions, Ms. Chong?"

A single headlight appeared in the rearview mirror, and Cho rolled down the window to wave the motor scooter by. The woman waited until the puttering engine had faded.

"I have nothing but my brother — "

"And your country."

"I'm a patriot, Mr. Hwan, don't insult me. But I can't go back. I'm twenty-eight and female. I'll be reassigned, not to the South but to some other country. Perhaps this time I'll be expected to use more than my skills at the keyboard."

"Patriotism has its price."

"My family has *paid* it, many times over. Now I want to be with what's left of that family. I will do what you ask, but then I want you to leave me at the cottage."

"So you can make your way to Japan?" Hwan shook his head. "I would be dishonorably dismissed, and I would deserve it."

"You'd rather risk your country going to war?"

"You seem ready enough to let thousands of young men like your brother die."

Kim looked away.

Hwan glanced at the dashboard clock. He motioned for Cho to drive on, and the car got under way with a squirt of mud.

"I'm not going to let anyone die," Kim said.

"I hoped you wouldn't." He watched her face, which was brightened dimly now and then by candlelight from huts and cottages they passed. The shadows of the rain-soaked window played on her face. "I'll do what I can for you, of course. I have friends in Japan . . . perhaps something can be worked out."

"Prison, there?"

"Not a jail. There are low-security facilities, like dormitories."

"It would be difficult to find my brother — even from a comfortable cell."

"I can help with that. He can visit, or maybe we can work something else out."

She looked at him. The dark rivulets on her cheeks resembled tears. "Thank you — that's something, I suppose. If it can be done."

She seemed open and vulnerable for the first time, and he felt drawn to her. She was strong and attractive, and he thought, and almost said, that he could always marry her and really complicate the South Korean legal system — but as tempting as the idea

was, it seemed unfair to tease her with free-
dom . . . or threaten her with him.

But it was on his mind as they drove
through the increasingly slippery road to
Kim's home in the hills. Had he not been
thinking of Kim, it is still unlikely that
Hwan would have noticed the scooter that
had passed them earlier, as it sat off to the
side of the road, its headlight off, engine
idling. . . .

FORTY-SEVEN

Tuesday, 10:50 A.M., Op-Center

Phil Katzen bumped into Hood on the way to his office and followed him in. He told the Director what they'd discovered, and that Stoll was already going through the first of the ROK diskettes.

"That would dovetail with what Gregory Donald told Martha," Hood said. "He and Kim Hwan at KCIA don't think it's North Korea, either." Hood felt good about having seen his son, and about the boy's prospects. He allowed himself a little grin. "How's it feel to get away from oil slicks and rain forests?"

"Strange," the Environmental Officer admitted, "but invigorating. Getting to use muscles that are a little atrophied."

"Spend too much time here, and that isn't all that'll atrophy."

Ann Farris strode into the room. "Paul — "

"Just the person I want to see."

"Maybe not. Do you know about the ROK files?"

"I'm the Director. They pay me to know those things."

"My" — she frowned — "we're feeling festive. Must've had a good meeting with the President."

"Not really. With my son. What about those files? I thought requisitions from the archives were privileged information."

"Sure. And by noon, the *Washington Post*'ll know. It's pathetic what good people will do for money or Super Bowl tickets. But that's not the problem we have to solve right now. Do you have any idea what kind of PR nightmare we'll have if word gets out that we suspect our *allies* of being behind this?"

"Can't you spin it?"

"Like a top, Paul. But mistrust is sexy, and that's what everyone's going to play up."

"Whatever happened to truth, justice, and the American way?"

"It died with Superman, friend," Phil said. "And when they brought him back, they forgot about the rest."

Ann tapped a pen on the small notebook she was holding. "What did you want to see me about?"

"Hold on, Ann." Hood had already pressed F6 and his assistant's face filled the screen. "Anything new from the KCIA, Bugs?"

"The lab report's in file BH/1."

"What's in the nutshell?"

"North Korean explosives, boot prints, petrol traces. How's Alexander?"

"Better, thanks. Do me a favor and ask Bob Herbert to come in at eleven." Hood punched the image off. He dragged a hand down his face. "Shit. The KCIA says it's North Korea, but Matty thinks we were invaded by a South Korean virus and Gregory Donald thinks we have South Koreans masquerading as North Koreans. Quite a circus."

"You're quite a ringmaster," Ann said. "What's wrong with Alexander?"

"Asthma attack."

"Poor kid," said Phil, shaking his head as he made for the door. "Freakin' smog doesn't help, this time of year. I'll be with Matty if you need me."

When they were alone, Hood noticed that Ann was looking at him intently. It wasn't the first time he had ever watched her watching him, but today there was something in those dark amber eyes that made him warm and uneasy — warm because there was compassion in those eyes, and uneasy because it was a feeling he didn't get often enough from his wife. But then, Ann Farris didn't have to live with him.

"Ann," he said, "the President — "

"Paul!" Lowell Coffey said as he swung in, his big hand still on the doorjamb as he nearly collided with Ann.

"Come in," Ann said. "No reason to shut the door with all the leaks around here."

"I hear you," said Coffey. "Paul, I need a second. About that ROK check Matty's running: you've *got* to make sure that the only words coming from this facility are 'No Comment.' There are confidentiality agreements with Seoul, possible defamation of character if we point the finger at a person or group, and we risk exposure on some of the questionable ways the information on those diskettes was collected."

"Have Martha read everyone the riot act. And have someone on Matt's staff set the computers to transcribe all phone conversations."

"Can't do that, Paul. Illegal as hell."

"Then do it illegally, and have Martha *tell* everyone we are."

"*Paul* — "

"*Do it*, Lowell. I'll deal with the goddamn ACLU later. I can't have my people worrying about plugging leaks, and *I* can't worry about who might be causing them!"

Lowell left, trailing disgust.

Hood looked at Ann, tried to recollect his thoughts. He noticed her kerchief now, casually knotted around her hair. He hated himself as he sat there thinking how nice it would be to tug gently at the end of the red and black cloth, and lose his hands in her long brown hair —

He pulled his thoughts together in a hurry. "Ann, I've, uh, I've got something else for your plate. You heard about the Mirage that was shot up?"

She nodded, the eyes suddenly looking sad. He wondered if she could possibly have known what he was thinking. Women never ceased to astound him that way.

"The White House is going to issue a statement to the effect that in light of North Korea overreacting to our flyover, our forces in the region are being put on Defcon 3 alert." He glanced at the countdown clock on the back wall. "That was fifty-two minutes ago. Pyongyang will do the equivalent, possibly one-up us, and my guess — my *hope* — is that the President will let things sit until we learn more about what happened at the Palace. At this stage of the game, if he escalates, God only knows what the North will do. When Bob gets here, we've got to talk to Ernie Colon and give the President a military options update. What I need you to do, Ann, is soften whatever the White House says."

"Give us a way out?"

"Exactly. Lawrence won't apologize for the surveillance plane, so we can't either. But if all we do is talk tough, eventually we're going to have to act tough. Let's get some regrets into our statement, so that if we have to back down at any point there's an open door. You know — they have the right of all sovereign nations to protect their territory, and we regret that circumstances forced us to take extreme measures to do the same."

"I'll have to run it past Lowell — "

"That's fine. I kind of sacked him before."

"He deserved it. He's a pain."

"He's a lawyer," Hood pointed out. "We pay him to play devil's advocate."

Ann folded away her pad, hesitated. "Have you eaten today?"

"Just a little crow."

"I noticed the feathery quality in your voice. You want something?"

"Maybe later." Hood heard Bob Herbert's voice as he rolled down the hall. He looked up at Ann. "Tell you what. If you're free around twelve-thirty, why don't you have them send over a couple of salads from the commissary. We'll do greens and strategy."

"It's a date," she said, in a way that shot electricity down his belly.

Ann turned to go and he watched her while pretending to look down. It was a dangerous little game, but it wasn't going anywhere — he wouldn't let it — and, right now, the attention felt fine.

He shifted gears quickly as Herbert spun into the office, buzzing Bugs and asking him to put the Secretary of Defense on teleconference.

FORTY-EIGHT

Wednesday, 1:10 A.M., the Diamond Mountains, North Korea

The Nodong missile site was just eighty miles as the crow flies, but the trip was slowed by deeply rutted dirt roads and foliage that crept across them as quickly as the North Koreans could clear it away. After nearly three hours of bumping and lurching, Colonel Sun and his aide Kong finally reached their destination.

Sun ordered Kong to stop the car as they came to the top of the hill that overlooked the valley where the mobile Nodongs were kept. He rose slowly and stood in the jeep, gazing down at the three trucks, which were arranged in a triangular formation. The long missiles were lying flat on the backs of the trucks, beneath tents of foliage erected to conceal them from above. In the dull light of the low gibbous moon, he could see pieces of the missiles' white skin peeping through the leaves.

"It's a thrilling sight," Sun said.

"I can hardly believe we've made it."

"Oh, we have," Sun said. He savored the view a moment longer. "And seeing them in flight will be even more thrilling."

It seemed so incredible: after a year of furtive contacts with the North, of working closely with Major Lee, with Captain Bock and his computer expert Private Koh, and even with the enemy himself, a second Korean War was about to become a reality. Privately, Sun and Lee both hoped that it would do more than mark a permanent end to reunification talks: they hoped that it would mark a full-scale U.S. commitment to their cause, and the destruction of the North as a military force. If reunification came then, it would not be a result of compromise but of strength.

"Drive on," Sun said as he sat back down.

The jeep rattled down the mountain road toward the nearest artillery emplacement. There were two ZSU-23-4 quad SPAAG anti-aircraft tanks looking out over the Nodong site, a soldier perched in the large, square steel turret with its four water-cooled 23mm cannons elevated at their maximum eighty-five-degree angle. Each had a range of 450 kilometers. Sun knew that six other tanks were positioned around the site, their large gun-dish radar antenna over the turret rear able to pick out planes day or night.

A sentry stopped the jeep. After carefully reviewing the Colonel's orders by flashlight, he respectfully asked him to kill his headlights before continuing. The guard saluted the officer and the jeep picked its way down the hill — blind, Sun knew, for their own protection. There might be enemy spies in the hills, and a colonel would be a prize for a sniper.

And that would be a pity, he thought, to be killed by one of his own countrymen. Because this Colonel was just hours away from doing more for South Korea than any soldier in its history.

FORTY-NINE

Wednesday, 1:15 A.M., the DMZ

Gregory Donald was met at the cargo bay of the TWA plane by a representative of the airline and by the Deputy Chief of Mission, both of whom saw to the customs paperwork and loading of the coffin onto the 727. Only when the plane was airborne, and Donald had gently touched his lips to the tip of a finger and pressed it to the sky, did he turn and board the Bell Iroquois.

The helicopter made the trip from the airstrip in Seoul to the DMZ in just over fifteen minutes. Donald was met at the landing field by a jeep, which escorted him to the headquarters of General M. J. Schneider.

Donald was looking forward to the reunion. In his eventful life, Donald had met a few people who were arguably insane, but Schneider was the only one who wore four stars.

A Depression baby who was literally left on the doorstep of the Adventurer's Club in Manhattan, Schneider had always fancied that his mother was returning to the scene of the crime and his father was a renowned hunter or explorer. He certainly had a build straight out of H. Rider Haggard: six-foot-three, lantern jaw, broad shoulders, and Mr. Olympia waist. He was adopted by a couple who lived and worked in the garment district, and enlisted when he was eighteen, just in time to fight in Korea. He was one of the first advisers into Vietnam, one of the last American soldiers to leave, and returned to Korea in 1976 when his daughter Cindy was killed in a skiing accident. At sixty-five, he still had what Donald once described as that "last Texican at the Alamo look": ready, willing, and able to go down fighting.

Schneider was a fitting counterpart to the North's General "Hair-trigger" Hong-koo, and worked surprisingly well with ROK's General Sam, with whom he co-commanded the Joint U.S./South Korean Forces here. Whereas Schneider was a man of flavorful language who believed in throwing everything he had at a problem, including tactical nuclear weapons, Sam was a cool, reserved fifty-two-year-old who favored dialogue and sabotage to head-to-head action. This being

South Korea, Sam had to sign off on any military action; but the Sinophobic Schneider scared the North Koreans, a role Donald had always felt he cherished . . . and played to the hilt.

It was ironic, Donald thought as he entered the General's headquarters, a small wooden structure consisting of three offices and a bedroom, set on the south side of the compound. The two of them — Schneider and Gregory — couldn't be more unalike, yet they'd always seemed to "fit" together better than matched socks. Maybe it was because they were contemporaries who had come up through hard times, through back-to-back-to-back wars, or maybe Schneider was right when he'd called it the Laurel and Hardy syndrome: the diplomats made the fine messes, then the army had to go in and clean them up.

The General was on the phone when Donald arrived, and waved him in. After brushing off his dusty seat, Donald sat on a white leather sofa along one wall. Schneider was a stickler for clean.

". . . don't give a foggy damn *what* the Pentagon says," Schneider was yelling, his voice surprisingly high and shrill for so big a man. "They killed a U.S. serviceman without so much as giving the aircraft a warning!

What? Yes, I know we were over their country. But I hear they used some kind of computer voodoo to poke a stick in our spy eyes, so what choice did we have? And doesn't that make the bastards invaders too — hi-tech saboteurs? Oh, not according to international treaties? Well, stuff those, Senator. Let me ask you this: What are we going to do when the next U.S. soldier dies?"

General Schneider fell silent, but he wasn't still. His bloodshot eyes moved like little machines, and his head hung on his sloped shoulders as if he were a bull waiting for the torero. He picked up a letter opener and began jabbing it in a much perforated USMC cushion that seemed to be there for just that purpose.

"Senator," he said, calmer after nearly a minute of silence, "I will not precipitate an incident, and if you were here I'd put my toe to your butt for suggesting I might. The safety of my troops is more important to me than my own life, or anyone else's for that matter. But, Senator, the honor of my country is more important to me than all those lives put together, and I won't sit still while it's shat on. If you don't agree, I *do* have the telephone number of your hometown newspaper. I think your constituents might see things differently. No . . . I'm not threatening you. All I'm saying is that I'll keep watering the seeds till you grow some stones. Uncle Sam's already got one black eye. Anyone closes up the second eye, we better do more than not apologize. Good morning to you, Senator."

The General slammed down the phone.

Donald took out his pipe and began poking in tobacco. "That was a good one . . . about watering the seeds."

"Thanks." The General inhaled, left the letter opener sticking from the pillow, and straightened. "That was the Chairman of the Armed Services Committee."

"I gathered."

"Got sunflowers in his shorts, thinks he farts daylight," the General said as he rose and came around his desk.

"I'm not sure what that means," Donald admitted, "but it sounds good."

"It means he gets all these lofty goddamn ideas and confuses being intellectual with being right." He extended both hands and clasped Donald's between them. "Screw him. How are *you* holding up?"

"I still feel like I can pick up that phone and call her."

"I know. I was that way with my daughter for months. Shit, sometimes I still punch her number without picking up the phone.

It's a natural thing, Greg. She should *be* there."

Donald blinked away tears. "Dammit — "

"Mister, if you need to cry, you go right ahead. Business can wait. You know that Washington doesn't like to get its ass to scrimmage till they've looked for every which way to punt."

Donald shook his head and resumed filling his pipe. "I'll be okay. I need to work."

"You sure?"

"Very."

"You hungry?"

"No. I ate with Howard."

"That must've been exciting." Schneider clapped a hand on his shoulder and squeezed. "I'm kidding. Norbom's a good man. Just a little cautious. He wouldn't send me more troops and matériel until he knew, for sure, that we'd be going to Defcon 3 — even after our Recon Officer was shot."

"I heard about that on the flight up. The officer was a woman — "

"She was. Now we're hearing on NK Army radio that they think we're cowards for hiding behind women. I'll say this for the North: It must be nice not to have to worry about the PC crowd. Shit, not like the old days when you were the only diplomat in town. Now we've all got to have golden tongues."

"Things are not like they were."

"No, they are not. I tell you, I sit here, Greg, and sometimes I want to give it all up and go back to sewing labels in shirts, like when I was a kid. If something was right in the old days, or necessary, you did it. You didn't have to go to the U.N. with your hat in your hand and ask the effing Ukraine for permission to test bombs in your own goddamn desert. Jesus, General Bellini at NATO says he saw a TV interview with some goddamn Frenchmen who're still pissed at us for accidentally shelling their houses on D-day. Who the hell pointed a TV camera at these assholes and told them to bitch? What the hell has happened to common sense?"

Donald was out of matches and lit his pipe with the hand-grenade lighter on the General's desk. Only after he pulled the pin did he realize it might not have been a lighter.

"You said it yourself, General. TV. Everybody's got a forum to say their say now, and there isn't a politician who's cocksure enough not to pay attention. You should have told the Senator you have a friend at *60 Minutes*. That might've shaken him up."

"Amen to that," Schneider said as the two of them sat on the sofa. "Well, maybe the wheel will turn again. It's like that slave in

315

The Ten Commandments who wanted to see the Deliverer before he died — and there was Charlton Moses Heston there to catch him when he took a hatchet in the gut. That's what I want. Just once before I die, I want to see the person who's going to deliver us from bullshit, who's going to do what's right even if he takes an ax in the belly. If I didn't care so much about my goddamn men, hell, I'd march right into Pyongyang and box their ears myself for Recon Officer Margolin."

The strategy session was brief. Donald would accompany the next patrol, taking a driver of his own, a recon officer, a night-vision digital video camera, and a jeep, and making two passes along two miles of the DMZ. They would phone the visuals to Op-Center, and he would make another pass in two hours — time enough for noticeable changes to have occurred along the heart of the border.

The thirty-five-minute round trip was uneventful, after which the digital videotape was given to a communications officer for transmission to Bob Herbert.

While he waited for the next pass, Donald ignored Schneider's suggestion that he get some rest and went to the radio center, a

316

shack with five cubicles, each of which was crammed with radios, telephones, and a computer with thick files of int-sigs — interval signals used to identify broadcasters — the exact location in degrees and minutes of every transmitter site in Asia and the Pacific — as well as the azimuth of maximum ra diation in degrees from true north of the site — a kiloHertz frequency schedule to help pinpoint particular signals, and a SINPO troubleshooter program to help clear up any problems with signal strength, interference, noise, propagation, and overall merit of the signal.

Taking the cubicle vacated by the Communications Officer to whom he'd given the CD, Donald only cared about one transmitter. And he knew he'd have no trouble getting a message to a point less than five miles away.

He ran a computer check of the transmitters at the DMZ. There were two: shortwave and medium wave. He selected the former, operating at 3350 kHz, picked up the small microphone, and sent a terse voice message:

"To General Hong-koo, Commander of the Forces of the Democratic People's Republic of Korea at Base One, DMZ. Ambassador

Gregory Donald sends greetings, and respectfully requests a meeting in the neutral zone at the General's convenience. Seek an end to hostilities and escalation, and hope you will favor us at your earliest convenience."

Donald repeated the message, then reported to General Schneider. The General's own people had already told him what Donald had seen: that ranks were being closed at the front, with tanks and light artillery being moved in along with support personnel.

Schneider was neither surprised nor worried by the buildup, though he wished that General Sam would allow his troops to do likewise. But Sam wouldn't act without an okay from Seoul, and Seoul wouldn't authorize it until President Lawrence had upgraded the situation to Defcon 2 and conferred with President Ohn Mong-Joon. Donald knew that the former wouldn't happen without another incident like the Mirage, and that the two men would avoid talking, officially, until they and their advisers had already decided what needed to be done. That way, they could reach a quick consensus and show the world that they were of one decisive mind.

Meanwhile, Donald sat and waited to see whether the North would accept his invitation . . . and if they did, whether Schneider would see that as the act of a coward or a Deliverer.

FIFTY

The cottage was made of stone, with a thatched roof and small wooden deck in the front. The door was held in place by a hook latch, no lock, and there were two windows with four-pane glass on either side. The structure seemed relatively new, neither the thatching nor stone looking like they'd been exposed to more than two rainy winters.

Cho looked back at Hwan, who nodded. The driver cut the lights, took a flashlight from the glove compartment, and stepped into what was once more a light drizzle. When he opened Kim's door, Hwan got out.

"I promise not to run," Kim said to Hwan with a hint of indignation. "There's nowhere to run *to*."

"But people run there all the time, Ms. Chong. Besides, it's policy. I've already bent the rules by taking you here without hand-cuffs."

She slid out, Cho standing close beside her. "I deserve the rebuke, Mr. Hwan, and I'm sorry." With that, she started ahead and was quickly swallowed by the dark, Cho snatching the keys from the ignition and hurrying after her with the light, Hwan coming close behind.

Kim lifted the latch and entered. She pulled a long wooden match from a glass bowl on a table beside the door, and lit several glass-domed candles scattered around the single room. While she wasn't looking, Hwan motioned for Cho to go outside and keep watch. He departed silently.

As an orange glow filled the small room, Hwan saw the piano, a twin bed neatly made, a small round table with one chair, and a desk covered with framed photographs. He followed her with his eyes as she moved about the room — gracefully, seemingly at peace with what the day had dealt her. He wondered if it was because her heart was never truly in the work, or because she had a pragmatic, Confucian nature.

Or if she was setting him up for the biggest fall of his life.

He walked closer. There were no pictures of Kim, but he wasn't surprised. If she'd ever had to flee unexpectedly, Pyongyang wouldn't want photographs of a spy lying around where the KCIA could find them. He picked up one of the photographs.

"Your brother and mother?"

Kim nodded.

"Very handsome. And that's your home?"

"It was."

He put the picture down. "What about this cottage. Was it built for you?"

"Please, Mr. Hwan — no more questions."

Now it was Hwan who felt rebuked. "Excuse me?"

"We have an agreement . . . a truce."

Hwan walked over. "Ms. Chong, there's no such deal. Perhaps you misunderstand our relationship."

"There's no misunderstanding. I'm your prisoner. But I will not betray my country by cooperating with the KCIA, and I resent your trying to charm your way into my confidence with questions about my home and family. I fear I may have already compromised myself by bringing you here."

Hwan felt stung. Not because he'd asked and been refused: it was his job to try to learn whether this cottage was built by locals or by infiltrators of whom the KCIA might not be aware, and it was her job to prevent him from finding out. That was the game. What made him angry was that she was dead right. Kim Chong might not be a spy at heart, but she was a patriot. He wouldn't make the mistake of underestimating her again.

As Hwan stood directly behind her, Kim sat on the green-velvet bench in front of the upright and played several treble measures of a jazzy piece Hwan did not recognize. When she was finished, she lifted the lid and reached inside with both hands. He watched her closely; if she noticed, she made no sign. With both hands, she carefully unscrewed the wingnut on a metal brace, swung it back, and lifted a small radio from the compartment. On the opposite side was a bracket with what appeared to be an explosive device wired to the lid.

Hwan recognized the radio as a state-of-the-art Israeli-made Kol 38. The KCIA was negotiating to buy them as well; with them, the user could reach distances of over 750 miles without using a satellite. One part was for listening, another for receiving, which made it possible for agents in the field to "conference call" with headquarters. The unit ran on lightweight cadmium batteries, which made it ideal for remote locations like this. Even the U.S. models weren't as reliable.

She went to the window, opened it, and set the radio on the sill. Before switching it on, she casually rested her hand on the LED readout on top so Hwan couldn't see the frequency to which it was set.

"If you say anything, it will be picked up. They must not know I've been compromised."

Hwan nodded.

Kim pushed a button and a red light came on beside the condensor microphone built into the top of the unit.

"Seoul Oh-Miyo to home, Seoul Oh-Miyo to home, over."

An operatic code name, Hwan thought. *It was somehow appropriate to the Wagnerian events that swirled around them.*

After a moment a voice came in so rich and clear that Hwan was startled.

"Home to Seoul Oh-Miyo. Ready. Over."

"Home, need to know if army boots, explosives, and other items have been stolen. KCIA found evidence of same at Palace today. Over."

"How recent was theft? Over."

Kim looked at Hwan. He flashed ten fingers and mouthed *month*.

"Ten months," she said. "Over."

"Will call with any information. Over and out."

Kim punched off the switch.

Hwan wanted to ask her if these things were computerized in the North as they were in the South. Instead, he asked, "How long might this take?"

"An hour . . . possibly longer."

He held his watch near a candle, then looked out at Cho's dark figure standing beside the car. "We'll take the radio and go back."

She didn't move. "I can't do that."

"You don't have a choice, Ms. Chong." He came closer. "I've tried to show you courtesy — "

"We both gain — "

"*No!* That keeps us from becoming animals. But I must stay on top of the investigation, and I can't do that from here. I promise that no one will look at your radio display. Will you give me what *I* need?"

Kim hesitated, then put the radio under her arm and shut the window. "All right. To keep from becoming animals."

They went outside. The flashlight snapped on to light the way, and the dark figure beside the car opened the door so that Kim could enter.

FIFTY-ONE

The faces of Ernesto Colon and Bugs Benet could not have been more unalike. Floating in a red border on Hood's computer monitor, the face of the sixty-three-year-old Defense Secretary was drawn, the deepset eyes ringed with shadows. The head of a major defense contractor who had served as Undersecretary of the Navy, he was Dorian Gray's portrait, reflecting every decision he'd had to make during two years in this office — the few that had gone well along with the many that had gone poorly.

Bugs was forty-four, with a round, angelic face and bright eyes that showed none of the pressure of managing Hood's schedule and document processing. He had been the executive assistant to the Republican Governor of California when the Democratic

Hood was Mayor, and they had gotten along extremely well — "conspiratorially" was the word the Governor had used more than once.

Hood had always found it strange how the pressures of sitting down and making a decision took a greater toll than running around and carrying them out. *The conscience was a killer taskmaster.*

Yet Hood had a deep respect for Bugs, who not only managed to deal with his boss's brooding but with the moods and demands of men like Colon — and Bob Herbert, who ran a close second to Lowell Coffey as a voice of caution at Op-Center. The difference was that Coffey feared lawsuits and censure, while Herbert had seen only too well the results of failing to consider every possibility.

Benet and Herbert mostly listened as Hood and Colon reviewed simulation papers on the computer and formulated the military options they would recommend to the President. Though the timing and particulars of execution would be left to the Joint Chiefs of Staff in consultation with their field commanders, the men felt that the naval and Marine forces already en route from the Indian Ocean should be supplemented by three battleships and two aircraft carriers from the Pacific fleet, as well as calling up reserves and redeploying fifty thousand troops drawn from Saudi Arabia, Germany, and the U.S. They also would call for the immediate airlifting of a half-dozen Patriot missile systems to South Korea. Although the Patriots had underperformed dramatically in the Persian Gulf War, they made good TV news visuals when they worked, and keeping the public's blood flowing red, white, and blue would be vital. Less visibly, tactical nuclear missiles were to be shifted by air from Hawaii to South Korea. DPRK might not be a nuclear power yet, but that wouldn't stop them from purchasing a bomb from any number of countries.

The men also calculated anticipated casualties of a "short war" of two or three weeks before a U.N. mandated armistice, and a "long war" of six months or more. With nonnuclear strikes, U.S. losses were expected to be at least four hundred dead and three thousand wounded in a short war, at least ten times that in a long war.

During this discussion, Bugs remained silent and Herbert made only three suggestions. The first was that until more was known about the terrorists, only a minimum number of troops should be diverted from the Middle East. He felt there might still be the possibility that this was a plot to involve the U.S. in a fake front so a real war could be started somewhere else. The second was that until the satellites were back on-line, he be given time to analyze whatever up-to-the-minute intelligence they and CIA Director Kidd were able to collect before committing troops. And the third was that no force be sent into the field without boofod up anti terrorist personnel. All three recommendations were put into the military options paper. Hood knew that Herbert could be crusty, but he'd hired him for his knowledge, not his charm.

While Bugs was putting the rough-draft document on the screen for the men to review, Herbert's chair phone beeped. Paul glanced over as Bob hit the speaker button.

"What have you got, Rachel?"

"We've heard from our operative at the military communications station in Pyongyang. He says that it's been difficult for him to get to us because the authorities there seem to be just as surprised by today's events as we were."

"That doesn't mean their hands are clean."

"No. But he does say that they just received a message from an operative in Seoul. She was requesting information about the possible theft of military boots and explosives from any base in the North."

"A *North* Korean agent was asking."

"Yes."

"The agent must have learned about the KCIA's suspicions. Inform Director Yung-Hoon there appears to be a leak in the pipeline. Did we pick up the transmission anywhere else?"

"No. I checked with Private Koh at the communications center at the DMZ. The message didn't come through a satellite up-link."

"Thanks, Rachel. Send the text of the transmission to Bugs." After hanging up, he looked at Hood who nodded. "DPRK is checking into the possible theft from one of their depots of the materials used in the bombing. Looks like we all may have been had, Chief, by someone who wants us at war."

Hood looked from Herbert to the monitor as the President's words returned to haunt him: *Whether or not the North was in it before, Paul, they're in it now — up to their necks.*

As the breakdowns of troop deployments were merged from the War Games file into the military options paper, Colon used his code to sign off on his section of the document. When he'd switched off, Hood said, "Bugs, I want that transmission placed up front, and I'd like you to add the notation

I'm going to type in. Ask Ann Farris to get on, would you?"

Hood thought for a moment. He didn't have Ann's gift for conciseness, but he wanted a cautionary note to be somewhere in the permanent crisis Task Force file. He made a window that she would be able to read on her monitor, and began pecking at the keyboard.

Herbert rolled to his side and read over Hood's shoulder.

"Mr. President: I share your outrage at the attack on our jet and the loss of an officer. However, I urge restraint from a position of strength. We stand to lose much and gain little fighting a foe who may not be our enemy."

"Good for you, chief," Herbert said. "You may not be speaking for the Task Force, but you speak for me."

"And me," Ann said. "I couldn't have said it better."

Hood saved the addendum and brought Ann's face on the screen. She was so good at selling ideas to reporters over the phone, he couldn't tell what she was really thinking unless he saw her face.

She was thinking exactly what she'd said.

In the six months he'd known her, that was the first time she hadn't noodled with something he'd written.

Herbert left the office, Ann returned to her conference with the White House Press Secretary, and Hood finished reviewing the options update before telling Bugs to fax it over the secure line. Alone and surprisingly relaxed for the first time that day, he rang the hospital where the news was not what he'd expected to hear.

FIFTY-TWO

Wednesday, 1:45 A.M., the DMZ

The soldiers in the radio center were joking with Private Koh when the message came from the headquarters of General Hong-koo, Commander of the Forces of the Democratic People's Republic of Korea. They were immediately alert, no longer teasing Koh about brown-nosing by taking a second shift; they replayed the coordinates recorded by their directional antennae to ascertain that the message had, in fact, come from just over the DMZ. That done, they checked their computer directory to confirm that the caller was, in fact, his adjutant Kim Hoh. The computer searched its files and, within seconds, had completed a voiceprint identification. Finally, less than thirty seconds after the signal had been received, they radioed back an acknowledgment and started the two-cassette recorder to tape the message and a copy. One man notified General Schneider that a communications from the North was being received. The private was told to bring it to him the instant it was complete.

Koh seemed the most intent of the five men, listening as the message came through:

"To former Ambassador Gregory Donald at Base Charlie. General Hong-koo, Commander of the Forces of the Democratic People's Republic of Korea at Base One, DMZ, returns greetings and accepts your invitation to a meeting in the neutral zone at 0800 hours."

While one of the men radioed that the message had been received, another ran a copy of the tape and a cassette player to General Schneider's quarters.

Koh said to the remaining two men that he *was* feeling a bit tired and was going to have some coffee and a smoke. Outside, he walked into the shadows of a nearby truck and undid his shirt. There was an M2 cellular phone strapped to his upper arm: undoing the buckle, he pulled up the antenna and punched in Lee's number.

"There better be a very short and enlightening explanation for this," Schneider said as Gregory entered, "because sleepy-eyed firing squads make me nervous."

The General was dressed in pajamas and a robe and was holding the cassette recorder and headset in his right hand.

Donald's heart quickened. He wasn't worried about General Schneider, but about the North Korean response.

He took the recorder, placed one side of the headset to his ear, and listened to the message. When it was finished, he said, "The explanation is that I asked for the meeting and I got one."

"So you really *did* this dumb-ass thing — illegally, from the radio center for which *I* am responsible."

"Yes. I'm hoping we can all be reasonable and avert a war."

"We? Gregory, I'm not going to sit across a table from Hong-koo. You may think you scored some kind of coup by getting him to a meeting, but he's going to use you. Why do you think he's waiting a couple of hours? So they can plan the whole thing out. You'll be photographed trying to make nice, and the President will look like he's talking out of both sides of his mouth — "

"Doesn't he?"

"Not on this. Colon's office says he's been

335

a tiger from the get-go, as well he should be. The bastards blew up downtown Seoul, killed your own wife, Gregory — ”

“We don't *know* that,” he said through his teeth.

“Well, we *do* know that they shot up one of our planes, Greg! We've got a body bag as proof!”

“They overreacted, which is precisely what we *shouldn't* do — ”

“Defcon 3 isn't an overreaction. It's good soldiering, and the President was going to stop there, make 'em sweat.” Schneider rose and jammed his big hands into his pocket. “Hell, who knows what he's going to do after your little love letter.”

“You're blowing it out of proportion.”

“No I'm not. You really don't see it, do you? You might very well put the President in a no-win situation.”

“How?”

“What happens if you hold out the olive branch and North Korea accepts in principle but doesn't withdraw any troops until the President does? If he refuses, it'll look like he squandered a chance for peace. And if he does back down, it'll look like he blinked.”

“Horse shit — ”

“Gregory, *think* about it! And what kind of credibility does he have if it looks like *you're* running his foreign policy? What do we do the next time a Saddam Hussein or Raoul Cedras makes a power grab, or some nutcase sends missiles to Cuba. Do we send for Gregory Donald?"

"You talk to them, yes — try and reason with them. While JFK was busy blockading Cuba, he was also negotiating like mad with Khrushchev about withdrawing some of our missiles in Turkey. That's what ended the crisis, not sea power. Talking is what civilized people do."

"Hong-koo isn't civilized."

"But his bosses are, and there have been no direct, high-level contacts with the North since this morning. Christ, you wouldn't believe that adults play games like this, but they do. The diplomats are playing chicken. If I can open a dialogue, even with Hong-koo — "

"And *I'm* telling you that talking to them won't do any good. He's somewhere to the right of Genghis Khan and as God is my witness, he'll snooker you."

"Then come with me. Help me."

"I can't. I told you, these people know their propaganda. They'll use grainy film, black and white, and shoot me looking like I'm sniffing horse apples, like I'm a POW. The doves in Washington will go berserk."

He popped the tape from the recorder and slapped it gently in his open palm. "Greg, I was sad for you when I heard about Soonji. But what you want to do isn't going to stop anyone from dying. There are still more than a billion Communists right around the corner, and a billion other radicals, religious fruitcakes, ethnic cleansers, cult psychos, and Jesus knows who else. It's me and mine who look after the other three billion, Gregory. All a diplomat is ever good for is buying time — sometimes for the wrong side, like Neville Chamberlain. You can't reason with sickos, Gregory."

Donald looked at his pipe. "Yes . . . I see that."

Schneider looked at him strangely, then glanced at his watch. "You still have about six hours. I suggest you sleep, wake up with a stomachache, and call this off. In the meantime, as far as this base is concerned, your original broadcast no longer exists. We erased your message from storage, took the coordinates you used out of the log." He held up the tape recorder. "This is the first any of us heard about a meeting — when they contacted you. If the North Koreans say you radioed first, we'll deny it. If they produce a tape, we'll say they faked it. If you contradict us, we'll tell the press you were crazy

338

with grief. I'm sorry, Greg, but that's the way it's got to be."

He looked down at his pipe. "And if I convince Hong-koo to withdraw?"

"You won't."

"But if I do?"

"In that case," Schneider said, "the President will take full credit for having sent you, you'll be a goddamn hero, and I'll personally pin the medal on you myself."

FIFTY-THREE

Wednesday, 2:00 A.M., Yanguu Village

Kim slid into the car, hugging the small radio to her to protect it from the light rain.

Hwan watched her carefully. A captive, his hands cuffed behind his back, had once used the spring in the seat-belt latch to pick the lock and get away. But he wasn't watching Kim because he feared an escape; she would have tried that before, when they were alone. He was watching her because she fascinated him. Patriotism and humanism rarely existed in perfect harmony, but Kim had that balance. He strove for that in his own life, and usually fell short: one couldn't dig into the darker side of people's lives without getting into the dirt —

His thoughts were cut off by a sudden movement to his right, the flashlight moving crazily, followed by a crippling pain in his side. He gurgled loudly as the sharp punch emptied his lungs, followed by another that caused his right leg to shake and fall out from under him. He tried to grab the open car door to brake his fall. He missed, twisted, and fell against the side of the car seat, on his back. As he fumbled to get to the .38 in his shoulder holster, he looked out at Cho.

Only it wasn't Cho. The light from the car cast a faint yellow glow on the hat and on a face he didn't recognize, a face that was taut and cruel.

Damn her, he thought through his pain. *She had someone here all the time. . . .*

His right hand was tingling and he couldn't get his fingers to close around the gun. His right side felt damp as he slid toward the ground.

Hwan saw the nine-inch blade stained with his blood. It went back, level with his stomach. He would be unable to stop the blow to his chest, up and under the sternum, a flash of agony and then death. He had often thought about how and when he would die, but it was never like this, flat on his back in the mud.

And feeling like a fool. He felt her lean over him. He trusted her, and he hoped they put that on his headstone as a warning.

Either that, or *What a sucker* —

Hwan's gun slipped from its holster as he landed on the wet earth. He reached over reflexively, squeezing the wounds with his left hand, fighting to keep his eyes open so he could face death with what little defiance remained in him. He saw the assassin in Cho's clothing grinning, and then there was a white flash like lightning, followed by a second and third. The quick bursts were just a foot or two above him and he shut his eyes as their heat rolled toward him. The thunder echoed for a moment and died, and then there was only the tapping of the rain on his face and the throbbing heat in his side.

Kim crawled over Hwan and knelt at his side. She reached past him for the knife, and for a confusing moment he didn't understand why he hadn't felt the shots . . . and why she was going to stab him instead of shoot him.

He must have been writhing because she told him to hold still. He tried to relax, and became aware of how painful it was to breathe.

Kim pulled his shirt from his belt, cut a slit up the side, then picked up the flashlight. After studying his wounds she rose and jumped over him; he craned to watch as she pulled the shoes and socks off the assassin, then undid his belt and yanked it off. Hwan collapsed, his breath now coming in gasps.

"Ch-Cho?" he said.

"I don't know where his body is."

His body. . . .

"This man must have followed us. Don't ask: I don't know who he is."

Not . . . with Kim . . . from the bombers. . . .

Kim slid the belt around Hwan's waist but didn't fasten it; she put a sock against each of the wounds. "This may hurt," she said as she buckled the belt tightly.

Hwan gasped as pain girdled him and shot from his right armpit to his knee. He lay back, wheezing now, as Kim moved behind him, grabbed him under the arms, and pulled him onto the backseat of the car.

As she put the radio on the floor, Hwan tried to raise himself on an elbow.

"W-wait — body."

She eased him back and tried to secure him with the seatbelt. "I don't know where Cho is!"

"No! Finger . . . prints."

Kim understood. She shut the door, opened the passenger's side in front, and pulled the dead man in. Then she hurried to the driver's side, started to get in, and stopped.

"I've got to find Cho!" she said as she backed out.

Snatching up the flashlight, she turned it toward the ground and followed the killer's footsteps. Though there was urgency in her movements, outwardly she was calm, focused. The prints led to a thickly wooded ravine some forty yards from the side of the hut, where she found a motor scooter and, beyond it, the driver. Cho was lying head down on a slope, on his back, the middle of his chest dark with blood.

Skidding down the muck to Cho's side, Kim frantically searched his pockets until she found the keys he'd taken with him, then ran back to the car.

Hwan was lying still, holding his side. His eyes were squeezed shut and he was panting. When he heard the engine rumble, he opened his eyes.

"Car . . . radio."

Kim eased the car into gear, then sped up quickly. "You want me to tell them what happened?"

"Yes. . . ." The belt dug into his flesh and he tried not to move. "Need . . . ID . . . fast."

"Of the killer. From his fingerprints."

Hwan didn't have the strength to speak. He nodded, wasn't sure Kim saw, then heard her speak into the radio. He tried to re-member exactly what he was thinking about her, but every little breath, each bump of the car, sent shocks through him now. He tried not to move, jabbing his right elbow into the crease behind the seat and putting his left hand against the front seatback in an effort to brace himself. He felt as though there were a strap inside of him, tighten-ing, bending him to the right. Thoughts and images swirled through his mind as he fought the pain and tried to stay awake.

Not North Korean . . . she wouldn't have shot him . . . but who in the South . . . why . . . ?

And then the fire spread to his brain, the pain hammering him mercifully into uncon-sciousness.

FIFTY-FOUR

Dr. Orlito Trias was there when Hood phoned Alexander's room. He had the bed-side manner of Dr. Frankenstein, but he was a good doctor and a devoted scientist.

"Paul," he said in his thick Philippine accent, "I'm glad you called. Your son has a virus."

Hood felt a chill. There was a time, before AIDS, when the word suggested a problem easily treated with antibiotics.

"What kind of virus? In laymanese, Orly."

"The boy had an acute bronchial infection two weeks ago. The infection appeared to be cured, but the adenovirus hid in his lungs. All it took to trigger the attack were allergens in the air, which is why the steroid drugs and bronchodilator medication failed to work. This isn't a typical asthma attack. It's a form

346

of obstructive lung disease."

"How do you treat it?" Hood asked.

"Antiviral therapy. We've caught the infection relatively early, and there's every reason to believe it will not spread."

"Reason to believe — "

"He's been weakened," Orly said, "and these viruses are very opportunistic. One never knows."

Jesus, Orly. "Is Sharon there?"

"Yes."

Hood asked, "Does she know?"

"Yes. I told her what I've told you."

"Let me talk to her — and thanks."

"You're welcome. I'll check back here every hour or so."

Sharon came on a moment later.

"Paul — "

"I know. Orly's got no future with the U.N."

"It isn't that," Sharon said. "I'd rather know than not know. It's the waiting. You know I was never good at that."

"Alex is going to be okay."

"You don't know that. I worked at a hospital, Paul. I know how these things can catch fire."

"Orly wouldn't leave if the situation was serious."

"Paul, there's nothing he can *do!* That's

347

why he's leaving."

Ann walked in, her hands full of lunch; she stopped just inside the door when she saw Hood's expression.

Bugs sent an E-mail message crawling across the screen: Defense Secretary Colon wanted to talk to him.

"Listen," Sharon said, "I didn't get on the phone because I want you to drop what you're doing and come here. I just needed an anchor, okay?"

Hood heard the catch in her voice; she was fighting not to cry. "Of course it's okay, Sharon. Call me if anything happens — or I'll call you as soon as I can."

She hung up, and Hood switched from the regular phone to the secure computer phone. He felt less than a husband, less than a father, and considerably less than a man.

"Paul," Colon said sullenly, "we've just learned that your man Donald sent an unauthorized radio transmission to the North, requesting a meeting with General Hong-koo."

"*What?*"

"Worse, they accepted. If it gets out, we'll spin it that the North contacted *him,* but you'd better get on the blower and try to talk him out of it. General Schneider gave it his best shot, but Donald intends to

348

be at the meeting."

"Thanks," Hood said, and buzzed Bugs. He told him to contact the DMZ on the secure line and get Gregory Donald on the phone. Then he rang Liz Gordon and asked her to come in.

"You want me to leave this and go?" Ann asked.

"No. I want you to stay."

Her expression brightened.

"We may have a PR nightmare on our hands."

Her expression darkened.

"Sure," she said. She sat across the desk from Hood and set the lunches between them.

"What happened with Alex?" she asked.

"Trias said he's got a lung infection. He thinks he's got it under control, but you know Orly — doesn't read people very well."

"Hmmmm," Ann said, her eyes darkening even more.

Hood picked up the fork and jabbed at a slice of tomato. "Any word from Matt on his own virus hunt?"

"Not that I've heard. Want me to check?"

"No thanks. I'll do it when I'm finished with Gregory. Poor guy must be going through hell. We get so wrapped up in events here, we forget the people sometimes."

The secure phone beeped just as Liz Gordon and Lowell Coffey walked in. Donald's prefix appeared with the number at the display along the bottom. Hood motioned for Liz to close the door. She sat and Coffey stood behind Ann, who shifted uncomfortably. Hood hit the speaker phone.

"Gregory — how are you?"

"All right. Paul, are you on the secure line?"

"Yes."

"Good. And you're on speaker?"

"Yes."

"Who's there, Liz, Ann, and Lowell?"

"That's the list."

"Of course. Then let's get right to it. I did radio Hong-koo, and he responded. I'm to meet him in five and a half hours. Why shoot bullets when you can shoot off your mouth, that's always been my motto."

"It's a good one, Greg, but not with the DPRK."

"That's what General Schneider said when he read me the riot act. He's going to leave me twisting in the wind. So is Washington, I'm told." He hesitated a moment. "Are you, Paul?"

"Give me a minute."

Hood hit the Mute button and looked at Liz. From the corner of his eye, he saw Ann nodding solemnly. Lowell stood motionless. The Staff Psychologist sucked on her upper lip and then shook her head.

"Why not?" Hood asked.

"As his ally, you have a chance of changing his mind. If you're his adversary, he'll shut you out."

"What if I fire him?"

"It won't change a thing. He's a man who's had a severe shock today, who thinks he's behaving with restraint and compassion — a common reaction — and won't be dissuaded."

"Lowell, what if Schneider charges him with something — misappropriation of government equipment when he made the radio broadcast, something like that — and arrests him."

"It'll be a hell of a messy trial, and we may have to reveal things we don't want to about the way we work."

"What if they only hold Greg twenty-four hours? Security reasons, some bullshit like that."

"He may sue you. Same result."

"But he won't," Liz said. "I went over his file when you appointed him, Paul. He's never done anything vindictive. That was one of his problems, as far as his diplomatic career was concerned. He was a true Christian."

"Ann, what kind of press is up there?"

"As a rule, no one, they're all based in Seoul. But I'm sure reporters are scrambling for credentials and are on the way. They'll be looking to file any and all kinds of stories. Especially the holding of a former high-level diplomat."

Lowell said, "And what will the press do to *us* if Donald goes to the meeting and they find out that he's connected with Op-Center? We'll be portrayed as a bunch of kooks working outside the establishment."

"I hate to agree with Lowell," Ann said, "but he has a point."

"Donald won't say anything," Liz said. "Not even in anger. As far as the world is concerned, he works only for the U.S./Korean Friendship Society."

"But Schneider knows the truth," Lowell said, "and he can't be happy about this."

"He isn't," Hood said.

"There! And *he* may leak the news to the press, just to put the brakes on."

"I don't think we have to worry about that," Hood said. "He won't want to embarrass the President by exposing an organization Lawrence himself established." Hood killed the Mute. "Greg, would you put this off if I could convince someone at the Embassy to join you?"

"Please, Paul. Ambassador Hall would never agree to that without Presidential approval, and you won't get that."

"Postpone the meeting and let me try. Mike Rodgers is en route to Japan. He'll be landing in Osaka around six. Let me talk to him about joining you."

"That's an 'A' for effort, but you know if I delay even a minute, the North Koreans will feel like I'm playing games with them. They're sensitive that way, and they won't give me a second turn at bat. I'm going. The only question remains, are you for me or against me?"

Hood sat perfectly still for a moment, then looked at the faces of his associates. "I'm with you, Greg."

There was a long silence on the other end. "You caught me by surprise there, Paul. I thought you were going to shoot me down."

"So did I, for a while."

"Thanks for holding your fire."

"I hired you for your experience. Let's see if I made the right choice. If you want to talk again, I'll be here."

Hood hung up. Noticing the slice of tomato still on his fork, he ate it. Liz gave him a little thumbs-up. Ann and Lowell just stared.

Hood touched the intercom. "Bugs, please

get me a progress report from Matt."

"Coming right up."

Lowell said, "Paul, this will finish off Donald . . . and us."

"What would you have had me do? He was going anyway, and I won't leave one of my people out there alone." Hood chewed slowly. "Besides, he may pull something off. He's a good man."

"Exactly," said Ann. "And everyone knows it. When video of Donald and the North Koreans is on the late night news tonight — video of a man who lost his wife and is *still* willing to forgive — we'll all be looking for jobs."

"That's okay," Coffey said. "We can go to work for North Korea. They'll owe us one."

"Have some faith," Hood said. He waved a finger between Coffey and Ann. "And you two have a plan in place in case he does screw up."

The phone beeped and Hood picked up. It was Stoll.

"Paul," he said, "I was about to call you. You'd better come over and see what I've found."

Hood was already out of his seat. "Give me the short of it."

"The short of it is, we've been had — big-time."

FIFTY-FIVE

Wednesday, 2:35 A.M., the Diamond Mountains

The Nodong missiles were modified North Korean Scuds.

The construction was virtually identical, one stage with a payload of up to two hundred pounds and a range of five hundred miles. With a payload of seventy-five pounds of high explosives, the Nodong could fly nearly six hundred miles. It was accurate within a half-mile radius of its target.

Like the Scuds, the Nodongs could be launched from fixed sites or mobile launchers. Silo launchers made it possible to launch multiple strikes within an hour, but were highly vulnerable to enemy retaliation. Mobile launchers could only carry one missile and had to be brought to hidden stockpiles for reloading.

Both the fixed and mobile launchers were

operated by a one-key system, once the launch coordinates were programmed into the computer. Turning the key began a two-minute countdown, during which time the launch command could only be stopped with both the key and a cancellation code. The code was known only to the officer in charge. In the event that he was unable to give it, the second in command had to get the code from Pyongyang.

The Nodong was a relatively unsophisticated system as missiles went. But it was effective in its purpose, which was to keep Seoul honest with the threat of sudden destruction from the skies. Even with Patriot missiles in place, the danger was still very real: designed to track and strike at the missile itself, the Patriot often left the warhead intact, allowing it to fall and explode somewhere in the target zone.

Colonel Ki-Soo was the ranking officer at the site in the Diamond Mountains, and when the guard post radioed ahead to tell him of the arrival of Colonel Sun, he was taken by surprise. Resting in his tent, which was situated at the foot of a steep hill, the bald, oval-faced officer rose and greeted the jeep as it arrived. Sun handed him his orders without being asked, and Ki-Soo retired to his blackout tent.

When the tent flap was secure, he switched on the lantern, withdrew the papers from the leather pouch, and unfolded the single sheet:

Office of the High Command
Pyongyang, June 15, 4:30 P.M.
From: Colonel Dho Oko
To: Colonel Kim Ki-Soo
Colonel Lee Sun has been dispatched by General Pil of Intelligence Operations to oversee the security of the missiles under your command. He will not interfere with your operation unless it directly affects the security of the site.

Affixed to the bottom of the document were the seals of the General of the Armed Forces and of General Pil.

Ki-Soo carefully folded the document and replaced it in the pouch. It was authentic, but something didn't seem right about it. Sun had come with two agents — one man to guard each missile, which was sensible enough. Yet something wasn't right.

He looked at the field phone and thought about calling headquarters. Boots crunched on the gravel outside. Ki-Soo doused the lantern and pulled the flap aside: Colonel Sun was standing in the dark, facing the tent. His hands were clasped behind his back and his body was rigid.

"Is everything all right?"

"It appears to be," said Ki-Soo, "though I'm curious about one thing."

"What is that?" Sun asked.

"Generally, orders such as these mention the number of men in the party. Yours do not."

"But they do. They mention me."

Ki-Soo looked at the other man, who was standing beside the jeep. He pointed with his thumb. "And this one?"

"Not an agent," Sun said. "Our department is hard-pressed right now. This man was sent to accompany me through the hills. He will remain to bring me back. That is his only function."

"I see," said Ki-Soo. He handed the folder to Sun. "Make yourself comfortable in my tent. If you'd like, I can have food brought over."

"Thank you, no," said Sun. "I'd prefer to tour the perimeter, see where we might be vulnerable. I'll let you know if there's anything I need."

Ki-Soo nodded as Sun returned to the jeep and took a hooded flashlight from a toolbox in the back. Then he set out with his men, away from the camp and across the small field to where the missiles sat.

FIFTY-SIX

Koh's warning reached Lee just after he'd finished tucking the cans of tabun into a niche in the tunnel. He went up from the tunnel to receive the call, then climbed back down the hemp line.

So Gregory Donald would be meeting with General Hong-koo in just a few hours. That must not be. It would attract sympathy for the North and might even convince some world leaders of their innocence. Phases two and three of the operation must go ahead while tension was at a peak.

Donald would have to die. Soon.

Lee briefed Private Yoo, the soldier who had remained with him. The other man had returned to the base with the truck; if it wasn't back when it was supposed to be, General Norbom might institute a search.

359

They would move the gas through to the North, as planned, but once there Yoo would have to place it alone while Lee took care of Donald. Yoo understood and accepted the task gratefully and promised that all would go as planned. Lee expected nothing less from any member of his team; each of whom had been trained to complete the mission if anything happened to a comrade. Crouching in the dark, the men began working on a job they had run through countless times on paper.

The tunnels had been dug by the North Koreans, and formed a complex network over a mile from north to south and a quarter mile east to west. While Military Intelligence knew about them and made occasional attempts to close them down, the North Koreans were like ants: when one entrance was shut, another was opened. When a tunnel was flooded or gassed, another was opened. The entire region was shelled on occasion, but while that collapsed large sections of the tunnel the North Koreans simply dug new sections, deeper.

Lee and his men had recently opened this connecting tunnel of their own, ostensibly to spy on the North. While the nine-yard vertical passageway was nearly four feet in diameter the tunnel itself was narrower, just under three feet, identical to the North Korean tunnels; this trunk linked up with the main Northern tunnel just ten yards from the border.

To get the four quarter-size drums of tabun down, one man had gone to the bottom of the passageway while the other lowered the drums in a sling and Lee kept watch. The drums were tucked into a niche they'd dug on the far side of the passageway, away from the tunnel; otherwise, there wouldn't have been room for them and the men. Now it would be necessary for Yoo to move backward through the tunnel, guiding each drum in turn while Lee rolled them ahead. The drums would just fit sideways, and where the tunnel wasn't wide enough, it would be necessary to shift them lengthwise and gently push them through.

Lee had calculated that each round-trip through the maze would take seventy-five minutes. That wouldn't leave him much time to get back to Donald, but it would have to do; he didn't dare stop to do it now, lest he get caught and fail to complete his mission here.

Major Lee took the small flashlight from the pocket of his uniform, turned it on, and clipped it to the strap on his shoulder. Yoo backed a short distance into the tunnel while

Lee gently took the first drum from the niche and walked it on end to the entrance. Getting on his hands and knees, he began rolling the drum after Yoo, who checked the tunnel for sharp outcroppings they may have missed on their earlier sweeps. . . .

FIFTY-SEVEN

Wednesday, 2:55 A.M., Seoul

The KCIA car screeched to a stop in front of the casualty entrance at the National University Hospital on Yulgongno. She left the car running and ran through the automatic doors demanding help for a wounded man. Two doctors hurried into the drizzle, one toward Hwan, the other to the figure in front.

"He's dead!" Kim yelled to the second medic. "Help this man!"

The physician opened the door anyway and felt for a pulse, then climbed half into the car to give him mouth-to-mouth resuscitation. In the backseat, the doctor carefully but quickly removed the belt and socks from Hwan's wound. Hwan had been pale and semiconscious when they arrived, but he was fully awake as two paramedics came racing out with a stretcher and lifted him on.

Hwan's hand shot out, clutching at the air. "Kim!"

"I'm here," she said, running over and catching his hand, then holding it as they wheeled him toward the doors.

"See to . . . other. . . ."

"I know," she said. "I'll take care of it." Letting go of his hand, she watched as they took him inside, then walked back toward the car where the doctor had given up trying to revive the assassin and was examining his gunshot wounds. He motioned toward the hospital door.

"What happened, miss?"

"It was awful," Kim said. "Mr. Hwan and I were driving to our cottage in Yanguu Village when we stopped to help this man. It appeared he'd had a scooter accident. The man stabbed Mr. Hwan, who shot him."

"You don't know why?"

She shook her head.

"Would you come inside, miss? You'll have to give us information about the wounded man, and the police will want to speak with you."

"Of course," she said as a stretcher was wheeled out. "Just let me park the car."

Two orderlies removed the body from the car, placed it on the stretcher, and covered it with a sheet. When they were gone, Kim slid behind the wheel and headed toward the parking lot. As she pulled into a spot, she picked up the phone and pressed the red button on the receiver. The desk officer at the KCIA answered.

"I'm calling on Kim Hwan's car phone," Kim said. "He was wounded by an assassin and is at the National University Hospital. The man who wounded him is dead. He's also at the hospital. Mr. Hwan believes that this man was involved with the bombers who attacked the Palace, and that you check his fingerprints to find out who he is."

Kim hung up and ignored the phone when it rang. Looking around the parking lot, she saw a car she knew: a Toyota Tercel. Taking her radio from the backseat, she put it on the floor, turned it on, and angled it so the light of the dial shined under the dashboard. Finding the ignition wires where her instructors had once told her they'd be, she knotted them together, started the car, and drove off, headed north.

FIFTY-EIGHT

Tuesday, 1:10 P.M., Op-Center

As Hood arrived in Matt Stoll's office, the Operations Support Officer was just finishing up his work. There was a big smile on his round, full face, and a look of triumph in his eyes.

"Paul, this was pure, wonderful genius," he said. "I set up all kinds of safeguards and diagnostics and checks and double checks to make sure incoming software wasn't tainted, and they got it past me anyway."

"Who did, and how?"

"The South Koreans. Or at least someone with access to their software. Here it is, in diskette SK-17."

Hood bent over the screen and watched as a series of numbers and characters flashed on and off.

"What am I looking at?"

"All the stuff that was dumped into our computer system from this one diskette. I'm flushing it out — told the computer to read the original program and take it out in its entirety."

"But how did it get *in?*"

"It was hidden in a routine personnel up date. That's the kind of file that can be thick or thin, and you wouldn't think to check on it. Not like a file on, say, agents based in the Mascarene Islands. If that one suddenly came in big as the deficit, you'd notice."

"So the virus was hidden in that file — "

"Right. And it was triggered to dump a new satellite program into our system exactly when it did. A program that scanned the Library, morphed it with incoming pictures, and created false images — the kind the saboteurs wanted us to see."

"How did it get to the NRO?"

"The virus attacked our phone line into them. It's secure from the outside . . . but not from the inside. We'll have to do something about that."

"But I still don't understand what *triggered* the virus."

Stoll's big smile grew even bigger. "That's the genius of what they did. Look at this." He pulled over a laptop and booted the diskette, after carefully, almost reverently popping it from the disk drive. The title screen appeared and Stoll held a hand toward it.

Hood read everything on the screen. "South Korea diskette number seventeen, filed by him, checked by her, okayed by a general, and sent by military courier five weeks ago. What does that tell you?"

"Nothing. Read the very bottom."

Hood looked. He had to move in a little to read the fine print. "Copyright 1988 by Angiras Software. What's unusual about that?"

"All government agencies write their own software. It's not like WordPerfect where there's something to copyright. But our computers sometimes *do* get software with copyright notices on them, and I told the system to ignore that."

Hood began to understand. "This one triggered the virus?"

"No. This one triggered the shutdown that allowed the virus to enter undetected. That date — 1988? It's a date but it's also a clock. Or rather, a tiny program buried in the date got its hooks into our clock and shut it down. For exactly nineteen point eight-seconds."

Hood nodded. "Good work, Matty."

"Shitty work, Paul. We see notices like

that on programs and they don't even register on the brain. They certainly didn't on mine, and someone in South Korea took advantage of that."

"Who, though?"

"The date may help us there. I checked our files. One of the highlights of 1988 was when radical students demanding reunification clashed with the police. The government put the movement down, hard. Someone who's either for or against unification may have picked that date as a symbol. You know — the same way the Riddler always used to leave clues for Batman out of some kind of twisted vanity."

Hood grinned. "I'd leave the Batman part out of my official report if I were you. But this is the extra push we may need to convince the President the South Koreans *are* behind this."

"Exactly."

"You really came through on this one. Send that title page to my computer and we'll see what Lawrence has to say now."

"How do we know it wasn't a North Korean mole working in the South?" Burkow asked.

"We don't, Mr. President," said Hood. He was listening on the secure phone while the President and Steve Burkow studied the document. "But why would the leaders in Pyongyang want to tinker with our satellites, make it *look* like they were preparing for war. They *can* move troops in the field, so why go through all this trouble?"

"To make us look like the aggressors," Burkow said.

"No, Steve. Paul's absolutely right. This doesn't smell like the work of the government. The DPRK isn't this subtle. It's a faction, and it could well be from either the North or South."

"Thank you," Hood said with obvious relief.

His E-mail indicator beeped. Bugs would never interrupt Hood when he was on the phone with the President, so he sent a message crawling across the computer monitor. Since the message was sent to the TV screen directly, not through the computer itself, the President wouldn't see it.

Hood's stomach tightened as he read the short memo:

From KCIA Director Yung-Hoon: Kim Hwan stabbed by assassin. In surgery. DPRK spy escaped. Assailant dead. Checking identity now.

Hood put his face in his hand. Some head

of the Korean Task Force he was turning out to be. Knowing everything that happened after the fact, knowing that some person or group very desperately wanted a war, and having no idea who the perpetrators were. He suddenly understood from where Orly got his bedside manner. He wasn't being inconsiderate to the patient: he was frustrated by an enemy that he couldn't get a handle on.

He memoed Bugs to stay on top of the situation, to pass the message on to Herbert and McCaskey, and to thank Yung-Hoon. He also requested that the KCIA Director let him know the moment they had any information on the assassin or on Hwan's condition.

". . . but, as I told you before, Paul," the President was saying, "we've gone beyond that now. It doesn't matter who started this phase of the confrontation: the fact is, we're in the middle of it."

Hood brought himself back into the conversation.

"There's no question about that," Burkow said. "Quite frankly, I'd go to the first strike scenario in the military options paper. Paul, you feel that would work — "

"Hell, yes. Christ, the Defense Secretary's plan would be a juggernaut! From what we're hearing, the North is expecting another Desert Storm, with a softening-up period. A half-million troops moving into the North, air strikes against communications centers, missiles dropping on every airstrip and military base in the nation — sure, Steve. It would work. We'd only lose three thousand troops, tops. Why settle this peacefully when we can lose soldiers and overrun a country that'll be a financial drain on the South for the next forty to sixty years?"

"Enough of that," the President said. "In light of the new information, I'll instruct the Ambassador to make inquiries about a diplomatic solution."

"Inquiries?" Hood's nonsecure phone rang. He looked at the readout: it was from the hospital. "Mr. President, I have to take this call. Would you excuse me?"

"Yes. Paul, I want the ass of the person who let this software through."

"Fine, Mr. President. But if you take his, mine comes with it."

The son of a bitch, Hood thought as he hung up the secure phone. *Everything's got to be a big gesture. You're in, you're out, we're at war, I've made peace.* He wished Lawrence would take up a hobby. A person lives any job twenty-four hours a day, their sense of proportion is bound to get screwed up.

Hood picked up the open line. "Sharon — how is he?"

"Much better," she said. "It was like a dam breaking: all of a sudden, he took a deep breath and the wheezing stopped. The doctor says his lungs are working twenty percent better now he's going to be all right, Paul."

Sharon's voice was relaxed, light, for the first time that day. He heard the girl in her, and he was glad to have her back.

Darrell McCaskey and Bob Herbert stopped just outside the door. Hood motioned them in.

"Shar, I love you both — "

"I know. You've got to go."

"I do," said Hood. "I'm sorry."

"Don't be. You did all right today. Have I thanked you for stopping by before?"

"I think so."

"If I didn't, thanks," Sharon said. "I love you."

"Kisses to Alex."

Sharon hung up and Hood lay the receiver gently in its cradle. "My son's okay and my wife's not mad at me," he said, looking from one man to the other. "If you've got bad news, now's the time to give it."

McCaskey stepped forward. "That Recon Officer who was killed, Judy Margolin? Seems

373

one of her last photos was a shot of the oncoming MiGs."

"Someone leak them to the press?"

"Worse," said McCaskey. "The computer guys at the Pentagon were able to read the numbers on the plane. They did a search through all the recent reconnaissance photos to find out where it's based."

"God, no — "

"Yes," said Herbert. "The President just authorized the Air Force to go in after it."

FIFTY-NINE

Wednesday, 3:30 A.M., Sariwon

Sariwon, North Korea, was located 150 miles west from the Sea of Japan, fifty miles east of the Yellow Sea, and fifty miles due south from Pyongyang.

The air base in Sariwon was the first line of defense against an air or missile strike from South Korea. It was one of the oldest bases in the country, having been built in 1952 during the war and being upgraded only as technology from China or the Soviet Union was made available. That wasn't as often as Pyongyang would have liked: it had always been the fear of North Korea's allies that eventual reunification with the South would give the West access to up-to-date military hardware and technology, so the North was always kept several steps behind Moscow and Beijing.

Sariwon had radar that was effective up to fifty miles, and able to read objects at least twenty feet in diameter. That gave them the capability of picking up virtually any aircraft headed their way. In drills, an attack from the west didn't give the base time to scramble their fighters, though even an assault from Mach 1 fighters gave them time to man the antiaircraft guns.

An aircraft's radar cross section — or RCS — read larger from the sides than from the front. Bombers like the old B-52s had a very high RCS value, up to one thousand square meters, which made them easy to spot and target. Even the F-4 Phantom II and F-15 Eagle were easy to spot, at RCS readings of one hundred for the Phantom and twenty-five for the Eagle. On the opposite end of the scale was the B-2 Advanced Technology bomber, with an RCS profile of one millionth of a square meter — roughly that of a hummingbird.

The Lockheed F-117A Nighthawk had an RCS of .01. Its profile was reduced by its unique "cut-diamond" architecture, which used thousands of flat surfaces, angled so as not to share a common reflective angle with other surfaces. The RCS was further cut by the material used in the plane's construction. Only ten percent of the airframe's weight was metal: the rest was reinforced carbon fiber that absorbed and dissipated radar energy as well as the F-117A's infrared reading, and Fibaloy, an outer-skin plastic filled with bubbles and glass fibers that also reduced the RCS reading.

The black aircraft was fifty-six feet long, sixteen feet high, and had a wingspan of forty feet. Operational since October 1983, the F-117A was assigned to the 4450th Tactical Group at Nellis AFB, Nevada; the Team One *Furtim Vigilans* unit — "Covert Vigilantes" — was permanently based at "the Mellon Strip" there, located in the northwest section of the Nellis Test Range. Since Desert Storm, however, planes from the unit had been much on the move. Its wings folded, the F-117A could be tucked into the body of a C-5A transport, which was the only way it could be moved long distances undetected, since the refueling receptacle would be picked up by radar if used in-flight.

Flying at a top speed of Mach 1, the Nighthawk could cover fifty miles in four minutes. Powered by two 12,500-pound GE F404-HB nonafterburning turbofans, it had a combat radius of four hundred miles.

The F-117A was onboard the aircraft carrier *Halsey*, which had sailed north from the Philippines at Defcon 4 and was deep in the East China Sea. Taking off and heading due north, lights out, the F-117A shot up along the west coast of South Korea, climbing all the while, and angled northwest into the Yellow Sea. Flying at just ten thousand feet, it accelerated from Mach .8 to Mach 1 and tore into North Korean airspace, its back-swept wings and upright swallowtail fins slicing the air with imperceptible resistance.

Radar picked up a blip at once. The radar technician called over a superior, who confirmed that the blip seemed like an aircraft. He radioed the command center. The process took seventy-five seconds. The base commander was wakened and authorized an alarm to be sounded. Exactly two minutes and five seconds had passed since the blip was first spotted.

The air base was surrounded by guns on four sides, though only the antiaircraft artillery on the east and west were manned to catch the intruder coming and going. Twenty-eight men were sent out, seven to a gun, two guns on each side; it took them one minute twenty seconds to get to their posts. One man at each gun slipped on earphones. Another five seconds.

"Southwest gun to tower," said one. "What is the reading on the intruder?"

"We've got it at 277 degrees, dropping

fast, closing at a speed of — "

There was an explosion in the distance as the Nighthawk's ABM-136A Tacit Rainbow antiradiation drone missile tracked, found, and destroyed the radar dish.

"What was that?" the gunner asked.

"We lost it!" the tower replied.

"The plane?"

"The radar!"

The men at the control panel punched in the last-known coordinates, and massive gears ground quietly as the massive black barrels were swung into position. They were still moving when a sonic boom announced that the arrowhead-shaped aircraft had arrived.

Guided by its forward-looking laser radar and a low-light TV screen, the F-117A easily found the ship that had attacked the Mirage. It was sitting on the runway with two other MiGs on either side.

The pilot reached to the left, right beside his knee, and pressed a red button set in a yellow square with diagonal black stripes. At once, the air outside the craft was torn by the loud hiss of the optically guided ABM-65 missile, the slender rocket ripping through the five thousand feet between the plane and the target in just under two seconds.

The MiG was lifted and torn apart in a titanic fireball that turned night into day and then day into flaming dusk. The planes on either side were flipped onto their backs and debris from the explosion was scattered in every direction, the blast itself shattering windows in the tower, the hangars, and in over half the twenty-two aircraft at the field. Flaming pieces of fabric and plastic fell everywhere, starting small fires in buildings and on the brush surrounding the landing strips.

One gunner was killed in the blast, his back pierced by a ten-inch shard of metal.

The commander managed to scramble four jets, but the F-117A had swung back toward the sea and was racing toward the *Halsey* before they were even airborne.

SIXTY

Director Im Yung-Hoon was exhausted. Another cup of coffee would keep him going, if it ever got to his office. Along with the report from the lab. They'd fingerprinted the bastard fifteen minutes ago, and scanned it into the computer immediately. The damn thing was *supposed* to work at the speed of light, or some crap like that.

Yung-Hoon rubbed his cadaverously deep eyes with spindly fingers. He pushed his long graying hair from his forehead and looked around his office. Here he was, the head of one of the up-and-coming intelligence agencies, four floors and three basements packed with the latest analysis and detection equipment, and nothing seemed to work right.

They had fingerprints of all kinds in their

381

database. From police blotters, college records, even pens and glasses and telephones touched by North Koreans. Agents of his had gone so far as to remove doorknobs from North Korean military bases.

How long should it take to find a match?

The phone rang. He poked the Speaker button.

"Yes?"

"Sir, it's Ri. I'd like to send these prints over to Op-Center in Washington."

Yung-Hoon exhaled hard through his nose. "Have you nothing?"

"So far, no. But these may not be North Koreans or known criminals. They could be from another country."

The second phone rang; his assistant Ryu's line. "Very well," the Director said. "Send them over." He punched off the first phone and poked on the second. "Yes?"

"Sir, General Sam's headquarters just phoned with news: a U.S. fighter just attacked the air base at Sariwon."

"One fighter?"

"Yes, sir. We believe a Nighthawk hit the MiG that attacked their Mirage."

Finally, thought Yung-Hoon, *something to smile about.* "Excellent. What's the latest on Kim Hwan?"

"There is no latest, sir. He's still in surgery."

382

"I see. Is the coffee ready yet?"

"Brewing, sir."

"Why is everything so slow around here, Ryu?"

"Because we're understaffed, sir?"

"Rubbish. One man successfully attacked Sariwon. We're complacent. This whole thing happened because we're fat and lack initiative. Perhaps we need some changes — "

"I'll pour whatever coffee is made, sir."

"You're catching on, Ryu."

The Director jabbed off the phone. He wanted his coffee, but he was right about what he'd said to Ryu. The organization had lost its edge, and the best of them was on his back in God only knew what condition. Yung-Hoon had been angry when he learned what Hwan had done, hauling in the spy and asking for her help. It just wasn't done that way. But maybe that's why it needed to be done.

Show compassion and trust where you usually show anger and doubt. Shake people up, keep them off balance.

He'd been raised by the old school, and Hwan was the new. If his Deputy Director survived, maybe it was time for a change.

Or maybe he was just balmy with exhaustion. He'd see how things looked after coffee. In the meantime, he lifted his long right hand and gave a small salute to the Americans for having done their part to keep the North off balance.

SIXTY-ONE

The laboratory at Op-Center was extremely small, only nine hundred square feet, but Dr. Cindy Merritt and her assistant Ralph didn't need much more room than that. The data and files were all computerized, and the various tools of the trade were tucked into cabinets and under tables, hooked into the computers for control and observation.

The fingerprints from the KCIA computer came to Merritt's computer over a secure modem; the instant it arrived, the loops and whorls were already being scanned and matched against similar patterns in files that had come from the CIA, Mossad, MI5, and other intelligence sources, along with files from Interpol, Scotland Yard, other police sources, and military intelligence groups.

Unlike the KCIA software that superimposed the entire fingerprint over prints in its file — processing twenty every second — the Op-Center software Matt Stoll had developed with Cindy divided each print into twenty-four equal parts and literally threw them to the wind: if any part of the pattern showed up in another print, the entire prints were compared. This technique allowed them to examine 480 prints a second for every machine being used.

Bob Herbert and Darrell McCaskey had arrived when the print did, and asked Cindy if she could put several computers on the job: the unflappable chemist was able to give them three, and told them to stick around — it wouldn't take long.

She wasn't wrong. The computer had found the print in three minutes six seconds: Ralph brought up the file.

"Private Jang Tae-un," he read. "Soldier for four years, assigned to Major Kim Lee's explosives unit — "

"There you go," said Herbert, an edge of triumph.

" — and is a specialist in hand-to-hand combat."

"As long as the other guy didn't have a gun," Herbert muttered.

McCaskey asked Ralph for a printout of the data, then said to the chemist, "You're a miracle worker, Cindy."

"Tell that to Paul," said the attractive brunette. "We could really use a part-time mathematician to help write software to improve the algorithms we use to model biomolecules."

"I'll be oure to tell him." MoCaoltoy winkod as he took the paper from Ralph. "In exactly those words."

"Do," she said. "His son will explain it to him."

Hood was more concerned with Major Lee than with Cindy's request. With Liz Gordon and Bob Herbert at his side, both looking at the computer monitor, he reviewed the Major's ROK file that General Sam had sent electronically from Seoul.

The Director was finding it difficult to concentrate. More than at any time since the crisis began, he felt enormous pressure to find out who was behind the bombing: not only had the rising tension taken on a life of its own, but he felt that his diplomatic approach had caused the President to push Op-Center aside. Steve Burkow had phoned and informed him about the attack on the airstrip in North Korea just two minutes before it happened. The head of the Korean Task Force hadn't even been a part of the strategy team; the President wanted a fight, and was doing everything he could to provoke one. Which would have been fine if a fight was warranted.

If he was wrong about North Korea's innocence, he'd have more to worry about than losing the President's confidence. He would start to wonder if he'd been in politics so long that he'd actually become the fence straddler he'd once pretended to be.

He forced himself to concentrate on what was on the monitor.

Lee was a twenty-year veteran with a justifiable dislike for the North. His father, General Kwon Lee, had been a field general who was killed at Inchon during the war. The Major's mother, Mei, was captured and hanged for spying on troop trains coming and going at the station in Pyongyang. He was raised in an orphanage in Seoul and joined the army when he was eighteen, and served under now-Colonel Lee Sun, who had been a separatist in high school, handing out leaflets and once having been arrested. Though Lee belonged to none of the underground movements like the Fraternity of the Division and Children of the Dead — the sons and daughters of soldiers who had died during the war — Lee was in charge of an elite counterintelligence group, was unmarried, and did a good deal of reconnoitering in the North to help calibrate U.S. spy satellites, measuring objects on the ground to give the NRO a frame of reference.

"What's it look like to you, Liz?" Hood asked.

"Nothing's ever open and shut in my end of the business, but this looks as close to it as you're going to get — "

Bugs beeped.

"What is it?"

"Urgent call on the secure line from Director Yung-Hoon at the KCIA."

"Thanks." Hood hit the lighted button. "This is Paul Hood."

"Director Hood," said Yung-Hoon, "I've just received a most interesting radio message from the North Korean spy whom Kim Hwan was with tonight. She says he asked her to radio the North and find out about a theft of boots and explosives from anywhere in the DPRK."

Herbert snapped his fingers and caught Hood's eye. "That was the broadcast Rachel called me about in your office," Herbert whispered.

Hood nodded. He covered his right ear to block out Liz's typing on the keyboard. "What did the North Koreans say, Mr. Yung-Hoon?"

"That several boots, explosives, and handguns were taken from a truck en route to the depot in Koksan four weeks ago."

"They radioed this information to her, and then she told you?"

"That's right. It's very strange, because after she brought Hwan to National University Hospital, she stole a car and left. We're looking for her now."

"Is there anything else, sir?"

"No. Hwan is still in surgery."

"Thanks. I'll be in touch — we may have something."

Reconnoitering in the North, Hood thought. He hung up the phone. "Bob, check with General Sam and find out if our friend Lee was doing any reconnoitering in the North four weeks ago."

"Of course," Herbert said. He wheeled himself from the office with enthusiasm Hood had never before seen.

Liz Gordon was looking at the computer. "You know, Paul, I think that if there is a plot, this Colonel Sun may be involved as well."

"Why?"

"I just had Sun's file sent over. It says that he doesn't delegate authority."

"So Lee is on a tight leash?"

"Quite the contrary. Sun doesn't appear

390

to have much to do with Lee's operation."

"Which means that he may *not* be involved — "

"Or that his trust in Lee is so complete he doesn't need to oversee him."

"That sounds like a reach to me — "

"It isn't. It's classic when two people are on the same wavelength. It's a textbook symbiotic relationship for a hands-on type of officer like Sun."

"All right. I'll have Bob check on Sun's whereabouts as well." Hood looked at the countdown clock, then at the partly eaten salad by his elbow. He picked up a piece of warm carrot and started chewing on it. "You know, it took us nearly ten hours to pick up our first real lead, and we needed help from a North Korean spy just to get that. What does that tell you about our operation?"

"That we're still learning."

"I don't buy that. We missed things along the way. *We* should have contacted the North about a theft. There should have been a channel of communications for that. We also should have had a file on the separatist South Koreans."

"That's Monday morning quarterbacking. We'll have one now. We're actually doing pretty well, considering we're working at

391

cross-purposes with the President and some of his closest advisers."

"Maybe." He smiled. "You were the first one to say that the North Korean President wasn't behind this. How do you feel now that the rest of us here have come around?"

"Scared," she said.

"Good. Just wanted to make sure I wasn't the only one." He saved the ROK files. "Now, I've got to bring Mike Rodgers up to speed, and see if we can use our little Striker force to get Op-Center a piece of the military pie. Who knows? Maybe Mike will have some ideas to surprise even the newly hatched hawks at Pennsylvania Avenue."

SIXTY-TWO

Tuesday, 8:40 A.M., East of Midway Island

Just over an hour before, in the skies over Hawaii, the thundering C-141A was refueled by a KC-135 tanker. It was good now for another four thousand miles, more than enough to make it to Osaka. And with the strong tail wind they were picking up in the South Pacific, Captain Harryhausen informed Lt. Col. Squires that they'd be reaching Japan up to an hour ahead of schedule; at roughly five A.M. Squires checked with the navigator: the sun wouldn't be rising in eastern North Korea until a few minutes after six. With any luck, they would be on the ground in the Diamond Mountains by then.

Mike Rodgers was sitting with his arms crossed and his eyes shut, thinking dreamily about any number of things. Disconnected bits of the past, of friends no longer with him, mingled with pictures of what the Diamond Mountains might be like. He thought about Op-Center, wondered what was going on, wished he were cracking the whip . . . but glad to be in the field.

By design, everything drifted in and out of his mind like clouds. He had learned that the best way to remember complex plans fast was to read them two or three times, let them float on top of his memory, then review them once again a couple of hours later. That technique, which he learned from an actor friend, burned the material into the brain for a few days, after which it evaporated. Rodgers liked it because it didn't take up much time and it didn't monopolize brain cells forever. He hated the fact that he could still remember useless information from exams he'd crammed for in junior high school, that Frances Folsom Cleveland, widow of President Grover Cleveland, was the first First Lady to remarry, and that the unseaworthy sister ship of the *Mayflower* was called the *Speedwell.*

Best of all, floating the game plans Squires had reviewed with him gave Rodgers time to kick back on long flights, to compose himself for the mission —

"General!"

— and take the occasional call from Paul Hood. Rodgers sat up and removed his earplugs. "Yes, Private Puckett."

"Mr. Hood, sir."

"Thank you, Private."

Puckett sat the radio on the bench beside Rodgers and returned to his seat. Rodgers slipped on the earphones as Lt. Col. Squires stirred from his nap.

"Rodgers, here."

"Mike, there are new developments. The North Koreans shot at one of our spy planes, killing a recon officer, and the President hit back by destroying the enemy plane on the ground."

"Good work, Mr. President!"

"Mike, we're not really in his camp on that one."

Rodgers's teeth closed tightly. "Oh?"

"We believe that the DPRK was set up," Hood said, "that a South Korean officer was behind this morning's bombing."

"Did he shoot our officer too?"

"No, Mike, but we were deep in North Korea."

"Then the procedure is to force the plane down without firing," Rodgers said. "They didn't do that, did they, the pricks?"

"They did not, and we'll debate this some other time. We're at Defcon 3, and we believe things are going to get hotter. If they do, we can get to all the fixed Nodongs by air. But it will be up to you to take care of the mobile units."

"At my own discretion?"

"Are you in command or Lt. Col. Squires?"

"He is. But we think alike. At *our* discretion, then?"

"There may not be time to clear your actions with the Pentagon, and the President doesn't want to know anything about it. Yes, Mike. If it looks like the missiles are going to be launched, you take them out. Quite frankly, Mike, we've got a little egg on our faces here. We've been pushing peace, but the strike against the airstrip in Sariwon is going to go over really big. I need something with a little gunpowder in it."

"Message received, Paul."

It was indeed. Once again, a politician in trouble wanted a military strike to blast his constituents — in this case the President — back onto his side. He was being tough on Hood; he really did like the man, as a fourth in poker or next to him at a Redskins game. But Rodgers was a charter member of the George Patton School of Diplomacy: kick their ass first, then negotiate with your foot on their neck. And he remained convinced that Op-Center would be more effective, respected, and feared if it stuffed its intelligence into a .45 Magnum instead of a Peer-2030 computer.

"I don't have to tell you to watch yourself," Hood said, "and good luck. If anything happens, no one can help you."

"We know. I'll tell the men you wished them well."

Rodgers signed off and Puckett was up in a flash to collect the radio.

Squires fished out an earplug. "Anything, sir?"

"Plenty." Rodgers reached under the seat and pulled out his grip, plunked it in his lap. "We may get to use our swords before the boss makes them rust."

"Sir?"

"Henry Ward Beecher. You know what he said about anxiety?"

"No, sir. Not offhand."

"He said, 'It's not work that kills men; it is worry. Work is healthy. Worry is rust upon the blade.' Paul worries too much, Charlie, but he told me that if a Nodong so much as raises its pointy little head, we're free to do more than just assess the situation for Op-Center."

"Sweet," Squires said.

Rodgers unzipped the bag. "Which is why it's time I showed you how to use these babies." He removed two spheres a half inch in diameter, one lawn-green, the other dull gray. "The EBCs. I've got twenty in here, half of them green, the other half gray. Each one has a range of a mile."

"That's great," Squires said, "but what do they do?"

"Just what the bread crumbs were supposed to do in 'Hansel and Gretel.' " He handed the orbs to Squires, reached back into the bag, and withdrew a device the size and shape of a small stapler. He opened it at the hinge: there was a tiny liquid crystal display on top and four buttons underneath, one green, one gray, one red, one yellow. There was an earplug attached to the side of the device and Rodgers removed it. He touched the red button and an arrow appeared, pointing to Squires and beeping loudly. "Move the balls up," Rodgers said.

Squires did, and the arrow followed him.

"If you move farther away, the beeping will grow fainter. Matt Stoll worked these up for me. Simple, but brilliant. As you make your initial incursion through an area, you put the balls down — green in a wooded region, gray in rocky terrain. When you have to make your way back, you just switch on the tracker, put the earplug in so the enemy doesn't hear the tones, and follow it from ball to ball."

"Like connect the dots," Squires said.

"You got it. With these things and our night-vision goggles, we can move like a goddamn mountain lion."

"Electronic bread crumbs" — Squires laughed, handing them back to Rodgers " 'Hansel and Gretel.' This isn't a business for grown-ups, sir, is it?"

"Children love to fight and rarely think about death. They're the perfect soldiers."

"Who said that?"

Rodgers smiled. "I did, Charlie. I did."

SIXTY-THREE

Wednesday, 5:20 A.M., the DMZ

Gregory Donald learned of the attack on Sariwon an hour before, after completing another surveillance sweep for Op-Center, and he still couldn't believe it. General Schneider had been wakened and told, and had passed the word to him: with relish that Donald found repugnant.

Another person had died, a life had been ended so that the President of the United States could look tough. Donald wondered if Lawrence would have been as willing to take a life if the airman had been standing three feet away, staring at him along the barrel of a gun.

Of course he wouldn't. A civilized person could *not*.

What was it, then, that made that same civilized person kill for a jolt in the polls, or to make a point? Lawrence would argue, as had presidents in the past, that casualties like these prevent greater losses in the future. But Donald maintained that dialogue prevented more losses still, if only one side or the other wasn't afraid of looking weak or conciliatory.

He looked into the distance, at the conference building straddling the borders, each side brightly lit and guarded to prevent anyone from trying to sneak through. The flags of the North and South hung limply at the end of their surreally tall flagpoles, the South's most recently capped with a spire instead of a ball to make it five inches taller than the North's. For now. No doubt a six-inch spire had been ordered and was on the way. At which point the South would put a taller one on top. Or maybe a weather vane or radio antenna. The possibilities were absurd and endless.

All of their problems could be solved within those four walls, if only the participants wanted them to be. Soonji had once given a speech on that subject to a meeting of Koreans and Blacks in New York in 1992, when tensions between the groups were at their peak.

"*Think of it as a chain letter,*" she'd said. "*If only one person from each side wants peace, and can convince another person on their side to want it, and those two can convince two more people, and those four, four more, we will have the beginning we need.*"

A beginning . . . not an end. Not more blood spilled and more resources squandered, not more hate branded into the psyche of a new generation.

Donald began walking away from the border, away from the compound. He turned his eyes toward the stars.

He was suddenly very tired, overwhelmed by hurt and a deep sense of despair and doubt. Maybe Schneider was correct. Maybe the North Koreans would use him and he'd do more harm than good trying to bring about "Peace in our time."

He stopped, sat down hard, and lay back, his head on a patch of grass. Soonji would have encouraged him to go ahead with this. She was an optimist, not a realist, but she had accomplished most of what she set out to do.

"I'm a pragmatist," he said, tears in his eyes, "and I always have been. You know that, Soon." He searched the skies for a familiar constellation, for a hint of order. There was only a jumble of stars. "If I back down from what I believe, then either I've lived a lie . . . or I'll be living one from now on. I don't think I've been wrong, so I have to go ahead. Help me, Soonji. Give me some of your confidence."

A warm breeze drifted over him, and Donald shut his eyes. She would never come to him again of course, but he could still go to her, if not in life, then in sleep. And as he lay in the dark, in the silence, lingering between wakefulness and dream, he no longer felt unsure or afraid or alone.

Two miles to the west, and a few feet underground, the last drum of death was inching its way to the north, carrying sleep of a different kind. . . .

SIXTY-FOUR

Tuesday, 4:00 P.M., Op-Center

"What's the weather outside?" Hood asked as he walked into Matt Stoll's office.

Stoll hit Shift/F8, then 3, then 2. "Sunny, seventy-eight degrees, wind from the southwest." When he was finished, he returned to the keyboard, inputting instructions, waiting, then inputting more.

"How's it coming, Matty?"

"I've got the system cleaned out, except for the satellites. I should have those back in about ninety minutes."

"Why so long? Don't you just write a program to erase it?"

"Not in this case. There are pieces of virus in every photo file we have from the region, going back to the 1970s. They've been lifting images from everywhere. We've got a Ken Burns history of North Korean hardware in

404

today's satellite pictures. And it's seamless. I want to meet the guy who wrote this before we shoot him."

"Can't promise you that." Hood rubbed his eyes. "Have you taken a break today?"

"Yeah, sure. Have you?"

"This is it "

"A working break. Stretch the legs. See if I'm screwing up again."

"Matty, no one blamed you for what happened — "

"Except me. Shit, I used to laugh at Shakespeare or whoever it was said that 'For want of a nail, the horseshoe was lost . . .' business. Well, he was right. I missed the nail and the kingdom came tumbling down. Can I ask you a question, though?"

"Shoot."

"Were you a little happy when the computers went banzai, or was it my imagination?"

"It wasn't your imagination. I wasn't happy, I was — "

"Smug. Sorry, Paul, but that's how it struck me."

"Maybe. I feel like we've all gotten into this speed trap, everything moving faster because it can. When communications were slower and reconnaissance took time, people had time to think and cool down before

405

they blasted hell out of each other."

"But they did it anyway. Fort Sumter would have happened with or without Dan Rather and Steve Jobs. I just think you like being a daddy, and these babies don't need us till they run the family car into a ditch."

Before Hood could protest — and when he thought about it later he was glad he didn't, because Stoll had a point — Bob Herbert paged him. He used Matt's phone and punched Herbert's number.

"Hood here."

"Bad news, Chief. We found out what Major Lee was up to today, at least part of the day."

"More terrorism?"

"Looks that way. He took four quarter-drums of poison gas — tabun — from the Hazardous Materials Vault at the army base in Seoul. All very legal, the paperwork in order. It says he's taking it up to the DMZ."

"When was this?"

"About three hours after the explosion."

"So he would have had enough time to set the blast, get to the base, and head north, assuming that's his real destination. And somewhere along the way he decided to waylay Kim Hwan."

"Sounds about right."

Hood looked at his watch. "If he did go

north, he's been there at least seven hours."

"But doing what? Tabun is a pretty heavy gas. Somebody'd notice if he was hauling a missile around, and he'd need a crop duster to use it on troops."

"Then there's the question of *which* troops. He could use it on ours to send Lawrence into a frenzy, or use it on the North Koreans to push them over the edge. Bob, I'm not going to go to the President with this. Call General Schneider at the DMZ. Wake him if you have to, and tell him about Lee. Ask him to find Donald as well, and have him call me."

"What are you going to tell Greg?"

"To radio General Hong-koo and tell him we've got a nut on the loose."

Herbert's gasp was audible over the phone. "Tell North Korea that the South Koreans are behind all this? Chief, the President'll have you shot deader'n Ike Clanton."

"If I'm wrong, I'll load the gun myself."

"What about the press? The Dee-Perks'll smear it everywhere."

"I'll talk to Ann about that. She'll have something ready to go. Besides, world opinion *may* slow the President down long enough for us to prove our case."

"Or get our asses royally kicked."

"Lives are worth that. Just do it, Bob.

We're short on time."

Hood hung up.

"I know," said Stoll without looking up, "my fingers are flying as fast as possible. Just find out what kind of truck Lee was driving: I'll get your satellites back as soon as possible."

SIXTY-FIVE

Wednesday, 6:30 A.M., the DMZ

In his long career of crawling through tunnels, Lee had never decided which was preferable: the rank, damp tunnels that filled your lungs with musk that stayed for weeks, and tickled your face with roots, or the dry, airless tunnels like this one, which filled your nose and eyes with sand and left your mouth painfully dry.

This is worse, he told himself. *You can get used to a smell, but not to thirst.*

At least his labors were nearly at an end. They were in the last section of tunnel with the last of the drums: in just a few minutes they would reach the niche they'd dug on the other side. He would help Yoo up with the drums, and then the rest was up to the Private, carrying them closer to the target and putting them in place before sunup.

Yoo had already brought his tools through; they had studied the course through the hills and shadows several nights before, and there was no way anyone could see him.

While Yoo worked, Lee would go back and take care of Mr. Gregory Donald before he could meet with Hong-koo. It was so typical of an American. Those who weren't empire builders were self-righteous meddlers. He hated them for that, and for having stopped short of victory in the war. When they finished helping him destroy the government of Pyongyang, he would work on expelling them at long last from his country.

His country. Not Harry Truman's or Michael Lawrence's, not General Norbom's or General Schneider's. The personality and industry of his people had been kept down and perverted for too many years, and it would stop now.

Despite the pads he wore, Lee's knees were rubbed raw by the crawling and chafing, and his eyepatch was soaked with sweat, his good eye burning. But he could barely keep from rushing through these final yards and minutes as the time of the second and third events neared, the moment they'd been planning since he first approached Colonel Sun with his idea two years before.

He continued to creep forward, balancing

himself on his left hand, rolling the drum with his right, his shoulders hunched. His good eye shifted slowly from side to side as he moved ahead, watching the walls of the tunnel. And then the yards were a few feet, and the minutes were seconds, and they stood the drum upright with its three companions.

Yoo took a rolled rope ladder from the niche they had dug, and with his back to the wall of the narrow passageway, he shinned to the top. Attaching the ladder to a rock, he lowered it down and they began bringing the drums up.

Major Lee moved back through the tunnel on all fours. Sometimes his knees didn't even touch down as he kicked off with the balls of his feet, his legs going past his elbows as he raced ahead. He pulled the flashlight from his shoulder and doused it as he neared the passageway on the southern side, then sprang onto the hemp line. He scurried up, hand over hand, then paused just below the rim.

There was no one around. Pulling himself through, Major Lee patted his left pocket, made sure the switchblade was still there, then ran into the night.

SIXTY-SIX

Wednesday, 7:00 A.M., the Diamond Mountains

The 7.65 × 17mm Browning, officially known as the Type 64, was a North Korean-made handgun. It was more or less a copy of the Belgian Fabrique Nationale Browning Mle. 1900 pistol, but what appealed to Colonel Sun, and why he had asked Colonel Oko to bring that weapon specifically, is that it was manufactured in a silenced version.

Bent over the backseat of the jeep, Sun's orderly handed the Colonel the 64 and kept one for himself. Sun had already checked to see that it was loaded when they left the beach. He trusted Colonel Oko only so far. Their fathers had served together in a unified Korea, fighting the Japanese, and they had played with each other as boys. But while any man who would allow his own soldiers to be killed for the furtherance of a cause was to be admired, he was never to be fully trusted.

And what am I doing that's any different? Sun asked himself. The soldiers who were working with him and Major Lee were all volunteers, but what of the thousands, perhaps tens of thousands who would die when war broke out? They weren't volunteers.

Yet, what they were doing *must* be done. He had known that since 1989, when he crystallized his thoughts and published an anonymous pamphlet called *The South Is Korea.* It enraged intellectuals and pro-unification activists, which told him he was on the right track. In the booklet, not only did he maintain that eventual reunification would be a cultural and economic disaster, it would destroy the lives and careers and political aspirations of officers on both sides of the border. That alone would create chaos, for soldiers like Oko would not take a mustering out and token post with grace and gratitude. He'd stage a coup that would plunge the peninsula into a war greater and more deadly than the relatively small conflagration they were planning. Besides, incontrovertible separation would prevent repeats of brutal confrontations like the 1994 riots in Seoul, where over seven thousand troops clashed with ten thousand pro-unification supporters and more than two hundred people were injured. Those protests would only grow worse as the U.S. continued its efforts to help the North replace its old graphite-moderated nuclear reactors. New nuclear reactors would decrease the amount of plutonium and atomic bombs the North could produce, thus making them more responsive to a mutual defense pact with the South.

In the long run, the course of action he and his cohorts were planning was preferable. And if the President of the United States insisted on meddling, on forcing reunification on the South, then he and his allies would find any victory to be a pyrrhic one.

It was getting late. Time to move. Sun and Kong cupped their left hands at their sides, the pistols cradled in them, barrel up, the silencer extension reaching nearly to their elbow. They walked through the darkness toward Ki-Soo's tent. They passed a sentry who was patrolling the area, a man with medals, a big scar across his forehead, and a sinister bearing. The man saluted with zest.

The tent flap was unfastened and the Colonel entered.

Sun did not hesitate, though he was not without regrets. He had read Ki-Soo's record and had a grudging respect for the man.

His father was a Japanese soldier and his mother had been a comfort girl during the Second World War. Ki-Soo had fought hard to overcome the stigma associated with his birth, obtaining a degree in communications and then joining the military, where he rose quickly. It was unfortunate that he would die at best, be dishonored at worst. But he had a wife and a daughter, and the Colonel hoped he would be reasonable.

Sun's orderly went to the holster hanging from the chair by Ki-Soo's desk and collected the TT33 Tokarev pistol. He tucked it in the back of his belt as Sun himself got down on one knee beside Ki-Soo's cot and put his free hand beside the Colonel's right ear, the barrel of the gun to his left ear.

Ki-Soo awoke with a start; Sun pushed the man's head against the barrel and held it there.

"Don't move, Colonel."

Ki-Soo jerked his head and tried to rise, but Sun held it firm.

"I said don't move."

He squinted into the darkness. "Sun?"

"Yes. Listen carefully, Colonel — "

"I don't understand — "

Ki-Soo tried to sit, then stopped as Sun pushed the gun harder.

"Colonel, I haven't time for this. I need your help."

"For what?"

"I want the code to change the launch coordinates of the Nodongs."

"But your orders! They said nothing about — "

"These are new orders, Colonel. Without your help, this will be difficult. With your help, this will be easier . . . and you live. Your choice?"

"I want to know who you're with."

"Your *choice*, Colonel?"

"I won't turn the missiles without knowing where!"

Sun stood, the gun still pointed at Ki-Soo's head. *He is doing what a good officer should do*, he thought. *Let him have that much.*

"They'll be aimed nowhere in this country, Colonel. That's all I'll tell you."

Ki-Soo looked from Sun to his aide. "Who are you with?"

Sun's arm shifted and there was a pop followed by the hiss of released gas as the silenced pistol discharged. Ki-Soo howled as his left hand was pushed into the cot. His right hand flew over, clutching the bloody wound.

After a moment, they heard hurried footsteps outside. Sun saw a flashlight approaching from a nearby tent. "Colonel, are you all right?"

Kong stepped beside the flap, the Tokarev and his own 17mm pistol both pointing toward it.

The Colonel moved his arm so the gun was once again pointing at Ki-Soo's head. "Tell your orderly that everything is fine."

Fighting back the pain, Ki-Soo said, "I — I stubbed my toe."

"Do you need to find something, sir? I have a flashlight."

"*No!* Thank you, I'm fine."

"Yes, sir."

The orderly turned and went back to his tent.

Sun glared down at the officer. "Kong, tear off a piece of the bedsheet and wrap his hand."

"Stay away!" Ki-Soo hissed. He pulled off his pillowcase and pushed it against his hand.

Sun gave him a moment, then said, "My next shot will be higher. Now, Colonel, the code."

Ki-Soo was struggling to stay composed. "Five-one-four-zero in the bottom row . . . lets you get into the system. Zero-zero-zero-zero in the middle row . . . erases the coordinates and allows you to change them. Once you've done that, any code you pick for the bottom row will lock the coordinates in."

The coordinates. That was something of a joke in the South. The American-built systems were operated by built-in topographic maps and photographic images provided by aerial or satellite surveillance. These missiles were able to find a particular jeep in a busy camp and could be dropped in the lap of any of the passengers. Conversely, the No-dongs could be aimed in 360 directions, and the elevation was selected by how many miles away the target was. Targeting specific city blocks was virtually impossible.

But Sun didn't need to hit a specific block. He just needed a particular city, and anywhere in it would be fine.

"What time do the men in the hills change shifts?" Sun asked.

"They'll be . . . relieved at eight."

"Will the officer in charge report to you?"

Ki-Soo nodded.

Sun said, "I'm leaving Kong with you. The flap is to remain closed, and you'll receive no one. If you do anything but what you're told, you'll die. We won't be here long, and when we're finished your camp will be returned to you."

Ki-Soo winced as he used the thumb of his right hand to press the pillowcase into

418

the wound. "I'll be disgraced."

"You have a family," Sun said. "You were right to think of them." He turned to leave the tent.

"The missiles are aimed at Seoul. What target . . . can be more important?"

Sun said nothing. Very soon, Ki-Soo and the rest of the world would know.

SIXTY-SEVEN

Wednesday, 7:10 A.M., Osaka

"General Rodgers, I thought the pilot was flying us into some warm sunshine!"

Even over the roar of the engines, Lt. Col. Squires along with the rest of the Striker team could hear the slashing rain as they crossed Ise Bay on their approach to Osaka. Rodgers was always fascinated and impressed by imbalances of that sort, like hearing a harp in the midst of an orchestra. In a way, it was similar to the philosophy behind the formation of the Striker unit. From David and Goliath to the American Revolution, size did not always mean dominance. Playwright Peter Barnes had once written about a puny weed that split the walk, and that image — not just the Andrew Jacksons and Joshua Chamberlains and Teddy Roosevelts of history — had kept Rodgers going in some of his darkest days. He'd even had his sister stitch the design onto his duffel bag, so he'd always be reminded of the image.

Private Puckett broke into Rodgers's reverie with a salute and a snappy "Sir!"

Rodgers removed his earplugs. "What's the word, Private Puckett?"

"Sir, Major General Campbell says he has a C-9A jet waiting to fly us over."

"Leave it to the army," Squires said. "We get an unarmed Nightingale to fly over North Korea."

"I'd rather have a nice, snug Black Hawk myself," Rodgers said, "but we've got a problem with range. Thanks, Private."

"You're welcome, sir."

Squires grinned as Puckett returned to his seat. "Johnny Puckett's a real good man, sir. Says his daddy used to have a Ham radio setup in his room when he was a baby — made him a mobile out of old knobs."

"There's something to be said for that. Like in the old days, when people learned one craft and became real good at it."

"True, sir. Only if you don't get quite good enough at it, like my daddy trying to be a soccer player, you're screwed."

"Are you?"

"Seems so to me."

"He passed that drive and ambition on to

you, didn't he? King Arthur couldn't search for the Holy Grail himself. Moses wasn't permitted to cross the River Jordan. But they inspired others to do those things."

Squires cocked his head. "You make me feel guilty about not writing home."

"You can send him a postcard from Osaka when we head back."

Rodgers felt the plane bank to the southwest. *Head back.* The words always caused his throat to tighten up. You never knew if you would come back; you just assumed it. But there were so many times that didn't happen, and even experienced soldiers were caught off-guard by that realization. The words of Tennyson came back to haunt him, as they often did:

Home they brought her warrior dead. She nor
  swoon'd, nor utter'd cry: All her maidens,
  watching said,
"She must weep or she will die."

The transport landed, and as Captain Harryhausen complained about the weather, the Striker warriors rushed out to the waiting aircraft. They were in and airborne four minutes after the door of the C-141 had been opened.

The sleek, narrow Military Airlift Com-

422

mand jet rose rapidly in the driving rain and headed northwest. The men were sitting as before, in benches along the sides, but the mood now was entirely different. Those who had slept or played cards or read on the trip to Osaka were now electrified. They were checking gear, giving each other pep talks, and a few were praying. Private Bass Moore was in charge of the parachute rigging, and he checked the lines as the jet flew in low over the Sea of Japan, bucking the heavy winds and thinning sheets of rain.

An officer from Seoul was onboard, reviewing the exit strategy with Squires. There would be a Sikorsky S-70 Black Hawk waiting to come and get them: the chopper could be over the DMZ and into the Diamond Mountains in a matter of minutes. More importantly, the eleven-seater had a pair of M-60 side-firing machine guns to help ensure that they'd get out again.

With just twenty minutes until drop time, Rodgers called Puckett over and asked him to raise Hood.

The Director was edgier than Rodgers had ever remembered hearing him, and it was refreshing.

"Mike, it's beginning to look like you're going to be in the thick of it."

"What happened?"

"The President doesn't buy it, but we're convinced that a South Korean team is behind all this, and we've also learned that a pilot took two men from a ferry in the Sea of Japan. Guy was so nervous he cracked up his plane on landing and spilled his guts to the sea patrol. He said he took the men to Kosong."

"Kosong? That's just a three-pointer from the Nodongs."

"Exactly. And there were two bodies on the ferry. The dead men were carrying gambling money from Japan to North Korea. Tens of thousands of dollars."

"That's decent bribe money up North. Most of those bastards would sell their kids for a grand."

"That's what Bob Herbert says. It's a big leap of faith to assume that someone from the South is planning to use that money to get control of the Nodong site, but we can't afford to overlook the possibility."

"Which means we've got to get in there and find out for sure."

"Right. I'm sorry, Mike."

"Don't be. This is what we signed on for. To paraphrase George Chapman, being threatened is what turns us into lions."

"Sure. And like Kirk Douglas said in *Champion*, 'Ours is like any other business, only

424

here the blood shows.' Take care of yourself, and tell Charlie and the boys to do the same."

"*Ten minutes!*" Squires called back.

"That's it, Paul," Rodgers said. "I'll radio you when we have something. And if it's any consolation, I'd rather be dodging bullets than the press on this one. Good luck to you too."

SIXTY-EIGHT

Wednesday, 7:20 A.M., the DMZ

General Schneider forgot his dream the instant his orderly entered. All he remembered was that he was on skis somewhere and liking it very much. Reality, and the dry night air, always brought him back with an unpleasant jolt.

"Sir, there's a phone call from Washington."

"The President?" he said.

"No, sir. Not *that* Washington. A Mr. Bob Herbert from Op-Center."

Schneider muttered an oath. "They probably want me to straitjacket poor Donald." Sliding into his slippers, the General went to his desk. With an air of relief, he inserted himself in the swivel chair and picked up the phone. "General Schneider."

"General, this is Bob Herbert, Intelligence

426

Officer at Op-Center."

"I've heard of you. Lebanon?"

"Yes. That's quite a memory you have."

"Bob, I never forget when we do something stupid. Goddamn Embassy had a 'kick me' sign on it for terrorists. No heavy barricades out front, nothing to stop a bomber bent on driving a truck to Allah's doorstep." He leaned back in the chair and raised his eyelids to stretch the sleep from them. "But enough about old mistakes. You're calling to stop a new one from being made."

"I hope so," said Herbert.

"Yeah, I don't know what the hell got into the man. Well, that's not true. He lost his wife yesterday. Donald's a good man. He's just not thinking clearly."

"Clear enough to go over there with official instructions, I hope."

Schneider shot forward in the seat. "Hold on! You're telling me you're sanctioning this idiotic little conference of his?"

"Director Hood has asked him to relay a message. That we believe a team of South Koreans masquerading as North Koreans are behind the blast . . . and that it may be the first of several terrorist acts designed to throw us into war."

"Our own side?" Schneider sat still as an oak. "Dammit, you're sure?"

"The pieces are coming together," Herbert said. "We think a Major Kim Lee is behind it."

"Lee? I've met him. Stony-faced bastard, superpatriot. I liked him."

"He seems to have put together a small team," Herbert said, "and he appears to be in your area now — with four quarter-drums of poison gas."

"I'll contact General Norbom, send out a search and destroy squad to find him."

"That's not all. Some of his men may be trying to gain control of a mobile Nodong site in the east."

"Ambitious," said Schneider. "You sure you want Donald to *tell* Hong-koo all this? They'll have it on all the wire services before the last word's out of his mouth."

"We know."

"They'll also shoot Lee's people on sight," Schneider said. "Have you thought about what'll happen when word gets out that the U.S. was responsible for the death of South Koreans? Seoul will explode. It'll be like goddamn Saigon."

"Hood knows about that too," Herbert said. "He's preparing something with our Press Officer."

"A double funeral would be my recommendation. You guys may actually be creating some kind of constitutional crisis by effectively obstructing the powers of the Oval Office to make war."

"Like I said," Herbert replied, "the boss knows."

"Well, Bob, I'll relay the message. And here's one for Mr. Hood. His tank may not be full in the brains department, but I haven't seen stones like his since Ollie North."

"Thanks," Herbert said. "I'm sure he'll understand that was a compliment."

Gregory awoke from his short sleep feeling remarkably refreshed and clearheaded.

Sitting up on the scrubby flats, he looked over at the brightly lighted border. How fitting it was that hate and suspicion should cause both sides to burn their fires. Distrust always leaves people in the dark.

He took out his pipe and filled it with the last of his Balkan Sobranie tobacco. After lighting it, he held the match to look at his watch.

It was nearly time.

He puffed slowly and reflected about the smoke, about the Balkans and how a single incident there, the assassination of Archduke Ferdinand, triggered the First World War. Would a single event here trigger a Third World War? It was conceivable. There was more than tension in the air; there was rampant insanity. Preserving ego with lives, painting images in blood. *What is wrong with us?*

From behind, headlights found the former diplomat. Donald turned and shielded his eyes as a jeep approached.

"Communing with the stars?" General Schneider said, climbing from the passenger's side. He walked over, an imposing silhouette.

"No, General. With my muse."

"You should have told me where you were going. If you didn't light up, we'd be searching till daylight."

"I haven't changed my mind, if that's what you've come about."

"No. I've got a message for you from your boss."

Donald felt his insides constrict. He hoped that the General hadn't gone to the White House.

General Schneider told him what Herbert had said, and Donald felt an enormous weight lift from his shoulders. Not only was there the satisfaction of his and Kim Hwan's initial hunch having been correct, but there was every chance that now this brushfire could be stamped out.

Strangely enough, he thought, he wasn't surprised about Major Lee. When they had

430

met earlier, there was something in his eye, in the last glance he gave, that wasn't quite right. There was intelligence, but also an edge — suspicion, perhaps, or maybe contempt.

"I won't pretend that I'm happy with this," Schneider concluded, "but I won't stand in your way now."

"Were you going to before?"

"I was leaning strongly in that direction, yes. I still plan to go on record as being opposed to conciliation, but it takes all kinds to make a world." Schneider headed back to the car. "Get in. I'll give you a ride back."

"I think I'll walk. Clear the head a bit."

Schneider didn't look back as he climbed into the jeep. His orderly swung it around and drove off, dust and diesel fumes hanging in their wake.

Donald walked after them, puffing with contentment, knowing that Soonji would be surprised and proud of how things had gone.

As he walked, he felt a prick at the back of his neck. He reached back to scratch it, touched steel, and froze.

"Ambassador Donald," said a familiar voice as the knife traced a sharp path from his nape to just beneath his chin.

431

Donald felt a trickle of blood slip down his neck and under the knot of his tie as he saw Major Lee's face burning a dull red in the glow of the pipe.

SIXTY-NINE

Tuesday, 5:30 P.M., Op-Center

As Ann Farris entered Matt Stoll's office, the operations Support Officer snickered.

"Gee, folks," Stoll said, "don't put too much pressure on me or anything."

Paul Hood was sitting on a small leather couch in the back of the room. There was a twenty-five-inch TV screen in the ceiling and a video-game console on a shelf, and Stoll retired to the well-worn piece of furniture whenever he needed to relax and think.

"Not trying to pressure you," Hood said. "Just want to know the instant you get the satellites back."

"We'll be quiet," Ann said as she sat down. She looked at Hood, her eyes full of sadness. "Paul, I can't lie to you. We're going to get murdered on this, even if we're right."

"I know. Donald meets with the North

433

in a half hour, after which the world press chews the President and Seoul to pieces for escalating when we knew Pyongyang might be innocent. Result? Lawrence has to hold his horses."

"Or look like a warmonger."

"Right. And if it turns out that Major Lee wasn't behind this, then the North has the ears of the world to apologize, punish the guilty party, and clean house themselves. Or if Pyongyang authorized the bombing, they can regroup and attack again. In any case, the President ends up helpless."

"You've pretty well summed it up," Ann said. "I hate to agree with Lowell, but he thinks you ought to tell Donald to postpone the meeting. The North will make PR hay of that too, but we can deal with it. Say he was acting alone."

"I won't do that to him, Ann." He looked at Stoll. "Matty, I need those satellites!"

"You said you weren't going to pressure me!"

"I made a mistake."

"What will reconnaissance do for you now?" Ann asked.

"There are soldiers looking for Lee, but no one's searching for the men who may have gone after the Nodongs. Mike and the Striker team will be there soon. If we can

434

find evidence of an incursion, and Mike can stop them, we prove that we were right — *and* the President gets a sexy military action that makes him look awfully good. The North will bitch that we sent men in, but it'll blow over like when the Israelis went into Entebbe."

Ann's eyes were wide. "That's brilliant, Paul. That's very good."

"Thanks. But it only works if I have — "

"You *have!*" Stoll said, pushing his chair back and clapping his hands once.

As Hood ran over, Stoll punched the button to ring the NRO. Stephen Viens came on at once and Stoll put it on speaker phone.

"Steve — you're back on-line!"

"I thought so," he said, "when I saw that old Soviet battleship vanish from the Sea of Japan."

"Steve, this is Paul Hood. Let me see the Nodong site in the Diamond Mountains. Close enough so that I can see all three missiles."

"That'd be about two hundred feet up. Inputting coordinates now and . . . she's responding. Night-vision lens in place, the picture has been taken, and the camera is digitizing the image now. Starting to scan on the monitor — "

"Send it over here while it's scanning."

"Will do, Paul," Viens said. "Matty, you

did a helluva job."

Stoll put the computer on the receive mode and Hood bent down to watch the monitor as the image came. It appeared in swift strokes from top to bottom — like a lightning-fast Etch-A-Sketch he always thought. Ann stood behind him and gently lay a hand on his shoulder. He ignored the arched-eyebrow look he got from Matty, was less successful ignoring the electricity from her touch as the black-and-white terrain materialized rapidly.

"The missile on the top is pointed south," Hood said, "the missiles on the left and right — "

"Jesus," Stoll cut in.

"You can say that again."

Ann bent over Hood. "The two on the sides are pointing in different directions."

"One to the South," said Stoll, "the other — "

"East," said Hood. "Which means someone's gotten in there." He straightened and hurried to the door, not meaning to throw Ann's hand off but managing to anyway.

"How can you tell?" Ann asked.

Hood said over his shoulder as he hurried into the hall, "Because not even the North Koreans would be mad enough to aim a Nodong at Japan."

SEVENTY

Wednesday, 7:35 A.M., the DMZ

"Major Lee," Donald said quietly. "Somehow, I'm not surprised."

"I am." Lee pushed the knife harder into the flesh under Donald's chin. "I thought I would be about my business by now. Instead, I'm here with you."

"And your business is to kill innocent people and start a war."

"There's no such thing as an innocent person — "

"You're wrong. My wife was innocent."

Donald raised his hand slowly. Lee pressed the knife deeper but Donald continued to lift his arm.

"Your wife and you, Mr. Ambassador, made life easier for those who abandoned their country. You are as corrupt as the rest, and it's time for you to join — "

Donald moved so swiftly that Lee hadn't time to react. The bowl of the pipe in his left hand, Donald swung the stem around, hooked the knife from above, and pushed it to the left. The bowl was facing Lee and, thrusting it forward, Donald pressed the hot tobacco against his right eye. Lee screamed and dropped the knife, which Donald hurried to recover.

"No!" Lee yelled as he turned and ran into the deep blue of the morning.

Donald ran after him, still holding the knife.

Lee was headed into the area where the North Koreans had been known to have tunnels. He wondered if the Major were leading him away from the South-side base intentionally. Was that where he was planning to use the gas?

Not likely, he thought. Lee was dressed in his own ROK uniform. He was going to the North, almost certainly to release the gas in some way: if he was spotted, the South would be blamed. Donald briefly considered stopping to alert Schneider, but what would the General do? He wouldn't follow him into the North.

No. Donald knew that he was the only one who could go. His breath came in painful wheezes as he half ran, half stumbled after the shrinking figure of the Major. Lee was putting more and more distance between them, at least two hundred yards, but he was running east. As night gave way to the blue morning, Donald might lose ground on Lee but at least he could still see where his quarry was headed.

And then Lee disappeared.

Donald slowed to catch his breath. It was as though the earth had swallowed Lee up, and Donald realized that he must have dropped into one of the tunnels. He noted the area, a thicket some twenty yards across, and walked swiftly toward it, counting the steps to take his mind off of how much his lungs and legs hurt.

Just a few minutes after Lee vanished, Donald was at the entrance to the tunnel. He didn't wait, figuring that if Lee had had a weapon he'd have used it back in the field. Folding the knife into a pocket and dropping to his knees, Donald grabbed the hemp line and lowered himself along the passage, bumping his back repeatedly as he tried to walk himself down. He reached bottom, nearly exhausted, and listened. There were shuffling and clawing sounds somewhere up ahead. He struck a match, saw the tunnel, and knew where Lee had gone.

If something happened to him, he wanted

Schneider to know where he'd gone. Turning and setting the hemp line on fire, he dropped to his belly as thick smoke filled the passageway. He crawled into the tunnel, hoping that the General would see the smoke and flames. He also hoped that he himself could reach the other side before he choked to death . . . and getting there, that he could find Lee before he was able to realize his insane vision.

SEVENTY-ONE

Wednesday, 7:48 A.M., the Diamond Mountains

A parachute jump is nothing like what most first-timers expect. The air is remarkably full and solid: free-falling through it is like riding a wave at the beach. During the daytime, there's very little sense of depth since objects are so flat and far away; at night, there's no sense of depth at all.

Though the other men had all gone first, Mike Rodgers was surprised at how alone he felt: he saw nothing, felt only the resistance of the wind, could barely hear his own voice as he counted out twenty seconds before pulling the ripcord. Then the pounding of the wind was reduced to a gentle gust, and everything else was silent.

They had jumped from only five thousand feet up, and the ground came up quickly, as the copilot had warned them it would.

Rodgers had picked out a landmark as soon as he pulled his ripcord, a high treetop aglow in the early morning light. He watched it as he descended. That was the only yardstick he had as to how high he was, and when he was level with it he prepared himself for landing. His legs were bent slightly, and when his feet hit ground he cushioned his landing by bending farther, then dropping and rolling. When he was on his side, he released his parachute, stood quickly, and bundled the fabric into his arms. He was only a bit sore where his Achilles tendons had stretched on landing; the spirit was willing, but the flesh wasn't as elastic as it had once been.

Bass Moore was already running toward him, followed by Johnny Puckett and his TAC SAT radio.

"How'd we do?" Rodgers asked Moore softly.

"Everyone's down and okay."

Puckett was unfolding the parabolic antenna and had fixed the uplink before the rest of the team arrived. While Moore took Rodgers's parachute and jogged to a nearby lake to sink it, Squires reached Rodgers's side.

"You all right, sir?"

"The old bones held out." Rodgers pointed to the radio. "Make the call. I told you, this is your mission."

"Thank you, sir," Squires said.

Crouching, the Lieutenant Colonel accepted the headset from Puckett and adjusted the mouthpiece while the Private punched in the frequency.

Bugs Benet answered, and Hood came on quickly.

"Mike, you're down?"

"It's Squires, sir, and yes, we all made it."

"Good. New development. Over the last ten minutes, all three of the Nodongs have been recalibrated. Instead of being aimed at Seoul, they're pointing toward Japan."

"All three missiles are aimed at Japan," Squires said, looking up at Rodgers. "I copy."

"Christ," said Rodgers.

"You're to get over there and, at my instruction, take them out."

"Yes, sir."

"Out," said Hood.

Squires removed the headset. As he briefed Rodgers, the members of the Striker team loaded their Beretta automatics. Sgt. Chick Grey, responsible for the maps, was checking the printouts Lt. Col. Squires had given him.

Upon hearing that they were almost certainly going to have to destroy the Nodongs,

Rodgers wished they had brought explosives. But while North Korea was known to negotiate for the release of men with guns, men with explosives, bent on heavy-duty sabotage, were shot on the spot. Still, it was one of those rare calls he wished he could take back. The control circuits for those missiles were locked in safe-strong boxes and would be extremely difficult to get to, especially if time was tight. If they couldn't pick up explosives at the site, he didn't know what they were going to do.

Sgt. Grey walked over to Squires. Using a pen-sized laser light, he pointed at the map in the fast-dissipating darkness.

"Sir, the pilot did a great job. We're less than four miles from the site — here." He pointed to a forest southeast of the depression where the missiles were located. "The march is mostly uphill, but the grade isn't a bad one."

Squires hitched up his own small backpack and loaded his pistol. "Let's move them out, Sergeant," he said barely above a whisper, "single file. Moore, you take point. First sign of life, you stop us."

"Sir!" Moore saluted, and went ahead of the line.

Squires went next, with Rodgers behind him.

As they walked through the field, the deep blue of the horizon shaded to azure and yellow. They marched up the sloping hill into increasingly thick woods.

This was the time Rodgers liked best. His senses, the air of anticipation, were at their peak; pure reflex, the survival instinct, had not yet kicked in and there was time to savor the challenge ahead. For Rodgers, as for most of the others they'd picked for the team, challenge was more important than security, than their lives and their families. The only thing more important than challenge was Country, and the synergy of daring and patriotism was what made these men unique. As much as each man wanted to go home, none would do so at the expense of a job unfinished or poorly done.

Rodgers was proud and thrilled to be with them, though he felt remarkably old as he looked around at the twenty-odd-year-old faces and walked on his aching forty-five-year-old heels. He hoped the flesh was up to the challenge and reminded himself that even Beowulf was able to defeat a fire-breathing dragon fifty years after his encounter with the monster Grendel. Of course, the aged Jute king perished as a result of that battle, though Rodgers told himself that when it came his time to die he wouldn't mind being consumed on a huge pyre with his thanes riding around him, singing his praises.

Twelve thanes, Rodgers remembered, trying not to dwell on the irony of that as Moore neared the top of the rise. He scurried forward on his belly, then raised his hand, extending five fingers twice.

There were ten men somewhere ahead.

As the men moved forward at a crouch, Rodgers knew that the savoring time was over. . . .

SEVENTY-TWO

Donald knew there was a point at which the body no longer supported the will of even the strongest spirit, and he was rapidly approaching that point.

Still breathing heavily from the run, Donald was perspiring madly and coughing dryly as he wormed his way through the tunnel, his elbows at his sides, chafed and bleeding inside his jacket — which he'd kept on in an effort to prevent just that from happening. The heat was oppressive, sweat and sand stung his eyes, and there was no light; each turn in the seemingly endless tunnel was discovered by his shoulder colliding hard with a dirt wall.

Yet all the while there were the sounds of Major Lee ahead, and that kept him going. And when there were no more sounds, he continued because he knew that Lee was free of the tunnel and the end was near.

Finally, with his body crying to rest, his arms and legs cramped from exertion, he saw the light and reached the passage that would take him from this hateful pit.

Standing with pain and difficulty, his lower back stabbing him as he tried to straighten up, Donald took a moment to suck down the cooler air — and then saw that there was no way out. If there had been a ladder, Lee had withdrawn it.

He looked around him. The passage was narrow, and putting his back against one side, his arms and legs stiff against the opposite wall, he began ascending crablike. Twice during the nine-foot climb he had to stop to keep from falling back down. He was carrying Lee's knife in his teeth and would dig it into the wall to use as a handhold, resting and collecting his strength before continuing. When he finally made it to the top, the sun was rising and he knew where he was; he'd seen the terrain from the other side of the fence. He was in North Korea.

Donald was in the middle of a crater that had obviously been caused by artillery practice. The exit was in a wall of the southwest side of the crater, where it was invisible from the base, approximately a quarter of a mile to the west, or the fence, some two hundred yards south. This had to be a new tunnel dug by Lee and his men; the North would have placed their entrance closer to the facilities, where people could come and go unseen from the South.

Lying flat against the wall of the crater, Donald looked over the lip. Lee was nowhere to be seen. There were low-lying hills to the north, with trees and plenty of rises and depressions for someone to hide. The hard, dry ground held no footprints, and Donald had no idea whether Lee had gone into the hills or to the base.

Not that it mattered, he told himself. It was more important to find the poison gas. Whether it went to the base or to the north — to Pyongyang, as a counterpoint to the blast in Seoul? — he had to go to General Hong-koo and tell him what was happening.

Donald started out, walking briskly, feeling better now that he was out of the tunnel and his muscles had had a chance to relax. He peered ahead, hoping to catch sight of Lee, but there was only stillness on this side of the base. To the south of the facility, patrols were coming in and fresh ones had begun to take their place.

Of course, Donald thought. That was why Lee had selected this time. Guards were always the most lax when a shift neared its end.

He looked toward the back of the barracks again, thought he saw something glint in the rising sun, behind a low hill. He stopped, squinted ahead. He saw it again, something metallic, and he ran a few yards to the south to get a better look at it.

There was a man crouching behind one of the barracks, deep in the shadows. There was something in the wall beside him — it might have been a small generator. His eyes on the man, Donald began running toward him, realized that it wasn't a generator but an air conditioner, and that what he'd seen glinting was the back of the unit. He also saw what looked like a box beneath it.

A box . . . or a drum. Donald started running slowly. Gas in the air-conditioning system would be fast and horribly effective. The patrols returning to the barracks would be tired, they'd fall asleep immediately, and they'd never know anything was wrong. He started running faster. As he approached, Donald saw that the back of the air conditioner was off. The object *was* a drum, and it was being lifted to the top of the unit.

Donald was running as fast as he could.

"Stop him!" he shouted. "Someone stop that man — behind the barracks!"

The man looked in his direction, then sank deeper into the shadows.

"*Saram sallyo!*" he shouted in Korean. "Somebody *help!* Don't let him get away!"

A searchlight flared on a tower in the South, and another came on in the North. The Southern light picked Donald out immediately; it was a moment longer before the Northern light had him.

Soldiers just heading out on patrol came from around the barracks. Donald waved his arms over his head.

"*Get everyone out of the barracks!* There's gas — *poison gas. . . .*"

The dozen men were animated, appeared confused. Several of them unshouldered their AKM assault rifles, and a few were aimed in Donald's direction.

"Dammit, *no!* Not *me!* I'm trying to help — "

The men were shouting among each other; Donald couldn't quite make out what they were saying. And then he heard one man yell that the General was coming and this man had *naifù.*

The knife. He was still holding the knife.

"No!" Donald shouted. "This isn't mine!" He raised it above his head where they could see and cocked his wrist to throw it down.

451

Two rifle shots tore through the early morning, the reports echoing through the hills long after Donald's pounding footsteps had stopped.

SEVENTY-THREE

Wednesday, 7:53 A.M., Seoul

Nearly five hours after he'd first gone into surgery, Kim Hwan was awake and somewhat alert. He looked around him, the events at the cottage coming back to him. He remembered the drive back . . . Kim . . . the arrival at the hospital.

He turned to his left. Just past the IV sack he saw the Call button hanging from a white cable. He lifted his left arm carefully and pressed the red button.

It wasn't a nurse who entered but Choi Hongtack, an agent from the Internal Security division of the KCIA. The young man was dressed in a smartly tailored black three-piece suit. He was a bright kid, an up-and-comer, but deep in Director Yung-Hoon's pocket and not to be trusted without serious threats to his career.

Hongtack picked up a chair and set it beside the bed. "How are you feeling, Mr. Hwan?"

"Stabbed."

"You were. Twice. You suffered wounds to your right lung and to the small intestine, also on the right. The surgeons were able to repair the damage."

"Where's . . . Miss Chong?"

"She left your car in the lot, stole another, and has since abandoned it for a third. There's been no report on a car being stolen in that area of the city, so we've no idea what she's driving or where she's headed."

"Good." Hwan smiled.

Hongtack regarded him strangely. "I'm sorry?"

"I said . . . good. She saved my life. The man . . . who attacked me?"

"He was ROK. We're chasing down what we believe are his commanders, who are also in the field, also ROK."

Hwan nodded weakly.

"Your driver, Cho. He didn't come back."

"I think . . . he's dead. Go to the cottage . . . Yanguu Village. Kim's home."

Hongtack slid a notepad from inside his jacket. "Yanguu Village," he wrote. "Do you think she went there?"

"No. Don't know where . . . she would go."

That wasn't true, but he didn't want to tell Hongtack that. She would make her way to Japan, to her brother, and he hoped with all his heart that she got there. But he knew that might not be enough, and her welfare must come first . . . just as she had put his first by bringing him here.

"If she's found . . . do not arrest her."

"I'm sorry?"

"You're to let her go wherever she wants." Hwan reached out and grabbed Hongtack's sleeve. "Do you . . . understand? She is not to be stopped."

From the ill-concealed fire in his eaglelike eyes, Hwan couldn't tell what bothered Hongtack more: the order or having his clothes touched.

"I — I understand, Mr. Hwan. But if she is found, you want her followed."

"No."

Hongtack's pager beeped. He looked down at the number.

"But then — what do I tell the Director?"

"Nothing." Hwan moved his hand from the sleeve to the lapel. "Don't . . . cross me on this one, Hongtack."

"All right, Mr. Hwan. If you'll excuse me now, I've got to call the office."

"Remember what I said."

"Yes. I will."

* * *

In the hall, Hongtack tugged his sleeve straight, then pulled the compact cellular phone from inside his jacket.

"Croaking little frog," he muttered as he walked to a corner near the soda machine. He punched in the number that had been on his pager, the office of Director Yung-Hoon.

"How is he?" Yung-Hoon asked. "Are they treating him well?"

Hongtack turned his back to the corridor and shielded his mouth with his open hand. "He's awake and the doctors tell me he'll recover fully. Sir — he also wants to protect the spy."

"Excuse me?"

"Protect the spy. He told me she's not to be apprehended."

"Let me speak with him — "

"Sir, he's sleeping."

"Does he expect us to let her go back to the North, having seen him and several of our agents?"

"Apparently, yes," said Hongtack, the aquiline eyes narrowing. "That's exactly what he expects."

"Did he give a reason why?"

"No. He said only that she was not to be taken, and that I was not to cross him on this."

"I see," Yung-Hoon said. "Unfortunately, that would create a problem. We found her stolen car abandoned at a BMW dealership, and everyone's looking for her. City police and highway authorities have joined our search and I've sent helicopters to cover the roads leading from the city. It would be impossible to recall them all."

"Very good. What shall I tell Mr. Hwan, if he asks?"

"The facts. I'm sure he'll understand when his thinking clears."

"Naturally," Hongtack said.

"Check in with me again in an hour. I want to know how he's doing."

"I will," Hongtack said, then returned to his chair outside Hwan's door, a smile on his ascetic face.

SEVENTY-FOUR

Wednesday, 7:59 A.M., the Diamond Mountains

Rodgers and Squires crept up to where Bass Moore was lying. He handed his field glasses to the Lieutenant Colonel.

"That's the unit guarding the eastern perimeter of the Nodong site," Squires said. "There are only supposed to be five of them."

Rodgers peered out. The hill sloped down sharply ahead, a rocky area of about a half mile to the ledge where the soldiers were sitting. Except for some large boulders, there was nothing to use as cover. On the ledge at the base of the hill were two mobile antiaircraft guns, the clips of two thousand rounds each stacked neatly to the left of each gun. Beyond them, in the valley below, the rising sun revealed the Nodongs beneath their foliage-covered canopies.

"Looks like we go in two-by-two," Squires

said. "Moore, go back and tell the men to pair off. You and Puckett'll go first. You'll go to that gumdrop-shaped rock sixty-odd yards down on the left. See it?"

"Yes, sir."

"After that, you cut right and down to the cluster on the right. You feel your way after that, and we'll all follow. When we're as low down as we're gonna get, the General and me will open fire from the back and give the enemy a chance to surrender. They won't, and when they come up after us we close in from the sides. I'll brief each pair as they come down."

Moore saluted, then went back up the hill to collect the Sergeant.

Rodgers continued to study the terrain. "What if the men down there do decide to surrender?"

"We disarm them and leave five of our men behind. But they won't."

"You're probably right," said Rodgers. "They'll fight. And when the soldiers at the missiles hear the gunshots, they'll pull men off the other stations and send them after us."

"We'll be out of here by then. I'll keep the men in pairs to spread the enemy out, pick 'em off as we can. We'll rendezvous at the command tent below and figure out a way to shut those birds down. I just hope they don't fly them prematurely."

Rodgers borrowed the glasses and looked down at the command tent. "You know, something's not right down there."

"Like what?"

"There's no one coming and going from the command tent, including the commander."

"Everything's set. Maybe he's having breakfast."

"I don't know. Hood said that two men flew into the North off that ferry. If this *is* a conspiracy against the DPRK, the commander wouldn't have just let them mosey in, take over, and retarget the missiles."

"Orders can be forged."

"Not here. They work on a double-check system. If the commander gets new orders, he radios Pyongyang for confirmation."

"Maybe they've got someone on the inside up there."

"Then why send two men here? Why not just change the orders from headquarters?"

Squires nodded as Moore and Puckett arrived. "I see your point."

Rodgers continued to study the command tent. It was still, the flap shut. "Charlie, I've got a feeling about this — would you let me take two men and go down there?"

"And do what?"

"I'd like to get down there and give a

listen, see if whoever's in charge is the person who's supposed to be in charge."

Squires shook his head. "You'll be eating up the clock, sir. It'll take you at least an hour to pick your way down there."

"I know, and it's your call. But we're facing twice the number of troops we were expecting, and there's going to be a lot of shooting without any guarantees."

Squires sucked on his upper lip. "I always wanted the chance to tell a general 'no,' and now that I've got it — I won't. Okay. Good luck down there, sir."

"Thanks. I'll contact you by field phone when I can."

Rodgers and Moore took a moment to chart a course the three of them could use to go around the artillery emplacements, while Puckett took off his radio backpack and left the unit with Squires.

"Oh, and Charlie," Rodgers said before leaving, "don't radio Op-Center unless something happens. You know how Hood gets about some of my schemes."

"I do, sir, yes." Squires smiled. "Like a terrier at a rib roast."

"You got it," Rodgers said.

With the sun high above the horizon and throwing long shadows behind the boulders, the three men started off.

SEVENTY-FIVE

Wednesday, 8:00 A.M., North Korean DMZ

The first shot hit Gregory Donald's left leg and brought him down, while the second rifle shot hit the top of his right shoulder as he fell, boring diagonally through his torso. As soon as he hit the ground he was pushing with his left arm, trying to get up. When that proved impossible, he began clawing with his hand, trying to pull himself ahead. The knife tumbled from his dead right hand as he scratched forward, inches at a time.

The soldiers came running over.

"Air . . ." Donald gasped in Korean. "Air. . . ."

Donald stopped moving, fell on his side. He felt a slight burning sensation in his left leg, waves of pain that ended at his waist. Above that, he felt nothing.

He knew he'd been shot, but that was in

the back of his mind. He tried to crane his head around, tried to lift his arm to point.

"The *air* con . . . condi— " he said, then realized that he was probably wasting whatever breath remained. No one was listening. Or maybe he wasn't talking loud enough.

A medic came rushing over. He knelt by Donald's side, examined his throat to make sure it was clear, then checked his pulse and examined his eyes.

Donald looked up into the man's bespectacled face. "The barracks," he said. "Listen to me . . . air-conditioning — "

"Rest," the medic said. He threw open Donald's jacket and unbuttoned his shirt. He used gauze to wipe away the blood and made a cursory examination of the entrance wound in the shoulder and the exit wound to the left of the naval.

Donald managed to get his left elbow under him and tried to rise.

"Keep still!" the medic snapped.

"You don't . . . see! *Poison* . . . gas . . . the barracks. . . ."

The medic stopped, regarded Donald curiously.

"Air . . . con . . . dition. . . ."

"The air conditioners? Someone is trying to poison the men in the barracks?" Understanding and sadness crossed the medic's features simultaneously. "You were trying to *stop* them?"

Donald nodded weakly, then fell back, struggling for breath. The medic relayed the information to the soldiers standing around him, then resumed working on his patient.

"You poor man," the doctor said. "I'm sorry. So very sorry."

Behind him, Donald could hear shouts, men running in the direction of the barracks. He tried to speak. "What. . . ?"

"What's happening?" the medic asked an aide.

"The soldiers are leaving the barracks, sir."

"Do you hear?" the doctor asked Donald.

Donald heard but couldn't move his head. He blinked slowly, looked past the medic at the bluing sky.

"Don't let go," the doctor said as he called for a stretcher. "I'm going to get you to the hospital."

Donald's chest was barely moving.

"What's happening now?" the medic asked as he straddled Donald's chest.

His aide turned back. "There are soldiers around the air conditioner. They're checking the other barracks now. Now the lights just went out — it looks like the electricity's been shut off."

"You're a hero," the doctor said to Donald.

Am I? he thought as the blue sky went gray and then black.

There were shots, but the doctor paid no attention to them as he pressed his mouth to Donald's, pinched his nose shut, and gave him four quick ventilations.

He felt for his cartoid pulse, found none, then repeated the procedure. There was still no pulse.

Sliding from Donald's chest, the medic knelt beside him and put the middle finger of his right hand on the notch where the sternum meets the bottom of the rib cage. Then he placed the heel of his left hand on the lower half of the sternum beside the index finger and pressed, counting out eighty pushes each minute. His assistant held Donald's wrist, checking it for a pulse.

Five minutes later the medic sat back on the balls of his feet. The stretcher lay beside him and he helped his aide place Donald's body on it. Two soldiers carried it away as an officer walked over. They ignored the soldiers from the South who were looking on.

"Does he have any identification?"

"I didn't check."

"Whoever he was, he deserves a citation. Someone had rigged valved drums of gas to the air-conditioning systems of the four barracks on the east side. We caught him as he was about to turn them on."

"Just one man?"

"Yes. He probably wasn't alone, though he won't be telling us anything."

"Suicide?"

"Not exactly. As we closed in, he tried to spill the gas. We were forced to shoot." The officer looked at his watch. "I'd better inform General Hong-koo. He's on his way to meet that American Ambassador, and this may change things."

Tucked behind the trunk of a large oak, he watched as the small convoy of three jeeps neared the northern entrance of the conference building. They had come from the far northern side of the base where the General had his headquarters, and would park right beside the door of the structure, wait for the contingent from South Korea to arrive, and not exit until then. At least, that was probably the plan.

But if Lee had seen what he thought he had — Donald gunned down as he ran toward the barracks — there would be no contingent from the South. It also appeared that there would be no gas attack on the barracks. Those other shots, the lack of excitement at what should have already occurred — it was obvious the plan had gone seriously wrong.

His palm was dry, his grip on the pistol sure. If only he had used that against Donald, instead of the knife. It would have attracted attention, but he could have fled

No matter. Fate had handed him another opportunity, one that was almost as rich.

The cars stopped, and Lee's eyes came to rest on General Hong-koo, a small man with a wide mouth like a snake and, he'd heard, a disposition to match. The General would wait no more than twenty minutes before entering: when no one showed up, he would announce to the world that the North wanted peace, the South did not, and he would return to his headquarters.

That was surely the plan, he thought again. For Lee didn't intend to give him the chance to do either.

Roughly 150 yards separated Lee from Hong-koo's convoy. The General was sitting stiffly in the back of the middle jeep, a poor target now but not for long. As soon as he emerged from his jeep, Lee would run over, gun him down, and shoot as many of the six other men as he could before running back toward the tunnel.

Yet he was prepared to die, if he had to,

emerge as either a leader or a martyr. All of them had been ready to give their lives for this cause, for even if the bombing, the assassination, and Sun's attack against Tokyo didn't start a war, their acts would strengthen the hearts of those opposed to reunification.

Hong-koo's driver looked at his watch, turned, and said something to the General. The General nodded.

It was almost time . . . time for the United States to be driven from the South, for patriotism to flourish, and for a new militarism to rise, making South Korea the most powerful, prosperous, and feared nation in the region.

SEVENTY-SIX

Wednesday, 8:02 A.M., the road to Yangyang

Kim had buried nearly four million won in a cemetery east of the city. The equivalent of roughly five thousand U.S. dollars, she had hidden the won while kneeling at footstones, sitting on benches, and resting beneath trees, tucking the coins and bills in small holes, under roots, beneath rocks. All of it had still been there. People didn't come to cemeteries to look for hidden treasure.

It took her nearly three hours to recover all the money in the dark, after which she'd filled the car with gas and followed the Pukangang River toward the northeast and Lake Soyang. There, she had rested while she looked through her notebook for the name of someone from whom she could buy a passport and passage to Japan.

Sitting in the car, Kim had kept the radio

on, tuned to the frequency Hwan had used in his car to communicate with the KCIA. She wanted to hear if they had anything to say about her, and for a time it appeared that they had no clue as to her whereabouts or even what kind of car she was driving. Then, just a few minutes before she was about to leave, the KCIA found her Tercel at the BMW dealership. They were in the process of determining which car she had stolen when she was back on the road, headed toward the sea.

The two-lane road led through beautiful countryside, but it was deserted, and she began to grow concerned that she might not find another car. Her only hope was reaching Sorak-san National Park before the authorities found her. There were usually a great many tourists there, and there was a spacious parking lot just north of the Paektam-sa Temple on the park's west side. She could get there by way of the Taesungnyong Pass and headed in that direction.

Kim was sorry she'd stopped to rest at the lake. It had been a stupid idea, but the day had seemed endless . . . and then there was her guilt over the man she had killed. It had been surprisingly easy at the time: a good man was in danger and she had shot the man who was attacking him. Only when it was done did she realize she knew nothing about the assailant, or if she'd even acted in time, or whether the man she killed would have turned on her . . . or helped her to escape.

All that really mattered was that she'd murdered someone. The spy who wasn't a spy, the North Korean who had been damned to come here because she had loved her brother, had now committed the ultimate sin. She would always see his face as she shot him, shock and pain lit by the flash of a gun, a body crumbling raggedly, not flailing and arching the way it did in the movies. . . .

A clear voice came in over the radio, which was nestled in the passenger's seat.

"Chopper Seven, this is Sgt. Eui-soon. Over."

"Chopper Seven copies, over."

"The white BMW was seen fueling near the Tongdaemum Stadium Station about ninety minutes ago. It left headed east, which would put it past Inje by now. That's in your area. Over."

"We'll check it out and report back, over and out."

Kim cursed. She was just past Inje, which was at the northeastern tip of the lake, and they would be on her within minutes. The police in South Korea loved issuing summonses, and she dared not speed up — not without a registration for the car and millions of won stuffed in the radio carrying case on the floor. She stayed under the speed limit, looking desperately for a parked car, finding none, and finally reaching the park, with its craggy peaks and thundering waterfalls visible in the distance. Park rangers were not as difficult as the police, and she was about to speed up to get to the parking lot when she heard the distant beating of a helicopter rotor.

She pushed the gas to the floor, looking for someplace to pull off the road. She had finally decided to abandon the car and continue on foot when the helicopter passed over her, made an arcing turn, and came back.

She braked hard.

The helicopter hovered some two hundred feet up, facing her, the two men inside pointing. She heard a shrill whistle as the loudspeaker was turned on.

"There are ground personnel on the way," the speaker said. "You are advised to remain where you are."

"And if I don't?" she said under her breath. "What are they going to do?"

She scanned the road ahead. About two miles off it started a sinuous course into the mountains, and it would be difficult for cars to chase or the chopper to follow.

To hell with them, she thought and, flooring the gas pedal, the BMW screamed out from under the helicopter toward the blue-gray peaks beyond.

SEVENTY-SEVEN

Wednesday, 6:05 A.M., Op-Center

Hood was in his office with Ann Farris and Lowell Coffey, debating about how to handle news of the Striker incursion in case the team was captured or killed. The White House would disavow the operation, as the President had said, and SOP was that Op-Center would do the same. But Ann felt there were some PR brownie points to be gained by letting the world know that they had been looking out for the well-being of Japan, and while Hood agreed she had a point, he was disinclined to go along with the idea.

When Bugs told Hood that General Schneider was calling with urgent news from Panmunjom, the debate came to a swift end.

"Hood here."

"Mr. Director," General Schneider said,

"I regret to inform you that your man Gregory Donald appears to have been shot to death by the Dee-Perks on their side of the border just a few minutes ago."

Hood's face paled. "General, they invited him to come over — "

"This wasn't that meeting. He wasn't in the meeting center."

"Then where was he?"

"He was running toward the barracks with a knife."

"Gregory was? Are you *sure?*"

"That's what the watch officer's putting in his report. And that he was screaming in Korean about the poison gas."

"Sweet Jesus." Hood shut his eyes. "That's what it was. Gregory, Jesus . . . why didn't he let the military handle it?"

"Paul," Ann said, "what happened?"

"Gregory Donald's dead. He was trying to stop the gas." He returned to Schneider. "General, Major Lee must have snuck the gas into the North — Gregory was probably following him."

"That's what we figure, but it was a damn foolish thing to do. He had to know those troops would shoot on sight."

It wasn't foolish, Hood knew. *It was Donald's way.* "What's the present situation?"

"Our lookouts say the soldiers appear to

475

have shot someone who may have been trying to flood the barracks with the tabun. As I just told Secretary Colon, they're running around like headless chickens over there. One of our towers is watching General Hong-koo. He's just sitting at their side of the conference hut in a jeep . . . waiting for we don't know what. He's got to know Donald isn't coming."

"He might not know that it was Donald who was killed."

The words sounded so wrong. Hood looked at Ann for support, saw only the same sadness that he felt.

"He'll find out soon enough. Our problem is this. The Pentagon has contacted Pyongyang and they don't believe that Lee and his team were acting alone; they think it's part of a plot hatched in Seoul. You can't reason with those pricks."

"What are we doing in response?"

"Matching them. General Norbom is shipping us just about everyone and everything he's got, direct orders from the President himself. Somebody sneezes up here and we're going to have ourselves a shooting war."

General Schneider excused himself then, leaving Hood sick and angry when he got off the phone. He felt like they'd been through a full season of winning football only to lose the championship on the last play of the last game. At this point, the only thing worse would be if Mike Rodgers and the Striker team did something that actually precipitated the final conflict. He thought briefly about recalling them, but knew that Rodgers wouldn't do anything rash. And there was still the fact that the missiles were pointed toward Japan. If Japan was hit, then war or no war the cry for remilitarization there would be unstoppable. That would cause China and both Koreas to build up their own military forces, creating an arms race that would rival the Cold War of the 1960s.

After bringing Ann and Coffey up-to-date, Hood asked them to brief the rest of Op-Center's department heads. When they were gone, he put his forehead in his hands —

And it hit him. *Pyongyang's not going to believe anyone from the South about this, but what about someone from the North?*

He buzzed his assistant.

"Bugs, Kim Hwan is at National University Hospital in Seoul. If he's out of surgery and awake, I want to talk to him."

"Yes, sir. Secure line?"

"There's no time to wait for one to be brought in. And, Bugs? Don't let any of the doctors or KCIA guys get in your way. Go

477

through Director Yung-Hoon if you have to."

As he waited for Bugs, Hood rang Herbert.

"Bob — I want you to arrange for a broadcast to that frequency from Yanguu."

"*To* it," Herbert repeated.

"That's right. We're going to try to set up a game of telephone that may stop a war."

SEVENTY-EIGHT

Wednesday, 8:10 A.M., Seoul

Kim Hwan was drowsing when Choi Hong-tack touched him on the shoulder.

"Mr. Hwan?"

Hwan opened his eyes slowly. "Yes — what is it?"

"I'm sorry to disturb you, but there's a telephone call from Mr. Paul Hood in Washington."

Hongtack was holding the telephone receiver toward him. With considerable effort, Hwan reached over and accepted it. He lay it on the pillow beside his ear and turned his head toward it.

"Hello, Paul," he said weakly.

"Kim — how do you feel?"

"It beats the alternative."

"Touché. Kim, time's short so I'll get right to the point. We found the man behind the

479

bombing, a South Korean officer, and —
I'm sorry to have to tell you this — but
Gregory Donald was killed trying to appre-
hend one of his cohorts."

Hwan felt like he'd been stabbed again.
He couldn't breathe and his insides burned.

"I wish there was some way I could have
softened this," Hood said, "or at least
waited. But the North Koreans don't believe that the group was acting alone and
are ready to go to war over this. Are you
with me?"

"Yes," Hwan said, choking.

"We intercepted a message from Seoul Oh-
Miyo before. Can you still reach her?"

"I — I don't know."

"Well, Kim, we need someone the North
Koreans trust to tell them that this is not
an official act of the South Korean government. We've got the frequency of the radio
she used and we think we can get to it. If
she's left it on, will you talk to her? Ask
her to radio the North and try to convince
them?"

"Yes," Hwan said. Tears trickling from
his eyes, he motioned for Hongtack to help
him sit up. "I'll do whatever I can."

"Good man," Hood said. "Hold on while
I make sure things are set on this end."

As he waited, Hwan ignored the questioning glances of Hongtack. Even if war was averted, what a monstrous tragedy this day had already been. And for what? The kind of military and political machinations that Gregory had always hated.

Talk, he said. *Talk and art are all that separate us from the other animals. Use them and savor them fully. . . .*

It was so unjust. And worst of all was the fact that the man to whom he would have turned for consolation was no longer here.

"Kim?"

Hwan pressed the phone to his ear and struggled against the lingering effects of the anesthesia that threatened to drag him back to sleep.

"I'm here, Paul."

"Kim, there's a problem — "

Over the crackle of static, a frantic voice cut Hood off.

"They're threatening to shoot me!"

Hwan was instantly alert as he recognized Kim Chong's voice. "Kim, this is Hwan. Can you hear me?"

"Yes — !"

"Who's threatening you?"

"There's a helicopter — and two motorcycles are on the way. I'm parked on a mountain . . . I can see them below."

481

Hwan's eyes fastened on Hongtack. "Are they ours?"

"I don't know," said Hongtack. "Director Yung-Hoon said there were too many agencies involved to — "

"I don't care if God himself is involved. Call them off."

"Sir — "

"Hongtack, you get on another telephone and tell Director Yung-Hoon that I accept full responsibility for Ms. Chong. Tell him that now, or tomorrow you join the U.S. team doing radio surveillance in McMurdo."

After hesitating, appearing to weigh his dignity against a tour in Antarctica, Hongtack left the hospital room.

Hwan returned to the phone. "I've taken care of it, Kim. Where are you?"

"I'm in the mountains of Sorak-san National Park. I've pulled under a ledge where the helicopter can't land."

"All right. You're to go see my uncle Zon Pak in Yangyang. He's a fisherman; no one likes him, but everyone knows him. I'll phone ahead and he'll get you safely where you need to go. Now, did Mr. Hood explain our problem?"

"Yes. He told me about Major Lee."

"Can you help? *Will* you help?"

"Yes, of course. Stay on the line and I'll

radio Pyongyang."

"Will you plug in the headset so you can hear Mr. Hood and me without them hearing us?"

Kim told Hwan she would, and he listened as the hospital-to-Op-Center-to-Sorak-san link took on one more participant: Captain Ahn Il at "Home," which Hwan knew was the North Korean Intelligence Agency's headquarters in the capital, located in the sub-basements of the Haebangsang Hotel on the west bank of the Taedong River.

"Home," Kim said, "I have received incontrovertible evidence that a cell of South Korean soldiers, and not — repeat, *not* — the government or military in Seoul, was behind today's bombing and the attempted gassing at the base. Major Lee, the officer with the eyepatch, is the person behind the entire operation."

There was a moment of silence, then: "Seoul Oh-Miyo, what man with the eyepatch?"

"The man who was handling the poison gas."

"No such man was involved."

Paul said, "Ms. Chong, please tell him to wait. I'm going to try and find Major Lee — and if I do, they'll have to act quickly to stop him."

483

SEVENTY-NINE

Wednesday, 6:17 A.M., Op-Center

Paul Hood put Kim Hwan on hold and rang Bob Herbert.

"Bob, do we have a photo of Major Lee?"

"It's in his dossier — "

"Scan it over to NRO fast, then come here with Lowell Coffey, McCaskey, and Mackall."

Hood called over to Stephen Viens at NRO.

"Steve, you've got a photo coming in from Bob Herbert. The man may still be on the North side of the DMZ in Panmunjom: I need to find and track him. Check the area near the conference center first — give me two satellites on it."

"Secretary Colon has authorized the second eye, right?"

"He would if he knew about it," Hood said dryly.

"That's what I figured," Viens said. "The mug shot's coming through now. Will the subject be alone?"

"Most likely," said Hood, "and in a ROK uniform. I want to watch as the pictures come in."

"Hold on."

Hood listened as Viens ordered a second satellite camera turned on the area, and ordered it to look down from a relative height of twenty-five feet. Then he had Major Lee's photograph fed into the satellite computer: it would search the area for anyone with those features and outline him in blue.

The roof of the conference center appeared; he wasn't there, or the watchtowers on both sides would have spotted him. Then, 4.4 seconds later, staggered with images from the first, the second satellite gave them a photograph of the area in front of the building — the small caravan and the jeep with what was probably General Hong-koo.

Bob Herbert came wheeling in, followed by Martha, Coffey, McCaskey, and Ann Farris. Hood had a feeling she'd come, not so much to check on the crisis but to look after him. Her mothering made him both uncomfortable and strangely content, though he let the discomfort go for now. He'd liked how her hand felt on his shoulder before.

"Darrell," Hood said, "why is Hong-koo just sitting there? He has to know by now what's happened."

"It wouldn't matter," Martha answered for him. Darrell shot her a look. "The North Koreans would still have a party even if the birthday boy was shot dead. They like being unflappable. A holdover of President Kim Il Sung's ideology of *juche* — self-reliance."

Ann said, "He'll probably use the forum to make a political statement of some kind."

"How they've been attacked and have exhibited enormous self-control by not responding," Martha said.

Darrell threw up his hands and sat down.

Hood watched intently as the pictures continued to come in, on the upper left and lower right of his computer, respectively. The arrival of each one was marked by a second-long whir of the hard disk as it stored the images; a code number in the bottom right of each picture — the sequential number followed by a "1S" for "First Sweep" — would allow it to be brought back instantly. The computer could also enhance the images with greater clarity, brightness, and even change the angle from directly above to head-on by extrapolating from information in the picture.

"Hold 17-1S," Hood barked, sitting up in

his chair. "The lone figure standing behind the tree one hundred and something yards from the caravan — "

Bob and Darrell came around to look.

"His face is hidden by leaves," said Viens. "Let me move the camera over a bit."

A bit meant thousandths of an inch that, magnified by the satellite's distance from the Earth, would give them a different angle by a foot or more.

The new picture came in and it immediately began to shine with a faint blue line.

"Canasta!" said Viens. "I'm locking on him with the other satellite."

"No. I want an overview of the area — give it to me from a quarter mile."

"Gotcha," said Viens.

Hood took the second phone line off hold, watched as the next photo showed Lee turning his body slightly toward the General's car. Hood had the same eerie feeling he got whenever he watched the Zapruder film of the Kennedy assassination: the event was happening and he was powerless to stop it.

The next photograph of Lee came up. He was clearly moving from behind the tree.

"Ms. Chong, can you hear me?" Hood said.

"Yes!"

"Tell your people that the rogue officer is emerging from behind an oak tree one

487

hundred and thirty or forty yards north of the conference area. We believe he intends to attack General Hong-koo. Tell your people to stop Major Lee by any means necessary."

"I understand," she said, and relayed the message.

While she did so, Hood told Bugs to get General Schneider on the phone. As Bugs hurried to make the connection, Hood watched Lee continue to move from behind the oak. He was holding a gun. The men below him were watching General Hong-koo as he stood in his jeep, ready to emerge. In the larger picture, Hood saw the entire conference area, and both the immediate north and south sides of the DMZ. What he had been hoping to see was there — on the South side, roughly three hundred yards southwest of Lee.

"I've got General Schneider!" Bugs said. He patched Hood through to the commander's field phone as he oversaw the deployment of the troops.

"Hood," the General snapped, "I wouldn't even be talking to you now if you weren't head of the crisis — "

"Major Lee is behind the conference center, North side."

"What?"

Hood said urgently, "You should be able to see it from your watchtowers southwest of the center. You've got a rifleman up there?"

"Yes — "

"Then use him. *Fast!*"

"You want me to shoot one of our own officers . . . *and* fire into North Korea?" Schneider said.

"Isn't that what you've been wanting? Lee is armed and he's going to kill Hong-koo. You've got to *stop* him or a minute from now you'll be up to your goddamn neck in bodies!"

"What about my man in the tower? They'll fire back — "

"Hopefully not. My people are talking to them now."

" 'Hopefully,' " Schneider snorted. "Mister, I'll give the order, but this one's entirely *your* ass."

Schneider signed off, and Hood asked Viens to keep one satellite on Lee, the other on the watchtower.

The second image moved in closer, showed one of the two soldiers picking up his phone, the other looking through field glasses.

The first image showed Lee boldly approaching Hong-koo.

The second image showed the man with

489

the binoculars lowering them.

Lee was closer now — close enough so that he and Hong-koo were in the same image. Hong-koo was stepping from the jeep on the passenger's side, his men forming a semicircle around him, an honor guard. Reporters and photographers were off to the sides.

The soldier in the watchtower picked up his rifle.

Lee raised his gun.

The soldier put the stock of the Colt M16 to his shoulder.

Hood's gut was a furnace, his mouth painfully dry. A second late, one word too many, might be what plunged the peninsula into war —

Photo flashes flared as Lee's gun went off. Hood's heart pushed against his throat as the watchtower soldier stood with the rifle in position. It seemed an eternity before the next set of pictures arrived.

Lee's face was turned away, apparently in response to the flashes. Hong-koo was falling backward with what appeared to be a splotch on his upper right arm.

The M16 spit smoke.

Hood had a curious flashback to when he was a kid, hiding in the muted, woolly quiet of his parents' cedar closet. The silence in his office was that thick.

The next photograph of the North Korean side showed General Hong-koo on his back, holding his arm. Nearby, Lee still stood, smoke rising from his gun . . . his head entirely obscured by a cloud of blood.

"They did it," Herbert said, clenching a fist and shaking it.

McCaskey patted Hood on the back.

In the next photograph, Lee was falling and Hong-koo was rising. To the south, the men in the watchtower were ducking.

"Mr. Hood?" Kim Chong said. "I've given them your message and they're relaying it to Panmunjom."

"Do you think they believed you?"

"Of course," she said. "I'm a spy, not a politician."

Hood rose and Ann came over and hugged him. "You did it, Paul."

Coffey watched unhappily. "Right. We killed a South Korean officer. There *will* be repercussions."

"He was crazy," said Herbert. "We shot a rabid dog."

"Who may have a family. Rabid dogs don't have rights; soldiers and next of kin do."

Bugs interrupted with a call from General Schneider. Hood told him to try to raise Mike Rodgers, then sat on the edge of his desk and picked up the phone.

"Yes, General?"

"Looks like you may have pulled this one out. There's no shooting — the North Koreans seem to be waiting."

"Can you see General Hong-koo?"

"No," said Schneider. "My boys up there are still ducking."

Hood looked at the monitor. "Well, the General's sitting up in the jeep, holding a handkerchief or cloth to a wound in his shoulder. Now they're driving away. Looks like he's okay."

"Colon's still going to shit."

"I don't know," said Hood. "The President may like how this worked out — self-policing plays well in the press. So does taking a hard line with an ally we've been underwriting for forty-plus — "

"Excuse me, sir," Bugs interrupted, "but I have Lt. Col. Squires on the TAC SAT. I think you'll want to talk to him."

Elation was replaced by a fresh wave of burning in his gut as Hood was plugged through and listened to what Rodgers was attempting. . . .

EIGHTY

Wednesday, 9:00 A.M., the Diamond Mountains

The trip down the hill was slower than Rodgers had hoped. They had gone over four hundred yards around the troops stationed below and had crept down on their bellies, feetfirst, to keep as low a profile as possible. Sharp rocks poked at them, thorny plants stabbed their bare arms, and the grade was exceedingly steep the lower they got. Several times, each man had lost his footing and had to dig at the rocks, hand and foot, to keep from sliding into the camp. Rodgers realized that that had to be the reason the command tent had been pitched where it was: in daylight it was difficult enough to approach. In the dark, even with night-vision glasses, it would have been virtually impossible to get to.

Rodgers was in front, Moore and then

Puckett behind; he stopped them behind a boulder twenty yards above the tent. With his two men behind the rock, Rodgers leaned around to watch for signs of activity below.

He heard soft, very muted voices, but saw no movement within.

Damn strange, he thought. This wasn't standard operating procedure at all. Once the Nodongs were raised and targeted, it was typical for commanders to be in the field: a launch order would never be given over the phone, but in person. It frustrated Rodgers that he couldn't make out what was being said in the tent, not that it really mattered. The only way they were going to stop the missiles from being launched was to get in there and persuade whoever was in charge to lower them. Though he couldn't hear, he was willing to bet his pension that it wasn't the North Koreans who were calling the shots.

He leaned back toward the others. "There are two or three men inside the tent," he whispered. "We'll go in right below, on the back side. Moore — you cut us a doorway, then step to the left. It'll have to be fast. I'll go in first, then Puckett, and you follow us. I'll cover the left side; Puckett, you take the right; and Moore covers the front. We go in with guns, not knives — we don't

494

want anyone even to think about calling for reinforcements."

Both men nodded. Drawing his knife, Moore inched down the last stretch of slope, feetfirst, his back to the rock. His Beretta drawn, Rodgers set out behind him with Puckett bringing up the rear.

Upon reaching the bottom, Moore waited for the others. The three men crouched in the relative dark behind the tent, Rodgers listening as Moore crept over.

". . . will find that I have a great deal of support here," someone was saying. "Your own people made this possible. Reunification, like remarriage, is a precious notion, but ultimately impractical."

The South Koreans have obviously taken over here, Rodgers thought. He watched as Moore rose slowly beside the tent, the long knife in his left hand, pointing down and ready to strike. Rodgers made his way over, Puckett behind him, both crouched on the balls of their feet, ready to jump in.

If only he knew who was the infiltrator and who was the DPRK officer. He would kill the former without hesitation.

Moore nodded once, then pushed the hilt bottom with his right hand. The blade tore through the fabric, Moore pulled down, and then he stepped aside. Rodgers leapt through, stepping to the left and pointing his gun at the Colonel sitting on the cot: he was bald and holding a bloody cloth around his hand. From his wound, and the fact that he was unarmed, Rodgers knew at once that this was the North Korean officer and that he was a prisoner of the other two. Puckett jumped through, pointing his gun at the officer standing on the right side of the tent. He grabbed the Type 64 pistol before it could be fired and put his own Beretta to the Colonel's forehead.

Moore came in next as Kong, beside the front flap, held up his left hand and dropped the Type 64 he was holding in it. His gun pointed at the big orderly's head, Moore stooped to pick up the gun.

His right hand behind him, Kong whipped the TT33 Tokarev from his belt and fired into Moore's left eye. The soldier fell back and Kong aimed at Puckett.

Rodgers had been watching Kong, and when he saw the big man's right hand slip behind his back, he had swung his own gun around. The General was not quick enough to save Moore, but he put a bullet into Kong's forehead before he could fire at Puckett. The orderly crumpled to the floor of the tent, slumped against the flap, causing it to bulge out.

Puckett's jaw was set like iron, his eyes aflame. "Don't you *move,* dirtbag."

Rodgers heard soldiers yelling outside. He looked down at the officer on the cot.

"I've got to trust you," Rodgers said, not sure he was being understood. "We need those missiles stopped."

He made a point of aiming the gun away and stepped back. He motioned for Ki-Soo to rise.

The officer bowed slightly.

"You traitors!" Colonel Sun shouted. "See how a patriot dies!"

Sun reached forward and pulled Puckett's arm toward him. Reacting as he'd been trained to do in an attack situation, the Private fired. Sun groaned, folded at the middle, and fell at Puckett's feet.

Rodgers dropped to his side and felt for a pulse. "He's gone," he said. He turned to Moore. He had known that the Private was dead, but picked up his wrist anyway. He pulled a blanket from the cot and handed it to Puckett, who draped it over Moore's body.

"Colonel," Rodgers said, "do you speak English?"

Ki-Soo shook his head.

"Pu-t'ak hamnida," Rodgers used one of the few Korean words he knew. "Please.

497

The Nodongs — Tokyo."

Ki-Soo nodded as soldiers appeared in the doorway. He held them back with a raised hand and barked command. Then he pointed to the dead man.

He said a word Rodgers didn't recognize. Then the Colonel thought for a moment and said, *"Il ha-na, i tul, sam set. . . ."*

"One, two, three," Rodgers said. "You're counting. Countdown? No — you'd go backward."

"Chil il-gop, sa net, il ha-na. . . ." Ki-Soo continued.

"Seven, four, one — a code? The password?" Rodgers felt a chill run up and down his back. He pointed to the dead officer. "You're telling me that *he* changed the passwords. That's why he killed himself, so we can't get them out of him." He thought quickly. The Nodong circuitry was in a box rigged to fire the missile if tampered with. There was no way to stop them unless they got the code. "How long?" Rodgers asked. *"On-che-im-ni-ka?"*

Ki-Soo looked at one of the soldiers standing in the door. He asked him the same question, and the soldier answered.

The only word Rodgers recognized was *"ship yol."*

Ten.

They had ten minutes until the three Nodongs were fired toward Tokyo.

Quickly he used Ki-Soo's radio to call Squires and asked to be patched into the TAC SAT.

EIGHTY-ONE

Wednesday, 7:20 P.M., Op-Center

Hood and his top aides were still in his office when the call came through from Rodgers. Hood put it on speaker and the others gathered around.

"Paul," said the Deputy Director, "I'm in the Nodong camp, using their radio through the TAC SAT up in the hills. South Koreans had taken over — we lost Bass Moore getting it back. Colonel Ki-Soo here is being very cooperative . . . but he does *not* know the cancel code. The South Koreans changed it, and they're dead. We've got just over eight minutes until the things take off, headed for Tokyo."

"Not enough time to bring in planes from the South or North," Hood said.

"Exactly."

"Give me a minute," Hood said and

punched up Matt Stoll on the computer. "Matty, bring up the file on the Nodongs. How do we stop them without a password?"

Stoll's face disappeared, replaced with the Nodong file. He scrolled through, past schematics and lists of specifics.

"Control circuits encased in two inches of steel to protect during launch . . . let me see. We've got three rows of numerals. The top row is a countdown clock. Middle row is the launch coordinates. The four numbers that allow you to change the target remain on display for one minute after inputting. That gives you a chance to change them before they lock in. After that, four numbers appear in the bottom row serving as a kind of double-lock system. You can't get to the middle numbers unless you input the bottom row first. They leave after a minute too. So . . . all you have to do is set the first four numbers, the middle numbers, at zero-zero-zero-zero and they won't fire."

"But you need to get into the program to do that."

"Correct."

"And we don't have that second set of four numbers."

"In that case, you can't do anything. And to input every possible combination of four numbers from zero through nine would take — "

"I've got about seven minutes."

"— longer than that," Stoll said. Suddenly his voice brightened. "Hold on a second, Paul. I may have something."

The Nodong file disappeared, replaced with a photograph of the site.

"Give me a second," Stoll said.

Over the phone, Hood heard the keys of Stoll's computer clicking. He looked at the countdown clock. He wanted to reach out and put his palms on the numbers, slow them down, give them more time to do this. Once again, to have come so far only to fail, for all those lives to have been wasted, was something you never found in the job description.

"Martha," Hood said while Stoll worked, "you'd better call Burkow at the White House. Brief him: the President may have to put in a call to Tokyo."

"Oh, they're both going to love that," Martha said as she walked to the door.

"I'll buzz you in your office when I have news," Hood said.

Bob Herbert said, "I have faith that somehow, the U.S. is going to end up getting blamed for everything that's happened today."

"Today's not over," Hood found himself pep-talking, refusing to allow himself to believe that the final gun had been fired.

Hood continued to watch the screen as the picture of the Nodongs was enlarged and enhanced. One of the missiles became larger by a factor of ten every five seconds.

"Damn, I'm good," Stoll said. "You see what we've got down there, Paul?"

"The Nodongs — "

"Yes, but this is the photograph I took when we came back on-line," Stoll said.

Hood learned forward. "You *are* brilliant, you son of a bitch." He examined the screen and frowned. *"Shit!"*

They could read three of the four numbers in the bottom row: one, nine, eight. Whoever had programmed the numbers was blocking the last one on the right.

"My guess is the last number's an eight," Stoll said. "That's been a recurring theme today."

"Let's hope you're right," Hood said as he got back on the phone to Rodgers.

"Mike, you've got to program the missiles as follows: one-nine-eight-eight on the bottom row, zero-zero-zero-zero in the middle row. Repeat — "

"Nineteen eighty-eight on bottom, four

503

zips in the center. Stay on the line."

"Don't worry," Hood said under his breath. "I'm not going anywhere."

EIGHTY-TWO

Wednesday, 9:24 A.M., the Diamond Mountains

The foliage canopies were lying beside the missiles, which glistened like polished ivory in the young sun.

Rodgers climbed up to the control panel of the nearest Nodong and told Puckett to punch the two codes into the second, Colonel Ki-Soo into the third. A medic was following him, snarling with rage as he tried to bandage his hand on the run.

Rodgers hit one-nine-eight-eight, then stood there expectantly waiting for the middle row of numbers to light up.

They didn't.

"Nothing happened here, sir," Puckett said.

"I know, soldier," Rodgers said.

He didn't bother trying the numbers again. Not with four minutes twenty-five seconds on the countdown clock. He ran back to the tent.

"Paul," he said, "it didn't work. You *sure* about those numbers?"

"The one-nine-eight part," he admitted. "We're not sure about the last one."

"Great," Rodgers snarled as he bolted from the tent.

He thought as he ran back to the Nodong. *Less than five minutes. Takes about five seconds for each goddamn number to click in. That doesn't leave much time.*

"Private Puckett," Rodgers yelled, "start with nineteen-eighty and — "

A soldier, festooned with medals, came running up to the Nodong on which Puckett was standing. He pushed the soldier off, where Rodgers couldn't see, whipped out his pistol, and fired once toward the ground. Then he turned and emptied several rounds into the keypad before Ki-Soo could order his men over. The North Koreans wrestled him to the ground, screaming.

Squires's voice crackled over the field radio. "We heard that shot. What was it?"

Rodgers whipped it from the strap on his belt. "Someone doesn't like us being here," he said. "Don't worry. They've got him."

"Sure feels useless up here, sir," Squires said.

Rodgers didn't answer; he understood. But he had bigger problems right now.

The medic left Ki-Soo's side and ran to Puckett. Fighting the urge to join him, Rodgers climbed up to the nearest Nodong and started punching in numbers.

One-nine-eight-zero.

Nothing.

One-nine-eight-one.

Nothing. Nothing until he reached one-nine-eight-nine. There was a beep, the middle row lit up, and he quickly changed the numbers to zero-zero-zero-zero. As he did so, the missile began to lower.

The top clock read two minutes two seconds. He ran to Puckett's missile. The keypad was shattered beyond repair, but at least Puckett was alive. The doctor had pulled away his shirt and was wiping blood from a shoulder wound.

"Colonel!" Rodgers said as he jumped off the missile. He put his hands against the side of the truck. "We've got to *push* . . . push it over so it fires into the hills out there." He pointed. "Deserted — no one dies."

Ki-Soo understood and ordered his men over. While the doctor dragged Puckett out of the way, fifteen men ran to one side of the missile and began pushing. Ki-Soo went around the truck and shot out the tires on that side. While the colonel's men pushed, Rodgers headed toward the last missile. *There's still time,* he told himself. *We're going to do it —*

Behind him, he heard a metal stanchion groan as the weight of the missile shifted. Without stopping, he looked back as the entire truck-and-rocket assembly slanted, the missile sliding to one side of its gantrylike support — and the men shouting as smoke began to pour from the back, followed by a jet of yellow-orange flame. The Nodong had ignited as the truck went over.

That's impossible! Rodgers thought as he hit the dirt and covered his head. Tipping the truck over wouldn't cause the missile to launch.

Men ran in all directions from the spire of flame as the missile left the overturned truck and rocketed along the ground, ripping up tents, jeeps, and trees as it blazed across the terrain. It shot through everything in its path for nearly a half a mile before impacting against the side of a hill, sending a fireball over a thousand feet in the air and a searing shock wave back toward the base.

When he felt the rolling heat pass over him, Rodgers was up and running toward the last of the Nodongs.

He had a sick feeling as he ran — a sense that the South Korean officer was going to have the last laugh. They'd all assumed that the missiles had been programmed to launch at the same time.

But what if they hadn't? Why would they? He went from one to the other to the other. There might be minutes between each one. The first missile programmed had just gone off. The one he'd deprogrammed could have been the second one the South Korean programmed or it might have been the third. Which meant he might have just a minute or so, or —

When Rodgers was just twenty yards from the Nodong, he saw the tail begin to smoke.

And then it hit him hard. *The timers were set differently.* Of course. Why *wouldn't* they be?

There wouldn't be time to scramble jets or fire air-to-air missiles, not with a missile capable of speeds of over two thousand miles an hour. And even Patriot missiles fired from Japan were chancy: what if the Nodong didn't pass near any of them?

"Colonel!" Rodgers shouted as he started running back toward Ki-Soo.

There was only one chance, and he suspected the officer was ahead of him. As the Nodong hissed on its launcher and erupted in flame, Ki-Soo was already shouting into his radio and his men were quickly seeking cover behind rocks and under ledges.

Good man, Rodgers thought as he literally dove over the smoking remains of a jeep destroyed by the last Nodong. He landed hard on his side and threw his arms over his head just as the last missile took off on a bright finger of flame, roaring like an unchained dragon as it sliced through the morning sky.

Then Rodgers thought about Squires and the Striker team, and he scrambled to pull the field radio from his belt. But it had been smashed when he fell on it, and all he could do was pray that they didn't misunderstand what they were seeing. . . .

EIGHTY-THREE

Wednesday, 7:35 P.M., Op-Center

"Bad news, Paul," Stephen Viens said over the phone from the NRO. "It looks to me like one of the Nodongs got away from them."

"When?"

"Seconds ago. We saw it light up — we're waiting for the next pictures."

"Is Hephaestus watching?" Hood asked.

"Yes. We'll let you know where she's headed."

"I'll stay on the line," Hood said, and put the secure line on speaker. He looked at Darrell McCaskey and Bob Herbert, who were both in his office.

"What is it, chief?" Herbert asked.

"One Nodong was launched," he said, "headed for Japan. Bob, find out if there's an AWACS in the area and tell the Pentagon they'd better scramble fighters out of Osaka."

"They'll never intercept it," Herbert said. "That's like finding a needle in a haystack the size of Georgia."

"I *know*," Hood said, "but we have to try. Coming right at it, they may get lucky. Darrell, NRO will pick up the missile's heat signature on the Hephaestus satellite. We'll get the trajectory so that at least we can give the flyboys a general vicinity to look." He fell silent for a moment. *All the lives,* he thought. *The President will have to be told at once so he can telephone the Japanese Prime Minister.* "Maybe we'll be able to give the people on the ground a few minutes to seek cover," Hood said. "At least that's something."

"Right," McCaskey said.

Hood was about to phone the White House on his second line when Viens stopped him short.

"Paul — we've got something else on the screen now."

"What?"

"Flashes," Viens said. "More than I've seen since Baghdad on the first night of Desert Storm."

"What kind?" Hood asked.

"I'm not sure — we're waiting for the next picture. But this is un-freaking-believable!"

EIGHTY-FOUR

Wednesday, 9:36 A.M., the Diamond Mountains

Perched behind his field glasses, Lt. Col. Squires watched as the Nodong rose and the antiaircraft guns opened fire.

His initial thought was that an aerial attack was underway, and his first impulse was to disperse the men and attack the gun positions. But why would they be firing the shells *into* one another? For incoming aircraft, they'd turn them in the direction from which the radar said the planes were coming. Then he saw the guns actually *lower* as they fired, and he understood.

The clip-fed 37mm shells zipped skyward from all sides of the perimeter, two guns on each side, setting up a shield of explosive fire roughly one thousand feet over the Nodong site. Radar-guided shells were colliding one into the other, replaced by new shells every half-second.

The North Koreans were erecting a barrier, trying to shoot down their own missile. The Nodong was speeding up — one hundred, two hundred feet up and accelerating, rising toward the cross fire. The shells stitched the morning sky as the barrels continued to descend, their loud "pops" sounding like firecrackers tossed into a barrel. The image reminded Squires of a trick candle burning down, the explosions getting lower as the rocket rose.

Only two or three seconds had passed since the Nodong was launched, but the missile was already just instants away from the flashing, sparking barrier. There was no guarantee that the antiaircraft fire could stop it, and there was always the chance that the bursts would only cripple it or knock it off course, send it hurtling down or toward villages in the North or South.

Fire rained down on the Nodong site, like the burning hail of the Bible, setting tents and vehicles afire. Squires hoped that Rodgers and the men were okay — and that if the missile did explode, the conflagration didn't take the men on the ground with it.

How many times had his heart beat since the Nodong took off? *Just a few,* he told himself. Now it felt like it had stopped as the nose of the missile rose into the ceiling of flak.

It was like a dream, a slow-motion hell of flame and metal as the shells crashed into the missile from top to bottom, kicking it from side to side like an ambushed hood in a gangster movie. The bursting sounds were replaced by a heavy drone of *pock-pock-pocks* each time a shell connected.

In an instant, the flak worked its way from top to middle to the fiery bottom of the missile, and then everything in front of Squires went from blue to red as the sky exploded.

EIGHTY-FIVE

Wednesday, 9:37 A.M., the Diamond Mountains

Rodgers had listened to the shells exploding, heard pieces of flak sizzle earthward around him. Though he knew that the face of the Medusa was not far behind, he had to see, had to know for sure what was happening, and so he lifted his arms from around his head and squinted skyward to watch.

The fury and spectacle of what he saw took his breath away.

Of all the historians and philosophers and playwrights he had studied and could quote from memory, only one figure, an attorney, came to mind as he witnessed the spectacle of the missile rising into the wall of popping shells.

"... *and the rocket's red glare, the bombs bursting in air ...*"

The brash Nodong tried to push its way

through the wall of explosives and was ripped and blasted, exploding with a fury that made it seem just feet away and not a quarter of a mile.

Rodgers covered his head again, the heat of the blast searing the hairs on the back of his hands and wrists, the sweat on his back going from cool to hot in an instant. He pressed his second and third fingers to his ears to block out the sound of the blast that came a moment later, slamming down so hard that his chest literally felt like a drum.

Then the flaming debris from the destroyed Nodong came pouring from the skies, some in coin-sized fragments, others in chunks the size of plates. They crashed and thudded around him as he tucked himself tightly against and partly under the destroyed jeep, screaming and jerking hard as a thumbnail-sized piece landed on his shin, burning through his pant leg.

Moments later there was silence, heavy and deep, followed by the sounds of men stirring and calling to one another.

Rodgers's bones creaked and popped as he extricated himself from the jeep, leaned back on the balls of his feet, and looked up at the sky. Save for fast-dissipating wisps of dark smoke, it was clear.

Rodgers rose, saw that Ki-Soo was all right, that most of his men were shaken, a few bloodied, but were also unhurt.

The American saluted the Colonel, and now it was Shakespeare who seemed appropriate:

"For never anything can be amiss,
When simpleness and duty tender it."

EIGHTY-SIX

Wednesday, 9:50 A.M., the Diamond Mountains

When Rodgers was able to make Ki-Soo understand that they had a team in the hills, the Colonel sent a truck up to collect the men. Most of the Americans were edgy as they arrived in the camp, but Squires was glad to see Rodgers and Puckett was happy to see his radio. The Lieutenant Colonel left it with him as the North Korean medic saw to his shoulder wound.

"Glad you held your fire," Rodgers said as he took a drink from Squires's canteen. "I was afraid you might try sharpshooting the men on the guns."

"I might've," Squires said, "if they hadn't been firing all the guns at once. Took a second, but I figured out what they were doing."

Puckett was the one who answered when

Hood called from Op-Center. Rodgers and Squires had been standing off by a jeep, with Moore's covered body in the back; when the call came through, Rodgers rushed over, followed by Squires.

"Yes, sir," said Puckett. "The General is right here."

He handed the headphones to Rodgers.

"Morning, Paul."

"Good evening, Mike. You guys pulled off a miracle there. Congratulations."

Rodgers was silent for a moment. "It cost us, Paul."

"I know but I don't want you second-guessing anything you did," Hood said. "We lost some good people today, but that's the lousy price of the business we're in."

"I know that," Rodgers said. "But that isn't what you tell yourself when you put your head on the pillow at night. I'll be replaying this for a good long time."

"Just make sure you factor in the lives you saved. The other soldier Charlie said was wounded — "

"Puckett. Shoulder wound, but he'll be fine. Listen, I gather that Colonel Ki-Soo wants to escort us to the pickup point so we'll be leaving here soon."

"It seems a little strange," Hood said, "this sudden détente."

"Only a little," Rodgers replied. "Robert Louis Stevenson once advised his readers to try the manners of different nations firsthand before forming an opinion about them. I've always felt he had something there."

"Something you'd never sell to Congress, the White House, or any other seat of government on the planet," Hood pointed out.

"True," Rodgers said. "Which is why Stevenson also wrote *Dr. Jekyll and Mr. Hyde*. I guess he didn't think human nature could change either. Paul, I'll contact you when we're heading back from Japan. I want to hear what the President has to say about all this."

Hood snickered. "Me too, Paul."

After asking Hood to check with Martha Mackall on a specific word, Rodgers and his men climbed into two of the four trucks that were to take them and Ki-Soo's party into the hills.

As they drove, Rodgers had his hand on the small staplerlike device he'd showed Squires earlier. Every two hundred yards or so, he pushed a small plunger on the back, and then released it.

"That's the EBC locator, isn't it, sir?" Squires asked.

Rodgers nodded.

"What are you doing?"

"Blowing them up," he said. "Trust is nice," said Rodgers, "but caution is good too."

Squires agreed as the open-top truck rumbled through the uneven terrain.

The Sikorsky S-70 Black Hawk flew into the Diamond Mountains as scheduled, the pilot expressing surprise when Squires told him to fly right in and land.

"No ladders, no quick turnaround?" he asked.

"No," Squires said, "set her down. We're leaving like proper gentlemen."

The eleven-seater landed on schedule, the M-60 machineguns ominously silent on the sides. While the men boarded, Rodgers and Ki-Soo made their farewells while Squires looked on.

Ki-Soo made a short speech to the American officers, the words foreign but the meaning clear: he was thanking them for all that they'd done to protect the integrity of his homeland.

When he was finished, Rodgers bowed and said, *"Annyong-hi ka-ship-shio."*

Ki-Soo seemed surprised and delighted, and said in response, *"Annyong ha-simni-ka."*

The two men saluted one another, Ki-Soo

holding his bandaged hand stiffly at his side, after which the Americans turned and left. As they boarded the helicopter, Squires checked on Puckett, who was lying on a stretcher on the floor. Then he sat heavily beside Rodgers.

"What did you two just say, anyway?" Squires asked.

"When I was on with Paul, I had him ask Martha Mackall how to say, 'Good-bye and may your home be well' in Korean."

"Nice sentiment."

"Of course," Rodgers said, "Martha and I don't get along too well . . . for all I know, I may've just told him I'm allergic to penicillin."

"I don't think so," Squires said. "What he answered sounded pretty much like what you said. Unless you're both allergic."

"It wouldn't surprise me," he said as the chopper door was shut and the Black Hawk rose into the gradually clearing sky. "Each day that I live, Charlie, less and less does."

EIGHTY-SEVEN

Wednesday, 10:30 A.M., Seoul

Kim Hwan sat on the bed, the back of the mattress raised and the pillow having fallen to the side. He wanted it, though after the physical and emotional upheavals of the last few hours, he seemed to lack the ambition and energy to reach over and get it.

The man who would save the peninsula was unable to lift his arm and recover his pillow. There was probably an irony in that, though he was in no mood to look for it.

The dull pain in Hwan's side kept him from sleeping, and the tight bandages made it difficult to breathe. But it was the events of the past few hours that kept him alert. The death of Gregory Donald held him like a nightmare he couldn't shake, yet while it still seemed unbelievable, it also seemed oddly inevitable. Donald's life had ended when his wife was killed — was it really less than a day before? — and at least now they were together. Donald wouldn't have believed that, but Soonji would have and Hwan did. So he was outvoted. The atheistic old goat was an angel whether he wanted to be or not.

As Hwan lay there, staring at the brick wall outside his window, Bob Herbert phoned to tell him about the events in the Diamond Mountains, and of the other men involved in the plot — the two the Striker team had killed at the Nodong site. Hwan knew that it wasn't likely the South would get the bodies of those men back soon, though the North was sure to send them fingerprints for identification.

"We haven't heard a peep out of anyone else," Herbert told Hwan, "so either we got the group or they've pulled in their claws to try again another day."

"I am sure," Hwan said quietly, "that we haven't heard the last of these people."

"You're probably right," Herbert said. "Radicals are like bananas — they come in bunches."

Hwan said he liked the image, after which Herbert repeated Hood's thanks for the KCIA's efforts and wished him a speedy recovery.

Hanging up the phone and deciding to

try to get his pillow, Hwan was surprised to find someone reach over and get it for him. The two strong hands gently lifted his head and slid the pillow under it, fluffing the sides to make sure he was nestled securely.

Hwan's eyes shifted to the side.

"Director Yung-Hoon," he said with surprise. "Where is — "

"Hongtack? On his way, by now, to his new post — a fishing boat monitoring Chinese broadcasts in the Yellow Sea. He seemed to believe that our different styles were a weakness and not a strength."

"Perhaps . . . you should reserve me a seat next to his," Hwan said. "I feel that way too."

Yung-Hoon winced. "We may have seemed to be working at cross-purposes from time to time. But after today, that won't happen again."

Someone in the government must have leaned on the Director about his handling of this case. It wouldn't surprise him to learn that Bob Herbert or Paul Hood had made a few calls on his behalf. Yung-Hoon had always responded to things like that.

The Director laid a hand on Hwan's. "When you get out of here, we'll see about arranging things differently, giving you responsibilities where you don't have to report to my office — "

Someone had definitely called him.

" — where you can work things your own way. I've also recommended to the President that we set up a scholarship at the University. Something for Mr. Donald in the political science department."

"Thanks," Hwan said. "Don't forget Cho's wife. She'll need help."

"Already done," said Yung-Hoon.

Hwan watched the Director carefully as he asked, "And how is Ms. Chong?"

Yung-Hoon looked as though his necktie was too tight. "She's gone. As you — requested, we allowed her to drive off."

"She saved my life. I owed her that. You followed her, though?"

"Well . . . yes," Yung-Hoon said. "We were interested to know where she'd go."

"And?"

"And," said the Director, "she ended up in Yangyang. At your uncle's house."

Hwan smiled. They'd never find her. Uncle Pak would sneak her out on his boat, which they wouldn't dare board, and he'd arrange somehow to get her into Japan.

"Don't you think she'll spy for the North again?" Yung-Hoon asked.

"No," Hwan said. "She never wanted to be doing this. I'm glad she'll be able to find

527

what it is she really wanted."

Yung-Hoon patted his hand. "If you're sure, Hwan." The Director rose. "I've put one of your men outside, Park. If you need anything let him know or call me."

Hwan said he would, and Yung-Hoon left him — not alone, but with his ghosts, the bittersweet memories of Soonji and Gregory Donald, of his poor driver Cho and the guarded but entrancing Ms. Chong. He wasn't sure his own uncle would tell him where he'd taken the woman, but he vowed he would find her somehow. As this day had underscored, there were friendships and allegiances that transcended political boundaries, and there wasn't always the time to explore them.

Time had to be made for those bonds to be strengthened. Because in the end, what he remembered about all of those people was what they had in their hearts, not in their dossiers.

EIGHTY-EIGHT

Wednesday, 9:00 P.M., Op-Center

The President arrived at Op-Center unannounced.

He came in his stretch, armor-plated limousine, with two Secret Service agents, his driver, and no one else — no aides, no reporters.

"No reporters?" Ann had remarked when the sentry at the front gate of Andrews AFB announced his arrival to Paul Hood. "Then it's got to be a *former* President."

"You're too cynical," Hood said, sitting back behind his desk. He had just finished bringing the heads of all the departments up-to-date — Bob Herbert, Martha Mackall, Darrell McCaskey, Matt Stoll, Lowell Coffey, Liz Gordon, Phil Katzen, and Ann — and also thanking them not only for their industry but for their ingenuity and cooperation: he told them he'd never seen a team mesh more effectively, on all fronts, and he was proud of the job they'd done . . . proud of *them,* individually.

He had been about to leave his office when the call came, and so he sat back down to wait.

Ann waited with him.

She couldn't stop smiling. Ann was not just happy because things had worked out for Op-Center; not just because the TV networks had all broken into the prime-time schedule with news of the destruction of the Nodong; not just because she and her counterpart at the Pentagon, Andrew Porter, had sold to the press that what Gregory Donald and General Michael Schneider did were the acts of humanists, not partisans. They had gotten out with that story fast enough, honest enough, and strong enough so that whatever the North Koreans said about Major Lee's plot would sound ungracious and vindictive.

Ann was also happy for Paul.

He had managed to handle both the responsibility of Op-Center and the responsibility of being a father and husband, neither job easy, neither job part-time. She didn't know how he had managed to hold up. Sharon Hood might never know how much this day had taken out of him, but Ann did. She wished there were some way she *could* let her know . . . but nothing occurred to her.

The Press Officer speechless! she laughed to herself.

No, that wasn't entirely true. What Ann had to say was nothing a devoted admirer had the right to tell a wife. It was that Paul Hood was a very special man, a man with a good heart, integrity, and what she knew was a deep reserve of love. What Ann would tell Sharon, if only in her fantasies, was to nurture Paul and let him nurture her . . . to remember that one day he would lay aside his work, the children would be grown, and the love they'd sustained would flower and enrich them.

Paul was telling them all about how he wanted a memorial service organized for both Gregory Donald and Bass Moore, though she didn't really hear much of what he had to say. Her mind, and her heart, were elsewhere . . . with Paul, in an imaginary world where he would hold her when they'd all left, take her to dinner at someplace fast and informal, and then drive her home and make love to her and fall asleep with his chest pressed against her back —

"Mr. Hood?" Bugs said through the computer.

"Yes?"

"The President is coming."

Hood laughed as Bugs put a picture from the corridor video camera on the screen. The President was waving at Op-Center employees in their cubicles, barely stopping to shake hands with people he didn't know, making eye contact only as long as it took to search out the next face.

Paul rose as the President walked into the room, along with those department heads who weren't already standing. The President made a *tut-tut* face and motioned for them all to sit down.

They did, save for Paul. The President made his way through the office and shook his hand.

"Nice job, Task Force head."

"Thank you, sir."

Behind them, Ann sizzled. *It wasn't the Task Force. It was Paul and Op-Center.*

The President turned, rubbing his hands together. "Excellent, excellent job. Everyone involved in this project, from Paul to the Striker team to Steve Burkow's National Security personnel to all of you, have performed beyond all reasonable expectations."

"We all had help," Hood said. "Gregory Donald, Kim Hwan at the KCIA, the North Korean officer at the Nodong missile — "

"Naturally, Paul. But it was you who put

that support system into place. The credit is yours, along with everything the various departments did to manage the crisis. Though General Schneider did say he plans to request a civilian citation for Mr. Donald. He says he wants to award it himself. There will also be commendations for the Striker men who made sacrifices."

Made sacrifices, Ann thought. That's what presidents say when they aren't sure how many people have died and how many were wounded. But she refused to let President Lawrence spoil this moment for her, and hoped Paul would keep plugging for the people who helped. Everything he did seemed to elevate him in her eyes.

"*Dear Sharon,*" she began composing the letter in her head, "*I hope you'll forgive me, but I've kidnapped your husband. I'll return him when I'm carrying his child, because I very desperately want a piece of this man to have for my own, forever. . . .*"

"But," the President was saying, "I didn't come here just to commend and thank you all. When I founded Op-Center six months ago, it was on a trial basis — what I and a few others like Secretary Colon and Steve Burkow felt might be a useful adjunct, a crisis management team interfacing with our existing intelligence and military operations.

None of us had any idea *if* it would work out." The President smiled broadly. "Certainly, none of us had any idea how *well* it would work out."

Lowell Coffey applauded softly.

The President continued, "As far as I and my advisors are concerned, Op-Center has earned its wings. You are no longer a provisional operation, and I'd like to formally and finally christen you tomorrow at a private lunch at the White House. After that, Paul, we can discuss what else you think you need to make your operation more effective. Not that Congress will give it to us, but we'll give it a damn good effort."

"Mr. President," Hood said, rising, "we all appreciate the vote of confidence. As long as the past six months have seemed at times, today seemed a whole lot longer . . . and we're happy it all worked out. But as for tomorrow, I'm afraid I can't make the lunch."

For the first time since she'd known the President, Ann Farris saw him recoil in surprise.

"Really?" the President remarked. He scratched his forehead. "If it's play-off tickets, I'd like to come."

"It isn't, sir," Hood said. "I'm going to be taking tomorrow off so I can teach my son to play chess and read a few violent comic books with him."

The President nodded and smiled sincerely.

Ann Farris applauded softly.

ABOUT THE CREATORS

Tom Clancy is the author of *The Hunt for Red October*, *Red Storm Rising*, *Patriot Games*, *The Cardinal of the Kremlin*, *Clear and Present Danger*, *The Sum of All Fears*, and *Without Remorse*. He is also the author of the nonfiction books *Submarine* and *Armored Cav*. He lives in Maryland.

Steve Pieczenik is a Harvard-trained psychiatrist with an M.D. from Cornell University Medical College. He has a Ph.D. in International Relations from M.I.T. and served as principal hostage negotiator and international crisis manager while Deputy Assistant Secretary of State under Henry Kissinger, Cyrus Vance and James Baker. He is also the best-selling novelist of the psycho-political thrillers *The Mind Palace*, *Blood Heat*, *Maximum Vigilance*, and *Pax Pacifica*.